THE LADY

THE VALENTINI FAMILY: OATH: PART TWO

SERENA AKEROYD

BON VINUTI A LA FAMIGGHIA!

WELCOME back to New York City, darlings!

Fionnabhair - *Fee-on-a-bar*
Luciu - *Loo-cee-you*
Custanzu - *Cust-an-zoo*
Aoife - *Ee-Fah*
Giovi - *Gee-oh-vee*
Cèilidh - *Type of Irish dance (kay-lee)*
Buttana - *whore/bitch*
Vicchiareddu - *old man*
Bona sira - *good evening*
Duci - *sweetheart*
Bedda mia - *my beautiful*
Gilatu - *ice cream*
Figghiu ri buttana - *son of a bitch*
Porca troia - *Goddammit*
Pezz'i miedda - *piece of shit*
Miedda - *shit*
Famigghia - *family (Sicilian spelling)*
T'amu - *I love you*

Grazii - *Thank you*
Se - *Yes*
Natali - *Christmas*
Vinu russu - *Red Wine*
Capisci? - *Understand?*
Russu - *red*
Pi favuri - *please*
Cielo - *heaven*
Culu biddicchiu - *cute ass*
Jornu - *day*
Me mugghieri - *My wife*
Tuttu boni - *everything okay*
Vinnitta - *vendetta*
Chista è da me - *you're mine*
Culu - *ass*
Aeiri - *yesterday*
Supra l'onori di mi matri - *On my mother's honor*
Matri - *mother*
Patri - *father*
Ti ficci na promissa - *I made you a promise*
Riggina - *queen*
Abbili - *deft*

Triggers:

- References to sexual assault,
- Torture,
- General violence

Much love,
Serena
xoxo

The
VALENTINI
FAMILY

THE CROSSOVER READING ORDER WITH THE FIVE POINTS

FILTHY
FILTHY SINNER
NYX
LINK
FILTHY RICH
SIN
STEEL
FILTHY DARK
CRUZ
MAVERICK
FILTHY SEX
HAWK
FILTHY HOT
STORM
THE DON
THE LADY
FILTHY SECRET
REX
RACHEL
FILTHY KING

PLAYLIST

If you'd like to hear a curated soundtrack, with songs that are featured in the book, as well as songs that inspired it, then here's the link:

https://open.spotify.com/playlist/oIOdaI4u243k6n6LMDtnHP?si=
1732b464f6cd4b8e

ONE

JEN

"THANKS FOR NOTHING, MOTHERFUCKERS!"

When I was dumped outside my building, bags shoved onto the sidewalk, I wanted to scream. The driver and the guard who'd driven me to my place had both refused to speak English the whole ride over here.

So, when I asked important questions like:

"What was Luciu arrested for?"

"Where the hell are you taking me?"

I didn't even receive a grunt for my pains.

They blanked me. Totally, completely, one hundred percent ignored me.

It was, in a word, *infuriating.*

With my shit dumped onto the sidewalk as if it were trash, the bastards drove off without a second glance, not even stopping when I hurled curse words at them.

By actions alone, they were telling me I was nothing more than a whore. They didn't know Luc had told me he loved me... why would they? I'd only just found out myself.

One minute we'd been flying into a private airfield after a trip to Aspen; the next, I saw flashing lights and took notice of the cops who were waiting on us to land.

I thought they were there for me.

I'd killed a man.

Why wouldn't they be after me?

But they'd taken Luc.

My mouth wobbled as I watched the town car's red lights glare against the blanket of snow that, in the morning, would be plowed. With them, any hope of understanding what the hell had happened melted away.

I had no idea why he'd been arrested, just knew that the only man I'd ever loved was with the cops right now.

Seeing as he wasn't a Boy Scout, I didn't think it boded well. Not when he had a reputation for cutting people's faces as a memoir, anyway.

The bitter cold ate into my bones as I stood there, frozen in place by the temperature and by my fears, as well as a bone deep dread of returning to my apartment where Vlad had died.

The combination of all three jolted me into action.

I couldn't just wait at home for news.

I had to find out more.

My first stop was *Russu*.

I got in because the bouncers remembered me pulling up to the front of the nightclub with Luc before Christmas, but it came with the cover fee—no perks without the boss on my arm. When I finally got inside, I tried to ask at the bar for help, but I got a bunch of shrugs.

From the lower levels, I had no idea how to get to the offices that were like a labyrinth at the back of the ex-meatpacking factory.

I could get to the VIP lounge, but that would only get me access to more Cristal, and now *wasn't* the time for champagne.

When that was a bust, I took an Uber to Luc's building.

For a second, I just stood there once the car drove off.

It was freezing.

So cold that I was pretty sure my nipples were gonna fall off even though I was tucked behind ten layers of wool.

While frostbite seemed to be on the cards, I just stared up at the gleaming bastion of wealth, aware that getting into a building like this wasn't easy.

On the border between the Financial District and Tribeca, the security here was insane. There was not only a doorman, but I'd need several codes in the elevator to access the penthouse. Those were just the things I knew about, never mind what the *Famiglia* did to keep their Don from being killed as he slept.

I'd met one of the guardians of the elevators before, but he didn't know who I was to Luc, and the whole point of a damn doorman was to keep uninvited people out.

Everyone other than Luc had made it abundantly clear that I was definitely a gatecrasher in his life.

Didn't mean I was going to listen to the haters, of course.

"Where's a radioactive spider when I need one?" I muttered to myself as I headed toward the building's grand entrance. "Scaling this motherfucker with a spider's web would probably be easier than getting the mafia to let me in."

Pushing the buzzer, the doorman made a swift appearance. I recognized him though. He recognized me too.

"Yes, ma'am?" he asked, speaking through an intercom in the fancy glass vestibule.

Out here, everything was cold and gray. In there, everything was warm and gold.

"I need to speak with the resident of the penthouse," I settled on, because it wasn't like I could ask for Luc when his butt was in a police precinct somewhere in the city.

He tipped his head to the side like we weren't both aware that the 'resident' was currently absent, and that he'd left with me yesterday morning. "Have you made arrangements to visit? There's nothing in my agenda."

"No." I was supposed to be staying here though. "Look, you know who I am."

"I do, but you're not on the approved visitor's list yet, ma'am."

My mouth twisted at the oversight. Was that someone down the line's fault? Or Luc's himself?

"I don't want to go to the penthouse, I just want to speak with someone in it."

"I'm afraid that isn't possible—"

"Please," I pleaded, then dropped the charade when I knew I wasn't getting anywhere. "The owner's in..." *Trouble?* That felt like a goddamn understatement. "I just watched him get arrested. I have to speak with someone in the penthouse." *If anyone was even there.*

I saw his hesitation, saw the shift of resolve in his eyes, but wanted to growl when he shook his head.

Mind racing with the need to find out what the hell was happening with the man *I loved*, I almost didn't hear him when he spoke next.

"Try the intercom," the doorman said softly. "I'm sorry, ma'am, but I can't afford to lose this job and the resident of the penthouse..." He cleared his throat, nerves making the cough break in two. "...is virulent in his demands for security. I'm sure you're aware that he isn't the kind of man you want to disobey."

No. I couldn't argue with that.

"Thank you," I told him, and I meant it.

It wasn't his fault.

Him and me, we were just little worker ants trudging along for the one percent. We had to stick together.

Hoping that Alina, Luc's housekeeper, lived in, I pushed the buzzer to the penthouse, but no one answered.

Tears gathered in my eyes, and they stung from the bitter cold, but I stayed there, holding down the button to the damn intercom, not wanting to give up.

Luc wouldn't give up on me.

He'd killed for me—he wouldn't just walk away when life got tough. I had to believe that.

"He has a lot more resources to call on though," I muttered to myself, and I wasn't just talking cash.

I had a feeling Luc would have the police commissioner in his pocket. As for me, I probably helped the commissioner evade taxes, but that was as personal as it got.

"Ma'am?" the doorman's voice broke into my worry.

"Yes?"

"If you try 14A, that's where Alina lives."

Now I wanted to cry for real.

"Thank you!" I blurted out, jamming my finger on the button.

He walked away, letting me know that was as much help as he was going to give me. But it was more than I'd expected, and I was beyond grateful.

"*Da?*" Alina's voice was groggy and pissed at being disturbed at this late hour.

Of course, that was when I remembered I didn't know if she spoke English.

"Alina? It's Jennifer. Luciu's in trouble."

A barrage of Russian, or what I assumed was Russian, came down the intercom. Luc had called it a dialect, never actually specifying—

Gah, what did it matter what language his housekeeper spoke?

"Luciu's in trouble," I repeated, louder this time, doing that irritating thing English-speakers did when they tried to make themselves understood—because raising the volume always cleared things right up.

Another voice appeared in the background. This was clearer as it tangled with the gruffer, older one. Then, I heard the softer voice murmur, "Hello? Who is this?"

"Hi, I'm Luciu's..." What was I? "...girlfriend—"

"We know nothing. I must go—"

"Wait! I don't want to go into the apartment. I just need to know if he's okay."

"I can't tell you—"

"He was arrested in front of me! I need to know what's going on."

"*Signor* Valentini was arrested?" came the confused reply.

"Yes! In front of me," I emphasized. "We'd just landed and there were cops at the airfield waiting to take him away."

There was the soft murmuring of *whatever* as the new voice translated. A part of me wondered if this was the girl my ex-boyfriend had tried to date rape, but my focus was elsewhere right now.

"My mother says that she still knows nothing. She'll know nothing tomorrow or next week either."

"Helpful," I sniped.

"Yes, she can be quite difficult when she chooses to be," the woman said with an impatient sigh. "But... I know that if there's an issue, Custanzu, *Signor* Valentini's younger brother, will deal with it and will be in touch."

"That's what I'm afraid of," I whispered. "Stan won't tell me anything."

"I'm sorry, Miss..."

"MacNeill," I prompted.

"I'm sorry, Miss MacNeill, there's nothing else I can do. If Custanzu won't help, then our hands are tied. Go home and get warm. It's freezing out there."

When the intercom clicked off, I reached up and rubbed at my tired eyes.

One thing out of this I *did* know—Stan wouldn't help me do dick.

But I couldn't, *wouldn't* let this lie.

I had friends. Friends who had connections. There had to be a way to find out what the hell was going on.

TWO

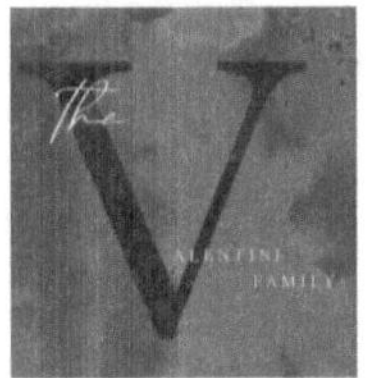

JEN

THE NEXT EVENING

I'D HAD to go to work.

Which had blown.

But after my boss had threatened to fire me when I emailed in the sick note Luc had had doctored for me, I didn't have much of a choice but to show up at the office.

The second I could get out of there, I'd raced over to Aoife's, and she was currently staring at me, brownie batter dripping from a whisk onto the counter as if I'd told her that I'd been probed by aliens.

"You killed someone?" she repeated, her voice fainter than when she'd first asked that question. This was her third time.

Progress was definitely slow, but I'd had to start somewhere, hadn't I? Not having mentioned to her that I was dating someone, period, never mind a mobster, I figured this was as good a place as any.

"Honey," I said carefully, "you're married to a Five Pointer. You're an Irish Mob wife. You're seriously giving me shade for killing that creep?"

I knew I sounded a lot more blasé than I actually was, but her reaction was starting to freak me out.

Killing Vlad Dubrov hadn't been the highlight of my week, even if he was a lowdown creep who whored out my mom. Aoife, my BFF, knew that, knew what my mom's boyfriends were like, but she looked as if she were going to faint on me.

I hadn't told her so she'd give me a round of applause, but so that she'd understand what Luciu had done for me when I got to that part of the story.

How couldn't I help him in return after what he'd done for me? How couldn't I use the limited connections I had with the Irish Mob to do something, *anything*, to work on liberating him?

Sure, Luc had his brother, but that woman who'd pretended to be his wife... with how she'd been there for his arrest, I knew something shady was going on and it scared me.

Luc needed help from the Five Points, and Aoife was the only person who could help me negotiate that.

"Well, no, I'm not giving you shade, but..." She gulped, dropped the whisk which splattered onto the counter, making one hell of a mess, then staggered back to sit at the kitchen table. I almost heard her ass make a 'thud' sound—that was how heavily she sank onto the seat.

"Do you need some water?" I didn't like her color. On an ordinary day, I'd say she looked like she'd eaten bad squid. But she was pregnant, and that changed things.

Her last pregnancy hadn't been easy, and I'd been along with her for the ride, so I knew the signs.

"No. I just—" Her brow furrowed. "Why did you kill him?"

"Because he was attacking me." I rolled my eyes as I squatted down in front of her. "I didn't do it for fun."

She rubbed her temple. "Why were you even with him?"

"He came to my place. I didn't shut the damn door properly. It was my fault for being stupid, but he barged in, and then..." I reached up and fingered the tiny Band-Aid on my earlobe. "He dragged my earring off so he could pawn it."

"You're joking." But it wasn't a question. Her gaze followed the passage of my fingers.

"No." I wished I were. The damn thing hurt like a bitch, and I had a tiny stitch there that was already starting to itch. One that had been inserted by a doctor who had spent more time sweating over Luciu breathing down his neck than concentrating on the injury itself. "He groped me, started saying shit like he'd make more money if he whored me out instead of my mother. So... I stopped him."

It seemed ridiculously simple now that I told her about it.

I hadn't realized that I needed to share this with her.

Aoife was my safe space though. She knew all my dirty secrets. I needed her to know this one and to still love me after.

"Why are you telling me this?" she choked.

Okay, so she didn't feel the same way...

But I hadn't told her I had a fetish for cock warming. I'd just confessed to murder. She needed time to process, but time was a luxury I couldn't afford right this second.

"I need your help with Conor."

She blinked. "Conor? O'Donnelly? Conor O'Donnelly?"

"How many Conors do we know?"

"Why do you need help with him?"

"Maybe I don't. Maybe Finn will help." I sucked in a breath that I released on a whoosh, alongside: "But... I started dating someone."

She gaped at me. "You're dating someone?!"

"I'm sorry I didn't tell you! It was just a fling, until it wasn't." I winced. "His name's Luciu Valentini. I think he's been arrested for Vlad's murder.

"I tried his place and the club he owns but... *nada*. I can't get any information. I need Conor, or Finn, to get me some."

"Why? Can't you just ask this Luciu's family?"

"I need to know what's happening and his brother's a dick."

"I can't believe you didn't tell me you were dating someone," she groused.

"I didn't think it was serious."

"It's serious enough that you're here asking for a favor from the Irish Mob," she sniped before she reached up and rubbed her forehead. "Why do I know that name?" The question appeared to be aimed more at herself than at me.

"He has ties to the mafia," I mumbled under my breath.

She clicked her fingers. "He's the Cheshire Cat guy."

What a rep.

How the hell did she know that anyway?

"He only does one cheek," I defended.

"One's ample. Are you sure you're not happy he's been arrested? I mean, it's one way to get rid of him—"

"No! Aoife, I don't want him locked up for something he didn't do. I-I..." I heaved a sigh. "You won't believe me."

"Babe, I didn't think you could kill someone, but I believe that," she said carefully. "Trust me, I don't think there's much you could say that would surprise me."

"I love him."

Three words.

The simple, stark truth.

I loved Luciu Valentini.

And that was when everything went to hell.

Aoife fainted.

She fucking fainted!

"Aoife!" I gasped, jumping upright to catch her as she slumped in front of me. "Are you being serious right now?"

My grousing didn't make her perk up with a laugh as if she'd tried to tease me—just in the least funny way. God, I'd prefer the worst joke in history to the reality.

But she didn't jump up and call me a nut, just slouched over even more.

I took most of her weight which left me in a precarious position. With my arms slotted through hers, I hovered in front of her, hoping she'd come to quickly so that I didn't have to call Finn or a doctor before I had to arrange her on the floor.

But luck was not on my side.

"Motherfucker," I growled under my breath when, from across the kitchen, Jake, my godson, started bawling his eyes out.

Twisting around with my limp friend in my arms, I found my godkid and called out, "Jake, dude, I'll buy you a goddamn Ferrari with Luc's money, but please, just stop crying! Lemme deal with your mommy, huh?"

Naturally, the toddler didn't understand what I was offering him.

At that moment, he could have leveraged a Bugatti out of me for his eighteenth, and I'd have given him it if he'd have stopped crying, but he sat there, in front of the TV in the kitchen, sobbing his heart out.

"Jesus Christ," I muttered as I twisted Aoife down and around, trying to be careful, but she was a deadweight—

Oh, God.

I knew what a deadweight really looked like now.

Vlad had gone down faster than a house of cards. The sound of his knees cracking against the floor beside my bed would haunt me for a lifetime. And when the knife I'd stabbed in his throat had pierced the other side as he slalomed face first—

No, I didn't need to think of that now.

It was already difficult stepping inside my apartment, never mind sleeping in that damn bed. I didn't need to add to today's woes.

Huffing under my breath as I struggled to get Aoife flat on the floor, I tried to remember the First Aid training I'd undergone when I started working with her at her tearoom all those years ago. Nursing had never been in my nature. I wasn't exactly a touchy-feely kind of person, but I remembered some bullcrap about the recovery position.

"I don't think I made this up," I mumbled to myself as I turned Aoife on her side, trying to decide if I was supposed to cross her leg over to the floor or if that was a yoga position. "Jacob, I swear, I'm coming, kid," I called out when his yowling didn't stop, and deciding that yoga was as good as First Aid, I left Aoife there and hustled over to the godchild that I loved but damn, he had some pipes on him.

Last year, they'd renovated this room and it was now a dining/kitchen/living space where Aoife could develop recipes for her bakery while keeping her eye on Jake.

When I made it over to where he was sobbing his heart out, I crouched down in front of him, unsure why he was crying, but he was holding his foot like it didn't belong to him and bawling at nothing.

In a commiserating tone, I rubbed his foot. "It's okay, baby," I crooned, picking him up, grateful when he scampered onto my lap without much of a fight and let me rock him.

Considering this wasn't my role as his godmother—I was the one who sneaked him Tootsie Rolls and other stuff he probably shouldn't be eating—it was kind of sweet that he clung to me even though he spread snot over my Gucci sweater.

As I began wondering if dry cleaners dealt with snot, then feeling guilty for worrying about something so inconsequential, I heard a soft moan come from the other side of the room, and though I was grateful Aoife was stirring, I groaned as I hauled Jake into my arms.

"Sorry, little dude, we gotta walk and talk," I told him as I hefted him across the space. He wasn't exactly small, either, but I managed to do it.

"Mommy's napping, Jake. You take a nap too," I half-begged as I plunked him beside his mom so that I could check on Aoife. Peering down at her, I whispered, "Aoife, please don't make me do CPR. I love you like a sister but I don't want to kiss you."

A soft moan escaped her, her eyelashes fluttered, and she slurred, "Probably...call—Finn."

I nodded even though she couldn't see me, because that was a smart thing to do. I grabbed the purse I'd dumped on the kitchen table when I'd come in earlier and scrolled through the numbers for Finn.

Who, of course, didn't pick up the fucking phone.

Four times I called the fucker.

Four.

And he ignored each one.

That was when I saw it.

The blood.

For a second, it froze me. I turned to literal ice as it seeped out of Aoife's body...

Shaking, trying not to think about the large pool that Vlad—

No. Aoife wasn't dying.

She wasn't *allowed* to die.

This wasn't from a vein or from a visible wound. It had to be the baby.

Breaking off from calling Finn, I shuffled Jake to the side when he started fussing as Aoife didn't give him the attention he figured he deserved.

Finally, I connected with 911 as I let Jake start braiding her and my hair together—i.e., making a massive knot—and gulping, I told them her symptoms, which had them sending an ambulance over.

The joy of wealth was that Aoife had purses that cost the same as an ambulance ride. For me, I'd have to haul my ass across the city gushing blood over the subway with every step.

Money really was the best.

The blood didn't seem to stop coming either, puddling under her butt, and because I had a choice of freeze further or carry on trying to locate Finn, I returned to my earlier mission.

Aoife needed Finn more than she needed me right now.

Desperation struck when I tried to open Aoife's phone by scanning her face, but because it failed each time, it required a passcode which I didn't have.

It was six now, so Finn should be coming home, but maybe he was in a meeting?

With the reasoning that Aidan could be with him, I called him too.

But the bastard ignored me as well.

Ten times.

Yes, I was still counting. Yes, I was pissed. Yes, I'd hold a grudge.

I growled under my breath when the only option open to me revealed itself. "Never let it be said that I don't love you."

She didn't even moan.

Fuck, oh, fuck, oh fuck—

I hit Savannah's number.

My second BFF.

The ex-BFF who I totally wasn't talking to.

She answered immediately.

Of course.

"Jen? Oh, God, I'm so glad you called."

I scowled at Aoife and muttered, "You owe me one."

She didn't answer.

The blood…

Could words trigger a miscarriage?

I mean, was my confession really that much for her to handle? Me telling her that I killed someone, she just got a little flustered, but that I loved someone triggered this?

I'd be offended if I wasn't shitting myself on her behalf.

"I owe you a thousand," Savannah declared, hearing my words but not understanding them. "I know I do. I'm so sorry—"

"Savannah, shut up," I growled. "Is Aidan there?"

"Aidan?" she said slowly.

"Yeah, Aidan. The fecker you're fucking. Big guy. Has a limp, nasty scowl that makes people piss themselves when they direct it at him... ya know? The O'Donnelly heir?" I snarled.

"I know who the fuck he is, Jen."

"Then what's the problem?" I snapped. "I've been trying to get in touch with Finn, but the prick won't answer the phone, and Aidan won't either."

"What's going on?"

"Aoife fainted."

"Shit! Is it the baby?" She knew about Aoife's pregnancy because my sappy best friend had told Finn on Christmas morning in front of us all.

I really wanted to say no, but logic dictated that it *was* the baby.

Because I didn't want to put it out there into the universe, I explained, "An ambulance is on the way, but she said I should call Finn and—"

"I'll call Aidan and get him to speak with Finn, tell him what's going on. Text me the hospital and I'll make sure they know what's what."

"Thanks."

Disconnecting the call, I rubbed my forehead, wondering why the hell Finn was letting her go through with this when carrying Jacob to term had been a problem. The idiot couldn't stand it when Aoife was upset, but he was okay with her putting herself through hell for nine months? What kind of logic was that?

And before Jake, she'd had two miscarriages.

Jacob was their miracle. Who asked for two miracles?

Fear hit me between the eyes.

Aoife...

She wasn't allowed to get sick.

"Jake," I rambled, "did you know that pregnancy is the worst thing a woman can put her body through? You owe your momma a gazillion, I swear."

He'd curled up at his mom's side on the floor by this point, his fingers tangling with her earrings as he tugged on them and played, and while I was regretting letting him knot my hair with Aoife's, it gave me something to do as I waited on the ambulance.

But that puddle of blood...

Where the hell were they?

When the intercom at the door sounded, I almost started sobbing as I scampered into the hall. Skidding in my haste to reach the elevator, I guided the EMTs to the right floor.

Which was how I ended up hauling ass across Hell's Kitchen with a toddler in tow to Bellevue Hospital.

And I thought this week couldn't get any worse...

THREE

LUC

EARLIER THAT DAY

AS THE CELL doors slammed shut, I turned away from the apologetic guard who returned my cell phone to me with a sleight of hand so *àbbili,* deft, that I tucked the knowledge away for future reference. Such a skill was not only rare but incredibly useful.

Slipping my phone into the pocket of my pants, I found one of the inmates peering at me from a bench, and I knew he was the guy my *consigliere* said was down for a bribe because he was the only one who looked up as the cell door opened.

Twenty by fifteen feet in size, stuffed full of fourteen men, the air stinking of piss and shit from a filthy toilet, I strode over to the bench, prepared to have to pull some moves if someone *did* deign to look up, to take note of my four-thousand-dollar suit, and decided they thought I looked like an easy target.

No one did, however.

Maybe because, until last night, no one knew my identity. Knew what I looked like.

My invisibility cloak had just been burned in the worst imaginable way, but I doubted these chumps had seen today's papers.

As I took a seat on the bench, the shiny metal cold beneath my ass, the guy from before approached me. "Mark Lorowitz," he whispered.

I dipped my chin in greeting.

"I appreciate this, man, I really do. My mom's broke and my kid needs braces—"

I raised a hand to still his words. "I will make certain your family is taken care of."

"You want me to do it now?"

"No. After ten. They're more likely to take me to Bellevue than deal with me in-house."

He blinked. "You really wanna go to that hospital, huh?"

My smile was soft. "You've no idea."

Lorowitz had leveraged the chance of being offered bail in exchange for forty thousand dollars, so I understood why he was nervous.

Time was the most precious commodity of all, and I sure as fuck didn't appreciate having mine wasted on trumped up charges.

The DA had been against me for years, but this was a pathetic attempt to throw me behind bars. The case would be tossed out in court because she didn't have a legal leg to stand on.

I *had* desecrated a cemetery, defaced a casket, and set fire to a corpse, however there was no proof of any of that.

This was maneuvering, but my *consigliere* and I were making it work for me with a quickly hashed out plan that had come to me via my attorney.

Bellevue Hospital had a dedicated ward for prisoners, and it housed someone I needed to see, a certain someone who had been ignoring my visitation requests for the last ten years.

Not even Aurora, my sister, had been able to get in to see him, and she had mad skills in making things happen.

As I stared up at a patch of the ceiling that was steadily growing damper with every second that passed, my top lip quirked up in a sneer of disgust, even as I wondered what Jen was going through.

Two days ago, she'd killed a man and I'd told her I'd protect her from the cops.

Yesterday, we were flying in from Aspen.

Today, I was in fucking jail.

It wasn't like she knew this was a temporary thing, and because my brother Stan was a *figghiu ri buttana,* only God knew what he was telling her...

If he scared her off, one of his fucking fingers would be doing a disappearing act before the day was over when I was released from this pit, that was for goddamn sure.

Imagining how I'd do it got me through to eight o'clock, which was when I finally stood up. Ten would be a better time to go through with this, but I'd had more than enough of the stench of piss and shit.

Lorowitz, jittery with nerves, rasped, "You wanna do it now?"

"I do."

"You won't fight back?"

"No. But you must break my wrist."

I cast a glance around, saw that most men had their heads tipped back and their gazes were averted; their disinterest was clear. Had each of them been bought off? I'd been prepared for a fight all day, but no one had given me any trouble.

While I wanted to go to the hospital, I didn't need to be in a coma from a severe beatdown by enemies or a shiv to the gut.

He cleared his throat, drawing my attention back to him. "Okay, man. I've done worse if that's what you want."

Well, that was reassuring.

I rolled my eyes. "I'm not looking to be hospitalized, Mark." Quite the contrary. "I want to get into Bellevue for treatment. At this time of the night, it should happen."

"I'm just saying, I'll do whatever you want. Your dime."

I heard the shrug in his voice and murmured, "I will shout out. Don't be surprised. I need the guards to hear."

"Yeah, I get it."

"You ready for solitary?"

"No, but I'll deal." He hesitated a second as he grabbed the arm I held out. "The money is with my mom, right?"

I reached into my pants where my cell was tucked away, handed back to me by the guard who'd locked me in here. Locating the email, I tapped on the receipt of payment and showed him.

"Twenty thousand. As agreed. The remaining twenty is for when I'm back on the outside."

"She can do a hell of a lot with forty grand. You ever need anyone for a beating again, I'm your man."

"I appreciate that," I said drolly, then I tensed my arm and told him, "No compound fractures. I don't want to deal with surgery."

Lorowitz grunted. "Your funeral."

FOUR

LUC

THE FOLLOWING MORNING

"THANK YOU," I told the officer who opened the door to the hospital room for me.

"My pleasure, sir." He cleared his throat. "The other guard just stepped out for breakfast. He said to tell you he needs to be back in here before seven AM."

Nodding, I headed into the pokey room, coming across a sight that had hope sinking in my chest.

I knew he was old, knew he was sick, but the lack of cuffs, the lack of straps that kept him immobilized to his bed...

This was worse than I could have anticipated.

It meant he was sick enough not to be a flight risk.

It meant he was close to death when I was here to try to encourage him to seek parole so he could live freely for however many years God blessed him with.

Currau Valentini, my great-uncle, my *prozio,* was the last remaining Valentini from my grandfather's generation, and the only reason he'd been kept alive was to be a patsy.

A fucking patsy.

Outrage had me balling my fists as I walked over to him—a gesture I immediately regretted when my wrist didn't appreciate the move. My fingers were like sausages, but it was a simple break that had taken hours to treat.

I wasn't used to medical care that took hours to fix something as simple as a broken wrist. As for Currau, that was all he was used to when he'd been a prince of the *Famiglia* once upon a time too.

Falls from grace were the hardest to accept.

Shoving aside the pain, as well as the bitterness on my *prozio's* behalf, I scanned the room.

He shared a ward with three fellow prisoners, each in various stages of illness. One peered at me over a book, alert even though it was five in the morning. The second I looked at him, he averted his attention. *Smart man.*

"Keep your eyes and ears closed," I warned, the threat of death by my hand far more treacherous to his wellbeing than whatever had him locked up in here.

His nod and hunched shoulders told me he received the message loud and fucking clear.

The other two prisoners were unconscious, heavy-duty equipment the only things keeping them alive.

Currau was either like them or deeply asleep. I wasn't sure if that was even possible in a hospital with the noise, the lighting, and the bustling in the halls, but if he *was* awake, he was good at playing possum.

"Great-uncle?"

Sixty-four years he'd been rotting away in prison, and for a crime he didn't commit.

Not for the first time, I resented that the O'Donnellys had taken Benito Fieri out.

The fucker might only be the son of the bastard who'd slaughtered my entire family, but I wished I'd been the one to gut him like a fish and not an Irish cunt.

Wearily, I reached up and rubbed my eyes. I was tired, and this entire farce was taking longer than I liked. I'd wasted hours awaiting basic treatment, but also waiting for my guard to get me in to visit Currau. I never thought it would take this much goddamn time.

I'd wanted to visit so I could convince him to try for parole again. It had been decades since his last attempt, and this time, we had people in the right places to make sure he was liberated, but if he was unconscious, yet another of the goals my family had been working toward for a decade had been denied us.

The door to the hospital room opened, a nurse making an appearance with the officer at her back. I caught his eye, and he nodded at me before he pulled aside and retreated to the hallway.

"You will be well compensated for your silence," I told her calmly, pleased when she didn't quiver with nerves, just stood her ground at the foot of the bed.

"If you intend to hurt him, I won't allow it. I don't care who you are or how well you'll compensate me."

"He's the only remaining family my siblings and I have on my father's side," I countered. "I'm trying to get him out of here, and I don't mean in a body bag. What's wrong with him?"

The stare she settled on me was less suspicious than before but still wary. "He just came out of emergency surgery."

"So he's unconscious, not sleeping?"

"He's in the process of waking up." Talk about ill-timed luck... *porca troia.* "In all honesty, he needs a new kidney, but that's not going to happen."

"Because he's a prisoner?"

"No, because he's too old and he isn't a viable candidate."

"What's wrong with him?"

"Chronic kidney disease." Her gaze turned softer, sadder. "It was re-classified as end-stage two days ago."

And there we had it.

That was why I was here.

That was why that farce had happened at the airfield.

Goddamn Aurora.

I felt it though, could share in my sister's urgency as dread filled me. "He's dying?"

"His kidneys are failing," she said flatly.

I gritted my teeth at her statement, but nodded. "He needs dialysis?"

"Yes."

"Is he strong enough for a transplant?"

"There's no chance of a transplant."

She didn't know who I was, that much was clear.

"If there were—"

"There isn't," she retorted.

"Humor me. Is he in good health?"

"Relatively speaking for a man whose kidneys are failing him."

I nodded. "Thank you for your candor."

"You really mean him no harm?" she asked, her voice warier than ever.

"I have no desire to hurt him. I want him to come home."

Her lips twisted. "That's exactly where he should be. I hope if you petition whoever you petition, they let him out."

I'd make sure of it.

When she trailed out, I was disappointed at the inability to speak to the man we'd struggled for years to communicate with. Even before we'd learned of his transfer here, getting our men in Rikers to talk to him had been hard.

Soldiers had come back to me with the news that he wouldn't speak to a stranger. That he was practically mute and only appeared to talk to two men—one a prison guard and the other his cell mate. The cell mate, another lifer, was just as close-mouthed and couldn't be bought, either.

Thinking of what he'd gone through had me wishing I could at least tell him we were fighting to liberate him, but there was no use when he was unconscious.

Forty-four years he'd spent seeking parole, only to be denied each and every time.

Reports indicated that was when he shut down. For the last two decades, he'd been on autopilot, just waiting for goddamn death while rotting away in *carcere.*

Now it was here, I guessed I understood why he wasn't willing to fight to live. What had his life been? One endless round of prison transfers, each day one long serving of dishonor and disrespect when he'd reigned over this city as my grandfather's right-hand man.

He'd been stabbed and shivved by Sicilians who believed he'd murdered *Nannu,* tormented by Fieri's men—had even lost a fucking ear in one of their fights—and had spent close to seven of those years in solitary confinement like he was an animal.

No, death heralded peace for him, but before that, I wanted him to have some time to live. Even if it only meant taking him back to Sicily to die there, I just wanted him to have a taste of freedom before he passed away.

A knock sounded at the door a second before it opened and my attorney stepped in—Rachel Laker did *not* stand on ceremony, so I didn't take offense.

"Rachel, thank you for coming."

She tilted her head to the side. "You're paying extra for this, Luciu. I didn't agree to make house calls to hospitals."

I ignored her prickly reply and instead asked, "You've secured my release?"

"What do you think?"

Rachel was a shark. A great white in a pond of surfers just looking to be eaten. She hid behind an ice princess facade, a sharp suit, and resting bitch face, but she was damn good at what she did.

Unfortunately for her, she didn't want to work for me, but I had a way of getting what I wanted.

Five years she'd been grousing and sniping at me. I'd take her shitty attitude every fucking time for the legal mayhem she was capable of unleashing on the unwitting courts that were her playground.

"I think you wouldn't be here if I wasn't allowed to go home."

Her chin dipped in assent before she scanned the room, settling on my *prozio*. "Is this your great-uncle?"

"Yes."

"He's refused every attempt at visitation with me."

"I know." I shot her a glance. "I don't blame you for that."

She was one of the few people who had nothing to fear from me, and I didn't want her to think that had changed because liberating Currau had taken longer than she'd first guesstimated.

The bastard was old and stubborn. Not much could be done when he was actively working against letting us help him.

Her fear definitely wasn't something I cultivated. Though she didn't want to work for me, I made it worth her while. Not only did I pay her a fortune, but I'd gotten her on board by hiring her through a charitable foundation that was one of her pet causes.

"Good. The man's more elusive than Casper." Her brow puckered as she took in the state of him. "If we can have his mental health evaluated, perhaps his power of attorney could be transferred over to his family."

"Would that matter? It's not like they care about that."

"It matters. I've already tried to have him released on compassionate grounds but so far, no dice. He's served sixty-four years, Luciu. With a life sentence where the judge stipulated the possibility of parole was only possible after seventy-five years served, the situation is more complicated than you understand. Especially after all his petitions for early parole were denied." She pursed her lips in irritation. "Leave it with me."

Nodding, I said, "Thank you."

"You're welcome." Rachel studied the men in the room, noticed how two of the three weren't conscious, so she stepped closer to me and, *sotto voce*, told me, "They're going to return you to the precinct, not Central Booking. There, you'll be presented in front of the arraignment judge and will be released on bail."

Surprised, I arched a brow. "They're taking this to court?"

She clucked her tongue. "Why are you so surprised? The DA has you in her line of sight." Her mouth firmed with disapproval. "We both know it's personal with her."

I smiled, agreeing, "Couldn't be more personal." Turning back to my great-uncle, smile fading, I murmured, "I don't want to leave him here."

Rachel hesitated. "I'd like to say it won't be for long, but these things take time and money."

"Use whatever you need to get him out," was my immediate reply. "I'll make the funds available."

Unsurprised, she nodded. "I'll leak the word out to the appropriate ears. His deterioration is severe... that might serve us some sympathy."

"Appreciated."

"There's a squad car waiting for you downstairs when you're ready," she told me.

"I'm ready now."

The words were true, but as I made to leave, I found I... *couldn't.*

A strange kind of nostalgia pulled at me.

This man had known my grandfather. He'd known my grandmother before life had made her bitter.

He'd attended their wedding, had been around when the Valentinis had reigned supreme over this city, and yet, here he was, lying in a hospital bed. Sickly and old, frail and forgotten. A nobody.

Just not to his *famigghia.*

I turned to Rachel and cooler this time, a warning lacing the words when I never threatened her, stated, "Get him out of here."

She arched a brow. "Your sister and I have been working on this for a while. We'll do what we can."

"Not good enough." I was pissed at Aurora for taking this long. "I want him out within the month, Rachel."

"I'm a miracle worker, but that might be more than I can pull off, Luciu."

"Make it happen," I said grimly, aware she harrumphed but gave me no promises.

Mouth tight, I gently patted the old man's hand, careful around the IV lines, before I headed out the door which the officer opened for me.

"There's a squad car waiting for *Signor* Valentini downstairs," Rachel directed him.

"I know, ma'am. I'm instructed to cuff him and place him in the officers' custody."

"How are you going to cuff him when he has a cast?" Rachel clucked her tongue in irritation.

"These are orders I need to follow, ma'am."

I held up my good hand for him to cuff, then watched as he tightened the other around his own wrist.

With a final glance at the ward and at my great-uncle through the window in the door, I moved down the hall with Rachel tagging along.

"Will you still be able to attend the FAST gala?" she asked me softly as we stepped into the elevator.

While posed as a polite question, both of us knew it wasn't.

Men in my position had few bosses, not even the IRS held us back, but a lawyer who could work miracles on the legal code? Better than a magic lamp with a genie in it.

"Of course. I'll have a plus one."

"You will?" She arched a brow. "That's unusual."

What was unusual was her commenting.

Rachel didn't do 'personal information' that wasn't relevant to a case.

She didn't appreciate being my lawyer, period.

While she worked mainly for the Satan's Sinners' MC, so wasn't averse to getting blood on her hands, I was well aware that as her client, I was her dirty little secret.

I didn't mind.

The woman was a wizard with loopholes.

I'd never known a legal mind like hers so would deal with her attitude and arrogance because a genius at work deserved room to breathe—maybe if she'd been around back in the sixties, my great-uncle wouldn't have wasted his life behind bars.

I studied her a second, then seeing her pallor was grayer than usual, queried, "Are you okay?"

She turned her gaze away from the doors. "Excuse me?"

"Are you okay?" I repeated. Her dislike of personal information being shared ran both ways.

Her jaw clenched—the muscles turning visibly white under the strain. "I just don't like elevators."

"You've never had a problem before."

"The motion has never made me feel nauseated before," she commented tightly.

"Are you sick?"

"No. Nothing that won't resolve itself after nine months, anyway."

"You're pregnant?"

"Yes." She cast me a withering glance. "Don't worry, I won't fail in my duties to the family."

"I didn't think you would," I disregarded. "After maternity leave, of course."

"Crime doesn't stop for childcare," she commented, her shoulders wriggling as she turned away from me again.

"I suppose it doesn't," I said, surprised because Rachel, though a beautiful woman, was the least sexual person I'd ever come across.

If Rachel had been, I'd have probably come onto her. If not me, then Stan. That spoke of how beautiful she was. But she had higher walls than a Supermax and was as impossible to breach as Alcatraz. Something both Stan and I had picked up on.

The noise of the elevator doors opening broke into the short silence that fell between us, and we started down the hall toward the lobby.

Which, incredibly enough, was where I saw her.

I braked to a halt and immediately turned to the guard. "I wish to speak with someone."

Awkwardly, he muttered, "It's unorthodox, sir."

"He isn't going to stage a breakout," Rachel drawled. "He's going directly to the precinct to be released." To me, she declared, "Five minutes, Luciu."

I almost smirked at the command because she was one of the few people in the world I'd actually listen to, but instead, I dipped my chin as the guard obeyed us both and released me.

Wasting no time, I strode over to the woman who, until I'd set eyes on my great-uncle, had been the only thing on my mind since I'd been taken to Central Booking.

"Jen?" I called out softly, then when she didn't hear me, I said her name again.

She physically jerked when her gaze collided with mine. Her eyes, round and big, frightened, had me bracing myself for what was to come. Then her face crumpled. *She* crumpled.

I never thought she'd hurl herself at me, arms slipping around my waist, face burrowing into my chest as she started sobbing.

Tangling the fingers of my good hand in her hair, holding her close to me with the broken one, I rasped, "*Cara mia*, what is it?" But she was too deep into whatever had happened that had brought her here...

What the hell could it be?

She was fine—otherwise she'd be in a hospital bed, not the lobby.

"Jen, please, *duci*, you're worrying me," I crooned when she cried for a solid two minutes.

Whatever I'd expected when I left my great-uncle's bedside, it wasn't this.

She shuddered in my arms, body heaving with the force of her tears before she pulled back and stared up at me and whimpered, "I told my BFF I loved you and it made her miscarry."

"*Vita mia*, that isn't why someone miscarries." At least, I didn't think so—Stan might know, but I'd never been interested in human biology. It didn't seem logical, however, but it didn't have to be, did it? Wincing on her behalf, I murmured, "I'm sorry for her."

Her bottom lip quivered. "Aoife was so happy."

Reaching up, I cupped the back of her head and drew her to me once more just as the guard mumbled, "Sir, it's been five minutes."

I shot him a glare and Rachel appeared, phone to her ear, one hand on his arm to hold him back. "She's clearly distraught."

He grimaced but nodded. "So long as no one comes looking for us."

Dipping my chin in understanding, I turned my focus back to where it mattered—Jen. My Fionnabhair.

Pressing my lips to the crown of her head, I whispered, "Fi, this isn't your fault. That you love me isn't to blame for what happened."

Had I anticipated she'd tell her friend that?

No.

Was I ecstatic that this flighty butterfly of a woman had pinned herself down for me?

Se.

Categorically, *se.*

"She fainted after I told her."

"Then there must have been an underlying reason." My tone was gentle even if the words were logical and I knew, more than anyone, that logic and feelings didn't always go hand in hand.

For all that I could be brutally cold in business, *sugnu siculo*—I was Sicilian.

Lava ran through my veins, devastating and destructive in its intensity, and where was that powerhouse founded? Emotions. There was nothing more powerful in the whole world than emotions.

She peered up at me, her arms still clinging in a way that Fi did not cling, and that was a testament to her state of mind. Her bottom lip wobbled, and it was right then, right there, that I knew I'd go to war for this woman.

I'd kill to make sure that bottom lip didn't tremble like that.

I'd tear this city apart to keep her safe.

Maybe she saw that, maybe she saw the peculiar resolve in my eyes that she could probably never understand because she didn't have the power to go to war, but she'd learn it.

I'd make sure she did.

"She's so sad, Luc. I want to help her, but I can't," she whispered, eyes closing, but a few teardrops slipped down her cheeks.

"Just being there for her will be enough," I tried to comfort.

However, her brow furrowed and she shook her head. "I-I, just, what are you doing here?" Then, she stared down at my arm. "What happened to you? Why aren't you—"

Pressing a finger to her lips to quiet her, I murmured, "My wrist is broken. I'm going back to the precinct, and I will be released shortly."

"For good?"

"They're pressing charges, but I'm out on bail. There'll be a court case."

"About..." She gulped, her eyes even bigger than before.

Porca troia, I could drown in those liquid orbs. Now wasn't the time for drowning, however, not when she thought I'd been arrested on a murder charge for killing her mother's boyfriend.

"No. Not about him. Something else."

Her lip was sucked in, and she did that thing that told me she was tugging on the underside.

"I tried to find you. Tried to get some information but—"

Fucking Stan.

"All will be well, *cara mia*," I crooned. "Did I not promise you that?"

She swallowed. "You did."

I hummed my appreciation of her ready agreement. "Now, I must leave. I will be back. Stay here, I'll return for you." I peered around, expecting to see a guard. "You have no one with you?"

"No. After you were arrested, they took me back to my apartment."

I gritted my teeth. "I'll make sure my men understand the error of their ways. My brother included."

Something gleamed in her eyes that diminished her sadness. "Can I be there for that argument?"

I had to laugh. The whip of amusement was so swift in comparison to the lash of anger from just a moment before. "I'll make sure you're a witness."

Her smile made an appearance and she darted onto tiptoe to kiss me. "Go now so you can come back soon."

I tugged on her fingers. "In this together?"

Maybe it was the nostalgia of seeing my great-uncle, maybe it was learning of Rachel's pregnancy, maybe it was the million other moments that had taken place over the last few days... but I needed to know.

Her voice was breathy when she whispered, "Yes."

I lifted her knuckles to my mouth and brushed them with my lips. "*Vita mia*, until later."

With a soft squeeze of her fingers, I turned away, found the guard hovering, his shifty eyes telling me he was nervous about being caught out, and I allowed him to cuff me, even as I vowed to myself that she'd never witness this again.

Not as long as we fucking lived.

Now, cuffed, Rachel at my side, we walked over to the cop car. Before I left the lobby, however, I turned to shoot her one final look and saw her watching me.

It was like she was lost. All alone...

I made another vow to her.

Never. Again.

She was, did she but know it, found, and I wasn't a man who lost the things he treasured.

FIVE

JEN

AS QUICKLY AS Luc broke into my misery as I sat, hunched over in the hospital lobby, trying not to lose my shit, he disappeared again.

Twelve hours I'd been here.

Twelve horrendous hours.

The first of which had been spent trying to appease a bawling Jake who wanted his mommy, all while getting no answers about Aoife's condition because, "You're not family, ma'am."

Finn had finally arrived, looking like a crazy person who was going to blow up the hospital if he didn't get answers about his *WIFE*. If he gritted that out between clenched teeth any more times, he'd need a dentist. Only Jake's sobbing had calmed him down because he'd had to focus on him. Then, the rest of the extended clan had turned up.

I'd been fine until Aidan Sr. had arrived, later than the others because he and his wife lived in upstate New York.

My focus had split from where it should be—Aoife—and had focused on him. Watching him. Wanting to see if the O'Donnelly patriarch looked at me with any recognition and I'd just never noticed it before.

Did he know who I was to him?

Did he know I was more than just Aoife's best friend, but his niece?

In the end, and feeling like I was losing my mind, I kept retreating to the lobby for some space.

I'd never imagined that decision would lead to seeing Luc appear from out of nowhere.

So vibrant, so alive, even though he looked more disreputable than I'd ever seen him in his wrinkled suit and with a cast on his arm.

God, had it only been two days since the last time I saw him?

Why did it feel like an eternity?

Needing to check in on Aoife before he came back for me, I returned to the floor where she was resting.

The reasons behind my anxiety attacks—the O'Donnellys—were hovering in the waiting room, looking more fractious than I was used to.

Clearly shaken, Aidan Sr. was a pale and pasty white. His head was tipped back against the wall, his expression averted as if it were a weakness to be seen to be grieving.

How sad was it that he was right?

The world these people inhabited wasn't the regular kind where men who cried were applauded on Tiktok for embracing their emotions.

Here, feelings were exploited.

Weaknesses were used as leverage.

Lena, his wife, had tears in her eyes that she didn't allow to fall as she sat under her husband's arm, while they held each other close.

Most of Finn's adopted family, Eoghan, Declan, Brennan, and Aidan Jr., were all in the waiting room too, their wives tucked close to their sides, making me wish Luc was back. Especially when I caught sight of Savannah sitting beside Aidan Jr., staring at me, willing me to make eye contact.

She'd helped me out last night, but I was in no frame of mind to get into anything with her here.

Aside from her, no one looked at me, adding to the feeling that I was invisible. It wasn't because they were focused on Aoife. It was simply how it always had been—I was a hanger on. Aoife's friend. But they were my family. My blood.

Savannah surged onto her feet like she couldn't contain herself, but my eyes flashed onto hers and I mouthed, "No!"

Pain creased her expression as she mouthed back, "Please?"

Aidan tugged on her hand, his gaze darting between the pair of us, but she didn't turn back to look at him.

Aware the rest of the family was staring at us now, I twisted around and away. I might want their attention but not like this.

Almost bumping into Conor who was sipping some coffee from a paper cup as he slouched down the hallway, I moved over to Aoife's hospital room, where I knocked on the door then stepped in, not waiting for permission to enter. I didn't need permission, just wanted to give them a warning someone was about to go inside.

Aoife had already made it clear earlier that I was welcome here when, after waking up, she'd screamed the house down for Finn, Jacob, and me.

Seeing her in a hospital bed sent flashbacks of the second-to-last time she'd been in one. Not when she'd given birth to Jacob, but the time before.

Talk about a red wedding.

Shivering at the memory of how her 'special day' had devolved, and how it was likely why she was back in a hospital bed now, I moved over to her bedside so I could take her hand.

Hating how pale she looked, how bright her red hair was against the pillows, I muttered, "Any news?"

"By the last check, she's..." His voice broke. "...fine. Just needs to rest."

Finn's tone was a low rasp, pain-filled, stricken with grief. It was in moments like these that he never failed to show me how much he loved his wife. Aoife deserved that kind of love. I gave her crap for it, but she deserved this.

Dedication.

Adoration.

Had I been jealous before and hadn't even known it?

Fuck, I was so selfish sometimes.

News of the pitiful update had me murmuring, "When can she go home?"

"They're saying later today. I'm going to send everyone away. They didn't need to spend the night." He rubbed at his eyes. The motion didn't disturb Jake who was sleeping on his lap.

"They didn't *need* to, Finn, but they wanted to," I chided him. "Wouldn't you and Aoife be here for them if the situation was reversed?"

His sigh said it all.

We fell silent, each of us studying Aoife's drawn features, but after a few minutes, he rasped, "It was..."

I turned to look at him. "What?"

The guilt in his eyes would have hurt me to behold but we both knew the truth—Aoife was only in this bed because of him and his ties to the Irish Mob. Which made me as much of a lunatic for getting involved with Luc, diving face first into this mess myself...

Releasing a breath, understanding and empathizing with Aoife in a way that I never had before—love made us do the craziest of things—I repeated, "What is it, Finn?" My tone was kinder than it would ordinarily have been. He deserved for me to give him a hard time, but his pain was too stark. Too raw.

He loved his wife. He loved his family.

If I hissed at him, condemned him for Aoife's health issues, what good would that do?

"The baby wasn't... it just wasn't meant to be."

"It wasn't because of her—" I struggled to choose a word that wouldn't make him defensive, finally settling on, "—problems?"

"No. Her OB/GYN said her bloodwork was off last Friday." His brow puckered. "This must be why."

"I'm sorry, Finn," I whispered, meaning it.

His eyes clashed with mine. "I thought you'd blame me."

Maybe Jen from Christmastime would have.

But I had a split personality now.

I was Fi as well, thanks to Luc.

I understood that meeting a man could turn your world upside down.

Until it happened to you, it was impossible to believe.

"You said it yourself, the baby just wasn't meant to be."

He swallowed, and I realized he'd been bracing himself for me to lob shit at him. "Thank you, Jen."

"For?"

"Not blaming this on me."

His relief had me taking him in, and I had to admit that the man who had walked into Aoife's tearoom all those years ago was still there, but he was different. Harder in some ways. More approachable in others. Jacob had done that, I thought.

The little boy was currently flat out asleep, resting against his chest, leaving a big drool patch on his daddy's expensive silk shirt, his feet crumpling the tailored pants with his wiggling toes.

At that moment, Finn wasn't the Five Points' money man. He was Aoife's husband and Jake's father. His tie was long gone, his jacket slung on the back of the chair. His eyes were red, his face was blanched, his sorrow etched onto his features...

Finn was hurting.

So, yes, I could be kind.

I didn't need to add to his pain.

"We're her family, Finn. I think it's a good thing that we're on the same side..."

And I wasn't lying.

Aoife would need us both to get her through this. If we were at each other's throats, that certainly wouldn't help her.

An hour later, Finn convinced everyone to go home.

I was pretty sure one of the O'Donnellys had bribed the administrator to let us stay in the waiting room outside of the appropriate hours, and I could see the nursing staff release a relieved sigh as we split up, each of us going our separate ways. Jake included—he went home with Lena and Aidan Sr.

As for myself, Luc had a car waiting for me—one without him in it.

"Where am I going?" I asked as I took a seat in a deliciously warm car.

The driver, one I recognized but not the guy with the extra bushy eyebrows who I knew spoke English, was either pretending not to speak it, or he just didn't want to talk to me. If this thing with Luc was going to become permanent, I needed to learn Sicilian just so these bastards couldn't ignore me.

For all that his rudeness was irksome, I was just grateful that I didn't have to take the subway home.

Tired, overwrought, grieving on my best friend's behalf, I stared out at the road as traffic whirled by us. That was when I realized I was being taken to Luc's apartment. Doubly relieved now, because I'd half-expected to be taken back to my place, I relaxed deeper into the seat.

My cell buzzed, and Savannah's name flashed on the screen.

Because she'd helped me, I connected the call.

"Hey."

"Jen..." Her voice waned.

"Yeah," I breathed, neither of us capable of putting into words what had gone down overnight and over the last couple weeks.

Then, as I thought about what she'd done, my eyes grew wet, and I rasped, "Why did you have to hurt me, Savvie?"

"I didn't mean to," she replied softly, but I heard her sniffles. "I really didn't, Jen. I promise. I was just... You know what it's like when I'm on the hunt for a story.

"I wanted answers, and I was willing to do anything to get them. But after I got the test results back, I didn't need to stick around."

Maybe I was tired, maybe sitting at Aoife's bedside had me in my feels, but I heard her sincerity and believed it.

Or maybe I was just a dumbass who *wanted* to believe, because I missed her more than she could ever have missed me.

"How do I know that's true?"

"You don't, but what you do know is how much I love you. You're my soul sister. You're the only person who's always got my back no matter what crazy shit I pull, who accepts me for me. Who doesn't care that I'm Dagger Daniels' daughter."

I gnawed on my bottom lip, the desire to let go and to keep my friend stronger than the need to hold a grudge.

But because I couldn't let her off the hook without giving her some shade, I told her, "That doesn't mean I don't expect concert tickets when he's next in town. Camden too." Her father and brother were rock stars. Their fame was of the mega variety.

Unlike Savannah, people didn't make a mistake with their surname.

My lips curved at the thought.

"You can have backstage passes for all I care. Please, Jen, please, don't cut me out. It's like..." A breath gusted down the line. "...hell, it's like I've lost my right arm."

"I thought I was the melodramatic one," I grumbled, even if, inside, I perked up.

"You are, but in this instance, that's how I'm feeling. I hate that you're mad at me, even as I understand it, but there was a lot less malice in it than you think."

Tiredly, I reached up and rubbed at my eyes. "You know this doesn't mean everything is back how it was, Savvie, don't you?"

"I have to earn your trust. I get it."

"Good," I mumbled. "Thank you for helping me last night."

"As if I wouldn't," she retorted with a huff. "Anyway, she's going to be my sister-in-law... and she's your ride or die."

A welter of love and grief walloped me in the chest. "I wish I could have done something to help her."

"You stood by her side."

"Aoife has had to deal with so much grief, Savannah. You've no idea. I just wish—"

"She's got a family like no other, Jen. I haven't been around the O'Donnellys as much as you have, but even I can see how close-knit they are."

"Close-knit and drowning in their secrets," I said with a huff.

"Isn't every family?"

"Maybe. Everyone has filthy secrets, I guess; it just seems as if theirs are worse."

"That'd make a good title for a book."

"What?"

"Filthy Secret."

I snorted. "Shuddup. You and books, I swear."

"Don't make out like you're a bimbette and don't read," Savannah drawled, making my lips curve.

"I read good books, none of that non-fiction crap." Then, what she said hit me. "Your sister-in-law?"

"What?"

"You said you were going to be sisters-in-law."

Silence tumbled down the line. Just enough for me to frown. "Well, you know how close Aidan and Finn are."

I blinked. "They're BFFs."

"Exactly."

Exactly?

Luciu's building surged into my line of sight, and I realized we were just down the street. Fatigue and exhaustion walloped me in the chest, as if I'd been keeping it together for this long and needed to let it all go.

Sagging into the seat, I murmured, "I have to go, hon. I'll text you later, okay?"

"You mean that?" she rushed out.

"Yeah. I mean that. You still gotta work yourself back into my good graces, but I don't want..." I sighed—why overcomplicate things? "I missed you." It was as simple as that. Before she could say a word, I scrambled to tell her, "Speak later." I cut the call.

Twisting the cell in my hand, the need to see Luc an ache in my soul, I waited as the driver pulled up outside his building and the doorman made an appearance to open the door for me.

Ordinarily, I'd have sashayed down the crimson carpet toward the downstairs lobby, but being turned away from his building still stung.

And after last night, the only place I wanted to sashay into was a bed.

Preferably one with Luc in it.

I needed to speak with him about his arm. He didn't look like he'd been in a fight, so I wasn't sure how he could have broken a bone unless the cops had done it.

God, if they had I'd be wicked pissed. Dirty fucking cops.

Agitated at the idea, and hurt that he hadn't come to pick me up like he'd said he would, I strode down the gleaming tiled entryway toward the bank of elevators and made my way inside. As I did, a screen I'd never noticed turned on, and I saw Luc's face peering back at me.

With another man, I'd never have said a word.

But this was Luc.

"Why didn't you come to the hospital?"

"It took longer than I'd have liked to be released." He pulled a face. "Plus..." He shook his head. "Never mind."

I eyed him, saw the weariness on his face, and asked, "Do you have to go out?"

Eight AM was on the horizon, and I knew he had his club to manage —and whatever else came as part of being the new Don in town, especially after being away from it for a few days—but he looked tired. As tired as I felt.

He sighed. "I should, but I don't want to. There's food waiting for us."

The doors opened a couple of seconds later, and I stepped out of the elevator and found him waiting there for me.

He had a towel around his hips and nothing else, which revealed a lot of delicious ab muscles that were just made to be salivated over. A few droplets of water trickled down his shoulders and his chest.

"You just got in?"

He grunted. "Came straight back here to wash off the stench of jail. That was the last time you'll have to touch me reeking of that place."

His melodramatic statement had my lips twitching, which felt good to be honest. Surrounded by melodramatic people, it made me feel like less of a drama llama.

After the last couple of chaotic days, I was starting to feel like I was living in a *telenovela*, and no one needed that.

I reached up and pressed a hand to his pec, moving closer into him, pleased when he looped his arms around my waist and tugged me deeper into his hold. Sure, his cast burrowed into my back, but it was worth it.

Looking into his eyes, staring into them for so long that I could have lost myself in them, I asked, "What charges did they arrest you on?"

He tilted his head to the side. "You sure you want to know?"

"Yes," I told him firmly, well aware that if I asked a question, then I should expect a truth that I might not appreciate.

"Desecration of a cemetery."

"Oh." My nose crinkled as I thought about the night I'd woken up and had found him sitting in my bedroom, watching me sleep. He'd passed me a Ziploc bag full of dirty jewelry that had come from his enemy's grave.

Yes, I was being embraced by a man who ransacked graves.

If I were a religious person, my knees would be sore from how much penitence I'd be seeking.

"They can't tie me to the crime."

Well, that was a relief. "Why?"

"No plates on the vehicle, no visuals. Nothing to indicate that it was us. Not affirmatively, anyway."

"So why are they going through with it?"

"The DA has a hard-on for me."

"Not in a good way?"

He smirked. "In the worst possible way." He didn't look too worried though, so that eased my concerns some.

"I'll bet. What happened with the arm?" I tossed out, needing to keep my voice cool because otherwise, I'd start squeaking.

Nobody needed to hear that.

"Paid someone to snap it."

Processing that took more than I was literally capable of right now. "I need food and then I need to sleep before I can unwrap the whys behind that."

And boy, was there a lot to unpack. So many things that had happened in the space of a few days, and out of nowhere, it was like a headache just morphed into being.

Ping.

Except it would have been nicer to get a hammer to the temple.

He brushed his lips against my forehead. "Both options are available to you." Wincing at the sudden onset of a headache, I hugged him back and as I did, he surprised me by rasping, "I'm sorry about Aoife."

"Me too." *Me fucking too.* "I don't think I can eat now."

He kissed my temple, and then, he did exactly what I needed.

Standing there, leaning against him, I couldn't move if my life depended on it, and the thought of food made me heave.

He seemed to sense that, and he shepherded me down the hall to his bedroom.

He undressed me, and slipped me between the sheets, then dropping the towel, curled up behind me.

After he whispered something in Sicilian, something that sounded a lot like, "*Bona nutti,*" I sighed as the words filtered into my mind and I let myself drift away.

Knowing that, for this short while, he'd keep the monsters at bay.

SIX

LUC

I WOKE up to the sound of chatter.

Chatter in my apartment wasn't normal.

Chatter at home was, which meant 'home' had come to me.

Heaving a sigh, I opened my eyes and found Fi fast asleep at my side.

Having always appreciated my space in bed, it surprised me how much I loathed that she did too. We'd started off glued together but now there was a good three feet between us.

That was the moment I accepted that I might have to get a new bed.

I wanted skin-to-skin touch.

I wanted her cleaved to me in the middle of the night—

"I can feel you watching me," she mumbled drowsily.

"Good. You should know when your man's eyes are on you."

That had hers popping open, and a smirk creasing her jaw. "We need to watch *Twilight* together." I groaned under my breath which had her cackling. "Oh, yeah, this has to happen. You'll get why it's weird then."

"I already watched it," I admitted, hiding a grin when she squealed with laughter and hurled herself at me.

Smugly satisfied that she was back in my arms without me having to do anything, she peered at me, demanding, "Well? You see why it's weird now?"

"It's weird when *he* did it. He's a boy."

"He was a hundred years old! You're a baby by comparison."

"He wasn't a man."

"Let me guess, they only breed men in Sicily?"

My eyes twinkled. "Where you're concerned, *se*."

She snorted. "Big head." Before I could say anything, she grumbled, "Yeah, yeah, yeah, big *everything*."

Grinning outright now, I told her, "I know it's strange to watch you sleep."

"But you do it anyway?"

"I know it's wrong to kill people, Fi," I drawled, "doesn't stop me from doing it."

That had her squinting at me. "Do you think reminding me that you kill people will stop me pressuring you to watch the sequel to *Twilight*?"

"Did it work?"

"Nope."

Groaning for real now, I was about to argue when I heard a soft laugh coming from the dining room, one that made my lips tip up at the edges.

"Who's that?" Fi bristled.

I turned to her, amused to find a hint of the green-eyed monster in her pout. "My mother."

She blinked. "Oh."

"I told you, no other woman has lain in this bed, *cara mia*. Unless—"

"Oh, my God! Luciu!" She sat up, the sheets dropping down to her waist, revealing her naked self that made me bitterly resent the presence of my family outside these walls. "I can't believe I forgot."

My focus on her tits, the tips like dark cherries that made my mouth water at the sight, I hummed, "Yes?"

"Luciu, this is serious." She snatched the sheet, dragging it off my upper body to cover herself. "The woman who told me she was your wife..."

Confused why she was bringing this up now, and why she was so hesitant, I asked, "*Se?*"

I'd had Stan look into the incident, and he'd told me the security footage showed only Fi fleeing the bathroom. Not trusting him with this, I'd watched it myself—Fi entered the bathroom, then ran out of it a few moments later.

Because a woman was allowed to change her mind, I hadn't investigated further, but it *hadn't* stopped me from attempting to court her.

That was before she'd told me about my so-called wife.

I'd sent Stan on the hunt for information once again. He showed me a list of the people who'd been in the VIP lounge that evening—an ex-lover's name was on there. As a result, I'd sent her a message, warning her to back the fuck out of my life or she'd reap the rewards of disobeying me.

I had no desire to reveal to Fi that I was capable of issuing those kinds of threats to a woman, however. Yet she remained silent, so I prodded, "What is it, *cara mia*?"

"That woman was at the airfield, Luc," she blurted out. "I know you have no reason to believe me, but I swear, she was waiting on you—"

And suddenly, everything made sense.

Fury swelled inside me. "She was?" I intoned grimly, pinning her gaze to mine.

"I promise I'm not lying. She was there when the cops read you your Mirandas."

Pezz'i miedda.

I'd been slow off the mark—he'd doctored the footage.

Stan was in on this conspiracy too.

I surged off the bed as if she'd just set the mattress on fire, and before she could say another word, I stalked into the bathroom, grabbed my robe, and hauled it on.

With Fi gaping at me, I stormed out of the room and hollered, "Aurora!"

If *Matri* was here, then she would be too.

I heard the sound of swiftly padding footsteps coming from behind me, and as I merged into the dining room, Fi collided into me in her haste to catch up.

"Luciu?" *Matri* asked calmly.

She was usually calm.

Her accent was no longer tinted with the hint of the West Country, but had morphed, over time, much as ours had. She sounded more British than we did, but Stan, Aurora and I had purposely adopted neutral American accents in the decade we'd been here.

Especially Aurora, who'd attended college at Brown then had gone on to Yale.

I shot *Matri* a tight smile before I snarled at my twin sister, "What the hell is your game?"

Fi's hand bunched in my robe as she peered around me, coming face-to-face with my family who were sitting, eating my food.

"It's her!" Fi exclaimed.

"Of course it is," I ground out, more at Rory who smirked at me, slouched back in her goddamn seat as if she owned the fucking place. "What right do you have to interfere in my life?"

Snapping off the end of a breadstick, she replied in Sicilian, "When it involves delousing you of whores, brother mine, I'll do whatever I have to. Our work isn't done yet."

My nostrils flared in outrage as I jabbed a finger in the air, but before I could say a word, Fi demanded, "Who is she?"

"She's my goddamn sister," I grated out, holding her behind me when I saw she wore the bedsheet and nothing else.

I'd cut out Stan's eyes before I let him see another inch of her beauty.

Like he could read my mind, he shot me a wolfish grin before he took an overly large bite of spaghetti loaded with ragú.

"*Duci*, go and get changed. Let me sort things out—"

"She told me you were her husband, Luciu," Fi hissed, her eyes snapping with fire. "And the bitch shoved me on my ass in your bathroom. She fucking slapped me."

I straightened at that, shooting my twin a glare over my shoulder. Unapologetically, she shrugged.

"*Cristo*, how dare you," I hissed at my sister. Twisting back around, I reached up and cupped Fi's chin, murmuring, "I will get to the bottom of this. Go and put some clothes on, *bedda mia*, hmm?"

She glowered at Rory and spat, "You hit me again, bitch, and I'll bring my A game. Surprise won't hold me back next time."

"There won't be a next time," I intoned grimly, earning myself a sniff from Fi.

"Bet your ass there won't."

With a final scowl, she grabbed the sheets, holding them tight to her much as if it were a fancy ballgown before storming down the hall with all the panache of a furious queen heading for her throne.

With her gone, I faced the dinner table and demanded, "What's your play, Aurora? And yours, fuckwit?"

I grabbed one of the bread rolls and hurled it at Stan. It bounced off his chest and plopped onto his plate.

"*Grazii*, Luciu. I needed that," he told me with a smirk before he tore into it and took a massive bite.

"If either of you were anyone else, your cheeks would be—" There was hell in my eyes, but I stopped before I could utter another word. *Matri* did *not* need to hear this. "I don't like you keeping *miedda* from me. First the bullshit with the grave, then this? I get that we're running out of time with Currau but pulling moves without consulting me is a no go."

She arched a brow at me, smiling as she murmured, "Technically, this came before the graveyard fiasco."

"Not a fiasco," Stan retorted. "We wore masks. No plates. You have no evidence."

"Exactly. The perfect crime to haul your ass into court over. I'm renowned for my tough stance on the mafia, Luciu," she drawled. "How would it look if I didn't ream you a new one from time to time?"

My mouth tightened. "You couldn't have coordinated it better?"

"With all that lovely press on hand? I'd say that I coordinated it perfectly. I told you on the plane what was going to happen."

"With minutes to spare," I snapped.

"Children, calm down," *Matri* attempted to soothe which had Rory smiling slyly at me while I glowered at her.

"Everyone knows his face now," Stan pointed out, spooning up more ragú like he hadn't eaten in months.

"Exactly. The city knows who he is. No more hiding in the shadows," my sister declared, her eyes gleaming with triumph. "Quite the entrée."

"You planned for that eventuality?" I boomed, hands gripping the back of the chair so I didn't try to strangle her instead.

"Luciu, there's no need to raise your voice," *Matri* tried to appease.

"Who do you think called in the press?" Rory inserted.

"You go too far," I snapped, ignoring Mother entirely. "Without my approval."

Outrage flashed in Rory's eyes. "*Your* approval? I don't need your approval to manage this *famigghia* and make sure we take back our rightful place in Manhattan."

Stan sniffed. "You're turning into a megalomaniac."

"I'm not," she immediately discounted, reaching for her glass of *vinu* and taking a deep sip of it. "You know I'm always ten steps ahead."

"I do, and I'd like to be informed of each of those steps. Especially if it involves you doxxing me."

"Is it doxxing?" Stan countered before he took another bite then pointed his fork at me. "Doxxing's an internet thing."

"Doxxing is a life thing, dear," *Matri* replied calmly, her fork sliding against the china as she picked at a green salad. Her limpid blue eyes drifted over her youngest son. "You really must keep up with today's slang."

Despite myself, I had to laugh, especially when Stan turned bug-eyed. "I'm twenty-nine, *Matri*, not a child."

"Well, apparently you need to get out more. All this beating people up, what about your spirit, dear? Hmm?"

"*Se*, Stan, what about your spirit?" I sniped.

Matri turned to look at me with an arched brow. "You think I haven't heard about your obsession with *Alice in Wonderland*? That's sick, Luciu. Sick."

As my siblings roared with laughter, I blustered, "I haven't even read the book, never mind seen the movie!"

"Cheshire Cat..." Rory prompted, her eyes sparkling with glee as she traced one finger over her lip and along the curve of her cheek.

My brow furrowed. "*Matri*, that has nothing to do with *Alice in Wonderland*. In fact, no." I heaved a sigh. "I prefer you thinking that I have a weird fetish rather than knowing what it actually is."

Stan cackled. "You think my spirit's in jeopardy, *Matri*..."

"Eat your fucking ragú." I folded my arms across my chest. "Look, we're getting away from the crux of the matter. You pretended to be my goddamn wife, Aurora. That's just wrong. On so many levels. And you helped her!"

I directed another roll of bread at Stan's head. This time, it hit its target and he huffed at me, barely managing to catch it before it collided with his wine glass.

"He has a point, Rory," *Matri* murmured before she tutted, "And you, Stan, getting involved. I think you all need to see a shrink."

Rory sniffed. "Lover boy over there was about to get led around by his dick. I had to stop that from happening. We had shit to do, and that doesn't involve him falling in love with a gold digger."

"Your grandfather told me that your father was a gold digger," *Matri* informed us. "He wasn't right, was he?"

The news had me slumping into my seat at the head of the dinner table. "Grandfather said that?"

"He didn't like your father."

"Was that why we visited alone?"

Nodding, *Matri* took a sip of some still water and told us, "He wouldn't have anything to do with him. I was surprised that he was so good with you three, but he loved you. Just didn't like your father." She shot Rory a pointed look. "Don't make things hard on Luciu. We fall in love when our hearts make the decision."

"I never want to fall in love," was Rory's grim reply.

"Yeah, we know," Stan said with a huff.

And we did.

Rory had been making the same declaration since she was twelve years old. That was why we'd been stunned when she'd gotten married while in college. It hadn't lasted long, but still.

"You think I asked to feel this way?" I demanded.

What I felt for Fi was riddled with peril. There were parts of me that were stirring to being that were far more dangerous than anything I'd experienced before.

Rage had fueled our rise to the top of NYC, but what I felt for Fi outweighed that rage.

Tenfold.

"There's nothing like it." *Matri's* misty smile turned sorrowful, which, of course, was why Rory and Stan began glaring at me.

"This isn't my fault," I mouthed at them, flipping them both the bird.

Twisting to the side when I heard Fi's approach, I held out a hand and found myself relieved that she was wearing clothes again. I didn't give her a choice about where she was sitting, instead, hauled her down onto my lap.

She scowled at me and immediately started struggling. "Luciu," she hissed. "Your mother's here! You haven't even introduced me!"

Unapologetically, I replied, "My lap is as good a seat as any."

Matri laughed and told Fi, "It's a pleasure to meet you. I'm Lauren."

"This is Jennifer MacNeill," I replied, satisfied when she stopped struggling and, with a huff, perched on my lap as if it were a chair—her back straighter than a knife's edge.

"Irish?" *Matri* asked with no small amount of surprise.

"American," Fi countered with a grimace.

Matri peered at me, and because I knew why—she was aware of some of our machinations, mostly because we argued about them over dinners with her—I replied, "She has ties to the Irish thanks to friends." I pointed a finger at my sister. "That is my twin. Aurora. I don't suppose you need the introduction seeing as you've already met." Rory sniffed, but Fi tensed. "Apologize, Aurora."

She glared at me. "I will not."

"Fucking apologize," I snarled in Sicilian. "I won't tolerate this bullshit."

The staring contest that unfurled between us only ended when Rory grumbled the least apologetic apology in history. "Sorry." The word was aimed at her *vinu russu* not Fi.

I squeezed Fi's waist, unsurprised when she didn't accept it. I wouldn't have either, but from my sister, this was a massive concession.

Wishing to change the subject, *fast*, because I was sure Fi's temper was barely appeased—rightfully so—I hollered, "Alina!"

Her head popped around the door to the kitchen. "Yes?"

"We'll have whatever they're having, *pi favuri.*"

Alina eyed us both, sniffed her disapproval at our position as well, I thought, at my lack of proper clothes, then retreated to the kitchen.

"I'm sure I didn't raise you to be so rude," *Matri* commented.

"No, you raised him to have a fetish for *Alice in Wonderland*," Stan said, sniggering as he made the comment.

I scowled at him then jabbed the air with my finger. "You were on my shit list before this, *frate*, for not bringing Jen here, so I wouldn't add—"

"You never told me to," he interrupted. "If you hadn't shoved my ass in coach, I could have handled things differently."

"I told your men that Luciu wanted me to come back here. They ignored me," Fi countered, her tone as fierce and angry as I'd expected.

Oh, fuck.

There was me, getting a boner at the dinner table, with my mother in attendance.

Fi knew as well.

The minx.

That straight-as-a-knife's edge spine of hers collapsed as she sank into me, and her butt nestled against my hardening cock.

I nipped her waist with my good hand, but she didn't even glance at me, just carried on glowering at Stan.

"Without direct orders from Luciu—"

"If it involves Jen's safety," I rumbled, "she might as well be talking for me. You got me?"

Stan rolled his eyes. "I got you."

"You'd better fucking do. Making her go back to her place after everything?" I scowled at him. "I want to know the guards who drove her as well. Those fuckers—"

"Luciu!" *Matri* barked. "Not in front of guests."

I wanted to tell her Fi wasn't a guest, that she was fucking mine, but I figured that was for another time.

Especially when my woman and twin sister collided with one another in a stare down that was worthy of a Western movie.

"Rory," *Matri* intoned, the warning stark. Then, in Sicilian, she remarked, "We love who we love."

I cast her a grateful glance. "I do love her, *Matri*."

"I can see that."

Jen shuffled on my lap, not because of my boner, but because we'd been speaking another language again.

"Sorry, Jennifer. It's second nature to flip between languages," *Matri* apologized.

"It's okay. And please, call me Jen."

"Jen, it is. It's wonderful to meet you. It's clear that you and Luciu know each other well."

"Only in the Biblical sense," Stan muttered.

"Stan, if you want to continue eating that ragú and don't want to wear it, then you'll shut up with your snide comments."

"He can afford to wear it," Rory retorted. "That's his third serving."

I shook my head. "I'm glad you're moving out. You cost me a fortune in food."

"Like your bank balance is suffering," Stan jeered, but he placed his forearm on the table, directly in front of his dish as if I were about to snatch it away from him.

"And you're not? Bitching about coach when you could have paid for the upgrade yourself?"

Alina bustled in, breaking up our argument, a tray in her arms, two dishes on the platter that she placed in front of Fi and me. Cutlery was laid down next, then she retreated to the kitchen, returning a minute later with glasses, followed by a jug of water.

"It's impractical to eat sitting like that, Luciu," *Matri* chided. "Let the girl up."

Though I huffed, I relinquished my hold on Fi's waist, but she surprised me by saying, "It's okay."

Naturally, I tightened my arm around her waist again.

Leaning forward, she started to toy with the pasta, and I tried not to focus on how her lips pursed around the tines, on how she—

Fuck.

"What happened to your wrist, Luciu?" *Matri* asked.

Forcing myself to focus on my food rather than on the sweetness of Fi's ass nestled against my cock, I answered, "Nothing."

"Nothing? Do you think I'm an idiot?"

Fi snickered a little, then she turned to me and asked, "Yes, Luciu, do you think your mother's an idiot?"

I shot her a warning glance that did nothing other than make her smirk at me. "No, I don't think you're an idiot, *Matri*, but there's nothing to tell. A small accident, that was all."

She cast me a disdainful glance then murmured, "I wonder why my children think I have no idea about the business they're involved in, Jen. Especially when they talk about it so freely in front of me."

Surprisingly, Jen retorted, "Because they equate motherhood with being a moron."

I arched a brow at her. "I don't think *Matri* is an idiot."

"Me either," Stan grumbled.

"I don't," Rory said with a sniff.

"You do," *Matri* countered, her tone musing as she studied Fi. "You're right, Jen. They do."

"I don't think it's intentional. More like inbred misogyny."

"Inbred misogyny?" Rory mocked. "Am I not a woman too?"

"Women can be misogynists. Take yourself, Aurora," Fi said sweetly. "Dismissing me as nothing other than a walking vagina because I like the finer things in life..."

Matri let loose a laugh. "She has you there, Rory."

"No, she doesn't—"

"Then why would you pretend to be your brother's wife if you didn't immediately judge me and disregard me? Was I not worthy of him because my dress was short? Because it was low cut?" She switched her glance between my siblings. "Men often judge women, but women can be even cattier. You judged me on the length of my skirt, not on my IQ."

"And how smart are you?" Rory scoffed.

"Smart enough to know that something shady is going on if you were present at your brother's arrest..." Her glance turned sly. "I'd imagine your surname isn't Valentini."

"It isn't," *Matri* agreed, her eyes twinkling as she watched Fi toy with Rory, an occurrence that rarely happened in our household. "It's Fitzwilliam. I was the last Fitzwilliam, and my father refused to leave me or them an inheritance unless they continued our surname."

"Only Stan and I are Valentinis now," I told her, even though this was definitely a family secret. "We go by our ancestral name."

"But your sister doesn't..." Fi's words waned as she weighed up my twin who, in turn, was eyeing her like she was trying to figure out if she could take her in a fight. "One-thirty-three, by the way."

Rory frowned. "One-thirty-three?"

"My IQ," Fi said sweetly. "My IQ is longer than the length of my hemlines."

Matri let loose a chuckle. "Smart enough to tangle with you, Rory; that means Luciu must have met his match. You're the only one who could ever twist him up in an argument."

I groused, "I let her win."

Stan shoved his dish away. "If you believe that, you really are more stupid than you look."

Glowering at him, I began eating, but Fi twisted on my lap and demanded, "Well? Is no one going to tell me who the hell she is? How was she there when you were arrested?"

There was silence for a moment as the entire family looked among each other, wondering who'd say it first.

Naturally, it was my dipshit brother who declared, "Meet the youngest District Attorney in NYC's history."

"She's the DA?" Fi gasped, her fork falling to her plate with a noisy clatter.

"That's one way to describe her," I said grimly. "Pain in my ass is the other."

SEVEN

"WHAT YOU ARE DOING?"

The thick, accented English had me twisting around to face Alina, Luc's disapproving housekeeper. I knew who it was from the accent alone, and I'd known she was there from the start because of her heavy footsteps.

She'd glared at me when she served me dinner, and she was glaring at me now, but I didn't have to answer her. I didn't have to do jack.

Instead, I averted my focus back to the tile that I was scrubbing with a toothbrush.

"What you are doing?" she repeated, and I heard her shoes clomp as she moved nearer to me.

"I'm cleaning," I answered on a huff as the scent of verbena perfume filled my nostrils.

Better than detergent, I guessed.

"Is no clean?"

"It's plenty clean." I scowled at her. "You speak some English, I see."

Which meant she'd totally understood me when I'd come to the building and had let her daughter translate for her on her behalf.

Bitch.

She ignored that. "Then why clean?"

Blowing a stream of air onto my forehead to cool down some, I stared up at her. "We got a problem?"

"You say is dirty?"

"No. I'm saying I *need* to clean."

She frowned at me, stared at the toilet bowl, then grunted something in her language as she wandered off.

Relieved to be alone again, I returned to my task, before I treated the entire bathroom floor to a toothbrushing.

It was pretty satisfying because Luc had one of those washroom floors with the tiny mosaic tiles so I could scrub around each corner, and it was big too, so as time passed, I was legit getting high on Lysol.

Sweaty and tired, I continued with my cleaning session, happy not to be thinking about stuff because my recent past had been weird.

Weird.

As.

Fuck.

And the simplicity of cleaning was just... *nice*. Not thinking about anything other than making sure the place was hygienic came as both a relief and a release because, somehow, I'd gotten myself involved in a real life conspiracy.

Somehow...

Jesus wept.

"I've been thinking—"

I let out a sharp gasp as I pivoted on my knees and found Luciu standing in the doorway, leaning against the door jamb, looking cool as fuck and as if he'd been watching me like I was a damn show on TLC.

"What the hell? I swear, you got a creep gene in your body or some-thing that lets you sneak around."

I'd heard Alina from a mile away, but him? He was such a ghost.

The edges of his mouth quirked up. "Is there a reason you're on your knees and it doesn't involve sucking my dick?"

I arched a brow at him. "I wanted to clean."

"Alina does that."

"She ratted me out, didn't she?"

"I think she was concerned that you were judging her cleaning skills." He eyed me. "Queens don't clean bathroom floors, Fionnabhair."

Ohh, he rolled out the full name.

I squinted at him. "Queens make their own decisions about how they get stress relief."

Angry with the world, I scrubbed the floor some more even though it no longer needed it. Well, to be fair, it hadn't needed it in the first place.

"The call with Aoife did not go well?" he hazarded a guess.

I'd called Finn earlier, but no dice.

"She was sleeping still." I let a stream of breath gust upward onto my sweaty forehead. "I feel bad for her."

"Of course you do," he crooned.

Learning that his sister was the motherfucking DA, that she'd been behind his arrest, that, somehow, the Italian mafia had infiltrated the goddamn DA's office…

Excuse me while I hyperventilated.

Was it any wonder I needed to clean?

He jarred me from my thoughts by stepping into the bathroom and holding out a hand for me.

"I'm dirty," I countered. "I need to shower."

"Then shower."

Despite the chaos in my mind, my lips twitched. "With you watching?"

He shrugged. "I'll turn around if you want."

"I should make you. It might discourage you from doing creepy things."

"Your creep, remember?" he teased, utterly unapologetic which was probably what I liked about him.

He owned up to his assholery. Not many men did that.

It made it easier to snatch up his hand, and I used it to get to my feet. The second I was standing, I dropped my hold on his fingers, then began stripping off in front of him, my eyes engaged with his.

He did a remarkable job of keeping his gaze above the tit line, and instead, moved over to the wall where the faucets were.

After I hastily folded the clothes and dropped them into the laundry hamper, he turned on the water, and I trailed my fingers through the rainfall spray, slipping under it when the temperature was right.

He appeared in front of me, uncaring that the cuffs of his jeans grew damp, and I snagged the bottle of body wash that he handed me.

As I washed up, I knew his focus shifted, sliding over my flesh like the water itself.

I didn't put on a show, because I wasn't in the mood for that. Just cleaned up because I hated being grimy, only I didn't bother using a sponge and used my hands to lather up so I guessed that was a prick-tease in and of itself.

His voice was gruff, two octaves lower by my calculations as he rumbled, "Rory's position concerns you."

Tension filled me. "Something like that."

"Why?" He tipped his head to the side. "You have to know your government is corrupt."

I did.

But...

I closed my eyes as I tipped my head under the spray. "Just ignore me. I'll get over this."

He was right. I knew cops were dirty, I knew officials were on the take, and then there was that shit with the New World Sparrows who'd infiltrated every part of the government...

So why was I freaking out about this?

"How attached are you to working for Crawford et al?" He couldn't have asked a better question to shatter my thoughts.

I arched a brow at him. "Not attached, but I need the salary."

He scoffed at that. "The salary that covers rent on that shithole you lived in is not a salary worth holding on to."

Lived in.

Past tense.

I knew I should argue, but spending a single night in my apartment had been hell. I had no desire to go back there. It might be so clean I could eat off the floor, but it would always be stained red in my memory.

"So says Mr. Bigshot," I sniped, trying to focus more on his arrogant comment than on the memory of Vlad bleeding out on my bedroom floor. "I worked my ass off for that position."

"I don't dispute that." He wafted a hand. "Your boss is a dick—"

"You're telling me," I interrupted glumly.

"—I looked into him."

"You did? Why?"

"Because he's in your life, of course."

That had me squinting at him with suspicion. "So's the barista at Starbucks. Did you go all J. Edgar Hoover on him?"

"No. But if you'd flirted with him, then maybe."

"You're nuts," I muttered, but I wouldn't deny—I liked him nuts.

"That didn't sound like a complaint, *vita mia*," he retorted, his voice more of a purr than my ovaries could handle.

"It was a statement of recognition. Acceptance. Not disapproval. But a warning that I'll only take so much bullshit."

His grin made an appearance, and it nearly floored me. So free and so expressive... When I thought back to that first night we'd met, when I'd seen him at The 68... so serious. Somber.

Had I done this?

Had I brought some levity to his life?

I wasn't sure how I had considering the last few days, but the readiness of his smile defrosted the ice around my heart.

"You like my bullshit," he declared, sounding so utterly Sicilian at that moment that I rolled my eyes hard enough it was a wonder they didn't fall out.

"You keep telling yourself that," I drawled. "Anyway, what did you find out about my boss? Anything worthy of blackmail?"

He laughed. "That's for another day. But I have an idea..."

Unease hit me.

"Luc, he's a jackass but he doesn't deserve to die," I stated, getting ready to save my boss's life even though he didn't know it was in danger.

"I'm not the Joker, Fi," he groused. "I don't just kill for fun."

"Good to know," I snarked.

"But I looked into his portfolio and yours... I have a proposition for you."

"I won't work for you if that's where this is going," I retorted, stomping over to turn off the water myself. "I won't tie my security to you."

He arched a brow. "I have legitimate fronts."

"So? You'd still be my boss." I scoffed. "Tying myself to any man for security would make me a damn fool."

"You have a skill I need. Why wouldn't I try to hire you to use it? And I'll pay better than Crawford, Lewis, and Jones. I'll make sure you have an ironclad contract too."

"How ironclad?" I demanded, grabbing one of the towels from the heated rail and tying it around my chest.

"Very ironclad. In case we don't work out—" A devilish gleam appeared in his eyes.

In another man, I might have thought he was trying to be funny, but Luc... I didn't think so.

I wasn't sure if that meant he'd kill me if we didn't work out, or if it was impossible that we wouldn't. Regardless, I folded my arms over my chest and cupped my elbows.

"—your job security won't be tied to the length of our relationship."

"Because you'll kill me so it's not a problem?"

He placed a hand on his heart. "You wound me, Fi."

"Yeah, you sound wounded."

"You're obsessed with death," he chided. "It isn't good for you."

My eyes rounded. "No, I know that."

He flicked his fingers. "Life is too short—"

"It is around you," I sniped.

"—to be worrying about death all the time. You should know that I'd never hurt you."

"I'm pretty sure Damian told me that at one point or another," I whispered, hating that my voice broke in the middle of that sentence. But I was freaking out. Today was one long round of crazy, and learning about his sister's job was just the icing on a shitty cake.

Luc's eyes darkened, but he clucked his tongue as he strode over to me. His good hand came to my shoulder, and he slipped it down over my upper arm while banding the other one at my back. "*Amore mia*, now you *do* wound me. Comparing me to that mutt... I will never hurt you. *Ever.*"

I released a sigh and rested my forehead against his chest.

I believed him. Call me crazy, but I did.

"When did things get so complicated, Luc? I can't even blame you for half of it."

His voice was amused as he told me, "That's good to know. You sure you won't bring it up in an argument when we're sixty?"

Something inside me seized up at the ease in which he spoke of the future.

Did he really mean that?

My mouth worked, my eyes burned, and I had no choice but to slide my arms around his waist and hold him.

He grounded me in that moment. Grounded me in a way that he'd never comprehend because I wasn't capable of describing it or explaining it to him.

"What is it, *duci?*" he asked me gently when I just stood there, not saying a word, only holding on for dear life like he was a life raft and I'd been tossed out onto the open sea.

How did I answer?

I was an O'Donnelly.

I'd murdered a man.

My sister from another mister had just lost her baby.

He'd been arrested.

I was in love.

His sister had pretended to be his wife.

I was in fucking love.

His sister had been pivotal in his arrest.

My BFF had betrayed me...

His sister was the mother-shitting-fucking DA.

So many things, *too many.*

Rome wasn't built in a day, however, and that was why I did what I always did in times of upheaval.

I focused on the green.

"What's the starting salary?"

TEARS LOOKED good on some women.

Diamond-like droplets spilled from their lashes, their cheeks didn't dare turn pink, their lips quivered, and their brows barely furrowed with emotion.

Rory was like that.

I'd seen her cry so rarely that it was close to a supernatural phenomenon, but every time it had happened, her face, the tears, her emotions had all been disconnected somehow.

The tears came because she hurt but her face didn't get with the program.

Fi, I'd thought, would be the same.

Thanks to her upbringing, I'd imagined she either wouldn't cry that much, or if she did, she'd remain icy cold.

Having seen her in the aftermath of a murder, without a single tear shed, I'd thought my summation was right on track. I'd thought she'd stare down emotion like it was the barrel of a gun, locking it away and hoarding it so that no one would know she'd felt anything.

That was why her admission that she loved me had triumph soaring through me.

A woman like this caved into her feelings for no man.

Until me.

When I woke that night, however, to soft sniffles, to the slightest of judders in the bed as she trembled and shook, my perception of her, and my sister, did a complete one-eighty.

Both of them were hard as nails. Both were smart—too smart for their own good. Both were arrogant and unafraid of life even though the lessons it had handed them should have taught them the opposite.

Yet here Fi was—*crying.*

In the stillness of the room, a dark that was only penetrated by the meager glow from stars that were strong enough to peer through the light pollution, even on the eighty-sixth floor, I turned on my side and watched my woman.

Hurting.

She was hurting.

In all honesty, people's feelings didn't matter that much to me. Not because I was a psychopath, but because feelings and business didn't go hand in hand. Half the decisions I made would never come to pass if I let other people's emotions get in the way, but this was Fi.

My Fi.

I slid across the bed, the silk sheets whispering with the motion of my limbs brushing across its surface, and I held her against me. One hand slid over her waist, the cast resting against her stomach, the other propped my head up on my fist.

Comfortable now, I pressed my lips to the ball of her heaving shoulder, and I waited.

I just waited.

But she didn't speak.

So I attempted to start the conversation for her, "You can cry in front of me, *bedda mia.*"

"I don't cry in front of anyone," she said a good thirty seconds later.

"Why not?"

"Because tears get you nowhere."

"They might get you somewhere with me."

A laugh that was more of a gurgle than anything else escaped her. "Will they take me to a vacation hot spot?"

"If that is what will stop their fall."

She sighed. "My Italian Darcy."

"Sicilian," I corrected.

"*Sicilian*," she agreed, but I knew she'd said Italian just to tease me.

My lips quirked. "Sicilians do everything better."

"I'm learning that."

I pressed another kiss to her shoulder, pleased when she tipped onto her back so that I was looming over her.

I liked having my eyes on her. She wasn't the kind of woman who was shy and timid, who'd fade without my attention, but if anything, she was the butterfly I'd likened her to. Bright and brash, loud and vibrant. I couldn't keep my eyes off her. Why would I want to miss out on whatever she said or did?

"You cry for Aoife?"

A low exhalation whispered from her lips. "I do. I really do. She was so happy at Christmas."

"She will be happy again. Not now, not tomorrow, and maybe not next week, but she will be."

"How very philosophical of you when you're still dealing with your vendetta because of your dad." There was no attitude to the words, but they stung for all that.

"*Vinnittas* aren't something you can just shut off. My father was butchered, Fi," I said thickly. "My brother found him—"

A shocked breath escaped her. "Jesus. Where?"

"In Catania, we have an estate. They dumped him outside the gates. Stan came back from class and... he was there."

"Oh, my God."

"He was eighteen, a man, but he cried like a boy when he called me to tell me." My throat felt choked with sorrow. "I was in fucking England. Thousands of miles away... I will bear that guilt until the day I die."

"You being there wouldn't have stopped anything."

"No," I agreed immediately, because she wasn't wrong. "If anything, I might be dead too."

She was quiet a second, then she whispered, "We'd never have met."

"No," I concurred before pressing another kiss to her shoulder.

We both processed that, and I thought she was going to drop it.

I'd never intended to dive into this conversation, but I wasn't about to apologize for the choices my siblings and I had made.

Our nuclear response to the Fieri's declaration of war was the only way we could avenge *Patri's* death, but more than that—we'd had to assure our own survival.

To do that, we'd tossed everything away—our goals, our dreams, our careers.

It wasn't something I could shut down like I could my laptop.

"Did you come straight to the US afterward?"

Her question jarred me from my thoughts, her interest soothing the part of me she'd riled up. "No. Rory and I... we were inconsolable. It took a while for us to figure out what to do. I returned from England, and she came back from Massachusetts. We moved to the UK shortly after the funeral though."

"She was in the States already?" she asked, surprised.

"*Se.* She'd started building a reputation for herself by that point. It was her first year out of law school and straight into the DA's office in Boston." I thought back to those horrific days and I rasped, "*Matri* didn't get out of bed after the move for six weeks. She was medicated for most of that time.

"Stan had a drug problem back when he was a teen—" That was how we'd gotten into this mess in the first place and was the biggest source of his guilt. "—I watched him struggle for close to a month until he gave in."

"He got high?"

"Yes. Nearly overdosed. That was when I knew I had to do something." I released a breath. "By that point, Rory had to return to the States for work or forfeit her position, but as I watched my family fall apart around me, I knew action was needed."

"What did you do?"

"I waited until my mother was awake and in need of another pill and I told her..." To this day, I remembered the words. Verbatim. "...I won't rest until the men who took him from us drown in their own blood."

It was so strange to say that now. To be here, in this position of power, knowing that *I* hadn't been the one to make those bastards pay.

Someone else had made them drown in their own blood.

"What did she say?" she breathed.

"Do it before I die."

A shocked laugh escaped her. "Your mother is hardcore. Who knew Brits had it in them?"

A smile appeared on my lips despite the subject. "She's stronger than she looks. Bloodthirstier too."

"You got Stan on board, clearly."

"I did. It kept him clean."

"What about your sister? Why didn't she dive into the family firm?"

"Because she had other plans."

"What kind of plans?" She sighed. "Sorry for all the questions."

"I'm glad you're interested. It means you care."

Fi was quiet a second before she whispered, "I really do."

I hummed, because I'd known that without her admitting to it. Otherwise I wouldn't have shared anything with her.

"When we were fourteen, we had to look into our family background for a school project. It led Aurora and I down two paths.

"Our *nanna* told us tales that filled our heads with..." I sighed. "*Patri* said it was nonsense, but I knew it wasn't. Rory knew it too. We both went looking, and from it, I became obsessed with our ancestry, and she learned about who we really were."

"That your line is royal?"

"No, I learned that. She learned about what happened to our grandfather and that we had a great-uncle who was still alive."

"I thought almost everyone in your family was killed?"

"They were. Great-uncle Currau was the patsy. The Fieris framed him." I closed my eyes. "The Fieris bombed the compound where my *famigghia* lived. Three generations were in that house, and every single one of them died.

"The fuckers had witnesses come forward who said they'd seen Currau plant the bomb because he wanted to take over the *Famiglia.*"

Her voice was small as she asked, "Your family burned to death?"

"*Se.* The worst of it is that Currau only survived because he managed to get my grandmother off the compound."

"How?"

"When we asked her, *Nanna* said that she had morning sickness throughout the course of the day. She was in the kitchen getting saltines and Currau came running in and dragged her out of there and off the compound.

"He shoved her in one of the cars, handed her a couple hundred dollars, and told her to drive until she ran out of gas, but not to stop moving until she was a thousand miles away." I heaved a sigh. "Ever since that school project, Rory's been on a crusade, working to get to a position where she can influence a retrial."

That had never panned out.

She'd been ten years too late for Currau to give much of a damn about getting out of prison in anything other than a casket.

"He's still alive?" she gasped.

"Barely. That was why I was at the hospital today."

"Not because of your arm?"

"Well, *se*, but when Rory had me arrested, the cogs were already in place, just waiting to start rolling. When my lawyer showed up at the precinct, she told me what she had planned. It was time to get him out."

"I don't understand why you had to go to jail for that."

I blew out a breath. "My sister has unusual ways of making things work."

"She's unusual all round," Fi groused.

"Currau has not sought parole in over two decades. The evidence was stacked against him perfectly. There was no way in hell she could start a retrial, and there was no need for her to visit him in a professional capacity as DA. She tried, *Cristo,* she tried, but it never happened.

"We couldn't get visits either. He wouldn't allow any. Getting to see him was harder than breaking into the Louvre."

"I guess you'd know..."

Wry laughter escaped me. "I've yet to resort to museum heists."

"*Yet* being the key word."

I hummed. "Currau is in Bellevue Hospital, and that meant it was easier to access him. To get into his hospital room, I needed to be treated there. There's a prison ward at Bellevue."

She peered up at me through the gloom. "You couldn't have just gone as a regular person? You had to get arrested?"

"Rory decided that it was time for my face to hit the papers."

She whistled. "It worked."

"She's annoying."

"I can see that." Fi paused. "You don't mind that she controls you like that?"

"I'm a strategist. I can see machinations at play, but Rory?" I shook my head. "She was not made for this generation."

"What do you mean?"

"I mean..." *Porca troia*, how did I explain what I meant without sounding crazy? "She's my *consigliere*—"

"That's like your advisor, right?" she interrupted to ask.

"*Se*. Her mind, the moves she's capable of planning, it's worthy of a conqueror."

"I guess she's good at chess."

I snorted. "Like you wouldn't believe. Her roles as DA and *consigliere* have been woven together from the start. She's taken a hard stance against the Italians since her career began back in Boston. It's how she made her rep.

"When she moved to New York after Stan, *Matri*, and I immigrated, her rep back there got her the job in the DA's office. She worked on taking the mafia down from a legal footing, and I worked behind the scenes."

"They really had no hope in hell of surviving, did they?" she breathed.

"No. But I didn't imagine it would take as long as it did. I'm not sure if we'd have achieved it without the political turmoil the country is going through."

"So, really, you're the one who owes Savannah a favor?"

My lips tugged up into a smile. "I suppose. Seeing as she's the one who broke the story wide open for the public to devour."

She had a point.

When Savannah Daniels had released evidence that there was a secret society working to undermine the US government, it had morphed from the plot of a Netflix show into reality.

People thought the Watergate scandal was bad. That was nothing in comparison to this. The public would be reeling from this for years.

"I won't tell her that when I convince her to help us."

I dipped down to press a kiss to her forehead. "*Grazii mille, cara mia.*"

Her hand shuffled higher to cup my cheek. "I'm glad you got your vengeance."

"It was denied to us. The Fieri line wasn't decimated by us, but there are perks to being the Don, I'll admit." I gently clasped her wrist. "Enough about me. I truly didn't mean to speak of such heavy subjects. What can I do to erase your sorrow?"

A soft laugh whispered from her lips. "Not long ago, I chided Aidan O'Donnelly Jr. for wanting to take away Savannah's hurt... now you're wanting to do the same for me. It's okay to hurt, Luc. It's okay—"

"I'm not saying that it isn't. You must always come to me when or if you're sad."

"Why? What are you going to do?"

"I don't know," I told her honestly. "But I can do something, can't I? I can be that soft place where you can land."

She reached up and traced her fingers over my jaw. "You're unexpected, Luc."

"*I'm* unexpected," I scoffed. "You think I wanted to feel this way for someone other than family. You're dangerous, Fionnabhair, and you don't even fucking know it."

"What do you mean? I'm not dangerous," she pshawed.

Tension and anger and concern battled inside me, but I could no more stop myself from looming over her, crowding her, than I could stop my heart from taking its next beat.

"I mean I will burn this city to the ground to find you if someone tries to take you from me. I mean New York City will shudder beneath my goddamn wrath if—"

She didn't let me finish.

"Luc!" Fi groaned, and her arms slipped around my neck as quick as lightning, and before I knew what the hell was happening, her mouth was on mine, and she was twisting against me, her legs spreading and coming to cup my hips.

Her tongue thrusted between my parted lips as she clung to me with her whole body, and I growled beneath my breath as I rolled onto my back and let her take charge, let her own this moment because if this was what it took to eradicate her tears, then I'd be a willing sacrifice.

Hips rocking against me, her panty-covered pussy jerking back and forth against my bare dick, I groaned as she ate at my lips, tearing into me. My hand moved to her ass, and I kneaded the taut curve while I manipulated her into grinding against me in a way that had my cock aching.

This woman shot my self-control and had me clawing to get inside that cunt that was home. More so than even Catania.

More than the entirety of fucking Sicily.

When she pulled back to bite at my bottom lip, her hair fell in swathes around us, and as her perfume loaded every breath I took, she rasped, "I like it when you go all caveman on me."

"I'd never have fucking noticed," I rumbled, rocking my ass up to grind into her some more because that felt like goddamn *cielo*— paradise.

She moaned at the motion, then surged upward, her hands falling to my pecs as she rubbed her slit against my cock. The silky fabric that separated us was both heaven and hell against my erection, and with my pre-cum and her pussy juices, it facilitated the rocking motion that had her head tipping back as she enjoyed the ride.

Grabbing the hem of the shirt she'd asked to borrow this evening, I dragged it up, higher and higher, to expose those delicious tits of hers.

I'd seen her dressed up, dressed down, naked and every which way in between, but when she was wearing my clothes, it was the only time I didn't mind that she was covered.

Palming one of the beauties, I squeezed and enjoyed the ripe swells, loving that they belonged to me before I tweaked a nipple.

Hard enough for her to moan, "I want you, Luc."

I could feel that. I didn't need her to tell me, but I knew she was trying to tell me something else.

Something that wasn't translating, but that had nothing to do with me not understanding English.

"I want you, *vita mia*—"

"No, you don't understand," she whispered, her nails digging into my pecs. "I don't care about the money, I don't care about the power, I want *you*."

"Aren't you lucky I come with both things?" I teased, surging upward to hug her to me. I left her tits alone and moved to cup her face. "You're not alone in this, *duci*. I want you too."

"Your family... I know your sister doesn't—"

"Screw what they think. I know what I know, and I want what I want."

She swallowed, and it was audible. "How can that be me? I'm everything they say—"

"You're nothing like what they say. The moment I first saw you, I felt the ground beneath my feet tremble. And seeing as we were seventy stories up, that was saying fucking something." I let my thumb swipe over her cheekbone. "That had nothing to do with what you are, but who. *Anime gemelle*."

"What does that mean?"

"Twin souls. Cleaved apart at birth."

"You believe in that?"

"No. Not until you came along."

She pushed her forehead against mine, and as our breath tangled, she reached between us. I felt her fingers fumbling with the gusset on her panties, before, suddenly, my dick was sliding through slick, slick folds, and she was guiding me inside her.

My low groan rattled along the sound waves just as her high-pitched moan tangled with it.

As I filled her full, her knees tightened around my hips, and she slipped her hands down and around my shoulders, holding me as close as she could.

"I-I need you, Luc," she whispered, a little hiccup to the words as she began the arch and fall that was the oldest and most beautiful of dances.

"I need you," I groaned, my hands clutching at her hips as I helped her find her rhythm.

My mouth dropped to her throat, and I sucked on the tender flesh there, suckling and tasting and teasing, loving her whimpers, the hitching in her breathing, how she clung to me and clutched at me. Owning this moment, owning us.

I lodged one hand between us and found her clit. Carefully, I stroked the small nub, needing her pussy to cling to my cock, to milk me, to take every fucking thing I had to give, and that was when her pace quickened.

Sweat glued us together. The heat made perspiration bead and the air around us turn humid as we stayed knotted into one whole being, tied as one, united in a way few would ever understand.

"I never thought I could feel like this," she cried out, a sob in the words.

"You weren't supposed to. This is mine. These feelings are mine," I snarled, possessiveness throbbing through me.

She'd tripped the switch in my head, and it had me twisting us around, rolling us so that I was on top and she was beneath me.

I rutted on her like the beast she made me, stripping away civilization, eradicating the charisma I was known for, replacing it with the raw, base man who wanted all of her. Who'd settle for no less than everything she had to give.

Her legs clung to me, her heels digging into my ass, her nails clawing at my back as she demanded no less than the same from me in return.

When she exploded around my cock, I felt the pulsation of those silken muscles and I didn't bother holding back anymore.

I came.

I came for so fucking long that I thought she sucked my goddamn heart out of my body at the same time, but I knew...

I knew what had just happened.

I let my forehead move to hers before I slipped down and pressed it into the mattress, staying close, letting her take my weight so I pinned her in place, keeping her impaled on my dick for as long as I could.

She didn't push me away; if anything, she clasped me as tightly as her spent body would allow, and then, she surprised me.

"You know what just happened, don't you?"

Tilting my head to the side, I brushed my lips over the curve of her ear and whispered, "We tempted fate and won."

NINE

LUC

THE FOLLOWING MORNING

"I GOT NEWS."

"So do I." I rustled the newspaper in my hands. "Can't you leave me in peace for breakfast?"

"No rest for the wicked."

Heaving a sigh, I peered over the paper and found my brother standing in the kitchen doorway, one of Alina's pastries shedding icing sugar everywhere with his next bite.

"What news?"

"The Anjou rubies we got on New Year's were fakes."

Slamming my hand down against the table, I hurled the paper at the wall as I grated out, "Dammit to hell."

He grunted. "My reaction entirely. I'm dealing with Laramie."

"Good. That fucker fleeced us. Get every cent back."

"They're real. Just not the Anjous."

"I could get any run of the mill ruby necklace," I snarled. "I want the Anjous."

"People will notice if he goes missing. He's a popular fence."

"Then make sure he returns, just not as whole as he once was."

Another grunt escaped him as he finished up the last bite of *sfogliatelle*.

"While you're at it," I ground out, "send men to deal with Lockhart. He didn't know that Martinez meant me no harm."

I'd visited Aspen with the intention of purchasing a tiara from a jewelry shop. Instead, a gangster had invited me into one of the town's most popular eateries and had leveraged the tiara for a favor.

A favor that saw my woman having to ask her friend to write a false exposé on Eva Kingston.

The notorious ex-NYPD detective had decapitated a fellow officer while undercover during an investigation into the *Lobos Rojos* gang.

I could only assume Martinez wanted the exposé to blame the New World Sparrows for framing his wife.

"He probably knew you weren't going to come into any harm," Stan countered. "Why would he send you into a dangerous situation when you're a good customer?"

His logic made sense, but I wasn't in the mood for logic right now.

Strolling into the dining room, he plunked his ass beside my chair and asked, "You done with that?"

I stared down at the fruit salad I'd been enjoying and shoved it at him. "*Matri* lied when she told me you'd stop stealing my food when you were an adult."

He smirked. "My role in life is to keep your kitchen cabinets empty and you on the straight and narrow, *frate*."

"Your mission, huh?"

"Exactly."

I waited until he picked up a piece of fruit and chewed on it to say, "I owe you a beating for what you helped Aurora do."

"Not going to apologize for protecting you."

"I'm not a child."

"You're the Don. We needed your eyes on the prize. Couldn't do that when they were on her fucking tits.

"But if it makes you feel better, you can give Aurora crap tasks and you can give me a Cheshire Cat grin... just know you'd be a hypocrite because if the situation were reversed, you'd protect us from ourselves too."

He wasn't wrong.

Fucker.

That was why I let him change the subject: "Heard whispers that the Hell's Rebels' MC drove up this past week. They entered Irish territory. It's been crazy or I'd have told you sooner."

I disregarded his excuses. "Aren't they based in Texas?"

"Yup."

"What were they doing up here then?"

He snagged a croissant then pointed the tip at me. "If I knew that, I'd tell you."

I snatched the croissant then tossed it onto my dish. "They're still producing ghost guns?"

"Fucking expensive ones," Stan muttered.

"Worth it though."

"Would have cost a fucking fortune to arm our men with their weapons. It made sense to buy our gear from the *Lobos Rojos*." He scrubbed his chin. "I'd be interested in arming my *stiddari* with them, to be honest."

The *stiddari* were the men a *capo* chose to work directly under him. After storming the Fieri compound, I knew he'd lost two men who he'd been eyeing up for the role.

"Arrange it."

"They pick and choose who they produce for. You know that."

I took a bite of the croissant. "Wonder who they came up to visit."

"They got a kid in Rhode Island," he pointed out. "In college. Maybe they were just riding through."

"Maybe." I grunted because I didn't think that was likely. For the information to have reached him, their arrival must have been noteworthy. "Must be arming the Feckers. They're top dog in the city right now."

"Seems likely." He cast a look around the room. "Where is she?"

"She has a name."

"I'm learning it."

"You're a jackass."

His smirk deepened as he popped a piece of cantaloupe into his mouth. "I own it."

"She's still sleeping."

"And so it begins," he grumbled. "She's going to take you for every cent."

"No, she isn't. She's going to work for us."

His scowl was instantaneous. "You're shitting me?"

"Did you or did you not compile the file on her boss's accounts?"

"Yeah, what does that have to do with anything?"

"He shoves his work onto her." I arched a brow. "That means she's the one with the skill and the contacts."

"You want her to become one of our CPAs," he rasped. "Are you fucking insane?"

"I want her to be one of our in-house tax advisors."

"Please, when you tell Rory, make sure I'm there," he said with a laugh, but he was shaking his head as he spoke. "I need to see her reaction. Maybe film it for posterity."

"The day you finally make a move on Evangeline, know that I'm going to ride your ass as hard as you're riding mine, Custanzu," I warned, which had the added bonus of shutting him the fuck up.

His crush on the housekeeper's daughter was his Achilles' heel and, like any good brother, I wasn't afraid to kick him there.

"Is it wise entangling her with our finances? When it goes south, we're fucked."

"It won't go south. I'm going to propose when we find the Anjou ring."

His eyes flared wide. "You can't be serious? Luciu, I thought this was a fucking fling."

"Never been more serious about anything in my goddamn life."

"You're doing this so she can't testify against you, right?"

"No. I'm doing it because I fucking love her, Stan. Why is that so impossible to understand?"

He shook his head. "This isn't like you."

"This is the new me." I slouched back against the seat, a warning to heed my words etched into my expression. "That reminds me. Did you collect the tiara from the safe on the jet?"

"No, I left it lying around for any fucking waif and stray to pick up." He scowled at me. "*Se*, of course, I had it collected. It's in the safe at *Matri's*."

"Good. Any joy in figuring out why the Triads are sniffing around our asses?"

"No. Jen said something that morning in Aspen—"

"Are you taking my name in vain, Stan?" Fi drawled, her voice husky from sleep as she rounded the corner and stepped into the dining room.

She wore a pair of tight-fitting tan chinos that she'd belted with a light brown leather belt which augmented the slim curves of her hips and waist, especially when paired with a slimline t-shirt with boxy sleeves. A chunky man's watch clung to her wrist, and she topped the masculine look off with a pair of heeled boots so high they defied gravity.

She surprised me further by striding over to me, all the sass and panache of a model strolling down the damn catwalk, then leaning down and pressing a kiss to my mouth.

"We don't approve of blasphemy in Irish households," she mocked as she took a seat opposite Stan.

Considering she'd been taking the seat at the other end of the table until now, I figured it was so she could mess with him.

An idea I was not averse to.

"Worshiping false idols is something we disapprove of in Sicilian households," Stan retorted as he snagged the last piece of grapefruit on the dish and took a large bite of it.

Jen shot him a smug smile as she reached for the French press and poured herself some coffee. "Anyway, what did I say in Aspen?"

"That Damian Headley didn't play Call of Duty but usually had it loaded on his computer."

She blinked. "That's relevant?"

I snagged her hand in mine and pressed a kiss to her knuckles. "The message boards are a good way to pass information that's difficult to log."

"Difficult, not impossible," Stan corrected.

"It can be hacked?" she asked, surprise lacing her tone.

"Sure, it can. With the right hacker." I pursed my lips. "Think we could hire Hunter again?"

Stan shook his head. "No. He's with the Camorra now."

"Jesus, when did that happen?"

"Last six months. He was always on the side lines, you know that. But they offered him an upgrade."

"Does Rory know?" I questioned carefully.

"Who the fuck knows what Rory knows?"

"True." I squinted at him as a thought occurred to me. "You learned that he's with the Camorra because you asked him to doctor that footage, didn't you?"

He smirked. "I always liked him, and he's usually willing to help Rory, whether she likes knowing that or not."

"*Porca troia.*" I barely refrained from hurling my coffee cup at him. "Don't go behind my back again, Stan. We'll have problems if you do."

He rolled his eyes. "It was in your best interests."

"Do it again, and it'll be in your *worst* interests." My mouth curved into a sneer as a thought occurred to me. "This isn't the first time you've done something like this, is it?"

I'd had very few girlfriends over the years, preferring hook-ups. No one had mattered enough to me to go hunting for answers when the women stopped answering my calls.

Not until Fi.

Stan's expression turned sheepish before, insistently, he repeated, "It was in your best interests."

I scoffed, "*Se,* it was, seeing as it meant I was single for when Fi came into my life."

"You're going to make me puke."

"*Bonu,*" I told him grimly.

"Yeah, so, I've been thinking about Rory..." Fi started, interrupting our spat, but I saw the interest in her eyes, as well as a gleam in them— she understood that she was different.

And so she should.

"What about her? Other than the fact that she's a pain in my *culu,*" I asked, turning to her. I jerked my thumb back at Stan. "Just as he is. Unfortunately for me, I can't kill them."

"I'm blessed," Stan grumbled.

"Ya know..." Fi cleared her throat. "The fact she arrested you?"

"She's a DA," Stan answered. "It's kind of what she does."

Fi frowned.

"What she *did*."

Stan nodded at my correction. "Wonder how long she'll stick it out for."

"Long enough to be worth our while."

Fi took a sip of coffee. "So, I mean... she's a plant, right?"

"She's the original plant," Stan drawled, but his pride was clear.

Hell, I couldn't blame him. I was proud too.

What Aurora had managed to achieve in this country was no less than our enemies' annihilation from a legal standpoint.

Singlehandedly, she'd made it her mission to take down the *Famiglia*, and it had worked.

With her targeting them through legal means, and us through illegal, the *Famiglia's* business hadn't been as viable for the past ten years as it had before. Wherever we could undercut them, we did. We outmaneuvered, fleeced, and manipulated their movements within the city.

Our first year, our businesses had turned over just under two million dollars. Now, we were veering toward two hundred million. Most of that had been snatched out of the Fieris' grasp.

"How hasn't she been found out?" Fi questioned.

"Grandmother had to buy a passport to flee to Sicily back in the sixties, and she chose a different name. *Patri* showed up ahead of schedule, and he was born here under that false name."

"So you're all US citizens?"

"Dual-nationals," I corrected. "Rory's background shows that she was raised in Sicily, came here for college, where she married another US citizen. There's no reason for her reputation to be entangled with the *Famiglia*."

"She's married?"

I wasn't sure why her question sounded dubious, but it clearly was. "He died."

"Or she killed him," Stan drawled with a grin.

Scowling at him, I grumbled, "She's going to think each of us has Jack the Ripper tendencies."

"Oh, I already think that," Fi retorted after she took another *deeper* sip of coffee. "I just have to brace myself and remember that I've joined the Ripper ranks."

Stan guffawed. "Ripper ranks." He waggled his finger. "I'll have to remember that one."

Rolling my eyes, I turned to her and snagged her hand with my good one again. I knew what Vlad's death had done to her... for her to make light of it, that couldn't be easy.

"So, you weren't raised with any connection to the Valentinis?" Fi queried, her confusion clear.

"No. Because his stepfather refused to adopt him—"

"*Pezz'i miedda*," Stan hissed under his breath.

"—*Patri* had the false name from *Nanna's* papers. Guerra." I smiled, knowing that surname translated to '*war*.' "Rory and I had that for two years until it was changed to Fitzwilliam to appease Grandfather.

"We only learned we were Valentinis when we asked her for information on our family. Her husband had just died. She had no fear of the repercussions, so out came the history of our line."

"That must have been a lot to take in," she muttered, eyes wide.

"It was."

"You're her brothers though. Surely that would come up if Aurora was investigated."

Oddly pleased by her persistence, I explained, "Legally, our surnames are a minefield."

"Purposely," Stan said with a laugh.

"I knew I wanted vengeance, and Aurora wanted to free Currau. To do so, we had to keep her name lily white. So, Stan and I changed ours from Fitzwilliam to Guerra in the UK and filed for a passport in the States."

"So you're Guerras?"

"No. We changed our names here to Valentini," Stan said.

"In Sicily, we never informed the authorities of our name change, so we're still Fitzwilliam on their records."

"So, if someone did a deep dive, they could find a fraternal connection, but they'd also find a rat's nests of different surnames?"

Stan chuckled. "*Se*. It's withstood a decade of scrutiny."

She whistled under her breath. "Talk about a tangle."

Though I nodded, I changed the subject and asked, "You're going to resign today?"

She stared at me. "You sure this is a wise decision?"

"Can you do for me what you did for Crawford, Lewis, and Jones?"

"With that starting salary, I can do better." Her smirk was loaded with enough self-confidence that even Stan kept his mouth shut.

"Don't bother with the two weeks' notice," I informed her. "If you decide to leave my firm, I'll give you a stellar recommendation regardless of what happens."

She cast me a look from under her lashes but remained silent, whereas Stan countered, "What will it say? She gives good head?"

Clipping him worked better when I had a cast.

"*Porca troia!*" He rubbed the back of his neck. "You just gave me brain damage."

"Only exacerbating what happened at birth," I sniped, before turning to her and pressing her knuckles to my mouth again. "Ignore him."

The smile dancing around the corners of her lips told me, if nothing else, that she wasn't offended...

"I will."

We lingered at the table for another forty or so minutes before she left for the office tucked up in a winter coat, gloves, and scarf, but with those insane boots still on her feet.

As I watched her leave, I turned to my brother and asked, "She has guards on her?"

He grunted. "*Se.*"

"How many?"

"Four."

"Is that enough after Rory's stunt?"

"No one really knows who she is yet. The press are interested in you for the moment, but with Ray waltzing around the city pretending to be you, they're under control."

"A fucking body double," I groused. *Goddamn Rory.* "They'll seek Jen out soon enough. You and I both know what those jackals are like. They'll hunt for a story even if there isn't one to be found."

He grabbed a pot of yogurt from the center of the table. "She'll be fine. Well, she will be if she doesn't break her neck in those boots. We can protect her from active threats, but not her footwear."

I ignored that because the same thought had crossed my mind. "She has access to the penthouse?"

"*Se.*"

"Her driver knows to bring her back here?"

"*Se.*"

"Her apartment's been packed up?"

"*Se,*" he snapped. "Everything is on its way here. For fuck's sake, Luciu, I did as you asked. She's safe."

"She'd better fucking be," I warned, and my mind raced as I thought back to that night and the guards who'd been on duty. "Who the fuck were the men who drove her back to her apartment? I want to speak with them."

"Calm down, Luciu. *Cristo.* How were they to know—"

"They knew the original plan was for us to return here. That they knew. So what the fuck had them taking her back to her place?"

He wriggled his shoulders. "I don't know."

"Rory?" I tossed out, because I couldn't blame him when he was fifty thousand feet in the sky.

"Maybe." As my mouth tightened, he muttered, "When you're in jail, or out of commission, she's second-in-command."

"I don't give a fuck." I slapped my hand against the table hard enough for everything to jolt. "A lesson needs to be taught. I want names. Especially if they're Italian." I had a mixed bag of men as guards now. I didn't like it, and I liked it even less now.

He heaved a sigh and begrudgingly told me, "I'll get you names."

Dipping my chin, content he'd do as I asked and that he'd done as I requested—upped her security and begun the transition of her moving into the penthouse permanently—I changed the subject. "We're going to Headley's apartment today, right?"

While he nodded in answer to my question, Stan commented, "She never eats."

"No. She doesn't," I concurred, though she had to at some point. It was just a rare occasion.

"No wonder she's got such a bad attitude."

I scoffed, "And what's your excuse with all you pack away?"

"I don't need an excuse."

"Neither does she." Scraping a hand over my chin, I heaved a sigh. "Today, we should take over the Fieri compound."

He just grunted, sounding as excited by the prospect as I was. "We need a hacker, Luciu. I've known it for a while but..." He shook his head. "That shit with Call of Duty... we need someone permanent."

Because I knew he was right, I didn't argue. "You got some names for me?"

"Couple of names. It won't happen, but I'd prefer Hunter."

"Not sure Rory would. You know she's weird around him."

"True. Never seen her get riled up over a man before. Not even that creep of a husband of hers."

I pulled a face because he wasn't wrong. I'd met the bastard twice and each time, he'd set my teeth on edge. "Set up interviews for me?"

"The hackers? Sure. You know they're not gonna start without a mil, min, in the bank, right?"

"They'll make it back for us though." I hummed. "I want to know what Headley and the Triads were up to."

"You and me both, *frate*. Whatever it was, it wasn't good."

I scrubbed a hand over my chin. "I wish Jen hadn't had to go through what she did that day, but it stopped me from meeting with Zhao."

"You know I never agreed with that. Meeting with the Dragon Head of the Triads would have made us look weak."

"I agree."

"*Now*." He huffed. "Rory isn't the only one with brains."

"Rory agreed with me at the time," I pointed out.

"Neither of you work the streets like I do."

"You make it sound like you're a whore," I argued.

"Maybe that's why I'm good in bed."

"I'm sure." I rolled my eyes.

His amusement faded. "If anything, Zhao should come to us for conciliation. Headley has no known ties to the Triads. They're in the wrong, not us."

I nodded. "Visit Headley's apartment first then deal with the Fieri compound?"

We shared a look.

"*Se.*"

JEN

SAVANNAH WAS WAITING on me when I made it out of my office building.

With her hands tucked into her form-fitting pants, she looked like the original lady boss in a man's suit, complete with a spic and span, bright red, seven-fold tie.

She wore a pair of heels as high as mine, the backs of which were as red as her necktie, but her deference to the colder temperatures were a double-breasted winter coat and a pair of scarlet leather gloves.

Though, today, we were both dressed for the weather; usually we made a striking picture when we went out together because she wore so much and I wore so little.

The thought made me smile, enough to warm up and open my arms to her. It shocked her. I could see that. She wasn't expecting an embrace, but she'd come when I asked her to. Last minute, as well.

Having decided that Luciu was right, and that I didn't have to work my two weeks' notice for a bunch of pricks if my new boss wouldn't think badly of me for it, I'd texted her before I'd gone into Jackass Jason's office to hand in my resignation.

That she was waiting on me told me she'd been close by. Not too surprising. This area was one of our haunts, and I knew she had a couple coffee shops around here that she liked writing in. Although, I wasn't sure how that would be working out now that she was more notorious than before.

Speaking of...

"Do people still get your surname wrong now that you're infamous?" I asked her, shuffling my bag around on my shoulder because it was full of the things from my desk, so that I could squeeze her in a tight hug.

"You know they do," she grumbled. "It's a phenomenon."

"Wouldn't it be funny if it was because of your dad?"

She tensed. "Huh?"

I shrugged as I pulled back. "I'm pretty sure your sisters have the same problem as you. Your brother's different. Everyone knows him. But you girls always get called the wrong surname. I noticed when they were in town last summer."

Her sisters were cats. Feral cats, at that.

"My God, you're not wrong." Her overlong lashes blinked double time as she stared at me. "How would he do that?"

I gave her another shrug. "I've learned a lot about what can be done this past month or so. I just think it's weird, that's all. A misinformation campaign on a mass level."

"I'm going to ream him a new one."

"I might be wrong."

"He probably deserves it for something else."

I laughed. "Full disclosure, I was talking conspiracy shit but it fits."

She pulled back to eye me. "You been trawling conspiracytok?"

No, I was living in a conspiracy.

"Maybe." I chuckled, but it disintegrated a tad as I mumbled, "I missed you, bitch."

"Missed you too."

"Get a room, lesbians," someone catcalled, breaking our moment.

I grinned up at her. "Want to give them a show?"

"No tongues," she retorted, but she gave me a smack on the lips to shut up the haters.

We received some wolf-whistles, but interest waned because, hell, this was NYC, and as we pulled back, I retorted, "We're a two-woman duet fighting the -ists of this world."

"Homophobic is an -ic, not an -ist," she pointed out.

"This is why you're the wordsmith and I'm the mathematician."

"Speaking of," she started, peering up at the expensive building behind me. "Why did you want to meet on a weekday at nine-thirty?"

"I quit. Plus, I wanted to talk to you."

Her head tipped to the side. "You quit? Why?"

"Got a new job. Why else?"

"Who with?"

"Luciu Valentini."

Recognition blared to life in her eyes. "You're really getting involved with him, huh?" she asked, her tone wary.

"I am. But the starting salary is six times what I make in a month here."

"You signed a contract yet?"

"No. It's on its way. We only talked about it last night."

"You trust him that much?"

A smile danced on my lips. "You trust Junior?"

She rolled her eyes. "I guess I deserved that one."

"You mean after the shortest courtship in history?"

"Well, it was kinda long. I knew him from before," she argued.

"Talk about 'wham, bam, thank you, ma'am,'" I teased, sliding my arm around her waist to diminish the bite to my words.

"He whams and bams very nicely," was her prim response.

"I'm sure he does. None of the O'Donnellys—" I broke off before I could continue.

She squeezed me back. "Weird thinking of them as cousins and not hot chunks of man meat, huh?"

"It's a tragedy," I confirmed drolly, but I squinted up at her because with us both in high heels, she was taller than me. "It's messed up."

"I know, babe. But it doesn't have to be. You just gotta not think about fucking them anymore."

"Not so much of a problem seeing as I've got someone hotter."

"You really serious with him? Didn't think you'd mix business with pleasure."

"I love him, Sav."

Her brows rose. "Thought you were the Ice Bitch?"

"I am."

"Not so much if you see birds every time he's near."

I groused, "I don't see birds."

"It's a song," she joked.

"I'll bet. But I don't see birds or stars or anything like that. He just…" I tried to put it into words. "I don't even know. He makes things feel right."

She stared at me, her gaze more direct than a laser, as if she were trying to scan my brain or give me a lobotomy—I wasn't sure which. "Maybe before Aidan, I wouldn't have understood."

I hummed. "Makes a difference when you feel it too. I thought you were nuts getting involved with Aidan, and with the lifestyle, but…"

"It chooses you, you don't choose it. Do I want him to be in the Irish Mob? Nope. Do I like that he could get us both killed? Hell, nah. But I managed to get my ass in danger all by myself, without the interference from a bunch of mobsters.

"Those mobsters have actually saved said ass from being toast more than once." She hitched a shoulder. "Some people just need the mob on their side."

I sniggered. "I'm mafia, not mob."

"We're two different factions," she wailed, her hand flopping upward as she smacked the back of it against her forehead. "How will we survive?"

"We're the Montagues and Capulets of NYC," I agreed.

"You know what that means, don't you?" she countered, a gleam making a swift appearance in her eye.

"What?" I asked warily.

"Your kid and my kid have to get married."

Bursting out laughing, I retorted, "I don't want kids. Do you?"

"Dunno. Aidan makes me think about weird shit."

"Weird shit like what goes in diapers? You forget, I've seen the holy hell that goes down inside those because of Jacob."

"True." She pulled a face. "Nannies exist for a reason, though, right?"

"Oh, my, Goddddd, could you be any more of a diva?"

A laugh escaped her. "Man, that did sound pretty diva-esque, didn't it? I'd put it to bed and stuff, I just don't want to wipe up crap."

"That 'it' is gonna be the future heir to the Five Points, babe."

Her nose crinkled. "Don't remind me." When I snickered, she pleaded, "No, please, don't."

Laughing, I asked, "When it's a creature that's half you and half Aidan, maybe that'll change?

"I doubt it. Does crap ever not stink?" she answered as we pulled back and started walking down the street to the coffee shop we both used when we met up on a lunch date.

"True."

"Plus, hell, Aidan and I, we're only a new thing. I don't need to be thinking about kids. He has issues of his own, and I have issues of mine—"

"You mean like having a target on your back from a secret society that took over the US government—"

"Remind me why I love you again?" she complained.

I shot her a smug smile. "Just keeping it real."

"Yeah, yeah." A breath gusted from her lips. "Can you *stahp* with the reality? I have enough of that biting me in the ass."

"Aidan's a biter, huh? Duly noted."

She shoved me but she was grinning as she did it. I saw her happiness and was glad for her.

Truly, I was.

"I was surprised when you called," Savannah said once we were sitting down in the coffee shop, waiting for a server to deign to find us.

The service here was shit, but somehow, the chef made a green salad taste good. That made this place worth its weight in gold.

"I'll bet you were," I retorted. "I'm surprised I did too." After yesterday, though, I was feeling a little more generous.

Her lips twisted. "I don't deserve you."

"Nope, you don't. But I need a favor, and I'll consider that repayment in full."

She arched a brow. "Anything apart from cheating on Aidan, getting you off, or robbing a bank."

"Girl, that's where your mind went? Jesus." I clucked my tongue.

"Doesn't involve any of those things. Just because I like to mess with phobics' heads doesn't mean I want in your panties."

"I know, I know. What's the favor?"

"I don't forgive you one-hundred percent, Savvie. You really hurt me. But after these past few days, it's been so goddamn hard that I just... life's too fucking short."

"You're telling me. This past month has been insane."

"Agreed." I plucked at my bottom lip as I cast a glance around the coffee shop. It was mostly empty and still the server was ignoring us. *You had to love NYC.* "Has Aidan heard from Finn? Aoife's still resting. I think, at least. She hasn't answered my messages."

She shook her head. "No. All quiet from Finn." Her mouth tipped down at the edges. "I feel so bad for them."

"Me too. Aoife was made to have a massive family, but I don't know if that's in the cards for her."

"She had problems with Jacob?"

"Only because she had some nasty abdominal surgery back when she and Finn got married.

"I don't think the miscarriage was because of that though, but it was rough with Jake. Toward the end, I'd go and visit her and Aoife would plop her ass on the floor and sit with her legs against the wall to keep him in."

Savvie blinked. "Is that how it works?"

"I dunno, but Aoife said it helped her ankles." We stared at each other and shrugged.

"Maybe I should get a surrogate," Savannah mused, which had me snorting.

"Yeah, I can see the O'Donnellys being down for that. Their crown prince schtupping some broad and knocking her up—"

"What century are you in? There's this invention called IVF, you know?" she grumbled. "Aidan's dick is going nowhere other than in me."

I sniggered. "The server totally heard that."

It was typical New York that we actually got some service at that moment.

After we were both reacquainted with java and its fortifying capabilities, Sav turned to me and murmured, "You gonna stop giving me shit now that your coffee beast has been fed?"

"No. You're going to get shit from me for at least a decade. I figure that can be your tribute."

"Well, *I* figure it's worth it." Her brow puckered. "I missed you, Jen. More than I even thought that I could miss you because you're a massive pain in the ass."

"It's all a part of my charm," I mocked as I took a deep sip of my cold brew. "My forgiveness is multi-faceted."

"Oh, I know. You're sad about Aoife and you need me to do something for you. I'll leverage both if it means you talk to me again."

I eyed her over the glass. "I'm here, aren't I?"

"Good." She released a gusted breath. "I can deal with getting you to trust me again, because the Savannah you know and love hasn't exactly changed. I was never putting on an act around you, Jen. That was the problem. I've..."

"You've...?" I questioned when her words faltered.

She grimaced. "I've never been so real as I am with you. You don't want Savannah Daniels—"

"Or Davies, as the case may be."

Without missing a beat, she flipped me the bird. "—you just want me. I love that. I've always loved that. It was beyond refreshing. You don't want to be around me because of my family. You just want to know me."

"I'm not averse to meeting with Camden from time to time."

"Done. If it speeds up the forgiveness part of the process."

I smirked at her. "That might have worked before I got a boo of my own."

"You. With a boo." She shook her head. "It beggars belief. Or, you'll beggar him..."

My smirk morphed into a grin. "I think crime pays well enough to keep me in Jimmy Choos."

"You sure it's wise to work for him?"

"Nope. But he gave me a credit card with fifty grand on it to get me out of debt and fifteen grand a month as a starting salary. You bet your butt that got my juices flowing."

Her nose crinkled. "Lovely imagery."

"You're the wordsmith so you'd know." I grinned wider.

"What happened to Damian?" she asked softly. "I haven't heard you complain about the court case."

"Luciu sorted that out for me."

Eyes flaring wide, she whispered, "'Sorted out' out?"

"I chose not to ask," I lied. "I know he beat his ass. Luciu found him doping some girl's drink at his club. That exacerbated matters."

Nostrils flaring with outrage, Sav straightened up. "You mean that fucker was doping a woman in a club and your man saved her?"

Damn, that sounded good.

'Your man.'

My possessiveness regarding a partner had always revolved around how well he treated me and how little I wanted to lose him and his bank account.

But Luc?

Nope.

This went bone deep.

Every part of me purred with glee at knowing Luc was mine. That he loved me in return. It was... wonderful. A wonderful, wonderful feeling to be loved.

The thought came out of nowhere, and even though future Jen might regret leaving Jackass Jason behind and the rest of the dipshits at Crawford, Lewis, and Jones, present Jen was really happy with her decision.

"He did save her," I concurred. "Damian dropped the suit."

In a manner of speaking...

"Huh. Maybe we've finally found a man who can keep you out of trouble."

My lips twitched. "Was that a dare?"

"Maybe." She laughed. Then, eyes twinkling, she asked, "What's the favor? Come on, hit me with it."

"It's a big one," I warned.

"I figure I owe you."

In complete agreement, I nodded. "You do. But this is... well, let's say it's going to fudge your journalistic integrity."

That had her brow furrowing. "What? You want me to write a piece on someone?"

Slowly, I nodded. "You ever heard of Eva Kingston?"

For a second, she fell silent, then she slowly murmured, "The cop. The one who went undercover, took down some of the biggest names in that street gang over in Bed-Stuy?"

Because I'd googled the name, I nodded. "That's her. She took down some of the big boys in the *Lobos Rojos*."

"She went missing four years ago, if I remember rightly." Her brow furrowed as her mind whirred. Savannah was something of a savant with news stories. I figured her head was like a Google search bar for the New York Times. "After some photos came forward of her holding a cop's head if I remember rightly?"

Yeah, that was where me selling this idea to Savannah got dicey. On the ride over to my firm—ex-firm—I'd looked into the woman Luciu needed to help, and her past was beyond cray cray.

Until, all of a sudden, Sav surprised me and made shit a lot easier.

"I always thought that was BS."

"What was?" I asked warily. "The decapitation or the photos?"

"Both. It was clearly work she did for the gang while undercover. Everyone knows that to get anywhere with the *Lobos*, there's wetwork involved—"

My eyes bugged. "Everyone knows that, huh?"

"Uh-huh. You do if you're in the know. The NYPD totally hung her out to dry."

"She did kinda slice off a cop's head, Sav," I muttered, well aware that I was biting myself in the ass by saying that.

"Street gangs don't go around targeting members of the NYPD unless there's a reason for it."

I took a sip of my cold brew. "You really are made to be a mobster's wife, aren't you?"

"You trying to say I have dubious morals?"

Laughing at her wry comment, I merely said, "Maybe." It wasn't like I was much better.

For a second, my mind flashed back to the puddle of blood on my bedroom floor, the one that seemed to seep closer and closer to my feet, but before the image could take over everything else, Savannah called out, "Ma'am?"

Taken aback, I watched as she waved down the server again and ordered us another round of drinks.

When we were replenished with liquids, she shot me a look. "What's this really about, Jen? This isn't a favor for you, but for Luciu." She reached out and gently circled my wrist with her hand. "Are you in some trouble with him, honey? We can get you out of there—"

Twisting my fingers around, I clasped mine with hers. Appreciation and gratitude for the offer filled me as I admitted, "I'm already deep down the rabbit hole, Sav. I love him. I'm not lying about that." I sucked in a breath. "Apparently, Eva wants to come home."

Sav narrowed her eyes. "What does that have to do with you? Or Luciu, should I say?"

"She and her husband have something he's been looking for for a long time." I bit my lip. "If they're going to give it to him, then they want something in return."

"Me to write an exposé, let me guess, that ties Eva's arrest to some shenanigans with the New World Sparrows?" was her shrewd reply.

Slowly, I nodded. "Blaming the NWS seems logical."

The question was, would she do that?

Dubious morals were one thing, but this was completely different.

Journalistic integrity really did matter to Sav.

She was one of those fools who believed in the power of the press, and who didn't think oligarchs, up high, controlled it in board meetings.

But that could just be conspiracytok talking again.

"What does he have of Luciu's?"

"A tiara."

Her eyes bugged. "I thought you were going to say drugs."

"Would make more sense, wouldn't it?"

"Damn straight it would." She squinted at me as I laughed. "What kind of tiara?"

"A special one?"

"I didn't think it was made of plastic, Jen," she scoffed.

"I've worn it," I told her softly. "The Valentinis' ancestors were from this royal household back in the day. Luciu's hunting all these pieces down, and Eva owned one of them."

"Just happened to have it lying around, huh?" she drawled, reminding me of why I loved her—her bullshit radar was spectacular.

"Yep, just something she liked to throw on every now and then," I teased.

"I'll bet."

"Eva and her husband knew that we're friends. I'm not sure how. But they asked Luciu for this favor."

"And you're asking me..." She narrowed her eyes at me. "Okay. I'll do it."

Stunned by her easy compliance, I straightened up. "You will?"

"I will. On two conditions."

"What?" I demanded.

"One, you don't owe me a damn thing. But Luciu? He does."

I felt no compunction in saying, "Not a problem. What's the second?"

She dipped her chin. "You're paying for this coffee."

"This is because you know my starting salary, isn't it?" I complained, but I was smiling as I joked around.

"It is and I know they charge fifteen bucks for a latte here."

I winked at her, but grumbled, "Cheapskate."

ELEVEN

LUC

"HOW OLD WAS HE AGAIN?"

Stan pulled on some gloves, snapping the latex against his wrist as he peered at me. "Forty-two."

My brow furrowed. "It's like a frat house. Just... *clean.*"

He snickered. "You're not wrong. I'd have killed for that pinball machine when I was younger."

Shoving my hands in my pockets, I mooched around Damian Headley's penthouse, staring at the lewd art on the walls, the white-on-white decor that was touched upon with bright primary colors that matched the odd furniture—a coffee table, for example, was made of two pieces of glass with a red sphere separating them.

But the glass wasn't parallel.

It was skewed.

Talk about nonsensical.

Impractical.

Clearly, it was expensive. Only the very, very rich would waste money on this overpriced trash.

Disinterested and interested at the same time, I studied the place of a man who, as far as I could tell, Fi appeared to have liked. Prior to his infidelity, of course.

Stan's report on Fi had indicated that she was often cheated on by the men with whom she had relationships, and I had to think that her taking a key to his Ferrari, but none of the others', meant her feelings were involved.

I didn't like that.

I had no reason to be jealous, but that didn't stop the green-eyed monster from stirring to life.

"What are you hoping to find? If Headley was involved with the Triads, wouldn't they have taken it by now? They clearly know we had him."

That was why they kept showing up at *Russu*.

Goddamn pains in the ass.

Stan grunted. "It depends."

"On what?"

"A working theory I have."

I stepped over to him, moving away from the guards who were hovering in the entryway to the large duplex that had sound carrying more than I'd like.

With thirty-feet high ceilings and walls of glass, privacy wasn't a premium here.

"What kind of theory?"

He shot a look at the mixed bunch of guards. Giovi, Vincenzu, then there were Martino and Giuseppe hovering in the back. The first two I trusted; the others were Italians.

For the sake of peace, I had them tag along, but I didn't like it. Neither did Stan. But eradicating every Italian made man in New York City just wasn't feasible. We all had to learn to live and work together.

If I was going to get my men on the ground doing that, I needed to lead by example.

No one ever said it was easy being the Don.

"I wonder if he was working for the Triads but was stepping out on them. It'd explain why he was being watched and how they knew we had him so quickly. Fuck, we'd barely started turning him over before they showed up, guns blazing."

I hummed. "Good point."

"Contrary to popular opinion, I am capable of critical thinking," he drawled, before he started going through the cabinets in the place. "It'd go quicker if we let the guards help."

"Do we trust them?" I said softly.

"Have to start somewhere."

True.

Turning to the four men, I ordered, "Giovi and Martino, Vincenzu and Giuseppe, pair up. Take a room each and anything of interest, bring it to me. Glove up," I warned. "Any fingerprints that are found here will have you hauled to jail, and because you were dumb fuck enough to leave marks behind, I'll let your asses rot."

Receiving a quartet of nods, I turned my attention back to Stan. He was of more interest to me than the others.

He'd always had a knack of finding shit that didn't stink but that stuck out to him as if it did.

Our very British grandmother had once hauled our butts across one of the family farms, and she'd handed us each two twigs and told us to entertain ourselves with them.

It wasn't as bizarre as it sounded—our English grandparents, for all that they were nobility, had been hicks, more content to be in the country than in the city.

Bored and frigid with the cold, I'd made a fire with my two sticks. Rory, unable to sit still, had used them to pin up her hair before she'd climbed a tree and had returned with as many apples as her pockets could contain. As for Stan, well, he'd found water.

A fucking stream.

My lips curved, especially when I remembered how we'd hauled our butts into that freezing liquid silver after we'd pushed Grandma in. Memories like that stopped me from strangling my siblings for the various shit they pulled on me.

"What are you smiling at?" Stan grumbled, casting me a look. "It's creepy."

"I'm hearing that a lot lately."

"You *are* creepy." He smirked. "*Nanna* said you had shifty eyes."

"She said you had donkey ears," I retorted, folding my arms across my chest.

He rubbed one of his ears. "She stopped saying that when I had them pinned back. You can't do anything about your problem."

I rolled my shifty eyes and said, "I was thinking about the time when you found water at Hinderfield."

He laughed. "I remember that." His laughter didn't fade, instead it morphed into a genuine smile. "Grandma let us push her in."

"She was good like that," I agreed.

"I miss her."

For some stupid reason, I had to clench my teeth before I managed to rasp, "I miss them all."

And I did.

We'd had so much family growing up, and then... it was just us four.

It had been that way for ten years, and I thought I was okay with that. Not once had I thought about getting a wife, making a family.

Now?

I wanted it all.

I wanted four to become five. Six if I was right about what had happened last night.

Like she knew I was thinking of her, my phone pinged.

Fi: *Savannah says she'll write the exposé.*

Me: *Fantastic news, vita mia. Thank you.*

Fi: *Don't thank me yet. You don't know what she wants in return.*

Me: *She can have it.*

Fi: *Don't tell her that. For now, she just wants a favor.*

Goddamn favors were becoming the bane of my existence.

Me: *Consider it done.*

Fi: *I already agreed. Oops.*

Me: *So apologetic.*

Fi: *Well, that's how I roll. Speak later. We're going shopping.* <3

Flipping my cell phone through my fingers, I rubbed my chin as I contemplated what a favor from a journalist might entail.

There was no point in borrowing trouble, however. That was tomorrow's problem.

As for today, we had enough issues on our hands with this mess with the Triads.

Sighing, I turned away from Stan, letting him work his magic.

For some reason, he'd ignored the laptop on the kitchen counter—as had the Triads if they'd even bothered to come here, but it didn't look as if they had—and I stared at the TV.

Just as boredom hit and I was about to glove up and turn it on, Stan muttered, "A-ha."

Twisting back, I found him on his hands and knees in front of a unit that was filled with more ugly art. Each shelf was loaded down with a statue that had me pulling a face because it was offensively bad.

Peering at Stan, I saw he was messing around with one of the statues on the stand, a glass prism that, when he tugged on it, pulled the bottom of the shelf away, revealing a hole in the floor.

I stepped over to him as he retrieved a Sig Sauer, a couple of baggies of coke, three baggies of goddamn Rohypnol, a computer, a cell phone, and a tablet.

"The motherlode," I said softly.

"Agreed. The Triads didn't find this."

"They were here?" I questioned, surprised by his surety.

"They were. But they covered their tracks." His eyes were narrowed as he glanced around the room.

"Why bother?"

"Because when the cops figure out he's dead, and someone calls him in as missing, they didn't want this place trashed. It'd raise suspicions. Whatever it was, they were willing to lose it rather than let it fall into the hands of the NYPD."

My brows lifted. "That's some guesswork. It could be the opposite. They're not willing to lose it, but don't want anyone to think they're on the hunt."

"True." He grunted. "Right, we got what we came for."

"If we can't use Hunter, do you have another hacker lined up to work on this stuff?"

"Se. Name's Lodestar. She's ex-CIA. She agreed to do this one job, but if I can get her interested in a full-time position, I'll let you know."

"How did you find out about her?" I questioned with a frown.

"I know people."

I snorted. "Sure you do."

He tucked the computer gear under one arm and flipped me the bird with his free hand. "Right, guys, we're heading out," he hollered up the stairs.

"You found something?" Giovi hollered back.

"Yeah. We got what we came for."

Not wanting to leave anything to chance, I meandered upstairs as they headed to the lower floor, wanting to assure myself that they'd left everything as neatly as the Triads apparently had.

The man's bad taste and wealth were even more apparent up here.

A couple of lines of coke had once decorated the nightstand because there were traces of white powder littering it, and some used condoms were slung on the floor.

Distaste for the man's pigsty living arrangements had me stepping out of the bedroom before I checked out the other spaces.

Finding nothing out of place—no open drawers or a bed that was skewed after they'd dragged it out to check behind the bedstead, for example—I returned to my men, and we left the way we came in—via the service elevator.

Giovi and Vincenzu rode with Stan and me, whereas the Italians had our backs in an SUV as we drove to the ex-Fieri compound.

Getting arrested meant I was dealing with this later than I'd have liked, but I knew the widow Fieri had left almost a week ago by this point. I prepared to get angry because I knew the bitch would have taken things I'd requested she leave behind, but more than anything, I was just in a bad mood because I knew, before Stan said a fucking word, what he was thinking.

We were both thinking it.

With every mile we drove toward the goddamn hellhole, it was the white elephant in the back of the car with us.

"You should move into the compound."

I grunted.

"You should. The symbolism of taking over it matters," he prodded as he pulled out a large Ziplocked bag from his pocket.

When I saw its contents, I scowled at him. "Christ, you've been carrying that around with you?"

"Only since this fucking morning," he grumbled. "Don't look at me like I'm a cannibal or something. I have a purpose for it."

"Picking your nose?" He glowered at me, but I was more interested in the lone finger. "Didn't even know you hacked it off."

He'd clearly pricked it with some kind of preservative, but then, that was his world—not mine, thank Christ. It was gray, the flesh dying even though he was trying to keep it fresh.

"Now I know why you kept your gloves on."

"Thought it was a new fashion trend?" He snickered as he retrieved the digit from the bag, releasing an odor that was distinctly chemical but not the scent of putrefying flesh, then pressed it to the button on the laptop that *didn't* react with the system. "*Pezz'i miedda*, I was hoping..."

"What?"

"I created a kind of serum that I hoped would make this work, but no dice."

"Back to the drawing board."

"Yeah. It would have been a hell of a lot easier than trying to figure out what his passcode was. I'll get in touch with my contact and see what she has to say about transferring the files over to her. I might have to send her the hardware."

I grunted in agreement, watching as he slammed the laptop screen closed. "You know, it would have been a lot easier if your talents had rested with computer science rather than chemistry. Then we wouldn't need a hacker."

He arched a brow at me. "You won't be saying that next year."

"Next year? Or the year after? I'm starting to think this C-L-O you promised me is nothing more than a pipe dream," I taunted him.

C-L-O, aka, *cielo*, was the 'paradise' Stan was trying to offer our patrons in the forms of chemical freedom. Ha.

"If you let me work in my goddamn lab for more than a few hours at a time, I'd be more hands on."

"Now things are settled, you'll be able to drown in your fucking lab if that's what you want. In fact," I mocked, "you can have the Fieri compound. Use it as your base."

He cocked a brow at me. "You being serious?"

"When am I not?"

"It might work."

"What might?"

"A lab there. I could really start work on C-L-O, instead of just dicking around with it." His gaze drifted away, like he was thinking about his work. "Have you seen that underground parking garage? That would make a good laboratory."

For all that I taunted him with this shit, the last thing I wanted was him concocting drugs.

The last time he'd gotten high, the only person who'd stopped Stan dying from an overdose was me, and I'd been in London at the time, not scheduled to come back to the family estate until the following morning.

Luck and an argument with one of our lawyers had seen me driving back home earlier than planned. *Luck and an argument* were the only reasons he was still alive.

"If you end up blowing the place to kingdom come, I won't complain, just make sure your ass is safe, hmm?" I sniped at him, trying to back away from this offer, as I wished I'd never said anything now.

"You're all heart."

"Do what you want with the damn place." Tilting my head to the side, I stared out onto the road, trying to appear disaffected as I said, "Remember when you got it fixed in your head that you wanted to work on making EpiPens more accessible to the public?"

"My plans have changed."

"They don't have to. You don't need to work on C-L-O."

"I'm telling you; it's the way forward. You want the Valentinis on the map? C-L-O is the new Molly, Luc."

It was a low blow to bring up his best friend, but that didn't stop me. "You going to be okay after what happened with Accursio?"

"Maybe not, but if that's the case, I really will blow the place to kingdom come."

"We could just sell it," I drawled, trying not to sound like I preferred that prospect.

"No. That place is either ours or it burns." He grunted. "You can take the art, though. I don't like that shit."

"Rembrandt, even if you hate the classics, could never be classified as shit."

He sniffed. "We have different tastes. Speaking of... you know I have my ear to the ground for the Anjous?"

"Don't we all?" I retorted. "What have you heard though?"

"Declan O'Donnelly is on the hunt for some specific works of art. He's the brother who—"

"*Se*," I drawled impatiently. "I don't need a reminder. I know he's the O'Donnelly son who handles their drugs."

"Well, he's into art in a big way."

I frowned. "So?"

"So, you have a Rembrandt," he drawled. "We want more of an in with the Irish…"

"You want me to give it to him?" I growled. "You want me to *give* him a fucking Rembrandt—"

"I think it would be a wise move."

"Since when were you the strategist?"

He shot me a withering glance. "Since I saw you lose your fucking head to Jennifer."

"When has that impacted business?"

"How about when you had us cleaning up the corpse of a known associate of the fucking Bratva?"

"You said it yourself—an associate. As if they'll care."

"That fucker's brother is Bratva. It's a problem waiting to happen."

"I'll deal with it. By that logic, I should give the fucking Rembrandt to Lyanov."

"If he was interested in art, sure. I don't think he is."

"You know what his vice is?"

"Money."

"Pleb."

He scoffed, "Snob. We were raised with it. Not everyone was so lucky, and his past is one of the worst I've come across."

"Money's boring," I countered. "It has nothing to do with being a snob."

"So says the fucking snob. You were a millionaire without becoming the Don. He was a *boyevik* for the Russians before he snatched the crown away."

"Takes guts to do that. You sure money's his vice?"

"I'm positive. He's making a lot of investments right now."

"Bitcoin?"

"Real estate, Bitcoin, regular stocks and shares, blue chip... waving his old Pakhan's cash around like he's got a printing press of his own that'll roll out dollar bills when he wants.

"Moscow isn't very happy about him taking over as far as I can figure out, but you know it's 'might is right' with those fuckers. He earned the throne, so he'll keep it until he shows a weakness, and they'll slit his throat when he's sleeping."

"If he *has* a weakness."

"Rumor has it he wants the Pakhan's daughter. As we're learning with you, even the greatest can fall prey to pussy."

"Shame for him that all the Vasov women are married to O'Donnellys," I mocked, ignoring his mockery, before I scowled as I remembered there was a third sister. "The youngest girl?"

Stan grunted. "Victoria Vasov. She's been living with the middle sister and her husband ever since her father was killed."

Giovi turned around and told us both, "I heard Lyanov chopped off some fucker's head and gave it to the girl as a gift."

"Get real, Giovi." Impatiently, I strummed my fingers on my thigh. "Who the fuck would send a head to a teenager?"

"A *boyevik*?" Stan joked, chuckling at my grimace.

"Those fucking Russians have no style."

"Says the man who slices and dices men's faces."

"There's an art form to up close and personal knife work," I retorted.

"You keep telling yourself that," Stan sniped. "They say the Vasovs had a pristine collection of jewels."

I'd heard that myself. "From that museum heist in Belgrade, wasn't it?"

"I heard it was a museum heist, but I don't know where. You know half those war stories are bullshit anyway."

I hummed. "Might be worth a meeting. A preemptive strike... if he likes money, I'll willingly drop it if he has what we want."

Stan caught my eye. "Want me to arrange a meeting?"

Rubbing my chin, I thought about the long term and said, "I'll be attending the FAST gala next week. Get him an invitation."

Stan whistled under his breath. "Smart move. He's trying to edge into society."

"How do you know?"

"He keeps trying to move up in circles, but it isn't happening. Manhattan isn't willing to open its door to just any rich man. He's only been a Pakhan for as much time as you've been the Don, and without the established ground that you have."

"If they aren't willing, then he's not doing it right," I mocked. "I'll be his Yoda."

"Now your name's been littered around in the press, he'll be more than interested in what you have to say."

I grunted because I'd seen the headlines this morning. Fi wasn't the only person calling me the Italian Darcy, except I doubted Jane Austen had armed her hero with an arrest record and upcoming appearances in court.

Fucking Rory.

Still, the talk soothed me like nothing else could. I had no desire to visit the Fieri compound, but I knew it was imperative. Staking a claim on it was posturing, but it mattered. In this world, machismo was everything.

Fuckwits.

"We'll have to call a gathering soon," I murmured, thinking out loud. "Once I've met with Lyanov, that'll cement things. Peace with the Irish, peace with the Russians... what better way to call together the remaining families and to get them on board?"

Stan nodded. "Now there's my brother. Thinking with his head and not his dick."

I shoved him hard against the door, enough for the thud to be audible, but he just chuckled.

Thankfully, Giovi and Vincenzu weren't so fucking stupid.

TWELVE

JEN

ALINA BLANKED me as she served me breakfast, and while her attitude was too much to take first thing in the morning, it could just be that she was a grumpy bitch like me without a cup of coffee in her.

But seeing as she'd left me alone for the most part, I stayed out of her path and she steered clear of me. That was the kind of impasse I could handle.

With my gaze on my phone, because I didn't have the ability to shoot lasers at Luc's housekeeper from my eyes yet—that would definitely end the impasse—I shot Aoife a message instead:

Me: *I quit Crawfords yesterday.*

I waited a couple minutes, but when she didn't reply, I typed:

Me: *I told Jackass Jason to suck my dick.*

Me: *I've grown a dick.*

Me: *I was abducted by aliens, and they gave me one.*

Me: *It curves to the left.*

Me: *Sigh.*

Me: *Nothing? NOTHING? OMG, Aoifeeeeee. WTF. Where are you?!*

Me: *If you're not interested in my war story, then I'll have to text you it.*

Me: *Let me set the scene.*

Me: *I was wearing those Tom Ford boots that make my ass pop, and that black shirt you bought me last year for Christmas. The one that makes my boobs look four sizes bigger than they are?*

Me: *You know the one, right?*

Me: *The one I wrote on my Christmas list? And specifically asked you to buy me?*

Me: *Okay, I get it, you're not playing.*

Me: *Anyway, I walked straight into Jackass Jason's office without knocking on the door first. He was watching porn. Haha. It was hilarious. Some dude getting his balls stretched. It looked sooo painful.*

Me: *He was embarrassed as hell, but I was the one who was traumatized. I might have seen his prick if he was jacking off.*

Me: *He blustered a lot, told me that I was in deep shit for not knocking on the door, and that was when I planted my hands on his desk and loomed over it. I felt like such a lady boss, I swear.*

Me: *I told him, "I'd say you can stick your warnings up your ass, but seeing as I know what you jack off to, maybe that would be too pleasurable. I'm done. I'm done with you, with this place, and with you taking the credit for all my work. So, you can suck my dick. I'm outta here."*

Me: *See? I really did tell him to suck my dick.*

Me: *He sent security after me, so I had two guys watching me as I packed up my desk.*

Me: *Such a jerk. And now I never have to see him again.*

Me: *Bet he loses his job without me there.*

Me: *Sucks to be him.*

Me: *Eef, you're worrying me, babe. Please, just drop me a message to say you're okay? I'll accept a fucking emoji at this point.*

I waited, and when she didn't answer, I sighed and put my phone on the table. As I reached for a banana, my screen lit up.

Aoife: <3

It wasn't much, but it was something.

"You look like you want to do devious things to that banana." Luc's remark drew my attention his way.

"Is that because *you* want me to do devious things to the banana?" I tossed the question back at him, smirking as I unpeeled it then sucked the tip of the fruit into my mouth, bared my teeth, then bit down with more ferocity than was required for the soft flesh.

His lips curved. "Are you all right?"

"Aoife's being quiet."

"She's grieving."

"I know." I scowled at him for the obvious reply. "But how can I make it better if she doesn't let me? That's what friends are for. Not men," I grumbled under my breath.

"You can't make this better."

"Sure I can. I can sit with her, and we can watch movies or *Grey's Anatomy*, and we can eat pizza or Chinese—"

"You eat takeout?" he queried, his shock clear.

"I eat," I muttered, taking another bite of my banana as if to prove to him that I was capable of the basic human function.

He hummed his disbelief, but asked, "Carry on. How else would you make her feel better?"

"Why do you want to know?"

"Future reference."

"For what?"

"If you hurt, then I'll know what to do. This is when I'll watch *Twilight* 2 with you."

The need to laugh hit me hard, and I whooshed out a breath rather than let it loose because he looked so damn serious as he said it.

Clearing my throat, I told him, "It's called *New Moon*. I'll make a list of shows and movies that'll cheer me up."

"*Bonu.*"

"You have to tell me what cheers you up too. And not—" I interrupted before he could speak. "—a blowjob."

He grinned at me. "We men are simple creatures."

"Nothing simple about you, babe."

A twinkle appeared in his eyes, but he said, "I don't watch much TV."

"I figured that out when I saw you have no unit in the living room. You really need to sort that out if I'm gonna live here."

A gaggle of Russian or whatever the hell it was Alina spoke burst from the doorway, and Luc, frowning, retorted in the same language.

His face darkened, features turning saturnine as Alina and he argued. About what, I had no idea. Aside from me, of course.

Luc growled, "This is her home, Alina."

Those words—did he know what they meant to me?

Home.

I let it sink in, absorbed what he was offering me—offering without asking—and while I wasn't a snitch by nature, she'd hurt me the other night, so I said, "After you were arrested, I came here... I needed to know what was happening, if you were safe, but I wasn't allowed in."

Temper flashed in his eyes. "The doorman didn't let you in?"

"No."

Anger burst into being, becoming a physical entity in the room.

For the first time, Alina gave him no sass when he turned on her, and while he didn't even raise his voice, she was meek as she turned to me, saying, "Sorry."

I thought I'd see hatred in her eyes when she apologized, that it would come across as false, but it wasn't. If anything, it appeared genuine. Maybe Luc shouting at her was a rarity, and it hammered home that he had feelings for me?

Whatever, I'd take it. I deserved an apology after the way she'd left me out in the damn cold that night.

"Stan has informed security that you are allowed entry at any time," he groused, his eyes narrowed with his temper. "I'll have a key code made up so that you can come here at will."

I blinked. "You don't have to do that."

"*Se,*" he hissed, "I do. How can this be your home if you have no key? I want..." He gritted his teeth as he shook his head, anger getting the best of him.

His temper might have frightened Alina, but it didn't frighten me. I'd been raised around burly Irish Americans who didn't understand that 100 volume was high and not a bar that needed to be topped.

Plus, I knew what a nasty temper was.

I'd been raised with it, had come across it far too many times in Mom's boyfriends.

Luciu's was mean—I saw that for myself. Alina was a strong-minded woman and yet she'd apologized after brushing up against his temper. I didn't think that happened often. But he cut her so much slack that I imagined when she triggered his anger, it came as a shock.

She hadn't cowered, though. He hadn't demanded that of her. Violence hadn't leaked into his words or his tone, just his outrage.

That was refreshing.

"What *do* you want?" I asked him quietly when his voice faded out and he didn't finish the sentence.

"I want you to consider this place your home." I smiled at him, and the sight of it had him continuing, "I shouldn't have left this to other people—"

"You were busy."

While there'd been no accusation in my voice, he flinched like *I'd* hit *him.* "A man makes time for those he wants in his life."

When he talked like that, I half expected him to quote someone's name, but nope.

Those words were all Luciu Valentini, and I was the lucky woman who he bestowed them upon.

As he stared at me, pounding the words home with every second that passed, I started to believe. But trust was a journey. It didn't just pop into being. It grew over time, and he'd just planted the seed in me.

"You wanted to make sure I was safe, *duci?*"

"How couldn't I?" I whispered. "I was so scared for you. But no one would give me any information..." I bit my lip. "The only reason I was at Aoife's that evening was because I wanted her help."

Fire gleamed in his eyes. "You wanted a favor from her?"

"From the Five Points," I muttered, my shoulders rounding.

"*T'amu,* Fionnabhair," he growled, his voice as sleek as silk but redolent with satisfaction.

I gulped. "I love you too."

"Never again will you have to worry about going to others for favors," he declared before his tone softened, "What plans do you have today, *cara mia?*"

My voice was croakier than I'd have liked as I murmured, "I don't know. Depends on when you show me where I work now."

He chuckled. "So eager for work. What every boss likes to hear. I have the contract for you to sign in my office, but seeing as it's Saturday, we'll do that on Monday. Today, if you have nothing arranged, I want to show you something."

"What is it?"

"*Matri's* place in Brooklyn. I want to show you those pictures of my grandparents."

"I'd love that," I breathed, meaning every word. Just seeing his home would be enough.

"Good. When you're finished, we'll head out."

"I'm finished."

He scowled at my plate. "You ate a banana. Not even a whole one."

"I'm done," I retorted, sliding out of the seat. "Just give me five minutes to get ready."

I heard him grunt, but I ignored him, choosing instead to go into the wardrobe that had so impressed me before.

Luc was proving himself to be a man of action, if few words.

He didn't ask, he took.

With another guy, I'd have been pissed. But Luc was different. Maybe it was the Sicilian caveman in him that I responded to. Maybe he brought out the Irish cavewoman in me.

Overnight, almost all of my clothes had made an appearance, and because Alina hadn't realized that I was moving in, I wondered if someone else had unpacked my things. Maybe her daughter?

Unlike the first time I visited, the closet now held many, *many* traces of evidence that a woman lived here.

Me.

Smirking at the thought, I dragged out my coat and shoved my feet into some boots. Grabbing a scarf and some gloves, I dressed in them. I proceeded to wince when I forgot about my damn ear as I curled the scarf around my throat, and the fabric tugged on the wound on the lobe.

With it still smarting, the memory of Vlad dragging the diamond solitaire stud off my ear hurting even more, I left the bedroom, and, on my way back to the dining room, found him standing in the hallway, on the phone with someone, already dressed for the bitter cold outside, with the elevator waiting on us.

He saw me, held out his hand, tucked my gloved one in his, and together, we stepped into the elevator. As he talked—Sicilian, this time. I was getting to recognize some of the nuances of the language—I studied us both.

We fit. Did he see that?

In my silk-lined trench coat that I had belted around my waist, with my slimline pants—no one had to know I wore thermal tights under them because I wasn't about to freeze my ass off for fashion when it wasn't for a party—tucked into high boots that made me look like I was a Domme on the side, my outfit was sleek and expensive. As expensive as him.

He knew how to fill out a suit, that was for damn sure.

Watching him in the reflection, seeing his expressions, studying the differences between him speaking Sicilian and English, they were fascinating to me. Far more interesting than checking my appearance to make sure I was perfectly presented.

I'd noticed that he was cooler toned when he spoke English. A tad more formal. Apathetic, even.

In Sicilian, he was loud. His expressions were like a lash of a whip as the volatile nature of the language made itself known.

When he caught me watching, I almost felt the flames flickering to life between us. If he'd slammed me against the wall at that moment, I wouldn't have complained.

The car was idling as we made it out of the lobby and into the biting chill of a miserable New York morning.

After Luciu made a point of introducing me to a doorman I hadn't met yet, who held the door for us, we found Lorenzo outside.

Dressed in a black topcoat, his face burrowed beneath the upright lapels, hands shrouded in leather gloves, the only parts of him on display were his forehead, bushy eyebrows, and his ears with a pair of beady eyes peeping out.

Steam curled around the vehicle, and I almost felt his sigh of relief to open the door for us and to let us get inside, so that he could hop in too.

The warmth in the back of the car was intoxicating after that brief stint outside, but I still stayed close to Luciu as we set off, heading out of Manhattan and over the bridge into Brooklyn.

He was on the phone for most of the journey, but I didn't mind. Viewing the city, at this time of the morning, from the back of a luxury car was pretty damn sweet. It got even sweeter when he raised his arm and slipped it around my shoulders.

When we arrived in Brooklyn Heights and pulled up outside the Renaissance Revival-style brownstone, I had to admit that knowing he was wealthy and seeing it in just one of his properties was mind blowing.

These were the kinds of places that were written off on company accounts with twenty-million-dollar price tags.

Five stories high, twenty or so feet wide, the house had an oval entranceway that ran symmetrically in between two bay windows with white curtains that shielded the interior from the outside. Ornate moldings decorated every one of the fourteen windows, spanning each of the five stories, adding touches of another era to the brownstone.

By this point, Luc was finally done on the phone, and he turned to me, muttering, "Sorry, Fi."

"You don't have to apologize all the time, Luc. You're a busy man. I don't expect or want or *need* your full attention." I winked at him. "Except in certain situations."

He laughed as I'd intended, but he tucked me into his side as we headed up the stairs toward the entrance. He keyed in a code on the door, something that was definitely not from the eighteen hundreds, and we walked into a large foyer that served no other purpose than to hold the staircase and a table with a bronze nude atop it.

Guiding me into a room off the side of the foyer, I sighed at the baby grand piano, which sat pride of place beside the windows, but as for the rest of the room, it was relatively modern even though most pieces were vintage.

From the set of four club chairs that were finished with brown leather, to the coffee table that was topped with Vogue picture books and a tray loaded with bowls of candy.

There was very little on the walls apart from a painting above the fireplace.

I didn't know my art, but I squinted at the portrait. "That looks expensive."

"It is." He tipped his head to the side. "It's a Rembrandt. I had it delivered here yesterday. I don't particularly like it but, from now on, when I walk in here, I'll see it and *that* I like."

"Why?"

"It used to belong to the Fieris."

"Oh. Wow. There's a lot of money to be made in the mafia, isn't there?"

He snorted. "Just a few dollars here and there. The Fieris were the front for the Sparrows as well, so I guess selling out came with a high price tag."

"Which you're reaping the benefits of..."

"Indeed." He turned to me. "Take a seat. Do you want tea? Coffee?"

"Coffee would be nice."

As he disappeared, I peered around, but not wanting to sit down, I stepped into the foyer to look at the other rooms on the first floor.

I came across two more seating areas and an office, but what I liked more than anything was the view from the back of the house where there was a yard that upped the price tag on this place alone.

It was bleak now, the fountain frozen, the grass covered with pristine patches of snow, but it made me hope I'd be able to see this in the spring.

With my back to the hall, I didn't sense Luc until, in full on ghost mode, he moved behind me. "In the summer," he noted, "there's a pool out there. It's just hidden by the snow."

"You guys have a pool?" I laughed. "Your neighbors must be so jealous."

This was the largest property on the road, and I got the feeling the other houses had been broken up into apartments a long time ago.

Only a mafioso would be able to afford this kind of place, that was for damn sure.

"It's tucked behind trees so they can't see it." He pointed to a corner of the garden that was darker than the rest thanks to the large cluster of trees he was talking about. "It's there. Come, I'll show you around. Coffee will be with us shortly."

"Where's your mom?"

"Church. It's busier than she likes on Sundays, so she goes on Saturdays.

"She picked it up when Dad died, which is ironic because she and

Nanna used to go head-to-head because *Matri* never made us attend services when we were kids."

"She probably finds comfort in it."

"I think it's the only thing that's kept her going for a long time," he agreed, his tone solemn as he led me up the grand staircase where I found more sitting rooms, a library, a billiards room, as well as a strange kind of terrace that Luc told me was a 'smoking balcony.'

But the library interested me the most, and that was where he guided me.

A fire blazed in the hearth, and he explained, "This is *Matri's* favorite room."

I could see why. "It's beautiful."

My apartment was smaller than this one room alone, and every corner had books tucked into shelves, with only the wall above the hearth exposed. A portrait of a couple dressed in older fashions sat there, pride of place.

"Fionnabhair," he said formally, staring up at them, "meet my *nannu* and *nanna.*"

"You look like him," I whispered, taken aback by the striking similarities between grandfather and grandson. Stan was like him too, but he was stockier. Luciu's face shared his *nannu's* noble characteristics.

As for his grandmother, it was clear she was pregnant, her belly just starting to show. Her smile was more Mona Lisa than overt, but there was a warmth to her expression that spoke of a contentment.

It hurt my heart to know that, shortly after this, everything had gone to shit for them both.

Luc grunted but stepped closer. "I'm pretty sure when that picture was taken it was the last time *Nanna* was happy. I think she loved him, but maybe she didn't. Maybe she was born for this kind of life, I don't know. Bitterness made her vindictive."

"I'll bet. She had to run for her and her son's life, Luc. That changes a person."

He cast me a glance as he stepped over to a wall and dragged out what I could see was a picture book. When he passed it to me, I was glad because I hated when people looked over your shoulder as you stared at their photos. But as I flipped the page, my heart was stolen straight from my chest.

I saw a wedding day that looked as if the bride and groom were royalty. His *nanna's* dress was made of silk and lace, and while it was old-fashioned, it was majestic, and she was wearing the tiara that I'd had on my head days earlier.

On her wrists, she had solid cuffs that, even though it was black and white, I could see were rubies.

At her throat, hand, and in her ears, she wore more of them. Some were easier to see than others, some blurred and some were faded with time, but she looked like a queen. The jewelry helped, but *she* was regal. It seeped from her pores.

I couldn't imagine how difficult it must have been to get married, be wealthy enough to dress that way, then, to survive, to have to marry a farmer.

Maybe I got it more because I'd been born with nothing and had always craved *something*, but at that moment, I felt sorrier for his *nanna* than his grandfather. He'd died, but she'd had to endure.

Curious about the farmer, I asked, "You didn't like your father's stepfather?"

"Hated him." His reply was immediate. His passion fierce. "He was a brute. I was glad when he died."

"I wish I'd met her," I rasped, unbelievably touched and surprised by my reaction to the family photos.

"She wasn't a very nice person," he said dryly.

"I still would have liked to have known her." I shot him a look. "She was a survivor. Survival is tough."

His gaze was level as it met mine. "She'd have liked you."

I had no idea why, but his words made me blush. So I tipped my head away and I stared at more of the family memorabilia, grateful for a glimpse into his past that very few would ever be afforded.

THIRTEEN

LUC

MONDAY

"FRANK, THIS IS JENNIFER." I reached out to shake his hand and beckoned at Fi with my other. As I did, I watched his gaze glance over my new 3D printed cast which I'd gotten yesterday, and which was much more comfortable than the plaster one I'd received on the NYPD's dime. "She's the tax specialist I was talking to you about."

Fi shot me a dour look, but I ignored it. If I heard her repeat that she wasn't a tax specialist one more time, I'd probably have to fuck her to shut her up.

Her boss was a tax specialist.

She did all his work.

Their bosses were more than content with his performance, ergo, she was a specialist.

Her credentials were in line, her bachelor's degree summa cum laude, and she'd recorded one of the highest scores on the CPA examination *ever*—something she didn't know, but I did after Stan's very thorough background check on her.

"Pleasure to meet you, Jennifer," Frank said, too warmly for my tastes, but his gaze was nervous as he glanced first at me then at her.

What could I say? I made people nervous when I came around.

It didn't stop the bastard from checking Fi out though, not until I flashed a warning at him that had him gulping.

Frank was in his mid-fifties, played squash once a week and thought that gave him free reign to consume as many late lunches as was physically possible. He had a bushy beard that was just beginning to be peppered with gray, and his mustache bobbed every time he exhaled from his nose.

He was like a dark-haired St. Nicholas who wore Huntsman-bespoke suits instead of a bright red one.

"The pleasure's mine," she replied politely, a professional smile curving her lips that made me want to kiss her, just to see her mussed up again.

Both of us were playing at being anything other than the predators we were, and that had never been rammed home more to me than seeing her dressed like a corporate doll again.

I didn't like it. Not that she was working, I didn't care about that. Rory was smarter than me and was fucking superb at what she did. I had no doubt that Fi was the same. I just liked seeing her in the raw, not tidied and prettied up.

"Once Mr. Valentini showed me your resumé and indicated some of the accounts you'd been working on for Crawfords, I'll admit your experience and time on the job have me curious."

"I worked for a lazy boss, Frank," she said candidly. "I leaped ahead of the game because of that. As a result, I have contacts in six tax havens, three of whom keep inviting me over to meet their family. I'm very good at what I do."

"I heard you were dealing with the Martinez account."

Martinez was a common name, but Frank's curiosity pricked my own.

"Yes, it was definitely unusual."

"Why was it?"

"Mr. Martinez has no first name on record."

I shook my head. "Impossible."

"No, it wasn't. I checked. Trust me," she drawled, smiling at my surprise. "I've never seen anything like it, and neither had the Cayman Islands."

"You managed to make arrangements for his shell company there?"

"To a degree," she hedged. "Some of the details are still up in the air because I left recently, but I managed to get the ball rolling."

"How?" I queried.

Her eyes narrowed on mine, and I knew she wanted me to drop it, but dammit to hell, this sounded like the Martinez I'd had business dealings with in Aspen. The one who was the ex-leader of the *Lobos Rojos*.

Talk about a small fucking world.

Was this how they'd found out about Fi? Because of where she worked?

Everyone always referred to him as Martinez. There was no mention of his first name. Ever.

"How?" I pressed, not willing to let this drop.

"By less than legal means," she admitted, casting a glance at Frank.

"Most of the ways in which we bend the rules are less than legal," Frank chortled.

"Agreed," she concurred. "But in the past, Mr. Martinez had apparently never run across the issue before."

"Irregular," Frank pointed out.

"Perhaps the paper trail was less stringent than it is now. Before I was accredited, I'd assume there were ways and means of making things work."

She meant bribes.

Still, the way she evaded the question had me prompting, "So, what did you do?"

Fi seemed to sense I wasn't going to give up and, on a sigh, admitted, "I made up a first name."

My lips twitched. "As simple as that?"

"Not so simple. A lot of certificates required forging." She shot a look at Frank. "My boss approved of the maneuver."

"He signed off on it?" Frank questioned.

"He did."

"Nice to know the mettle of the men Crawfords hire," he replied, casting me a look.

Nodding, I said, "Indeed." I turned to him. "Is Jennifer's office ready?"

"Yes." Frank's smile was tight. "Could I speak with you a moment?"

"No—"

"I'll just wait outside," Fi said easily, glaring at me to force my compliance.

Folding my arms against my chest, I stared at Frank as he pointed out, "Her work experience is less than half of what we require as a standard from our employees, Mr. Valentini."

"I'm sure it is."

"We have graduates from Yale, Harvard, Princeton..." He blew out a breath. "I understand that she's your... *partner*, sir, but—"

The intonation on the word 'partner' pissed me off as much as if he'd called her my whore.

The twenty-first century label held a dismissive note when uttered from this fool's lips.

"To be here, holding CPA credentials is a standard, correct? Beyond anything else, that is the standard. *Se?*"

"Of course, Mr. Valentini."

"And to pass the CPA exam, one requires a score of seventy-five. Is that right?"

He sighed. "If memory serves, yes."

I turned away from him and headed over to the corner window that gave me a glimpse of the snow-blistered streets surrounding Grand Central station. "With the Financial Accounting and Reporting being one of the hardest sections to pass, no?"

"The FAR section is the hardest, yes. But sir, this is irrelevant—"

"It isn't. Not only did she pass the CPA exam the first time, but her FAR score was ninety-nine, Frank. A perfect score. As for the rest, she came out with a ninety-eight.

"Whether she's boning me or has a fiancé over in Long Island and a vacation home in the Hamptons, you can't deny her scores are good."

"It takes more than that to make a great accountant."

"Not according to the law." I turned back to face him just so he could see me arch my damn brow at him. "Whether or not you approve of her schooling, I don't care. Whether or not you have to fire someone so she can have a position, I don't care.

"Your opinion doesn't matter to me, Frank. I put you in this swanky office to do as I ask, not for you to have an opinion. Do you understand?"

His jaw tightened, and as he exhaled noisily down his nose, his mustache bobbed again. "I understand, sir."

"Now, you can be difficult and try to outmaneuver me by giving her projects that are worthy of an intern, but if you do that, you'll find yourself out of a job." I leaned back against the window. Frank had an addiction to high class hookers—I knew because the Valentinis owned one of the brothels he frequented. "So, I'd think twice before making a move against her.

"She can stand on her own two feet, but I won't have you making things harder on her just because you're annoyed that you lost this pissing contest."

Annoyance flashed in his eyes before it was quickly stamped out—I did appreciate a beta male sometimes.

They said alphas dominated the boardrooms, but *real* alphas couldn't work in boardrooms.

Period.

"I'll show her to her office."

"No. I will. Which one is it?"

His face cleared of all expression. "Six A."

"Pleasure speaking with you, Frank. I'll make sure that your annual bonus reflects upon the aftermath of this conversation."

Meaning that his money was tied to Fi's contentment in her job here.

His gulp said he understood my position loud and clear, and I stepped out, leaving him behind without another word.

Finding Fi sitting in the seating area outside his office, her knees primly tucked together, her spine barely touching the back of her chair as she stared out into the middle distance, I said, "Come, *cara mia*, I'll show you to your new workspace."

Once standing, she moved over to my side and let me lead her to the other end of the floor, one that was away from Frank.

I didn't mind because I'd seen the fucker's eyes on her, but also because rank and office placement weren't an obvious factor here. The corner offices went to the partners, with Frank being the most senior and the only one I dealt with. As for the offices in between that came with windows, they weren't preferential or rank related.

"He doesn't want me to work here, does he?"

I hummed. "I clarified things for him."

Fi peered up at me. "He'll resent me."

"No, he won't," I assured her. "I made certain of it."

"Threaten his cheeks?"

"No, I should have thought of that though," I drawled, breaking off the conversation when we reached six A.

Opening the door, I waited for her to step inside, but she had barely a foot in the room before she sucked in a breath and froze. She stepped back, collided with me, then twisted around to stare up at me.

"This is better than Jackass Jason's office."

"Is that a problem?"

Remaining silent, she stepped into the room, headed over to the window, then grimaced. "No, not until everyone realizes I'm an impostor." Then she raised a hand. "Don't give me any BS about how I'm so good at what I do. I'm not really."

"I see it like this. You can work here and prove yourself, earn what you should be earning, have a life outside of the office, and not kowtow to some piece of shit boss who exploited his position...

"You can see if you're as crap at accounting as you seem to think you are. No better way to learn a lesson than by seeing for yourself what you can do."

"I never said I was crap at accounting," she denied. "I said I wasn't the expert you make out that I am."

Closing the door behind me, I strolled over to her just so I could tap her nose with my fingertip. "I'll just keep on believing in you until you do that for yourself."

Her mouth twisted but she laughed. "I almost get vertigo from looking out the window."

"It's a nice view, isn't it?" I teased.

"It's beautiful." She twisted around, took in the space, then murmured, "I worked in a cubicle before. I could get used to this."

I intended to make sure she did.

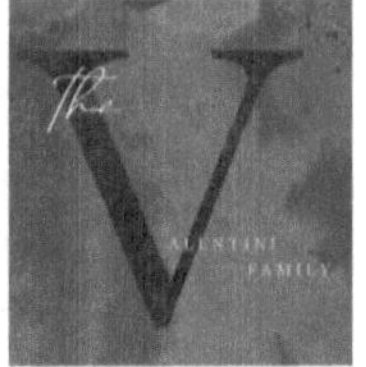

FOURTEEN

THE FOLLOWING week seemed to pass at an odd pace. Both too quick and too slow.

Going back to Luciu's apartment every evening was beyond awesome, such a pleasure by comparison to the dump I'd called home for months now.

Sleeping in his bed, beside him, was as much of a luxury as his penthouse. Waking up with him was a pleasure I'd never imagined, especially when his face was between my thighs.

As for the job he'd shoved me in? I didn't hate it, which I considered a bonus.

His team of accountants worked out of an Acuig building in Hell's Kitchen, ironically enough, and I'd been shuffled in as a tax expert when I really wasn't.

Not in the eyes of my peers, at any rate.

It meant that I didn't exactly have a place yet, and though I could have been on the receiving end of a lot of sneers because it was clear that I'd been slotted in here as I was Luciu Valentini's 'girlfriend,' everyone was too scared to say jack to me.

Sitting in an office that was better than Jackass Jason's at Crawford, Lewis, and Jones's, staring out onto Hell's Kitchen from an ergonomic leather chair that had probably cost more than a month's rent in my shit-hole apartment, I wasn't going to complain that I hadn't exactly found my sweet spot yet.

Today was better than yesterday though.

Today, I'd been tasked with setting up a corporation in a tax haven based in Europe, one that required some... shall we say... lubrication to make sure that the Valentinis got what they wanted.

This far, what they wanted appeared to be an apartment in which-ever haven I could find, and unlimited access to it.

And we weren't talking about Schengen visas here.

I had no idea why they'd want something like that, and I really didn't want to know either.

Rolling through my usual suspects, I was about to start reaching out to some of my contacts when my personal cell phone rang.

Immediately answering it because it was the first time Aoife had called me, I demanded, "Where the hell have you been?"

"Sleeping mostly," Aoife replied, her tone odd, like she was trying to sound neutral.

Only she was failing.

"I tried to visit but the doorman said you weren't in," I complained.

"Finn told me."

"Five times this week, Aoife," I grumbled. "I know you're sad, sweet-heart, but that's what I'm for. I cheer you up. It's like my job."

Her chuckle was half-hearted, but it was a chuckle nonetheless. "Better than Prozac, that's you."

"Damn straight," I joked before my tone softened and I asked, "How are you feeling?"

"Been better, been worse."

"Only natural." A knock sounded at my door, and I quickly called out, "One second."

"You're busy," she said flatly. "I should go."

"No, it's okay—"

"I'll speak with you later. I just wanted you to know I was fine."

Fine.

As in... Frantic. Insecure. Nervous. Erratic?

I believed that more than the other.

"Take care, darling," I told her softly, frowning as she cut the line.

When the knock sounded at the door again, I called out, "Come in!"

One of the receptionists appeared, a large box in her hand. In fact, several large boxes. I frowned at the sight, getting to my feet as anticipation made my heart beat double time.

The boxes were red.

Blood red.

Gifts from Luciu.

"Thank you," I told the receptionist, Narinda, who smiled at me politely before retreating.

With my cell still in my hand, I immediately dialed Luc's number and when he accepted the call, I demanded, "What did you buy me?"

His soft chuckle was the aural equivalent of hot chocolate sliding down my throat after a long, cold day of exploring Fifth Avenue like the Brave New World it was. "You could just open them and find out?"

"Where would be the fun in that?"

A cry of pain sounded in the background, and I grimaced, especially when he snarled something in Sicilian.

I heard footsteps, a door closing, and I muttered, "Sorry. I shouldn't have called—"

"You can always call me," he interrupted immediately. "Why wouldn't I prefer to hear your voice instead of some idiot crying out for his mama?"

"You're the reason the idiot is crying out for his mama," I pointed out with a snort.

"People have to learn not to cross me. And you," he said flatly, making shivers dance down my spine.

"Me?" I spluttered.

"You weren't taken back to my apartment. You were treated like you were my whore. I'm not about to stand for that."

When he reminded me of his position... it was like being zapped with a Taser—unpleasant—and yet, the weird streak in my nature that appreciated this shit had me getting turned on.

That first night back at his place, when he'd told me he'd burn New York to the ground for me... God, that was the best kind of dirty talk I'd ever heard.

As much as the news of his sister's position had freaked me out, there was no denying that his power aroused me like little else ever had.

"Fionnabhair," he crooned, seeming to know where my mind had taken me, but misinterpreting it. "I will never hurt you."

"I know you won't," I rasped.

Even though he was one big, flashing red warning sign, I could no more avoid him than I could stop myself from taking my next breath.

"Then why do you fall silent on me?"

"Because I'm disturbed by how turned on I am."

He chuckled, and the sound radiated with his satisfaction. "Don't be disturbed. I'm not."

"I'm not disturbed." *I wasn't.*

Maybe I should be.

But he was showing up.

Putting action behind the words.

His men *had* treated me like I was lesser, had treated my bags like they were trash when they dumped them outside my building, and I'd felt that to my core. I'd been terrified about him, his safety, and I'd had nowhere to turn other than the Irish Mob.

He was making sure that wouldn't happen again, and I loved him for it.

"Thank you," I whispered, finding it crazy that I was thanking him for torturing someone, but hell, it meant something to me.

"You shouldn't have to thank me for this. They disobeyed me. I've resolved the situation with Rory too."

"She was behind it?"

"*Se,*" he said gruffly, but I heard his irritation.

I guessed I couldn't expect him to torture her... that might be asking too much.

"Open the box, *bedda mia?*"

I joked, "You're not gonna talk me off now that you've got me all riled up inside? You're so bad at phone sex."

"Phone sex is for long distances. I don't consider Hell's Kitchen to be long distance."

"This is true," I teased, but I put the phone on speaker then moved over to the boxes. As I did, my charm necklace peeped out from behind the neckline of my vest, and I smiled as it whacked me on the chin. "Okay, so, big box first?"

He hummed.

"I still haven't worn the Morticia dress," I pointed out.

"I know, but that's for a special occasion."

"What kind of special occasion?"

"One where I can eat you out while you wear it."

Every internal muscle below the waist clenched down at his words. "You're obsessed with oral."

"Is that a complaint?"

"No. But you don't share." I pouted.

"Your mouth is divine, *vita mia,* but why would I want that when I can have your pussy?"

"Stop turning me on. You make it sound like I have the golden gates between my legs."

A soft laugh escaped him. "*Fossi,* perhaps, for me, you do. Open the box."

Grumbling, I did as he asked, revealing a bright green—

"Is this an Elie Saab?" I squeaked. If I hadn't been getting hot before, now I really was.

I heard the creak of his chair. "You like it?"

"I fucking love it."

I squealed as I let it flow out against the leather sofa—didn't mention those, did I? Yep, I had an office with two sofas now as well as a massive desk—and drooled at the exquisite lines of the gown.

It was bright green, a color that would look banging against my skin. It had sharp padded shoulders, long sleeves, a deep V that would cup my tits to perfection before it gathered at the waist with three gold buttons. Then, there was a deep slit that would reveal every inch of my legs.

"I can't wait to see you in it, *duci,*" he half-purred down the line.

I released a soft sigh. "It's perfect. I love it."

"Look at the other boxes."

Who was I to argue?

Finding a pair of Jimmy Choos, I nearly wept. They were strappy with zero arch support and walking paradise.

But it was the purse, a silver Judith Leiber clutch, that had me shedding tears of ecstasy.

"You've gone silent on me, *bedda mia*," he drawled. "Does that mean you're happy?"

I sniffled. "I'm in heaven."

He laughed outright. "I will be tonight when I collect you from work in it."

"Tonight?"

"Yes. Tonight."

"What's happening?" I questioned, the fog from this delicious haul fading at his caginess.

"There's a gala I must attend."

"Okay. What's the problem?" I asked, surprised that he hadn't mentioned it before.

"No problem."

"Then why am I only just hearing about it now?"

"Because I didn't think you'd want to go."

"Are you kidding me?" I laughed. "I love galas. Where else can you wear ridiculously delicious outfits like this?" A thought occurred to me. "Are you wearing a tuxedo? Please tell me you're wearing a tuxedo?"

"I'm wearing a tux," he confirmed.

"I don't think this day could get any better. Unless you appeared in breeches, a cravat, and Hessians."

"I'm going to get a complex. My being compared to Austen's Darcy is not good for business."

"Make sure you slice both sides of the face from now on and then people won't be able to mock you for it if they can't smile," I joked.

"That's not a bad idea," he mused.

"Luciu!" I barked, eyes widening. "I was kidding."

"I wasn't."

"Jesus. I was only teasing!"

He chuckled. "Fret not, *cara mia*, I was teasing in return."

I huffed. "Don't do that to me."

"I'll do many things to you. Teasing will be some of them, but it won't be in this sense."

"I look forward to it."

"I bet you do. I have to go, but I think you missed a box. I'll expect you to wear everything tonight, *duci*."

With that, he cut the call.

I frowned at his parting farewell, a little uneasy about the poor bastards who could be walking around Manhattan with two slits in their cheeks because of me, but I shoved the thought aside.

Symmetry made it highly likely that two slits were always how Luciu's methods were going to evolve...

Preferring to find the boxes he was talking about than ponder the evolution of his A game, I grabbed them, opened them, and smiled to myself.

"If that's the way you want to play it then game on."

FIFTEEN

LUC

CLEANING up involved soaking my hands to get rid of the blood drenching them before I could even think about getting a shower.

As I eyed the clock, I accepted that I was going to be late, and that I was going to teach Fi several lessons I didn't want her to learn—that I was always late, that she wasn't a priority, that when I said I'd pick her up, what that meant was I'd send a car for her.

My *travagghiu*, my work, wasn't exactly nine-to-five. Still, I didn't like the guilt that hit me, mostly because it was earned.

A man didn't treat his woman like she was a dog who came when called.

A man treated his woman like the goddamn queen she was.

When the water was running free and clear, no more pink tinges lacing it, I dried off, then grabbed my phone and texted her:

Me: *I'll be late, vita mia. A thousand apologies.*

Fi: *No worries. Meet you at the gala?*

Me: *A car is on its way. It will take you to the gala, but wait for me. I shouldn't be long. I'm closer to the event than you are.*

Fi: *Okay. I'll see you then.*

Fi: *xox*

I studied those letters with surprise.

Then, I did the damnedest thing.

I typed:

Me: *xox*

The message received two ticks, so I knew that she'd seen it, and I stared at the three letters that truly proved I'd had my dick handed to me.

Recognizing that I needed to haul ass, I stopped gawping at the most emasculating letters in the English language and dove into the shower.

Washing up as quickly as I could, I shaved off most of my scruff, then dressed in the tuxedo I'd promised her, grateful that my new cast allowed for a lot more freedom of movement.

When I was tying the laces on my Berluti Oxfords, I straightened up, strapped on my father's Rolex, then used one of the amber Valentini cuff links to finish off the outfit once my bow tie was knotted.

Now dressed, I left the bathroom and entered the hall, grimacing at the large blood stain on the floor.

"For fuck's sake," I yelled. "Clean this goddamn mess up, would you?"

It was like a slaughtered pig had been dragged down the corridor.

Giovi made an appearance, sweat beading his brow as he called out, "Whassup, boss?"

"There's fucking blood everywhere."

That had him hitching a shoulder. "He bled."

I rolled my eyes. "I know. I was the one who stabbed him. Clean this up, would you?"

He scrubbed his forearm over his forehead. "Will do, boss."

Stepping around the streaks of blood, satisfaction welled in me even as I felt distaste for the mess they'd made during clean up.

A lesson had been taught today—*Jen was a priority.*

I hadn't sliced the cheeks of the two men who'd driven her to her building, but when one, an Italian, had called her a whore? My temper had gotten the better of me.

Hence the corpse that was on its way to our pig farm.

As I strode into my office, I found Rory sitting at my desk, which had me growling under my breath.

Before she could say a word, I spat, "What the hell are you doing here? If this is to give me shit about Jen working at our firm, then you can fuck off."

I was *not* in the mood to be dealing with my siblings' disapproval about Fi. And I had three things to be furious with my twin about.

"Manners maketh man," she mocked, using the same saying that our grandfather had rammed into us since we were young. A rule Stan and I had to abide by, and one that she had to seek out in a life partner. Not my words: *his.* "I think you're insane, but you will make your mistakes whether I try to stop you or not."

Her holier-than-thou tone had me gritting my teeth. "I'm still pissed at you," I retorted before I strode over to the drinks tray and poured myself a brandy.

"None for me?"

"No. You want to get drunk, head into *Russu* and drink what's behind the bar."

She pouted. "If I'd warned you, it wouldn't have been as effective."

"If you'd warned me, I could have made better arrangements instead of needing to get my wrist goddamn broken so I could visit with Great-uncle."

"You'd always have needed a substantial injury to get into Bellevue," she disregarded my argument. "As it was, you were lucky—"

I raised my cast-covered arm. "I feel really fucking lucky."

She sniffed. "Anyway, that's in the past."

"It's hardly ancient history." A thought occurred to me, and I pointed a finger at her. "Do *not* go behind my back to fuck with the security details I'm implementing around Jennifer."

Her eyes narrowed at me. "She's a—"

"Watch your mouth!" I snarled before she could finish. "Did I say anything to you when you married that fucking cunt of a husband of yours? When you damn near broke Hunter's heart? No. I didn't."

"Don't bring him into this!"

"Then stop trying to fuck around with the woman I love. *Capisci?*"

Her mouth flatlined. "Everything I do, I do for the *famigghia.* Just as you do, *frate.*"

Her dedication to the cause was different than mine but no less stringent, so I raised my glass to her and said, "Don't come between

Jen and me, *again*," I added with a hiss, "and we won't have a problem."

Begrudgingly, she nodded.

"Why are you here, *soru*? This is, what? The third time in four weeks?"

Six months passed by without me seeing her in the flesh sometimes. We spoke every day, on several occasions, but actual visits required a lot of maneuvering on her part.

She shrugged. "I'm allowed to have a social life."

"Not when you're trying to take me down in the public eye. You're flying too close to the sun."

"I'll tell them I was scoping the place out for signs of under-the-counter activity. It worked on New Year's."

"I knew it was you who called in the cops." I heaved a sigh. "Knowing you, you'd sell that bullshit to them and have them paying for it."

Her smile was sweet. "You and I both know it."

"I have to run. So cut to it, Rory."

"The FAST gala?" she questioned.

"*Se.*"

She hummed. "I spoke with Currau today. Seeing as Rachel Laker put in the papers for release on compassionate grounds, he allowed me visitation. He doesn't want to leave." Her mouth tightened, and for all that her face was expressionless, I saw through the mask.

"We knew that was a possibility," I told her softly. "That was why he never wanted to see any of us. His whole life has been behind bars. That doesn't mean we're not going to work on giving him some freedom, though, does it?"

Her mouth tightened. "I just thought he'd recognize me, but he didn't."

"He's a sick old man, Rory," I said gruffly. "He's in pain. He's been locked up with animals his whole life. He probably wouldn't recognize his mother anymore."

"I just... it was tough." She blew out a breath. "I needed to see you."

"I understand, *soru*." I stepped over to the desk, rounded it, then placed a hand on her shoulder. "When are you quitting the DA's office?"

"I don't know," she admitted.

"You do know, you just don't like what you'll have to do in the aftermath."

A hiss escaped her, and she shoved away from me. "It's barbaric, making me marry just so that I can take my rightful place at your side."

Unoffended, I finished off my brandy and murmured, "Not my rules. You know it. We've always known it. I have to abide by the same dictates as you so don't make out that it's sexist. The second I made it to this position, we were always going to have to start looking at viable candidates for partners."

Her scowl made a reappearance as realization settled in. "If you think that Jennifer—"

Not about to argue over a *fait* accompli, I spoke over her, "But the DA's office isn't going to serve you forever. You're already itching to get out of that world, and with Currau close to freedom, what reason do you have for staying?"

"How about the fact I know more men I'd like to kill than I'd like to marry?"

My lips twitched. "Stan told me Hunter's joined the Camorra," I cast out there, watching her stiffen up like I'd shocked her with a cattle prod. Every mention of Hunter tended to do that.

"Fool," she hissed, jumping to her feet, all bristling temper and outrage.

It didn't take much to get my sister back on track.

I hated seeing her sad. Always had. She dealt better with anger than with sorrow.

It occurred to me then that that could be why I rarely saw her cry.

She knew I preferred her mad than tearful.

As guilt stirred, I shoved it aside, saying, "Hardly. He lives on the West Coast, and he's damn good at what he does. Best to get himself the appropriate protection." I let that percolate. "Wish he'd come to us first. We need someone who's good with computers."

She sniffed. "That's all the fool is good with. I'll see you around," she retorted, storming out of the office via the door that led to the club, letting the roar of the music from *Russu* flood the space for a second.

That was a conversation we'd needed to have, but second guessing how we dealt with one another wasn't ideal right now.

With my car waiting outside, I checked the time, saw that I wasn't too late, and felt slightly more at ease as I slipped into the backseat and we headed toward the event.

When I arrived, I saw that Vincenzu had parked me close to another of my town cars, and I climbed out, then headed over to the backseat, opening it and peering down into the dark expanse.

Her face was illuminated by the screen of her cell phone, and though I expected her to sulk, at the door opening, Fi turned to look at me and graced me with such a beautiful smile that I almost rocked back on my heels and wished we were anywhere but here.

Rachel Laker insisted on my attendance at these galas, mostly because there was always some kind of fundraiser and I knew she expected me to donate generously. It was an unwritten part of our contract, and considering the cause, I was more than willing to comply.

Regardless, undressing Fi seemed more of a priority at that moment.

I held out my hand for her, and she took it, her gloved fingers slipping against mine as I helped her stand.

Though the light was meager, the sight of her had my cock getting hard as I rasped, "You look fucking gorgeous." And I couldn't even see most of the dress. In a floor-length silk cape, the drama of her outfit stole my breath.

She placed her other hand on my chest. "You sure we can't just go straight home?"

Laughing because I wanted that as much as her, I told her instead, "The *crème de la crème* is inside this building, *cara mia*. You think I don't want them to know that you're taken?"

A shaky breath escaped her, and she leaned into me before she moved onto tiptoe and pressed her lips to mine. "You're better at phone sex when there's no phone to distract you."

I chuckled, and if it sounded hoarse, so be it, then directed, "Come, *duci*, we'll eat bad food, bid on overpriced donations, maybe dance, then be on our way. I have an appointment in our bed tonight—"

She tightened her fingers around mine. "Our bed?"

A grunt escaped me because I knew she liked the sound of that. "*Se, vita mia,* our bed." I let that register. "I'd ordinarily take you in through the front entrance, but with the Italian Darcy bullshit in the papers..."

She cackled. "I'll spare you the indignity of being labeled Italian."

"You're too kind," I grumbled, but I was smiling as I said it, was even smiling as Lorenzo appeared from the driver's seat of her car and guided us toward an entrance that took us to the kitchens. I passed him my coat and tugged the cape from her shoulders, then handed it to him.

When I allowed myself to take her in, the need to fuck her became an imminent problem.

She looked like walking sin: slick and elegant, but so sensual that just looking at her was better than ten minutes of hardcore porn. And those fucking gloves. *Cristo.*

Needing to touch her, I curved my arm around her, sliding my good hand around her waist, holding her tightly against me.

"I apologize for being late, *cara mia.*"

"You're a busy man, I get it."

"And your time is not precious too?" I countered, even knowing I was digging my own grave.

"Well, sure, it is, but—"

"Then you should be mad."

She blinked at me. "Well, I—"

"You need to value yourself more," I replied, curving her tighter into me so I could press a kiss to her cheek. On the verge of whispering in her ear, a flicker of rage whirled through me as I saw the small scar on her earlobe. My voice, as a result, was gruffer than I'd have liked as I told her, "Or I'll do it for you."

"What will that entail?"

"Grandiose apologies."

"And this would be a problem, why?"

I shrugged. "If you don't value yourself, how can I figure out what I need to apologize for?"

"You have a point," she replied, making me smile. "What kind of grandiose apologies are we talking here? Vacations in the Bahamas?"

I pulled a face. "Short vacations."

"Naturally. But a vacation? Overseas?" she prodded.

Something about her eagerness had me asking, "Have you ever left America?"

"No."

A huff escaped me. "Then screw the Bahamas. I'll take you to Europe." I raised my fingers to my lips and nearly ate a mouthful of plastic from my goddamn cast as I tried to chef's kiss them. "Why are you laughing?" I grumbled, but she had me grinning yet again.

"Because you're not nearly as suave and debonair with a cast as you are without it."

"And you're not so good for my ego."

"You mean the sexy as fuck dress and me being on your arm don't help matters?"

I eyed her up and down. "I'd like the dress more if it was on our bedroom floor."

"That can be arranged. Later."

"Are you wearing everything I bought for you?"

"Yes."

"How do they feel?"

"Delicious," she purred before she shot me a wink. "This feels very *Fifty Shades*. I'm just missing the mask."

"You read a lot of romance, don't you?" I drawled.

"I do. Aoife got me hooked on it. I'm surprised you know what *Fifty Shades* is." Her giggle made my heart skip a beat. "Does that mean you read it too?"

Snickering, I reasoned, "*Matri* has devoured the trilogy."

"That explains it. Shame, I'd get off on you reading the same stuff as me."

"I shall graduate to *New Moon* first, then, when things are really bad, I shall read one of your books." Only a man who wasn't secure in his sexuality wouldn't read something like that. "I'll look forward to seeing you get off on me doing that."

I could tell she liked the idea because she blushed, but instead of remarking on it, she explained, "Aoife, Inessa O'Donnelly, and I are supposed to be going to a book convention this weekend. I'm not sure if that's going to happen or not though. You know, what with everything."

"A book convention?"

"One with romance authors."

"You knew what the Ben Wa balls were, then?"

"Of course." She shot me a wink. "I lurve the nipple shields too. If you look carefully, you can see them through the dress."

A groan rumbled from my lips at that, and I immediately stared down at her chest just as we were graced with the sweeping music from an orchestra in the background.

"I'm sure that's the music from *Bridgerton*," Fi said in my ear.

"What's *Bridgerton*?"

She laughed. "I'll let you watch that with me too."

"Oh, you'll let me, hmm?" I mocked, but I smiled at her laughter and figured it was something a mob boss definitely shouldn't be watching.

"What's this gala for?"

"It's a pet project of my lawyer's."

"That doesn't give me any specifics."

"It's for teenaged mothers who find themselves without support—financial or custodial."

"And you donate to this charity?" she queried.

"Haven't you realized yet, *bedda mia*?"

"Realized what?"

"I'm a feminist."

That had her lips curving, but she didn't counter my words, just allowed me to swing her into a dance as we made it into the ballroom via the dance floor. I made a mental note to arrive that way in the future because it was a damn sight better than having to go through the tedious meet and greet.

Having her in my arms, looking like a million dollars, sure as hell brightened my evening up too.

We danced for a good half hour before I moved us over to the top table to take our seats for the speeches.

A cavalcade of people who worked for the foundation spoke briefly about how the donations helped the cause. Interest was minimal when the reason most of the attendees were here was as a tax write-off and because they'd come to owe Rachel Laker at one time or another.

For a woman who didn't even have her own offices in the city, she'd managed to collect a menagerie of clients and businessmen who owed her a debt of some kind.

For the first time in five years of my attending this gala, however, Rachel took to the stage, and I tuned in, curious as to why she was speaking now when she never had before.

"I see very few strangers amid the crowd and know most of you intimately. Your repeated support of FAST means more than you could possibly know, and to be fair, more than a lot of you even care to know. I'm aware that your support is tied to your work with me, and I don't begrudge that. You're here, that's all that matters.

"But, this year, my life has changed dramatically. I lost a man who was like a second father to me, and my own personal circumstances are changing. It reminds me of a time when I was eighteen and I was pregnant... I was terrified. Absolutely petrified. I had no idea where to go, what to do, who to turn to. A foundation like this one would have meant the world to me."

To say I was stunned was an understatement. Not only did Rachel never share private information, this went above and beyond anything I'd ever heard her discuss before.

She pursed her lips. "Life being what it is, things didn't work out for me, but I'd like to think that some women out there get to have their child and an education at the same time.

"That's why FAST exists. To make sure that women have options. They can have both. This isn't the Dark Ages. It doesn't have to be either/or. So, that's why I'm grateful to each of you. Because you help make that happen." Her smile was strained. "Thank you for being here."

In that five-minute speech, Rachel revealed more of herself to me—and the rest of her clientele—than she had in five years.

Turning to Fi to discuss my lawyer's unusual behavior, I found her looking elsewhere. As my gaze drifted along her line of sight, she murmured, "That guy's been watching you since we sat down."

Spying Maxim Lyanov, I reached over and pressed a kiss to her cheek. "Business, *vita mia.*"

"Who is he?" she inquired, then she rolled her eyes. "Yes, I'm sure I want to know."

Lips quirking, I replied, "This is information you might prefer *not* knowing."

"I'm a big girl," she groused. "Who is he? He doesn't look dangerous. More curious."

"He's Bratva," I drawled. "He's the new leader after he pulled a coup. I don't think I'll trust your instincts where first impressions count, *duci*."

She laughed. "Oops."

"Oops is the word," I retorted with a grin.

With the speeches finished, the master of ceremonies returned to the podium, and so commenced the fundraising part of the night.

Bored, I let my attention coast along the lots while I placed my hand on Fi's leg, finding her far more interesting than anything in the auction.

She leaned into me, her side pressing into my arm as she rested her chin on my shoulder. Her tactile nature was unexpected but not unappreciated, especially when she placed her hand on my stomach.

As I traced my finger along the slit in her skirt, forming circles with the tip, I heard when her breath turned raspy, shaky with desire. Before I could reach the sweet spot, however, she tensed up.

"Hell," she whispered.

On red alert, I sought out the threat, then felt like a dick when I realized she was looking at the stage where a woman in a black dress and wearing white gloves was holding up a bag.

Rolling my eyes at myself, I focused on the purse. I didn't appreciate it, but Fi clearly did.

"Here we have a rare *bleu du nord* swift leather and osier mini picnic Hermès Kelly, ladies and gentlemen. The hardware is palladium. Do we have a starting bid of, shall we say, forty thousand dollars?"

As the auctioneer's gaze drifted around the room, I raised my hand.

She nodded and said, "Forty-five?"

"What are you doing?" Fi breathed in my ear.

"You want it," I said with a shrug.

She gulped. "I think you may be the best boyfriend in the world."

A laugh drifted from my lips, but the ugly bag was worth double my bid for the soft kiss she pressed to the side of my jaw.

"Fifty?"

I raised my finger.

The auctioneer cast another glance, and a flurry of bids came in.

"Sixty?"

"Seventy?"

I nodded.

"Eighty-five? Do we see eighty-five thousand dollars?"

"A hundred," someone called out from the back.

"Jesus Christ, a hundred thousand dollars for a purse?" Fi rasped.

"One-twenty," I counter-offered.

"We have a bid of one hundred and twenty from Mr. Valentini." The auctioneer smiled. "Do we have any more interest...?" Another glance around the room and she declared, "Going once, going twice, going to Mr. Valentini for one hundred and twenty thousand dollars."

A smattering of applause made its way around the event hall, but nothing beat Fi's soft squeal as she hugged me harder into her.

"Thank you!"

I twisted around and smiled at her, chuckling when she planted a kiss on my lips that devolved quickly...

"Fuck, we need to get a room," she ground out against my mouth as she bit down on my bottom lip.

I wasn't about to argue. "Leave it with me," I rumbled, pulling back only when the woman to my right shot me a pointed, definitely *prudish* look.

With a glower at her, I reached into my tux for my cell phone and arranged with Lorenzo to reserve us a room here.

As the auction ran down, Rachel made an appearance with the bag in her hand which she passed over to Fi. "For you I assume?"

She squealed again, making me laugh, and I watched as she took possession of the bag, holding it like it were made of glass.

Rachel's lips twitched. "You beat me to it."

"You were the one who raised the bid?" I shook my head. "That should be illegal."

Her eyes glinted with amusement. "You can afford it. Thank you for the donation."

I smiled, discerning a sense of hesitation around her which, I assumed, was tied to her recent revelations regarding her troubled youth, but merely said, "You're welcome."

She dipped her chin. "I should have news regarding your great-uncle soon."

"Pleased to hear it."

"Enjoy the rest of your evening, Luciu and... *guest*."

As she faded into the crowd, I watched her go, then turned to find Fi cooing over her gift. "*Cara mia?*"

She hummed. "Yeah?"

"I have some business to attend to." I cast a glance at my phone. "The penthouse is ours for the evening, so when you're ready to go upstairs, Lorenzo will take you up there, okay?"

Fi leaned forward then pressed a kiss to my lips. "You're in for a very, very, very long night."

Resting one hand on the back of her chair, I leaned over her. "We could go upstairs and sleep and you'd still be worthy of that bag."

"*Mon cher*," she retorted with a wicked smile, "to call this a bag is sacrilegious."

I pressed a kiss to her forehead. "See you in a short while, *duci*."

Fastening the button on the waist of my tux, I caught Maxim Lyanov's eye and headed over to the bar.

Ordering myself a Vilafonte Malbec, I waited for the Bratva Pakhan to reach my side. Once he was there, he predictably ordered a vodka, and I turned around to look over the ballroom.

The Victoria was one of the few six-star hotels in Hell's Kitchen. Rumor had it that it was owned by Acuig—the legitimate front of the Irish Mob—but if it was, there were no records of it ever having passed hands from the original owners.

And when I said original, I meant it. Since eighteen forty-four, this establishment had been in the Sinclair family.

Allegedly.

The place was a grandiose nod to the *Belle Époque*, something that shone through in this ballroom. Over two thousand square feet of prime Manhattan real estate was wasted on it, but it had to make the Victoria money otherwise it would have been converted into something more profitable.

Panels with gilt edges decorated the walls, paintings at the center of some, small console tables lining others with massive bouquets of flowers perched precariously atop them.

Over forty tables filled this space with some of Manhattan's richest and most corrupt.

Of course, in my experience, wealth and corruption went hand in hand.

Lyanov moved closer to me once he'd taken back his shot of vodka, and I tipped my head at him. "Pleasure to make your acquaintance."

"The pleasure's all mine seeing as you managed to get me a ticket." His brows rose. "I'm just not sure why you extended the invitation."

"Fresh blood has to stick together."

"Does it though?" He pursed his lips. "Has nothing to do with Vlad Dubrov, I guess?"

My mind whirred, but I merely said, "You do your homework."

Did we have a fucking mole? How the hell did he know about our involvement with Dubrov?

"My rise to the top might have been shaky, but my wits are anything but."

"My *capo* tells me you're looking to make a name for yourself among Manhattan's elite."

"I have plans, yes."

"To legitimize?"

"No," he countered with a laugh. "But I wish to appear legitimate."

"Such a delicate balance," I concurred. "I'd apologize for Dubrov's disappearance, but he hurt my woman. That's something I can't tolerate."

"Naturally." His mouth tightened, his displeasure clear. "That information was not given to me."

"Why would it be? The circumstances behind a man's... *disappearance*... are known only to the man himself and the one behind the act." I sipped my wine, making a point by not apologizing. "Now, to business. It's well known that the old Pakhan appreciated museum-quality gems."

Lyanov nodded. "He did."

"I'm interested in acquiring some. For the right price."

"What kind?"

"Rubies."

"I heard you were hunting for rubies."

"Had feelers out for me?" I arched a brow at him. "Your men are very good, seeing as that was supposed to be hush-hush."

"My men are like me. Born in an orphanage, nothing more than a life of misery ahead of us, hard work our only consolation, and bitter poverty our one promise." His smile was dark. "We chose another path. Not everyone can be born with silver spoons in their mouth."

I didn't bother correcting him. Rory and I hadn't been born into that life. Not until Grandfather's visit to Catania when we were toddlers had our lives changed trajectory. "Only the lucky ones."

"Agreed." He shot me a look. "Have your people speak with my people." He wafted a hand at the ballroom. "If you can arrange more invitations to events such as these, you can have your pick of the gems."

What the hell was it with people who didn't want money for things?

First Martinez, then Savannah Daniels, now Lyanov... was I turning into a bank of favors?

"I prefer to pay," I told him, taking a deep sip of my wine.

"And I prefer to gain access to this side of society, something that isn't open to me just yet."

"I can only hold your hand for so long. If you don't legitimize your fronts, *fast*, then there's nothing I can do about it. I'm not Henry Higgins," I drawled.

Lyanov grunted. "And I'm not Eliza Doolittle."

I arched a brow. "Who'd have thought a Russian orphan would know *My Fair Lady*?"

"TVs exist in Russia."

"I somehow can't see them broadcasting old British movies," I drawled before I straightened up. "Rubies. A necklace, ring, bracelets, anklet, earrings. That's what I'm interested in."

He bowed his head. "I'll see what the Vasov collection holds."

"What about the Dubrov situation?"

"I'll deal with his brother. Explain things." He smiled a little. "I thought this invitation was an apology."

"I have no desire to be at war with you again," was all I said.

Lyanov rubbed his chin. "Neither do I. Our predecessors were old, foolish men. We are not old, nor are we fools."

"I'd like to think not," I agreed. "My *capo* will be in touch."

"I'll tell my *obschak* to await his call."

Nodding, I drifted away, my wine glass in hand as I left the party.

It wasn't ideal, but nothing about the hunt for the Anjou rubies was. That people were leveraging my desire to own them for favors was a weakness just waiting to be exploited and that irritated me like nothing else.

Peace, however, remained brokered between us despite the Dubrov situation, and I considered that to be the one goddamn positive from that particular meeting.

Especially if we uncovered a mole because of it.

SIXTEEN

JEN

THE SUITE WAS EXQUISITE. Everything about it luxurious; from the view that rubbed shoulders with the Empire State Building to the Carrera marble on the damn walls, a carpet that was so deep my shoes got stuck in it, and a baby grand piano that just made me want to have sex on it.

But for all that it was six-star glorious and that I had weighted balls in my vajayjay, and my nipples were being teased and tormented by silver shields, my interest was the purse.

Once Lorenzo delivered me into the suite, then disappeared, I quickly placed the Kelly onto the baby grand and stared at it.

I just...

I had to stare at it.

It was a work of art, and works of art required appreciation.

The clutch he'd gifted me this morning was beautiful, but not as interesting as this delicacy, and because Savannah was the only person who'd get why I was excited, I dragged off my silk gloves so that I could send her a photo.

When she'd seen it, I wasn't surprised to get a flurry of text messages from her.

Savannah: *Is that a Kelly?*
Savannah: *Is it?*
Savannah: *Did Luciu buy you that?*

When my cell rang, I laughed, but the number that flashed up on screen wasn't her.

My mother.

I thought about Vlad, I thought about the money he said they owed, and I thought about that damn credit card I had burning a hole in my pocket—not literally, but the security was still there...

How could I not help her out when Luciu had just gifted me a purse worth more than a Ferrari?

I did the stupid thing—I accepted the call.

"Mom?"

"Oh, thank Christ, Fionnabhair. I was worried you wouldn't answer."

"Well, I did. What do you want?"

"Did Vlad come and see you? He said he was going to, but he didn't call, and he's... well, I don't know where he is."

"I haven't seen him."

"He said he was going to visit you because you wouldn't answer my calls," she snapped. "Did you give him anything? Some money? Maybe he ran off with it. We owe some bad people, Fionnabhair."

"When don't you? You can't just owe Wells Fargo, can you? Nope, that would be too easy." I twisted around, staring at the luxury surrounding me, trying to reconcile how my past and present were colliding.

In all her forty-eight years, she'd strived toward this kind of lifestyle, fucking anyone who had enough cash on the hip, and she'd trained me to do the same.

A part of me had been terrified I'd end up like her, and I'd endeavored to stop that from happening.

That it could be within my grasp, that a future with Luciu could be possible, a man who thought nothing of buying me something like the Kelly purse... I couldn't allow her to keep on wrecking things for me.

"Look, I need help. You're my daughter. You're supposed to help your mother."

Because that was hilarious, I shook my head and leaned an elbow on the piano. "I owe you nothing, which is exactly what you gave me. Well, you gave me an eating disorder, I don't suppose that counts," I drawled.

"Fionnabhair—"

Hearing the name that Luc called me—that he insisted I suited—on her lips just heightened my temper. "If you want my help, you should start calling me what I ask you to call me."

"You're not understanding how urgent this—"

"I am," I countered, "but I'm not letting your timetable affect mine. I have some cash. I'll meet with you tomorrow. Where are you living?"

"Thank you, Fionnabhair—"

"What did I just tell you?" I snapped. "Call me Jennifer."

"I'm the one who named you—"

"And I'm the one who's giving you the cash you need so stop pissing me off if you want something from me.

"While we're at it, don't contact me again. I'll give you enough to get you out of the city. You should do that anyway if the people you owe are dangerous. Vlad apparently thought that was the best option if he dumped your ass and left you behind."

A sharp breath escaped her at words I'd uttered to wound her, but she rasped, "The bastard."

"You always could pick well."

I thought about Padraig O'Donnelly, my father, who was probably the worst kind of man she could have gotten involved with, but who was I to judge?

Maybe she'd loved him, and maybe he'd loved her.

Maybe he'd given her the same promises that Luc had given me. Expensive purses and sweet words, loving touches and the promise of more...

"Men always break their promises, don't they?" my mother rasped, and I heard her heartache.

Heard it and knew that, in her own weird way, she'd probably loved Vlad.

I wasn't sure how a woman could love the man who whored her out, but again, I wasn't going to judge, not after Damian.

"They do." I didn't tell her that I hoped not all men were like the ones we'd tangled with in the past. Nor did I tell her that I hoped I'd found one who kept his promises. Instead, I requested, "Text me where you're living. I'll be there tomorrow."

I didn't wait for her to reply, just cut the call. I stared at the Kelly purse, trying to feel as excited about it as I had a minute ago, but as with everything, my mother had a habit of draining me of my joy.

She was only ever interested in herself, and that was a trait I shared with her. A trait that I needed to cut from my life if I didn't want to mess things up with Luc.

Would he leave me like Padraig had Diana?

Had Padraig known she was pregnant when he'd left?

I pressed a hand to my belly, wondering if life stirred in there, and I prayed Luc was a better man than my father.

I'd never wanted kids, but Luc... I could imagine trusting him enough to become a mother.

"You look pensive, *vita mia*."

When I twisted around, I jolted when I saw him sitting there. A yelp flooded from my lips so deep was my shock, and I rested a hand against my chest as if that could still my beating heart.

He was drinking a glass of wine, sipping from it as he watched me like I was a show on television.

"You scared me, Casper," I grumbled.

Finishing the wine, he rested the glass on the coffee table before he sank back, saying, "The family house in Catania is riddled with creaks. One learns to move silently or one never gets to sneak out to parties."

I blinked. "The royal 'one?'"

His smile was grim, and he surprised me by patting his knee. The smile and the gesture were at odds with one another, but because I was feeling a little heart sore after that shitty conversation with my mother, I strode over to him and perched on his lap. He slipped his cast-covered arm around my waist and tugged me back against him.

"Now, you look sad, *duci*."

Nodding, I tipped my face against his throat and rasped, "How much did you hear?"

"Enough to know that you're going to meet with her tomorrow." He reached up and tipped my chin down. "Were you going to tell me?"

"Why would I? I don't have to tell you everything."

"Because she's toxic?"

Well, he had a point...

I frowned at him. "I want to get rid of her."

"You want to kill her?"

Huffing, I muttered, "I meant in a non-lethal way."

"If you say so."

"I do. I just don't want to have to deal with her anymore. That's all."

"That can be arranged without you having to meet her."

"I need to do this," I said softly.

"You want to say goodbye; I understand, *cara mia*. Tomorrow, *se?* I'll clear my schedule and come with you."

"You don't have to. I know you have some eyes on me. I figured that would be enough."

"And it *would* be enough to keep you safe, but, *duci*, after the farce with my siblings, I trust no one entirely with you. Only me." The pad of his thumb rubbed against my chin. "We will go tomorrow—"

A flush of heat burned along my cheeks, so powerful that it didn't even diminish how my heart flopped around in my chest at his protective stance. "It's embarrassing, Luc. I don't want you to have to see where she lives."

"You think I care about her home?"

"No, but I do," I groused. "Where I came from... it isn't pretty, and she hasn't moved up in the world."

"My past is loaded with misery. You heard my mother yourself—my grandfather thought *Patri* was a gold digger. For a while, when I was very young, I remember living in a tiny apartment in Catania. Grandfather must have seen where we were living, though, because we moved not long after he came to visit."

"You remember that far back?"

"The neighborhood we lived in makes the Meatpacking District look friendly," he drawled. "It was rough enough to leave a lasting memory. *Patri* made his own path though. His business was very successful."

"Mom doesn't have a rags to riches story," I said sadly. "She's just a two-bit whore who tried to strike it rich and failed."

My mouth trembled as my fears began to choke me, but he pressed a thumb to my quivering bottom lip and rasped, "You are not her, *bedda mia.*"

Gaze darting to his, I mumbled, "I wasn't thinking that."

"Don't lie. I know you were. Sometimes, you're as transparent to me as glass."

"Charming," I sniped, shoving away from his chest and making to stand, but he hauled me back down and tightened his arm around my waist.

"You're my *riggina,* my queen, Fi. I told you earlier that you need to figure out your worth, and I mean it. Sometimes, before you can take stock of your value, you need to think about what you mean to others. I told you I'd burn Manhattan to the ground to keep you safe... what does that say about your worth to me?"

His words resonated on a soul-deep level, and I slung my arms around his neck as I turned into him and kissed him, lips sliding over his, teeth biting until he let me in, his mouth parting so I could rub my tongue against his.

A sharp cry escaped me as I dragged my tits along his chest, the tips suddenly so sensitive that I felt a burning heat slide through my veins and settle right at my core.

The sensation was so powerful that I stopped kissing him, and instead, I rested my forehead against his as I panted through the experience.

That was when his good hand cupped my left breast, and as he did, I groaned and wriggled so that I was straddling him, eager for more as he delved underneath the deep V of my dress and began to tug on the nipple that was held fast by a torque ring.

Slippery pleasure unfurled through my system, making me cry out when he yanked on the buttons of the dress, the ones that gathered the fabric taut around my waist and hips and dragged them apart.

With that one move, the gown draped around my shoulders, exposing the fact that I wasn't wearing a bra and had barely there panties on.

The growl that rumbled from his lips was like a pinch to my clit, but it was compounded when he sucked on my nipple, and the vibrations slalomed through me. He pulled back to stare at the silver shields that covered the puckered flesh. They were circular, decorated with filigree work around the ring, and could be tightened to whatever size was required.

Apparently, they'd gotten my tits revved for action because they were beyond hypersensitive. Earlier, the pinch had been pleasant, but now, there was a pain to the pressure that felt good.

When he released one, I screamed. Hazy lights flickered in and out of my vision, sparks glittered into being too, and the Ben Wa balls in my pussy added a peculiar weight as well as a strange kind of jiggle that had my lower half contracting in rhythmic pulses that stole my breath.

That was before he nipped the tip, and it was then I realized that I was about to orgasm from nipple play alone.

When he sucked it into his mouth, and with his good hand, released the other from the shield, I started sobbing. Raking my hands through his hair, I ground into him, my pussy chasing the fullness of his dick that couldn't be appeased by the weighted balls inside me.

As he rubbed the other, soothing the tormented flesh, flicking it back and forth with his thumb, needing more, I found myself oddly breathless at the prospect of him getting me off this way.

I screamed when he sucked down harder than before, adding pressure where there hadn't been until now. Head falling back, I let my hair dance down my spine as I rocked against him, letting the sparks rage into an outright inferno.

As the pleasure seemed to flow endlessly, he encouraged me to rise up so he could drop his hand between my legs. Slipping the tips along my clit, he tugged on the string that was connected to the balls.

My scream warbled off as I choked, rearing forward as he played with it, changing where the weight laid, adding to it, making me feel as if he were going to pull them out, before he thrust them back in by plunging his finger into me.

Needing the torture to stop, I ceased scraping my hands through his hair and, instead, scrambled to unfasten his zipper. I pulled out his shaft through the gap, the throbbing flesh a beautiful agonized ruddy purple, before I reared up higher onto my knees.

He pulled on the tiny ribbons at the sides of my hips, growling, "I love these panties," before he tossed them aside.

Hell, I loved them too.

Talk about easy access.

He tugged on the Ben Wa balls, but my pussy clung to them, not appreciating the prospect of being empty, and I groaned as he grumbled, "Relax, *cara mia*."

"I c-can't," I wailed, nails digging into his shoulders before he darted forward and bit the tip of my nipple again.

As my cunt pulsed in response, he tugged on the Ben Wa balls, pulling them free, tossing them aside now that they'd worked their mischief on me.

Needing the fullness once again, feeling rabid, I grabbed his dick, slotted it against my gate and let him sink into me.

The second he was inside, all the way, I moaned. This fullness was *right*. Slick, heated flesh, not cold metal and latex.

Just as I got used to the delicious fullness, he stunned the shit out of me by banding both arms around my back, and surging upright.

With that, he walked us over to the window, and each step made my eyes roll further back into my head. This close to coming, I felt the chill from the glass as he pressed me against it.

Appreciating the dip in temperature against my heated flesh, I rested my hands against the cool glass as he hitched one leg higher, around his waist, then the other, before he started to rock his hips back and forth.

The motion was tight.

Each thrust was shallow, and it seemed to focus the pressure onto one particular spot. I had no idea why that drove me crazy, but it did.

My lungs suddenly couldn't chase enough air, and I could hear my heartbeat in my ears, which left me feeling as if it were about to explode there and then.

At this angle, we were a similar height, so when he nipped my bottom lip then murmured something in Sicilian, he did so with our eyes glued to each other's. "*Tisoru mia*."

His voice was thick with lust and need, making me whisper back, "I love you, Luc." I had no fancy words because, to me, those were the fanciest of all.

He growled beneath his breath, then he thrust his tongue between my lips and began to fuck my mouth as hard as he fucked my pussy.

I knew I wouldn't get off like this, but I didn't say anything, content to harness his strength, his power, happy that his control was a wreck around me.

Then, he played dirty.

He angled his body differently and put pressure on my tits.

I squirmed against him, the weight of him against them close to painful, but there was no denying that I could feel the ecstasy of before chasing through my system like a shot of neat vodka.

As he cried out his release, I felt him scald me from the inside out as he sped up, his cum making each thrust slicker and messier, then he stopped and gravity shoved him deeper into me before he pulled back, cupped one of my breasts, and treated them to the same torture of before.

Around his cock, my pussy suddenly clutched at him, so tight that it hurt as he sucked on my nipple, and I screamed again, so close, so close.

It hit me like a bomb detonating my retinas, and I knew that I'd never experienced anything more powerful in my life.

He groaned around the tip, making those goddamn vibrations throb through the tender flesh, each vibration in turn seeming to have been amplified because of the pinch from the silver shield, and I squealed, arching back against the glass both needing more and needing to escape.

My pussy throbbed around his still-hard dick, and I started sobbing, my hands leaving the window of their own accord to rake through his hair and to drag him away from my poor nipple.

Panting, he peered up at me and snarled something, but the only words I picked out were, "*Jornu... me mugghieri.*"

Whatever he said, the light of madness in his eyes had me resting my arms on his shoulders and pressing a soft kiss to his mouth.

Though I felt just as frantic, I pecked at his lips, gentle caresses, soft licks that had his unsteady breathing calming down, that stopped the flaring of his nostrils, that soothed whatever the hell it was that had riled him.

And with each kiss, I just fell more and more for him.

For this man who was undoubtedly insane, but who was equally crazy for me.

What more could a woman ask for?

Aside from a purse worth a hundred and twenty grand, of course...

LUC

"CONCERN IS *at an all-time high for the missing NHL player, Liam Donnghal. Donnghal went missing after—"*

Switching off the news, I watched Fi at the breakfast table the following morning, noticing that she was paler than usual, and that, for once, she was actually eating.

Her focus was on her cell phone as she munched on a piece of croissant that she'd cut into fifteen pieces—yes, I'd counted—and which she was eating one at a time and with as much care as if she'd shoved a whole apple into her mouth.

Stan had showed up this morning with a change of clothes for us both, but though the act was kind, I knew why he was here—the Victoria was famous for its French toast. The fucker had eaten two portions of it already.

"I was watching that," Stan complained, twisting around from the sofa where he was sitting in front of the television to glower at me.

"Go and watch it in your own apartment."

"Regular sex is supposed to make you less crabby," he muttered in Sicilian.

"Regular sex would be happening more often if my brother wasn't cockblocking me all the fucking time."

"You two bicker a lot, don't you?" Fi mused, peering up from her cell, the pucker in her brow warring with the smile she split between my brother and me.

"It's a Sicilian thing," I told her.

"Bickering? Isn't it a people thing?"

"We sound like we're arguing when we're not," I explained, reaching forward to pour her some more orange juice, curious to see if she'd drink it. "Are you okay?"

She hummed. "Aoife's still quiet. I sent her a picture of the purse, and normally she'd tell me I was crazy for letting you buy it, but she's seen the text only she hasn't replied to it."

"She's grieving. Some quiet reflection is to be expected," I reasoned.

"Maybe. We share most things though. Plus, this weekend, there is that author convention—"

"*Se*, I remember."

Her lips twitched. "You listen. How novel."

I laughed. "I listen to every word that spills from your lips—"

Stan made a gagging noise.

"Fuck you," I called out.

"No, thanks," he said, gagging some more.

As I grunted with irritation, Fi's smile deepened, shifting into her eyes, making them grow warmer even as a tinge of sadness softened it when she explained, "Aoife just canceled. Her favorite author will be there, but she doesn't want to go."

"She might not be up to it."

"Trust me, I figured that out." She shivered. "I was there when the bleeding started."

I snagged her hand with mine and kissed her knuckles. "You saved her."

She blew out a breath. "Or caused the miscarriage in the first place."

"We talked about this," I chided, squeezing her fingers.

"Maybe that's why she doesn't want to talk though. She might blame me." She shoved her damn plate away.

Pushing it back, I told her, "Eat your breakfast, *cara mia*."

She nodded but didn't pick up another piece. She did, however, sip at her orange juice.

I had a brother who ate too much and a woman who ate too little.

Was this the future the fates granted me?

Speaking of...

Stan grumbled, "Are we leaving? I have shit to do today for the lab."

"Speak English in front of her. Don't be a rude jackass," I told him in English.

Stan heaved a sigh but repeated, "I got shit to do. Can we get on with our day seeing as you won't let me enjoy my breakfast with the news?"

"Poor baby," I mocked, getting to my feet once I accepted that Fi wasn't going to eat another bite, and I was finished with my breakfast too. To Stan, I said, "We'll go to Jen's mother's first, then I'll drop Jen off at the office and we'll head into the city."

Fi nodded, Stan did too, and we left the hotel room after we dressed for the frigid temperatures outside and headed down to the underground garage where Lorenzo was waiting on us.

Before Stan's arrival and as we were ordering breakfast, Fi had told me she was going to give her mother the credit card I'd gifted her because she could earn enough to pay off her debts with her new position in less than six months.

Though I didn't approve, I'd merely told her to contact her parent and to arrange an earlier meeting that would fit in better with my schedule.

The ride into Port Morris was as grim as anticipated, and with the cold, blustery day making everything that much grimmer, I understood Fi's discomfort as we headed into an even more impoverished section of the district.

Grateful that the Spirit of Ecstasy on the front of my car retracted into the hood when the alarm clicked on, I fully expected for the town car and the SUV riding behind us to be cleaned out of tire rims when we parked.

As we pulled into an alleyway that was loaded with trash, I maintained a neutral expression so as not to upset Fi, but the notion that she might have been raised in such a dump had anger filtering through me.

Even though the wind was bitter, the cold numbing, the stench in this place couldn't be avoided. Dirty needles were tossed here and there, ten tons of trash were piled up in the corners, and I identified the stench as coming from an unfurled, *full* diaper that looked as if it had been tossed out of a window.

"I'll go up by myself," Fi said quickly, once she was standing beside the car.

Stan snorted at her futile suggestion, but I didn't bother arguing with her.

As he slipped me a gun, I arched a brow at the silencer on the weapon. I preferred knives, but guns had a place in our work so I tucked it inside my coat in the inner pocket that was crafted for this explicit purpose and walked with her as she headed for the front door.

As I moved, Stan, and the guards from the SUV behind us, followed.

She huffed when she took note of our presence, but though she took off at a fast clip, I stuck close to her, heading into the dark stairwell that, somehow, was even more disgusting than her old place.

"Fuck, it stinks of piss in here," Stan muttered under his breath, making me grateful that he ignored my earlier dictate to speak English around her.

He wasn't wrong.

Clumps of newspaper littered the stairs covering only God knew what, and music vibrated through the walls along with shouts from couples who were evidently madly in love. Not.

Four floors up, Fi moved away from the stairs and walked down the hall to the end unit. She knocked on the door before I reached it, and it opened, revealing a woman who was clearly her mother from likeness alone.

Though she was bony and her skin withered with either age or drug use, or maybe even both, she was still beautiful.

The second, however, she saw me, her eyes flared in shock.

Distress.

The emotion was so alien in this situation that I immediately scented a rat, and I grabbed Fi, tucking her behind me before she could step deeper into the room. As I did, I heard the cocking of guns and saw two guys leaping off the couch.

Fi screamed, but I knew exactly what was going down.

The ink on their faces declared them as *Chorros*, a small Argentinian group who ran women and ecstasy in this side of the city. Brutal motherfuckers whose stable of hookers often ended up addicted to their product and who worked for drugs until they found peace in an overdose.

Without a second's fucking thought, I pulled out the gun my brother had just handed me and slammed one of them in the chest with a bullet. He staggered back, hands flying to the wound, while Stan shoved me aside, and the guards took off after him as they launched themselves into the fray.

I fought to keep Jen tucked behind me, but she batted my hands away, storming forward to grab the pitifully cowering bag of bones that was her mother who'd slammed herself against the wall as my first bullet found a new home.

"This was a set up?" she yelled, shaking her when the old bitch didn't say a word.

A couple of grunts followed by more gunshots had me casting a look at the fight, and when I saw Martino had been shot, my mouth tightened with displeasure.

Arms and legs flew until I could barely distinguish between the guys fighting, then I heard Stan grunt as he grabbed one of the *Chorros* by the hair and he used his hold on it to twist his neck around in a brutal crunch.

The other guy, wound gushing blood on his chest, let out a shrill cry when Vincenzu punched him there. He wobbled forward, just in time to meet Vincenzu's knee on the way up.

"Get that piece of shit out of here," I snapped at my men before I eyed Martino and demanded, "You okay?"

"*Se*, Don. *Se*."

"Get your ass to the clinic in Brooklyn Heights." We had a deal worked out with a doctor there.

He shook his head. "I'm good. *Tuttu beni*."

Brow furrowed, I just nodded. "You know when to get your ass to the clinic." I wasn't his mama. I wasn't going to hold his fucking hand.

Turning to Fi, I saw her hissing something at her mother, but the woman's shoulders were huddled, her chest almost caving in on itself as she tried to hide from her daughter.

As well she should.

I stepped forward, deeper into the pigsty of an apartment.

Poverty was one thing, living in this kind of filth was another. Had they never heard of trash bags in this fucking building?

Wading through pizza boxes and empty packets of cigarettes, I stepped over dirty clothes and only the fuck knew what else before I carefully grabbed Fi's arm and murmured, "Let me handle this, *vita mia*."

She twisted around to glower at me. "This is my mom. My problem."

"Seems to me like your *mom* was about to use you to pay off her debts, *duci*," I told her, the words cold even if my voice was calm.

"We don't know that," Fi rasped, her eyes filled with devastation, her earlier anger having faded, breaking down with her sorrow. "She hasn't said shit—"

"That's because she's ashamed." I tugged at her arm. "Come, *bedda mia*. I will get you the answers you need."

Her mouth trembled. "She can't have meant—"

"I will find out," I crooned, reaching up and cupping her chin as she turned toward me.

Tears hovered at the lash line, but she sniffled and rasped, "It's a mistake."

I didn't think so.

For the *Chorros* to be sitting here, waiting, at the exact time Jen had texted her mom to say we'd be stopping by was too large a coincidence.

Unless, of course, the old bitch had been servicing them...

That was a possibility.

One I actually preferred.

"Stand over there, *amore mia*."

Her lips wobbled but she did as I asked. When I pulled out the Honyaki steel blade, the one I'd appropriated from Eva Martinez, she released a shaky breath, and I half-expected her to turn back to me, to drag on my arm and to stop me, but she didn't. I felt her hesitation though. Felt it and knew that she would always be weak where this woman was concerned.

I, more than anyone, could understand family loyalty, but it had to be earned. As far as I could see, and from what Stan's reports had keyed me in on, this woman deserved nothing more than the fucking noose.

With the knife in my hand, I told the whore, "Diana—" Both women gasped as I used her name. "—you should speak freely with me because if you don't, I'll have to hurt you. I don't want to have to do that in front of your daughter, but I will if I need to."

"T-They made me do this." She shot a terrified look at the *Chorros*, one of whom was dead and the other unconscious so they couldn't back up her story.

Yet, giving her the benefit of the doubt for Fi's sake, I could well believe that.

I could even believe that they might have forced themselves into her apartment.

As big of a dump as this place was, a quick glance at the door confirmed that it had been kicked repeatedly over the years, was scuffed, and the locks had been changed several times leaving behind patches where the paint hadn't covered the mechanisms, but it hadn't been busted open.

"How did they do that?"

When she didn't reply, I raised the knife and prodded the tip against my finger. Her eyes followed the move, eyes so like my Fi's, but these were loaded with terror.

I felt her fear and reveled in it because Fi, like any neglected child, longed for her mother's attention and this was how it was given to her. Diana deserved to be afraid. She deserved to feel the memory of this moment until the day she died.

"Vlad owed them money," Diana whispered. "T-They came this morning to collect. I've been trying to phone her for weeks," she cried, her voice surging with her fear. "She didn't answer! Then Vlad cut and ran, he disappeared and I—"

"You decided to use your daughter as collateral?" I grated out.

"No! I'd never do that—"

"So why didn't you send her a text to warn her not to come?" I reasoned.

She blinked up at me, all big brown eyes that, on her child, had the power to make me burn, but this bag of bones merely made me want to set fire to this building, leaving her to melt in the flames.

"No answer?" I rasped.

"Luciu?" Stan called out, just as Diana's bony knee kicked high. I knocked it aside with a bat of my own leg before she could kick me in the balls, and as she tried to run off, I pinned her against the wall with my arm, digging the cast hard into her throat until she was choking.

"What?" I snapped at my brother, twisting around as she struggled against my grasp. Seeing he was looking through their phones, I arched a brow. "Anything interesting?"

"Ignacio's asking where they are and, I quote, 'Where's the *puta* at?'"

Ignacio—the leader of the *Chorros.*

Confirmation that I was right gave me no satisfaction, especially when Fi started crying. "I can't believe you'd do this to me."

"Desperate," Diana croaked, her fingers scrabbling against the hold I had on her throat. The 3D-printed cast came with a honeycomb-like pattern on it and her fingers dug into the exposed flesh but the discomfort was minimal because adrenaline and fury diminished any pain she caused. "Owed too much."

Out of curiosity, I asked, "How much?"

"Twenty-five."

A soft laugh escaped me. "If you'd waited, your daughter would have handed you fifty." Misery slithered into the old cunt's expression. "You won't need a penny—"

"Don't kill her, Luc," Fi whispered, which had me twisting around to gape at her.

"You can't be serious. She almost sold you!"

"I don't want her death to come between us."

"It only will if you allow it," I rumbled.

"I don't want her to die—"

I shook my head at her, but now that the words had been spilled, I knew she *might* hold a grudge against me if I did the world a favor and scrubbed this bitch out of existence.

Well, I could listen, but it would be on my terms.

Tossing the knife in my hand, I leaned in close, digging the cast even harder into her gullet. "Your daughter's more generous than I am, Diana. I'd erase you if she let me, but I'm going to leave you with a lasting memory," I ground out as I placed the tip of the knife at the corner of her eye.

She released a soft whimper as her gaze chased the blade's passage as I trailed it along to the highest part of her cheek. She started struggling, but I ground the cast into her throat, harder than before. As she struggled for breath, I lodged it into the softness under her chin and used that to keep her head in place.

Diana screamed as I dug the tip in, the sharp steel slicing through the flesh like it was butter. But she choked on the blood, gargling on it as her teeth provided a natural barrier, then I tilted the knife and did something I'd never done before—I moved the blade back up, taking the cut at a right angle, and carried on until I hit her nose.

Pulling back, I let her cascade to the floor, her ragged cheek sliced into a 'V.'

A 'V' that, from this moment on, meant whoever had been given one was no longer welcome in NYC.

"If I see you in this fucking city again, I won't listen to your daughter. If you call her, I'll hunt you down, cuff you and throw you in the nearest river. If you so much as breathe the same air on the same goddamn coast as her, I'll do more than slice your fucking cheek. You leave her alone, do you hear me?"

Her hand clapped to her face, covering the gaping wound, but she nodded, a pitiful bloody mess on the floor.

I turned away, purposely tilted at an angle so that Fi couldn't see me, and I strode through the shithole, looking for a bathroom.

Finding one, a room that was impossibly filthier than the rest of this dump, I let the water pour from the faucet and used it to scrub at the blood spatter that had hit my face and hands. My coat was dark for this reason, and my shirt could be covered when I buttoned it up.

My coat sleeve covered the cast, but I knew blood would have seeped onto it which was, in a word, inconvenient. Washing it off as quickly as I could, I sensed movement in the doorway and turned to find Fi standing there.

Half-expecting to find hatred hidden in her gaze, I was surprised to uncover only grief.

Her mother might still be living, but she was dead to Fi.

And that had nothing to do with my actions, but Diana's.

I had no words for her, none at all, other than, "You're safe. You will always be safe with me."

Her bottom lip trembled, and she nodded, accepting what I had to say because actions spoke louder than words, and Fi had just been handed proof that I wouldn't only kill for her...

At her command, I'd let people who deserved to die, *live*.

EIGHTEEN

I STARED AT MY MOTHER, at the gaping wound, at the tumble of bony limbs on the ground and I wept.

I was the friend who wasn't supposed to give a damn.

Who existed on Cristal and five hundred calories a day.

Who gave Jake the good candy because I was an awesome godmother.

Who the IRS should fear because I knew more loopholes than a seamstress.

All my life, I'd lived as if I had zero fucks to give, and here was the reason why.

Because *she'd* had zero fucks to give *me*.

Lips wobbling with the need to cry, I stared at the 'V' on her cheek for so long that she hissed, "Aren't you going to help me?"

She must have thought I was horrified by what Luc had done. She must have thought I was scared.

Instead, I had an epiphany.

It unfurled slowly inside my mind, my goddamn heart, making it far too easy to whisper, "I let you live, Diana, so that you could know what it feels like to be dead to me."

"You think I'd give a damn?" she sneered.

I had no idea what made me say it, no idea why the words even came to me. "I don't. I don't think you care if you see me again or not. But you're marked now. That 'V' means something to the worst kind of people, and you have to live with that for the rest of your life."

I could feel the holy hell in my eyes, could feel it burning inside me as if my soul were on fire, and the best thing of all?

She saw it too.

Her shoulders rounded as she sniped, "It means he's a sick fuck. That's it. Nothing more, nothing less."

"No," I taunted. "It means you come back into the city, you *will* die. You're alive because I asked him to let you live, Diana. You should remember that. You owe me your life, and I can snatch it away the second I want to because the mafia's everywhere. And that means you breathe because I asked *him* to let you."

I witnessed the actual moment that she recognized what she'd gotten herself mixed up in, and like any cornered alley cat, she swiped her claws at me in self-defense. "You're just like your father," she hissed, her still-beautiful features pinching and revealing her true ugliness.

From the moment I knew what a father was, I'd asked where mine lived. When I was eight, I'd learned that the photo she gave me of him came from one of those picture frame inserts. That was when I'd stopped asking. When I'd stopped caring.

"You know who he is, then?" I drawled, so goddamn grateful that Savannah had armed me with this knowledge before she could weaponize it. "I thought you fucked your way around Manhattan so many times you didn't have a clue?"

"Like you're any better."

"I'm what you made me, Diana," I replied simply, unoffended, not even hurt by her words. "I don't eat and I drink too much. I wear too little and I party too hard, but I will always, *always,* be better than you because lying on my back isn't enough for me.

"I'm a CPA. And I'm good at it. I'm damn good at it. I struggled to get my degree, I worked dead end jobs, pulling two, sometimes three shifts a day, and I studied instead of sleeping to get to this point in my life. I'm more than just a pussy. But you? You're not. That's all you are. You're only a whore. Nothing more, nothing less."

The resolve in my voice felt good. Made me feel strong. *Powerful.*

I didn't need her.

I'd never needed her.

And now she was out of my life for good. Just like I'd wanted this morning.

As I turned to walk away, she whimpered, "Are you just going to leave me here? The *Chorros* still want their money."

"Patience never was your virtue." Then, I lobbed over my shoulder, "I'd prefer to dump my money in the Hudson than give it to you—"

"You bitch!"

I winked at her, and I smiled. "You know it."

"Don't you want to know who your father is? I'll tell you," Diana pleaded.

"For a price? I don't need to know." I didn't, but not for the reason she thought.

"If you don't want your other cheek carved out, I'd leave if I were you, *buttana*," Stan commented, stepping forward.

I shot him a look, expecting to see him sneer at me, but his expression was blank. Relieved by that, I walked toward the bathroom Luciu was using and heard her whining at him.

Cutting out her words, her pleas for help, I saw the guards rolling the gangbanger, the one who was unconscious, into a rug. I had no desire to even question why they were doing that or where they were taking him.

If anything, I focused on the grime and the dirt that my mother existed in.

The shame that hit me was painful, but when I headed into the bathroom and saw the outright filth... I wanted to puke.

A cry sounded from the living room, and when I twisted around, I saw Stan had picked Diana up and was dragging her out of the apartment.

The part of me that had wanted her attention for so long, that foolish, foolish girl, almost wept at the sight. Stan dragged her away, though, and one of the guards lifted the rug onto his shoulder and carried the gangbanger out, moving into my line of sight, providing me with a physical reminder of what she'd done.

Of how little I meant to her.

The soft splash of water drew my attention back to the man who'd just protected me from the fate she wished on me.

"You're safe. You will always be safe with me."

His words glued my gaze to his.

"I know," I whispered, and I did.

The truth settled deep in my bones, scoring my soul with the promise.

"*Bonu.*"

There was no guilt on his face, no shame. Why did I feel both?

He raised his arms to me, and for the tiniest moment, I hesitated. Just a fraction of a second.

His arms began to lower.

I hurled myself at him.

And they were raised again. Folding around me, he held me tight. So tight.

I didn't know where I started and he ended.

His hold on me *hurt* that was how tight his embrace was. I felt the individual holes on the plastic cast digging into my back, that was how closely he held me, but I needed it.

I needed it so badly.

I needed him to never let me go.

"She tried to sell me," I whispered, like he didn't already know.

Like he hadn't seen the most shameful moment of my entire life.

"She did," he replied softly, his good hand coming up to cup my head before he started stroking my hair. "I know you thought I was foolish this morning for coming with you, but this world... it's a bad place, *vita mia.* When I arm you with guards, I need you not to question me."

How *could* I argue?

I'd seen the guards hovering around Aoife for years, Savannah as well now, and I'd understood. I'd seen the violence of this life. I got it. I'd just never been the target of it.

If Luc and I weren't together, I'd be...

My mouth worked. "You saved me."

"I will always save you. Even when you don't know how to save yourself." He pressed a kiss to my temple, then murmured, "It's time to go home, *bedda mia*."

I didn't bother arguing. I just let him lead me out of that place that could have been the location of my last moments of freedom. He curved his arm around my shoulders, held me so close that the warmth from his body penetrated my frozen one, and we walked away from the crime scene.

The blood on the floor, spattered on the walls and furniture, it was so alien to me. Yet in the past two months, I'd seen more of it than I was sure I'd seen in a lifetime.

I'd spilled it, shed it, and bled it.

Dazed, I let him lead me to the car we'd left less than a half hour ago, a half hour in which my life had changed forever, and we drove home like nothing had happened.

But everything had changed.

Everything.

He knew, too. My strength had whispered away with the bite of reality, and I let him look after me. Today, I could be weak. Tomorrow, I had to be Jen again.

So, when he guided me into the penthouse, and when he stripped me down and himself, I let him clean me up. It wasn't sensual, it was almost paternal. Mostly one-handed, he washed my hair, scrubbed my hands and feet, then cleaned the rest of me.

When he was done, he wrapped me in a towel, then sat me down on the toilet seat before he returned to the spray.

Absentmindedly, I watched him do the same, and though he was rougher with himself, handling his body a lot more harshly than he did mine, the solid strength of him was something I knew I could lean on.

He would allow me to be weak, because he was strong enough to hold us both upright.

I'd never had that before. Ever. I'd leaned on Aoife and Savannah, but not like I could Luciu.

Was I capable of being that for him though?

When his world was so dark? When the ground beneath his feet was pooled with the blood and the bones of his enemies?

I knew the answer was yes, and that was somehow more terrifying than anything else that had happened today.

LUC

"I'M A HYPOCRITE."

As I buttoned the shirt I tucked her in, I arched a brow at her. "Isn't everyone a hypocrite?"

"You're not. You know what you are," she whispered.

"What am I?"

She swallowed. "A mobster."

"You knew that too."

"I did, but I..."

Because I knew what she was talking about, I tipped my head to the side. "You judged me for it."

"I did," she admitted.

"I know."

"You didn't mind?"

I shrugged. "What I do for a living isn't acceptable to the rest of the world. I didn't expect you to like it."

"The power you have turns me on. Your wealth..." She blinked at me. "I'm the worst kind of hypocrite."

My lips wanted to curve because she sounded so horrified, but I didn't let them, just chided her, "The worst kind? No. Are you against abortion but agree with the death sentence? Do you believe Hitler should have won the war? Do you think people should go to jail for assisting the suicide of their terminally ill loved one?"

Her shoulders straightened. "No."

"Well, then. You're not the worst kind."

"Is there a best kind?"

"No, but you're too exhausted for philosophy."

Her eyes were big in her pale face. "I'm glad, Luciu, that you did that to her cheek." She made the admission like it was a confession to cleanse her soul.

"Me too." Satisfaction filled me. "She'll never be able to forget today. Neither should she."

"You want them all to remember the day you did that to them, don't you?"

"I do. Every single one of them. Time makes a memory fade, but when you tie in pain? And a scar?" Now, I smiled. "That's why I do it. They should never forget when they crossed me." I gently tweaked her chin. "And now you."

She gulped. "I'm a bad person."

"*Chista è da me*," was my reply as I finished fastening the shirt at last and led her to the bed.

You're mine.

Docilely, when Fi was the opposite of docile, she climbed beneath the sheets, letting me arrange her there.

She didn't question what I was doing as I dressed, didn't ask where I was going.

Fi closed her eyes and shut out the world.

Shut out the fact that, today, her self-image had changed.

Forever.

I'd been raised around strong women. My grandmothers, my mother, and my sister were some of the strongest women I'd ever known.

Their presence in my life had shaped how I ruled, had made me the man I was today.

Women were *not* the weaker sex.

Women were different, but not weak.

If a woman stole from me, I cut off her hand just as I would cut off the hand of a man who stole from me.

I knew the power of women, and I never underestimated it because I'd seen what they could do.

Fi's strength was evolving, and I knew she was only just coming to realize her capabilities.

Some might say that she didn't need to realize them. That the underworld was a place she didn't have to inhabit, but every part of society was touched by it.

Drugs and whores and guns might be the base products, but the mafia brushed upon every part of capitalism, because it was inherently corrupt, and the mafia played those corruption games like no other.

Her eyes had been opened years before to the harsh realities of life in NYC, but I knew that hadn't prepared her for what was barreling her way.

So, I could give her time to adapt as I knew what she would be when she could embrace this side of life.

Once I was ready, I left her in bed after I dipped down to press a kiss to her temple, hoping she was sleeping for real.

Clean and exhausted even though she'd only woken up a couple of hours before, I knew she needed the rest.

Her clothes were bagged up alongside mine, ready to be incinerated just in case. Stan was waiting on me as I headed out of the bedroom, and after I shoved the bags at him, together, in silence, we returned to the lobby and climbed into the town car. Brooklyn Heights was our destination.

As Lorenzo drove off, Stan was the first to say, "She okay?"

"No."

"Understandable."

"Then why ask?"

"What else am I supposed to ask?" he countered.

"True."

"Her mother's a piece of work," he grunted.

"Doesn't deserve the name 'mother,'" I agreed.

"Surprised you let her live."

"Me too." I didn't want to talk about this. "The *Chorros* are going to be a problem."

"No. Ignacio and I have a rapport."

"Since when?"

"Since I threatened to blow out his brains if his people didn't stop entering our territory without permission."

My lips twitched. "That doesn't sound like much of a rapport to me."

"It was. His kid was the one doing the entering. I told him you'd carve his face up as a greeting, then would slice the rest of him up as a farewell."

"Where did the blowing his brains out come into play?"

"If he let any other fucker travel into our territory, that'd be the parting gift."

I outright grinned at that.

"They've dumped the body outside his shop in Queens. We'll probably see Martino at the clinic. He finally caved in and went for treatment after he left the rug with Ignacio."

"How bad is it?"

"Wouldn't be too bad, but the bullet's still in him."

Nodding, I asked, "The other fucker is at *Russu?*"

"*Se.*"

"*Bonu.*" He'd be tonight's stress relief.

"Got a team in to clean up the *buttana*'s place in Port Morris. Shouldn't take long."

"Keep me updated."

"Will do."

My mind raced as I thought about how differently this morning could have gone, about how I'd be tearing the fucking city apart to find her *if...*

Hands balling into fists, the pain from my broken wrist was grounding me because just thinking of her being whored out by those cunts made me want to annihilate every *Chorros'* member in NYC.

Maybe that was why my brain switched gears, and a memory from last night hit me. I'd had other priorities after my meeting with Lyanov.

"Last night, when I spoke with Lyanov, he already knew about Dubrov."

Stan stilled. "What?"

I turned to him. "He knew that Dubrov was dead."

"How?"

"I don't know. One of the men you sent in must have been a mole for the Russians."

I heard his teeth grinding. "I'll deal with it."

Nodding, I murmured simply, "See that you do," as I passed the duty over to him.

The rest of the fifteen-minute journey from East Broadway to Brooklyn Heights took longer thanks to a snafu on Brooklyn Bridge, but when we pulled up at the clinic, my arm was checked out and the cast removed and handed to Stan for incineration. It was another precautionary measure, but a man like me stayed out of jail by being precautious.

The bad news was that I'd need the bastard for another four to five weeks. It was healing, just slowly.

"Do you need pain meds?" the doctor asked me.

Stan snorted at that, but I shook my head.

"Aren't you in any pain?"

The doctor knew what and who I was, and we paid him a lot of money to keep his mouth shut, but clearly, he didn't understand that your pain tolerance increased when you were in our line of work.

My ascension to power hadn't been clean. Neither had Stan's. Our wealth afforded us some protection, but not a lot.

We'd both been stabbed, beaten, shot. Christ, both of us had almost died twice—him in a shooting, me with a stab wound that had led to blood poisoning, and we'd nearly been rammed off a fucking bridge a few years back.

"I'm fine," I told him. And I was. More annoyed at needing the damn thing for longer than I'd originally been told.

With a new, DNA-free cast covering my wrist, Stan and I returned to *Russu*.

As we pulled into the yard, Stan grunted as his cell rang. "It's Ignacio."

"I'll deal with him."

Accepting the call, I placed it on speaker.

"You got my *primo*, Valentini. I want him back."

"That sounded like a demand, Custanzu."

"It did," Stan agreed. "It also sounded like the *figghiu ri buttana* doesn't realize you're the Don now."

"Oh, I fucking realize. You just don't understand that your shitty goddamn titles mean nothing to me—"

"I'll make sure your cousin learns the lesson for you then." I used my thumb to crack my knuckles.

"You touch him, and I'll fucking—"

"You'll what?" I snarled, breaking him off. "Your tiny, piece of shit gang will come for one of the biggest factions in the goddamn city?" Even with the purge, we were still twenty times larger than the *Chorros*. "You were going to take *my* woman, Ignacio. You were going to trade her in and use her as a fucking whore—"

"I wasn't going to do nothin'," Ignacio retorted, but I heard the confusion in his voice, heard it *and* the hesitation.

"You fucking were. Her bitch of a mother was going to sell her to you to pay off her debts, and you didn't do your homework.

"I'd back the fuck away from this battle if I were you, *jefe*," I mocked, then hissed, "Because if you don't, I'll be the one who comes for *you*."

"I didn't know she was your *mujer*," the *Chorros* leader retorted. "How the fuck would I know?"

"Isn't my problem that you didn't do your homework. My problem is that you were going to take what didn't belong to you."

Ignacio's gulp was audible. "I swear I didn't fucking know, man. My *tia* is sick. You kill my cousin, it's gonna kill *her*."

"Should have thought about that when you were arranging to whore out my woman."

"Look, I'm sorry, man. I'm fucking sorry."

"So you goddamn should be." My top lip curled as I climbed out of the car and rasped, "Guess you'd better get down on your hands and knees and pray your *tia* doesn't pay for your mistake."

Cutting the call, I tossed the cell back at Stan and stormed into *Russu*.

If Ignacio thought his cousin was coming back to him in anything other than a body bag, then he was a moron.

TWENTY

WITH AOIFE DEALING with her own grief, I knew I couldn't unload my problems onto her, and I'd never shared all that much with Savannah about my mother because, in truth, there wasn't much to share. What little there was, was bad, and this was the worst.

She'd tried to sell me.

How was this my reality?

Four days later, and I was still dealing with the fact that if Luciu hadn't overheard our phone conversation, if he hadn't been with me...

It changed how I looked at him.

I already knew what he was. Knew what he was capable of. Knew what he was willing to do.

Seeing it was believing.

Witnessing him shoot a man, watching him carve the letter 'V' into Mom's cheek, seeing him wash off her blood...

Shuddering as if someone had walked over my grave, I turned my focus to my computer where I was working up a deal with a broker in Monte Carlo and jumped when there was a rapping at my door.

"Come in," I called out, hating that my voice sounded hoarse.

As if I'd been crying.

Which I totally hadn't been.

Quickly patting my cheeks, I shot a false smile at whoever was behind the door and blinked when I saw it was Lauren, Luc's mom.

Shoving my chair away from my desk, I got to my feet and awkwardly hovered as I said, "Lauren! How are you?"

She smiled at me, and her radiance hit me like a ray of sunlight after a long winter. "Do you mind if I come in? I was in the neighborhood and thought I'd drop by."

"You did?" I wasn't sure why, but I smiled back at her. "How did you know I worked here?"

"Luc mentioned it the last time we spoke." She stepped into the office, her coat swishing around her calves as she closed the door.

There was an openness in her expression that immediately set me at ease. She wasn't here to tell me to back off her son; if anything, she appeared friendly.

God, I needed that right now.

"He spoke about me?" I questioned.

"Of course." Lauren's eyes twinkled like she was hiding a secret. "I wondered if you'd like to come to lunch with me?"

"I'd really enjoy that."

I wasn't lying.

I really would.

Lauren was so... well, *normal*. Which was a lie because, from what Luc had told me, and Lauren herself, of course, she'd grown up wealthy.

But Savannah was a rock star's daughter, Luc carved letters into people's faces, Stan ate more than his body weight in cupcakes while breaking men's necks, and... well, Aoife was normal, but she didn't need my crap which was a walk in the park in comparison to what she was going through.

"Good! I hope you don't mind, but I preempted your agreement and reserved a table at *Le Chat Noir*."

"I've heard good things about that place."

"You've eaten there?"

"No." It was too expensive. That was usually my jam, but damn, I didn't even feel a buzz at getting to go there with her. "But I know people really like it."

She beamed at me. "Great."

Picking up my cell phone, I stepped away from my desk and headed to the door where my winter coat and purse were hanging. Tucking my cell into the purse, I turned around and found her watching me.

There was an odd expression on her face, one that she'd been shielding...

After what had happened with Diana, it put me on edge and I demanded, "What is it?" in a forceful tone that I'd never have used with a boyfriend's mother. But, of course, I knew. I knew 'what it was.' "He told you?"

Her smile was tight. "He explained that your mother had to leave town."

Or her son would throw my mom in a river and let her drown...

"He told me once that he'd burn the city to the ground if it meant keeping me safe." I swallowed. "I've known him six weeks."

For some reason, that made the genuine smile of moments before return at a high wattage. "His father was like that." She sighed. "Well, a lot less violent, but as protective. Custantinu would say those things, and he'd mean them, but he never had to act on them. Luciu's life..." She hesitated. "I'd say I regret the man he's had to become, but I can't."

"Wouldn't you have preferred for him to have become a professor? To do something normal?"

"Perhaps. I know this sounds strange, but if he had followed that career path, if his father hadn't been killed, I'd never have seen him."

"Why wouldn't you?"

"He'd have been in England. He'd have made his life there, and because his father was so pigheaded at times, and they weren't talking because Luciu changed career paths..." She shrugged. "I wouldn't know my son. There is no compromise here for me. No future where I wouldn't have lost someone I need to be in my life."

"He's a killer," I rasped, daring to say the words.

Needing to.

Desperate to hear them out loud with someone who wouldn't go to the cops. Because hearing them might be the wake-up call I needed.

Did Savannah and Aoife feel like this?

As if the truth gagged them?

Though we were inhabiting the same world, and a problem shared was a problem halved, I knew we'd never be able to talk about what our men did in detail, even if it affected us personally—we were protecting the men we loved.

But protection meant being silenced, and the silence was choking me.

Growing up around violence was one thing, seeing it with my own two eyes was another matter entirely. And if that made me weak, then so be it.

"Yes, he is a killer," she agreed with an ease that had me wobbling back against the sofa nearest the door and perching on it. "Does that frighten you? Or does it frighten you that you can deal with that side of him? That it doesn't terrify you? I had that same 'come to Jesus' moment, dear. It's frightening, but what's even more frightening?

"We're taught good and bad from a young age. Bad people go to jail; good people get to live happy lives. But what happens when the bad people don't go to jail, and the good people are killed by them? When there's no justice? When there's no punishment?" She swallowed. "My Custantinu was butchered like a pig, and he was dumped outside the family estate like he was roadkill.

"He'd done nothing wrong other than be the son of a man the Fieris had already burned alive. He was a good man, in fact, no, he was a *great* man.

"He came to the Fieris' attention because Stan had gotten himself in trouble, and Custantinu paid off his debts by offering to handle Stan's dealer's accounts."

Eyes flaring wide in surprise, I whispered, "That's tragic."

Her face turned to stone as she replied, "The dealer morphed from backstreet sales to becoming a big player... he did a deal with the Fieris and that was how they learned about Custantinu.

"He didn't have the same surname, didn't show in any way, shape, or form that he was his father's son, but somehow, they knew.

"Our lives changed from that moment, veering off course, ricocheting until this point in time.

"So, yes, I'd have liked for Luciu to have had a normal life, but he didn't have a choice. Just as you didn't."

"Is this why you go to church? Luciu told me that you didn't go when he was younger."

"It makes me feel like I can still speak with Tinu. He wasn't religious, but..." She sighed. "It's silly. I hope there's a heaven so that I can find my way back to him."

Tears stung my eyes because I knew how that felt. She'd been married for decades, had a family with her Tinu, and I'd only been with Luc for a ridiculously short length of time, but I'd always want to find my way back to him.

Regardless of everything, the mafia bullshit, my heritage and his, the love I had for him was real and raw.

She angled her head to the side. "What's the problem, child? You can speak candidly with me. I won't tell him."

I stared at her, wondering if she meant that or if she'd recount every word to him, but it didn't stop me from telling her, "I love him." I needed her to know that.

"Then what's the problem?"

"The problem is with me."

"You know he's concerned about you? He's a very private man, but he shared what happened with your mother..."

"She tried to use me to pay off her debts." Pain filtered through me. "Her boyfriend was going to do the same. I guess she got the idea from him."

"I'm surprised Luciu didn't kill her."

"He wanted to. I stopped him."

"Why?"

"Because..." I licked my lips as the words remained lodged in my throat.

"Because you didn't want her to die?"

Oh, if only I was so kind.

"No."

"Then, what?"

I dreaded that question and dreaded the answer even more. "Because she'll suffer more if she's alive." And this way, I wouldn't have her death on my conscience.

Lauren studied me for so long that I thought I might have grown two heads, and just as I wondered if she was going to convince Luc to leave me because I was evil, she merely said, "Ah." Then, she stepped over to me and slid her arm through mine. Tugging me close, she said, "A friend told me *Le Chat Noir* does a superb Caesar salad. They make it with sun dried tomatoes."

I blinked at her a couple times, then rasped, "Sun dried tomatoes?"

"Yes." She smiled as she patted my hand. "We'll have a nice lunch, share a bottle of wine, and I'll tell you about Luciu when he was growing up. I'll make sure they're nice and embarrassing stories so that you have ammunition for another time.

"Luciu might seem like a divine being to women, but I'm his mother, and there was nothing divine about him when he was fifteen."

My smile peeped out. "I'd bet the girls in his class didn't agree."

Her nose crinkled at the bridge. "Well, no," she admitted dryly. "My children were kissed by Cupid. At least, Custantinu used to say that when we had flocks of boys hovering around Rory and girls around Stan and Luciu. You couldn't move for their crushes." Her smile turned nostalgic, but it wasn't sad. More redolent with a warmth that came from sweeter times.

I was glad the family had had those, even as I was sad that I hadn't.

"We were blessed," she murmured before she patted me again and continued, "Come, dear. Lunch awaits."

Her words left me feeling shaken, my admission shaming me, but her hug, a caring embrace from someone who didn't have to like me, who didn't have to care, who was tied to Luc, meant more than she could know.

I wasn't hungry, at all, but that hug made me go with her. Made me follow her like she was Mary, and I was a lost, little lamb.

We grabbed a taxi to the restaurant, where a fawning maitre d' led us to a private dining room. It was actually very cutesy rather than swanky.

The walls were dripping with plants. Some were on vines that criss-crossed over a twenty-foot expanse, others were in ornate hanging baskets or tucked away in decorative pots.

With some plants brushing the glass ceiling of the internal terrace, the contrast between the miserable day outside and the colorful display inside was quite comforting.

As we were seated, servers brought us water and wine and spread out taster dishes from the menu.

"I can't drink," I said around a laugh. "I have to get back to work."

"There have to be some perks to putting up with Luciu," Lauren drawled. "We can call this a working lunch."

"We're not working."

"That's where you're wrong. This is work," she argued, stuffing a chip of harissa-flavored pita into some red pepper hummus.

"If this is work, then I've got a crappy job," I teased. "Although, I have to admit, that's not fair."

"How are you enjoying the new position?"

"It's good. I'm starting to find my footing. People are scared of me because of Luciu—"

"Child, just wait until you marry him. Then they'll be piddling themselves whenever they see you."

Unsure if it was her ease in talking about Luc and I marrying or her choice of word that took me aback more, I warbled, "Piddling?"

She wafted a hand. "I'm sure you can figure out what I mean. They do it all the time around me. I'm not even sure how they know he's my son, but it seems as if everyone does."

"He must tell people."

"The entirety of Manhattan?" she scoffed. "The boy's been incognito for nearly a decade. No one's seen hide nor hair of him. He's been like Batman, but it's as if the whole city knows to be cautious around me.

"That's why it's so refreshing talking with you, child. You know all the grim details." She beamed a smile at me that sharply contrasted her words.

I shoved some moussaka into my mouth so I didn't have to reply.

"Have you ever been to Italy, Jen?"

"No. I've never left the States," I told her once I'd finished chewing. "I hadn't even traveled outside of New York until recently."

She leaned forward and patted my hand. "He'll take you. The boy's dying to go home. He just doesn't realize it."

"He said it's been ten years since he was back there."

"A decade, God. We moved back to the UK that year Tinu..." Lauren heaved a sigh then took a deep sip of her wine. "They never tell you when you're your age how quickly time passes. Either that, or you just don't believe it.

"I left Sicily after he passed away, vowing that I'd never return, but I only lasted three years. I had to go back.

"Sicily was always home, and that was only compounded when I met him. All three of them miss it, but they're stubborn." She tutted. "Maybe you can convince him to go back sooner rather than later."

I shrugged. "I'm not sure if I can convince Luciu to do anything he doesn't want to."

"I think you're very wrong, and you know it."

Her gaze was measured upon mine, and I switched focus to the moussaka on my dish.

Because she was right.

He hadn't killed Mom, had he? Because I'd asked.

Rather than be a compliment, that seemed like such a dangerous ability.

As if I had a rabid dog on a leash...

But Luciu wasn't rabid. If anything, he was one of the most controlled men I knew.

"Did he frighten you, Jen?" Lauren asked kindly. "Is that the problem? If you're truly scared, and you want to leave him, I'll help—"

But I shook my head decisively, rejecting the very idea of leaving him. I didn't want that. At all. Funny how all the women in my life had offered to help me escape him when that was the last thing I wanted.

"I'm being a big baby."

"Everyone is entitled to act up when we've been through something traumatic."

"It would have been far more traumatic if Luciu hadn't saved me. I should be thanking him instead of giving him the cold shoulder, but I'm just—"

"New equilibriums take time to find."

Her lack of judgment eased something in me. "I think it's the difference between him telling me how he works, me believing it, then seeing it with my own eyes."

"Always tough to take."

"Yeah. It is." I pressed the tines of my fork into the moussaka, pulling the tender eggplant apart. "I love him. I accept what he does, oddly enough, it's..."

"That you can handle his work, that you can even enjoy its benefits, that disturbs you," she stated, no question within her words.

I had no choice but to nod.

She was right.

The rabid dog, when unleashed, came to heel at my command.

That was more power than I'd ever dreamed of having. Than I'd ever wanted.

And it was wonderful.

Safety was wonderful.

I was safe because of him.

"Did you hear that his case has been thrown out?" she asked when I didn't answer. I *couldn't* answer.

"Insufficient evidence," I quoted, the words a croak.

"Rory won't like her plans being messed with. She does like her day in court," Lauren teased. "But I'm sure Luciu didn't appreciate being thrown behind bars either."

"Who would?" I drawled.

She hummed, then rather than continue with that subject, switched back to speaking about Catania. To the family estate. Faded salmon pink stucco, gates framed with roaring lions forged in cast iron that gleamed green thanks to years of exposure to the elements, a small forest that sheltered the property from the blistering heat in the summer, two dozen rooms, half of them overlooking the ocean...

It sounded like heaven.

A heaven I wanted to visit.

My cell phone buzzed as she talked about the place her father had bought her and Tinu when Luciu was two years old, and seeing it was the man himself, asking if I was okay, I typed out:

Me: *I'm eating lunch with your mom.*

Luc: *I told her to leave you alone.*

Me: *She ignored you.*

Luc: *Apparently. Sorry, cara mia. If she's annoying you, I'll get someone to collect you now.*

Me: *Actually, I'm enjoying it.*

"The sign of love," Lauren said on a sigh. She made a motion with her hand, which had the white wine sloshing in the glass. "The soft smile when you're apart, the sweet joy of missing them and reconnecting with them... There's nothing like it."

Me: *She turns poetic when she's had a few too many.*

Luc: *I'm sure she'll regret that in the morning.*

Me: *You'd best come before she gets to the really gruesome stories about you.*

Luc: *I'm invited?*

Me: *Don't see why not. Are you hungry?*

Luc: *I can be.*

That had me laughing, and I shot Lauren a look. "Luciu is on his way."

"Why do you think I hired the private dining room, dear? I knew he'd come." She wagged her finger. "If Stan doesn't show up too, I'd be surprised.

"I'll be glad when Rory quits the DA's office. They're all like magnets. Glued together, I tell you. Not long apart. Rory broke Luciu's heart when she elected to go to college here rather than in the UK."

Interest piqued, I asked, "Didn't he want to come to the States?"

She shook her head. "My father was still alive at the time. Luciu wanted to be close at hand if he was needed. He's a good boy."

That made me smile, but what made me smile more? When Luc showed up, shooting me a sheepish glance as Stan bustled in behind him, much as Lauren predicted.

Luc took the seat beside me. Stan sat down next to his mother and proceeded to demolish every dish in sight.

As the two of them talked about the food on the table, Luc tilted toward me, leaning closer so they couldn't hear as he asked, "Everything okay?"

I looked from his mom to Stan, then to Luc, and the space at the table that some day soon might seat Rory, and I nodded.

That horrible morning when Aoife had miscarried, and I'd walked into the waiting room and had seen the O'Donnellys sitting there, I'd felt a little less alone.

But they weren't my family.

Not really.

I was a nuisance, a pest. A hanger on.

Here? Maybe Stan didn't like me, but he tolerated me, and Rory didn't know anything other than the fact I wore really short skirts midwinter, but Lauren seemed to like me. And Luc loved me.

To my mother, I might be discardable. To Luc, I was not.

Maybe someday, to Stan, Rory, and Lauren, I wouldn't be either.

And that was enough.

I pressed a kiss to his cheek and whispered, "Thank you for being you."

He reared back at that, the words clearly coming as a surprise, but his smile, when it came, was like the dawning sun. It started small, just a tiny gleam in his eyes, before it overtook his features and I found myself basking in his warmth.

Security... for someone who'd been painfully insecure as well as *un-secure* all my life, was it any wonder it was so alien to me?

It wasn't his fault that I was scared by the power he handed me. It was something I'd have to grow accustomed to, something I was lucky to have. Something more precious than a hundred-and-twenty-thousand-dollar purses and an expensive wardrobe, and something he'd never be able to understand.

But that was okay.

It was fine.

Today, more so than back in that shithole apartment of my mother's, accepting that she'd have sold me like I was a used car, I recognized that he was right—I had to value my worth. And if I based my estimation on my value to him, I was priceless.

TWENTY-ONE

LUC

EIGHT DAYS LATER

"LUCIU, I have that hacker on the line."

I looked away from my computer and saw Stan standing in the doorway. "She wants to talk to me?"

He nodded, but his expression was peeved. "Says you're the man funding the operation, so she wants to speak with you."

Shrugging, I held out a hand. "It's about time she has news for us," I grumbled as he gave me the phone. I tipped it up, tapped on the speaker, just in time to hear the hacker say:

"If you're going to whine about my work ethic, at least have the decency to put me on mute."

"Maybe I wanted you to hear me whine. I expected results sooner than this."

"It was coded in C++."

"So? I'm paying you to break it wide open."

"Look, I'm used to esoteric languages, the tough stuff to crack like Haskell and Prolog. Throw something normal at me, and my brain has to rewire itself. You could have given this to someone at Alphabet and he'd have known what was what. I like the complicated shit—"

"You're complaining that it was too easy to crack after I complained that it took you too long to crack?" I demanded, trying to understand if that was the bullshit she was selling.

"Exactly."

"Exactly what?"

"I know you're Italian so do we need a translator here or something? You don't seem to be getting what I'm saying. What the fuck is it with people who don't understand me? AM. I. SPEAKING. A. LANGUAGE. YOU. UNDERSTAND?"

"I'm Sicilian," I corrected. "I'm getting what you're saying, just not buying what you're selling."

The woman huffed. "Yeah, that makes two of us. I didn't sign on for kidnapping. I like to think my moral code is as complex as INTERCAL, but if you're gonna get me flagged by the Feds again, it had better be worth it—"

"Kidnapping?" I inserted quickly, wondering what the fuck she was talking about.

"Uh-huh. Didn't know?" was her mock-sympathetic retort. "You and me both. Fuck knows what you've gotten us into. Canada itself is about to go to war over that Donnghal dude going missing. Can you imagine going through life with a surname like that?"

What world was this woman from?

"Look, I don't know what the hell you're talking about—"

"Donnghal?" Stan repeated. "You mean the hockey player?"

"Not just any hockey player. He's the Mounties' golden boy. Got all those French-Canadians panting whenever he skates onto the ice. He's on the Olympic team and everything.

"Then you go and hand me the computer with the fucker's location and everything. It's just too much, man. I think you owe me danger money. Those Canadians come across as polite, but get in the way of their fucking hockey—"

"What the hell are you talking about? His location is on that computer?"

"Dude, I'm looking at live footage of him as we speak. He's in some kind of cell. They're using infrared cameras to monitor him and the kid."

"What kid?" I demanded, totally confused.

"Dunno. Some kid. Chinese, I think. Little. Who the fuck kidnaps a kid?" It seemed to be a rhetorical question because she muttered, "There are some real sick bastards out there."

I shot Stan a look, and I knew why the Triads had suddenly been haunting our asses.

Headley had something to do with both kidnappings, and one of the victims was evidently a relative of a Triad.

Cristo.

I rubbed my forehead, trying to figure out our next move, but as much of a strategist as I was, this came out of nowhere. Whatever I might have anticipated, this was not it.

Damian Headley was supposed to be a trust fund baby with a coke problem, one who worked at his daddy's firm of brokers until the older Headley had croaked and he was left to run through his inheritance unchecked.

Nowhere in that backstory was there even a hint that Headley could be funding his various pastimes with hostage payments.

"You were right, Custanzu," the hacker mumbled, breaking into my thoughts. "They were using Call of Duty to communicate, but Headley was being greedy. Every time the Triads offered to pay, he kept upping the price. The kid must belong to one of the upper ranks for how easily they kept capitulating to his demands."

"*Miedda,*" I rumbled under my breath.

No wonder they'd been sending soldiers over to my warehouse.

One of their sons had been kidnapped.

What the fuck was going on with the crime families in this city if they couldn't go to another leader and explain the situation?

There was no honor in this world anymore. Fieri had seen to that, but I was damned if I was going to lead my life that way.

"Is either hostage injured?" Stan questioned.

"No. Well, I mean, not as far as I can see, but the news said they cut off Donnghal's earlobe for proof of life although how that proves the poor bastard's still alive, I don't know. But if I can't see *that*, then I guess I could be missing other injuries. The resolution is really low on these cameras.

"The boy appears to be okay, but I don't think he's doing that well seeing as he hasn't moved in the last twenty minutes."

"Lodestar, that's your name, right?"

She hummed. "Don't wear it out."

"I won't," I grunted. "Is there a location on the computer or are you using the infrared cameras to extrapolate their whereabouts?"

"Well, I used the cameras' signal at first, but there's plenty of information on the computer that tells me where they're being kept.

"This is an advanced kidnapping operation, Valentini. The crew has several places to store victims dotted across the country. They swoop into a certain area, snatch two people, then collect the ransom and get the hell out."

"How do you know that?"

"Because the guy who owned this computer was anal with his filing system. He's got all kinds of information on the victims, their schedules, their families, and their bank accounts.

"As for the Triads, to be honest, I think he misunderstood who he was dealing with. Zhao's the leader of the Triads, but I think Headley thought he was just a businessman. That's why he got greedy. What he was asking for was chump change to Zhao."

"I need you to transfer the information over to me."

Lodestar grunted. "Which part of me thinking you should pay me more didn't you hear?"

"How much do you want?"

"Double."

"Fine."

"Shit. Is it too late to say triple?"

"It's too late, unless you're going to be greedy like Headley," I drawled.

"Damn, I walked right into that, didn't I?"

"You did. But I'll give you a bonus for your silence."

"Lucky for you that my silence can be bought."

"Lucky's the word. How many men are on the crew?"

"Sexist."

"I beg your pardon?"

"That's sexist. Women can be kidnappers too."

"Christ, are you always this annoying?"

"Invariably."

"How many *people* are on the crew?"

"Better. It depends."

"On what?"

"Well, I've got records here that span the past fifteen years."

"Fifteen?"

"Yeah. Told you, the guy was anal. For around seven, the crew was always the same."

"He lists the names?"

"Yep. Each one has an account with how much they've earned, plus he had info on them too. He clearly investigated them as much as he had their targets.

"Anyway, for those initial years, the crew never changed. Then, he archived the file on this one particular woman, Scarlet O'Shea, and ever since, the crew switches up. Never the same continuous people on each job.

"This time, there are ten men. No women. Think that's because of how big Donnghal is. You should see his thighs. They make 'em *big* in Canada."

Patience well and truly worn, I muttered, "Okay, Lodestar, I need you to work with my brother on transferring the files you've uncoded onto our servers." I pressed the mute button, then shoved the cell phone at him. "I want all that information, including their location, before lunchtime."

If I was going to broker a new future for the city, then we needed to get that kid out of there—yesterday.

TWENTY-TWO

JEN

THAT SAME AFTERNOON...

I GRINNED as Savannah moved to the seat opposite me at the coffee shop and made a serious point of placing the Kelly purse directly in front of me so that she could see it.

Only, her gaze drifted over it like it was a Walmart knock-off, and she started dragging off her coat as she focused on me. Her expression was serious, somber, and it had me straightening up because the last time she'd looked at me as if the world was ending...

Dammit to hell.

Jaw clenched, I snapped, "What have you lied to me about this time?"

Sinking into her seat, she winced. "It wasn't a lie."

"No? How about a falsehood? A mistruth? A lie by any other name still stinks, Savannah."

"It wasn't... I..." She reached up and rubbed her forehead. "This is insane, Jen. Seriously, insane."

"You thinking I'm going to forgive your lying ass again is what's really insane here."

"Jen, this is serious."

"*I'm* being serious. As serious as a heart attack."

She leaned deeper over the coffee table and hissed, "Have you heard about the hockey player who went missing?"

Her question had me frowning. "You know I don't follow sports' news."

"This isn't sports' news, Jen. This is headline-grabbing shit. This is stuff that even *you* couldn't avoid."

My brow puckered as I thought about the little news I'd absorbed lately. "It's your fault. Everything's about the Sparrows now, and it's super boring."

That had her huffing. "The story of my career is super boring. Thanks, babe. Really appreciate that."

I clucked my tongue. "Don't turn this around on me when you're the one who's clearly done something if that guilty expression of yours is anything to go by." Clicking my fingers in front of her face, I retorted, "Classic narcissistic behavior."

She narrowed her eyes at me. "I'm not a narcissist."

"You're a liar is what you are."

"I'm not a fucking liar. I just... I like to evade the truth."

I scowled at her. "I evade nice things, like taxes. You evade the truth, that's not nice."

"Well, boohoo. This is the real world, Jen, and it's fucking danger-ous." She sucked in a breath and glowered at the server who dithered after he served us our coffee. "No, we don't want your number; we're both with boyfriends who are nastier than you and who'll beat your ass up if you keep bothering us."

The guy blinked. "I just wanted to thank you for having the guts to publish your exposés, Ms. Davis."

She blinked back. "It's Daniels. You know? Like Dagger Daniels? Camden Daniels?"

His cheeks burned bright red. "Sorry to disturb you."

At his apology, Savannah heaved a sigh. "No, I'm sorry for being a bitch. It's just been a really stressful day." She eyed the bill he'd placed beside the coffees, and she put a fifty dollar tip on there. "Sorry."

He perked up at the tip. "No worries. You can bitch at me again if it'll get me a fifty-dollar tip."

Her smile was forced, but he went away happy.

But that was Savannah.

Act first, think later.

I pursed my lips at her, wondering what she'd done this time. I'd squint at her if it wouldn't give me wrinkles. "Do I get fifty dollars every time you lie to me?"

She glared back at me. "I don't lie to you. Often. When I do, it's a big deal."

"Gee, that's great to know. Thanks!"

"Look, I never told you how Aidan and I met, did I?"

"No. Not sure I want to know either," I said with a huff. "Not if it's another goddamn lie."

Her hand snapped out to grab mine. "I swear to you, Jen, everything I'm about to tell you is the truth. You have to believe that. You have to believe that I was protecting you and *me*."

Her tone was serious, but that was nothing to the fear in her eyes.

"Okay, I'll listen," I agreed, but only because her fear scared me.

Savannah was pretty badass. I figured it was the journalist in her. She put herself in dangerous situations and thought nothing of it because a story was a story, and it needed to be revealed to the world.

By comparison, I was a fucking wimp. This far in my life, I'd managed to keep my ass alive without outside help. It was only recently that it had gone to shit.

"Five years ago, I was in between jobs. I'd gotten fired from another paper and I was at a loss." She sucked in a breath. "I've always been super interested in the mafia—"

"Why?"

She wafted a hand. "Something happened when I was a kid, and I learned at a young age that bad people wear really good suits." The analogy reminded me of something Lauren had told me, and it had me zooming in on her as she admitted, "I got fascinated with the O'Donnellys. I studied them, I researched them, and I had time on my hands. It became something to get up in the morning for. I got it in my head that I wanted to do a biography on Aidan O'Donnelly Sr."

"I remember you telling me that. I thought you were crazy. Still do."

"Agreed. Anyway, I thought that if I solved a family mystery, it would give me an in."

"What family mystery?"

"How your father died."

Surprised, I almost dropped my cup. It clattered against the saucer, but I saved it from spilling by snatching it back up. "How he died wasn't a mystery," I said softly enough so that no one would hear. "Everyone knows that was the Albanians."

"It doesn't matter how, but I knew it was bullshit. I knew something wasn't right. I kept digging, and eventually, I came to Sr.'s attention." Savannah gulped. "He sent Jr. after me. He was supposed to have me killed, but instead, he met me, and we talked, and I explained why I thought what the police believed was wrong."

Mouth agape, it took a few seconds for me to croak, "Jr. was sent to kill you and you're marrying him now?"

She winced. "It's complicated."

"I'll bet." I wasn't sure my brows could get any higher. I didn't even care about the premature wrinkles anymore.

"I-I figured out something worse. Something that I couldn't tell anyone, but I'm obsessive, and it led me to taking risks I shouldn't have taken, but out of it, I met a friend who became a sister to me. The best friend a woman could ask for..."

"Me?" I mumbled dumbly.

"You." She nodded, before she whispered, "I figured out that Padraig staged his own death."

For a second, I just stared at her.

Then I laughed.

I laughed so much that everyone in the coffee shop took notice. I laughed so hard my belly ached with it as whoops of amusement cascaded from me like water down the Niagara Falls.

But when she didn't laugh back, when she didn't join in, slowly, it resonated that she wasn't amused.

Which meant she was being serious.

Which meant...

My laughter died as abruptly as it had begun.

"You're not joking, are you?" I grated out.

"I wish I were."

"He's really alive?"

"He is." Savannah swallowed. "And he's back."

"What? Why?" I straightened up. "He's in New York?"

"He is." She ran a hand over her face. "His son's the hockey player who was kidnapped, Jen."

Mouth gaping harder than before, I whispered, "Are you for real?"

"I-I wish I weren't. I'd have told you he was alive, but I couldn't..." She closed her eyes. "If you went looking for him, you'd have been like me—on Sr.'s shit list.

"He thought everything I was doing was casting aspersions on his brother's legacy, so what would he think you were doing?" She shook her head. "I had to protect you. Even if it was only from yourself."

Reaching up, I rubbed at my eyes which were still watery from the tears I'd shed while laughing. "He's really alive?"

"He really is. H-He was at the compound yesterday. Showed up at Sunday dinner. I swear to God I thought Aidan Sr. was going to have a heart attack or something.

"I'd have told you sooner, but I couldn't. I needed to see you face-to-face, explain what was happening."

I swallowed. "Why is he back?"

"Because the kidnappers want more money than he has."

"He wants Aidan Sr. to pay it?"

She nodded. "He does."

"Will he?"

"I mean, I don't know, but I'd guess so. It's not like they're poor, is it? Plus, they're all about the family, aren't they?"

Her sarcastic tone of voice had me studying her but, slowly, I nodded. "This is crazy."

She reached out for my hand. "It really is. Do you forgive me?"

"I wouldn't have gone looking for him," I told her.

"I couldn't risk it. And you can't say that you wouldn't have because when you found out, there was nothing to go hunting for."

"I didn't visit his grave or anything. I'm not like that. What's in the past is in the past. He didn't want me, so I don't want him," I insisted, because I wanted her to know that. I *needed* her to know that she was wrong.

Adopted kids around the world might want to hunt down their birth parents, but I'd already been raised with one and, to be frank, that was more than enough.

This revelation just hit too close to home after what had happened with my mother...

I couldn't deal with this.

I really couldn't.

"I just couldn't risk your safety," she insisted right back. "You might have, you might not have. Either way, I couldn't afford for you to ask questions."

"Savannah, this means that I have a brother."

A famous brother who'd been goddamn kidnapped.

Slowly, she nodded. "You do, babe."

Staring at the creamy bubbles on the top of my coffee, I whispered, "I need to speak with Luciu." I jerked to my feet, and without a second look at her, I grabbed my purse and dialed his number. "Where are you? I need to speak with you."

LUC

"I'M IN A MEETING, *CARA MIA*," I murmured, my voice low so as to avoid detection from the Triads who, quite frankly, were up in arms about what I was showing them.

Cantonese flew around the back office of the restaurant where the Dragon Head, Zhao, had agreed to speak with me. He was the only silent man in the room. His subordinates had broken down the minute I'd showed them the footage Lodestar had sent us.

"It's important," she whispered, her voice shaky.

"I swear to you, the second this meeting is over, I'll call."

"Is that... Can I hear Cantonese? Are you at a Chinese restaurant?"

I didn't answer. "Give me twenty minutes. I'll call back."

"I'll go to *Russu*. Meet you there."

"Okay. I'm in Chinatown. So once I'm out of here, I'll be fifteen minutes max."

"It's... you know the hockey player who's gone missing?"

I straightened at her words. "Yeah?"

"It's about him," she said on a rush.

What the hell could she know about him?

"*Vita mia*, I swear to you, I'll give you all my attention when I'm not in a precarious situation."

"Thank you, Luc. Really, thank you." Then, she swallowed. "Are you safe?"

"*Se.*"

A relieved sigh whispered down the line. "Good."

Fi cut the call the second Zhao demanded, "How much?"

I shook my head. "I don't want a cent. I told you, I have nothing to do with this. Headley is the one behind the kidnapping."

"You brought him in to your club. My men saw yours taking him," Zhao snarled. "You dealt with him—"

"Because he was drugging the drink of a girl in *Russu* who is under my family's protection."

"He was a date-raper?" Zhao's mouth folded into a sneer. "If I didn't already think he was scum, he just went down a few feet in my estimations." He motioned to the tablet that was propped on the table in front of him. "Where is he?"

"We have coordinates—"

"How much?"

I shot Stan a look, and he tossed a burner cell to Zhao. "Free of charge."

"Nothing comes for free in this life."

No, I was learning that. "Consider it a favor." People were collecting them from me, I didn't see why I shouldn't do the same goddamn thing in return.

Zhao's chin dipped before he ground out something in Cantonese.

Was I surprised when he got to his feet and raced out of the restaurant? Maybe.

I guessed we had proof that the kid was directly related to Zhao. His concern was for family. For his blood. Not for one of his men's.

"Do you think they'd let me have some takeout?"

"For fuck's sake, Stan, is there ever a moment you don't think about food?"

He scowled at me. "No."

I rolled my eyes as I got to my feet. "If you're so fucking starving, stay here and eat. I'll head back to *Russu*."

"Because Jen called. I swear, you're pussy-whipped."

"And you're treading on thin ice," I replied softly. "I'd watch myself if I were you."

"What are you going to do? Stab me with one of her heels?"

"No, stab you with one of Evangeline's. Glass houses, *frate*, glass houses."

"You can throw stones at me, and I wouldn't shatter."

"No, because all the carbs you eat would protect you," I sneered. "I'm *not* pussy-whipped. She said she has information on the hockey player."

His brows rose. "*Our* hockey player?"

"Well, not exactly." I connected the call with Fi. "I'm on my way, *duci*. Can you tell me more over the phone?"

"The hockey player is related to the O'Donnellys."

Stunned, I snapped my fingers at Stan. "Get Aidan O'Donnelly Jr. on the line."

He frowned. "Why?"

"Just fucking do it," I sniped before I averted my attention to Fi. "How do you know this, *cara mia*?"

"Savannah just told me. Padraig O'Donnelly—"

"O'Donnelly Sr.'s brother? Isn't he dead?"

"Well, apparently, he isn't."

"What?" I boomed. "He's alive?"

"Yeah, comes as a surprise to me too."

"How does Savannah know this?"

"She's a journalist, remember? It's her job to uncover people's secrets."

I grimaced as distaste for her friend's profession filled me. I wasn't altogether certain why she'd forgiven Savannah, just knew that she'd been happier as a result.

For all that I loathed journalists, I knew bitching about Savannah's career wouldn't go down well.

"What do you wish me to do with this information, *vita mia*?" I asked her, keeping my attention on Stan as he struggled to get through to Aidan Jr.

"I-I don't know. Luc, I have to tell you something..." She swallowed. "At the beginning of the year, Savannah and I... you know we fell out?"

"I do."

"We fell out because she lied to me about how we met. Basically—and trust me, there's nothing basic about any of this—she told me she knew who my birth father was."

Of the many things I could have anticipated from her, that was the last thing I was prepared to hear.

It was one of those goddamn days—it didn't rain, but it poured.

"Your birth father?" I questioned warily. There'd been nothing in her file about a birth father. No name on the birth certificate aside from Diana's. Considering her profession, which Stan's investigation revealed she'd recommenced two months after giving birth, I'd thought Fi was the biological daughter of a john. "Who was he?"

She waited a beat before she whispered, "Padraig O'Donnelly."

Porca troia.

Mind whirring, I put two and two together quickly. "The hockey player is Padraig's son? Your half-brother?"

"Yes." She gulped. "Savannah told me that Padraig is in town. He's come to ask his brother for help with the ransom."

"I'll deal with this, Fi. Don't worry about it."

"I-I don't want to meet him, Luc." She sucked in a breath. "I just... if you know anything and can protect him, please, can you help?"

"I'll make sure nothing happens to him."

"Thank you," she whispered.

I heard the tension in her voice and hated it. "Fi?"

"Yes.

It was ridiculous. The need to stake a claim was pathetic. But she was *not* and never would be an O'Donnelly. *Over my dead body.* So I rumbled, "You're mine, *duci.* Remember that. You're mine; you're not an O'Donnelly. No matter who your birth father is. Say it."

After a moment's hesitation, she whispered, "I'm yours, Luc. I'm yours."

"*Se,*" I hissed, the welter of possessiveness that flooded me at her admission was borderline insane.

Stan ruptured the moment with, "Luciu, I've got Aidan Jr. on the phone."

"*Bedda mia*, go straight home. I'll meet you there and will bring you news."

I didn't wait for her to reply, just snagged the cell from my brother's hands as I cut our call. "I may have some interesting information for you."

I felt the Five Points' heir's hesitation down the end of the line, but since our initial meeting, a lot had changed.

As a gift, we'd handed him New York's archbishop on a platter.

"Your wariness grows irritating," I told him. "I bring you the man who covered up your brother's sexual abuse by one of the clergy, nicely trussed up as a gift just in time for *Natali*, and you greet me with such distrust?"

He exhaled roughly. "What is it?"

"The balance of favors is tipping evermore on my side," I informed him. "I'd appreciate a meeting with your father at some point to cement ties."

"Depends on how good the information you have for me is." He sighed. "I'm going to assume that you've heard about Liam Donnghal?"

"I have."

"Goddamn Savannah."

"These women of ours are not afraid to meddle where they should fear to tread," I concurred, mouth twitching. "They have big balls—"

"—and they're not afraid to fucking swing them," he snapped. "Okay, what is it?"

"I know where he is."

"You're shitting me?!"

"No. If I'd known you were connected to him, I'd have come to you first. As it stands, the Triads are heading there now."

"You sold him out?" Aidan snapped.

"Calm yourself, O'Donnelly," I grumbled. "A child of the Triads was also kidnapped. He's being held hostage with Donnghal."

"Jesus Christ, they took kids?"

"They did. It's why I came here first. We have access to a feed—the boy isn't doing so well."

"Shit, this is fucked up." A noisy exhalation rumbled in my ear. "Can you give me access to the location?"

"Of course. I'll send over the coordinates now."

There was silence, then, a pissed off: "We owe you."

"I'm glad you know it," I stated calmly. "But as our women are friends, I see no reason for our alliance not to hold firm. Do you? Alliances don't require favors to function."

He was quiet a second. "I agree."

"Good."

"I appreciate this."

"I'd still like a meeting with your father."

"I'll make it happen."

I cut the line, turned to Stan and said, "Send him the coordinates."

He nodded as I tossed the phone back to him. "They owe us."

"He knows it."

"*Bonu.* He agreed to the meeting with his father?"

"He did," I confirmed. "Once we've met with him, peace among the factions will be confirmed."

"Only after there's another Summit," Stan said with a shake of his head. "Until another meeting is called where the Triads, Irish, Bratva, and *Famiglia* get together, things are still unsanctioned."

I thought about how the Triads and now the Irish owed us. "After the past couple of weeks, you doubt that my position is cemented?"

"No," he countered. "But I'd like one of the men who owe us fucking favors to call a Summit to make shit official in the city. The news will spread then, better than whatever Rory can do with the press."

He wasn't wrong, but I had more important matters to deal with than speculating on this. "Once you've dealt with the O'Donnellys, stay here and eat."

With his focus on the screen, he replied, "I will. If you don't need me for anything else, I'll work on kitting out the laboratory."

"Okay, you deal with that."

"At least now, the Triads will leave us the fuck alone."

"I'm surprised they didn't send in their whole army—"

"No, they didn't want anyone to know. Who could blame them? Once struck, the weakness is exposed."

"True." I rubbed my chin. "They lost a lot of men."

"Unnecessarily."

I hummed, in complete agreement with my brother for once.

"Enjoy your food," I told him before I headed out of the back office and into the restaurant.

It was busy, lunch was being served, but there was a difference. Before, when we'd stepped through the door, I'd known there was a red alert as our identities were registered—every soldier in here had felt up their weapons.

Now?

The place was free of soldiers.

The Triads had taken their army to go and free Zhao's relative.

Bonu.

I hoped the fuckers who thought snatching a child was a business opportunity burned for their sins.

TWENTY-FOUR

JEN

IN A WAY that was oddly similar to how I'd come to his apartment the second time, I was waiting for him in the hallway as he stepped out of the elevator.

From between the opening doors, I caught him in the act of dragging off his winter coat and sliding it over his arm. The move tugged on his jacket, pulling taut against delicious muscles I slept against, had licked, and liked to drool over when I caught him coming out of the shower.

How was it that, in the shortest space of time, he'd become my safe place?

We were days into February, but the second I saw him, it was like I could breathe again. Like my lungs were capable of taking deeper inhalations now he was here.

After Savannah's revelation, I'd just needed to take this problem to him because I knew he'd fix it for me.

His gaze caught on mine, and he shot me a gentle smile. "I learned some information about the kidnappers behind your..." He hesitated. "...behind your half-brother's abduction. The O'Donnellys are retrieving him as we speak."

"I'm glad," I rasped, not even questioning this miracle because that was Luc. I knew he'd fix things, and he had.

I stepped forward as he dumped the coat on the floor, lifted his arms, and tucked me into his embrace.

Home.

God, *this* was home.

Not even caring that he'd left a mess on the floor, I sucked in a breath that was loaded with his scent, reveling in the sweet citrus notes of his aftershave while wanting to drown in the sandalwood that made it all the headier to inhale, and I murmured, "I'm sorry for the drama."

A soft laugh escaped him. I felt the vibrations against my cheek. "It was unexpected after a day of unexpected revelations, but I am *siculo*, Fi. Remember? We Sicilians live for this kind of thing."

"You do, huh? Well, here, this is shit that belongs on CBS or something. Daytime TV for the win."

"Mafia would be prime time, no?"

"Maybe. More likely to be picked up by Netflix."

"Would you sell your rights?"

Why was I surprised that he could make me grin? "Hell, yeah." I pulled back so he could see that he'd made me smile. "I can be bought."

"Good to know," he said with a snort. "Purses and vacations?"

I nodded. "Other things too now."

"Now? Not before?"

"Yep."

"What kind of things?" he inquired, his tone curious.

"Orgasms work."

He arched a brow. "You've orgasmed before, don't lie, *duci*."

"Jilling off is a lot different than a tongue fuck by you."

"See this face?" he asked.

"I see it."

"Consider it your throne, *riggina mia*."

I shuddered. "Well, there we go. You can bribe me by saying stuff like that."

He pressed a kiss to my lips. "Feel like sitting down?"

Groaning, I muttered, "I'm supposed to be upset."

"You can be upset later."

"I just found out my dad's alive," I chided.

He shrugged. "You're not going to tell him."

I scowled. "How do you know that?"

"Because I know you."

That made me huff. "Savannah didn't know that."

"Well, I'm different. I *see* you, Fi. I have from the very beginning. I see the wildcat and the drama queen, the shopaholic and the lost, little girl who wants to be loved. I want them all. Each one is like a facet in a diamond."

"Sicilian Darcy is at work, I see," I whispered, peering up at him with big eyes that, I'd admit, were loaded with need.

A need for him.

A desire for him.

A craving that was for this man alone.

"Do you ever just want to feel?"

He blinked. "Sometimes. I'm... I'll admit, I'm too controlled for that. I like everything in its proper place."

"I don't fit that."

"No. It's why I like you."

"Because I rock your world?"

He laughed. "*Se.*"

"On New Year's Eve, Savannah told me about my real biological father. That was why I came to you. I needed to feel. To fuck. I needed to be snapped out of the headspace I was in because I felt like I was in a tailspin and it wasn't going to improve with time." I sucked in a breath. "But I've never found pleasure in sex. Not until you. That's more of a gift than you know."

"Are you being serious?" he rasped.

"I really am. It was a tool, something to use to manipulate men, but I don't need to do that with you. I just... I was teasing before. I want you to know that." I licked my lips. "You have my loyalty, Luc. I will never betray you. *Ever.*"

"I knew that too," he whispered, reaching up to cup my cheek while he left his other one banded against my back. "I know you better than you know yourself."

"That's no fair," I said with a teasing pout. "I'm pretty sure I don't know you better than you know yourself."

"I think you know what matters most."

"That you like ice cream for breakfast, love fiercely, will spoil me rotten, and are cuddly in bed?"

He sniggered. "If you tell Stan any of those things, I will deny it."

I beamed a smile at him. "Our secret?"

"Our secret." Luc stroked his hand over my hair and whispered, "Want to sit on your throne, *riggina mia?*"

I really, really did.

My sex pulsed with the heat his words triggered in me, and I groaned when he let go of me then dipped down and hauled me into his arms.

"Your wrist," I yelped.

"It's fine."

"It won't be if you keep on abusing it," I grumbled, even as I tucked my arms around his neck.

"The day I can't carry you to bed is the day that I'm ready to die."

"I see that I'm not the only melodramatic one in this relationship."

He laughed. "I'm Sicilian...

"...you're Sicilian."

We both said at the same time.

Smiling, I hid my face in his throat but as I did, I saw Alina peering at me from the living room door, and before I looked away, I saw she was staring at Luciu with no small amount of surprise.

Was his laughter such a rarity?

When it fell so freely from his lips when we were together?

I hoped I made him happy. I really did.

Maneuvering us around the furniture once we were in the bedroom, he carefully lowered me to the bed, and as he did, he stared down at me.

"No more pants," he complained.

"Going to start wearing skirts, are you?" I mocked.

"When Brioni starts making them for men, sure."

Laughing, I reached down and unfastened the fly to my khakis.

They weren't as fashionable as I'd like, but damn, it had been cold this morning. I rocked up and off the bed, wriggled out of them, then hauled my turtleneck overhead.

It was a testament to how damn cold it was, that I wore a woolen vest. Beneath it, of course, there was a La Perla bra, which matched my cream and rose gold panties—I'd bought a couple more pairs with the ribbons at the sides because they were sexy as hell.

By the time I was naked, he was too, and I stared at him, watching as he flopped back onto the bed, his dick already hard against his abs.

Mouth watering at the sight, I stepped around the bed, approaching from the other side. His head rocked back to watch me, so I rolled my hips and gave him a show, then I climbed onto the mattress and crawled toward him.

When I reached him, I spread my legs and shimmied so that my pussy was over his face, and I got access to that delicious shaft that dicked me so, so, *so* good.

He grabbed at my ass and just as I was about to start licking the mess he'd made on his stomach, he rearranged me, using the fingers of his good hand to direct while using his cast to force me to move.

The position had me pressed up close and personal with his face, and I gulped, admitting, "Didn't think you meant it when you said you were my throne."

He didn't answer, just found my clit and immediately sent me soaring through the air.

What this man could do with his tongue...

Jesus wept.

For a second, my sight was fuzzy as I stared down at nothing, his dick there, an angry, throbbing red, but I was just focused on the zero-to-one hundred speed in which he'd found the right spot.

Rocking my pussy against his face, I didn't even wince when I felt his nose brush against me, didn't grimace at the slick sounds of my wetness making an appearance—I was all-in.

Then he nibbled one of my labia, and I squirmed, grinding into his face. He growled, and the vibration ripped through me like a bullet vibe. Except this was better because his tongue curled around my clit, making every inch of my sex throb in response.

It took me far too long to focus on his dick, but by the time I did, pre-cum bubbled out of his slit faster and faster.

I'd never known a guy as messy as this, but God, I loved it. I loved every fucking thing about him.

Laying the flat of my tongue against his taut abs, I lapped up his seed, then I flexed it along his length at the back, nipping here and there at the thick vein that traversed the nine inches of cock that always got me off.

When he growled again, I whimpered because damn, that felt so good. Too good.

Moaning, I sucked all the way down, focusing on the base before I sucked one of his balls into my mouth. I palmed them then, twisting them in my grasp, as I used my other hand to spread his legs wider, arching his leg up, then spreading them so that I could get further down below.

Not a lot of guys would let me do this, but when they did, they came harder and faster, which was exactly what I'd wanted in the past. If they got off quickly, then I didn't need to be pawed at.

This time, I was just focused on the pleasure it would give him.

Luc was... well, he was nothing I could have expected, everything I wasn't sure I deserved, but I'd take him, and love him, and hold him for forever if he'd let me.

As I licked my tongue around his balls again, he surprised me by arching his hips and...

Damn.

Well, there went my ovaries just exploding.

He rocked his ass back and widened his legs.

Fuck.

Just... fuck.

Was there anything this man wasn't down for?

God, I hoped we had decades to explore that theory.

Telling myself I was priceless was one thing, but here and now, I just hoped that he didn't get bored of me. That he didn't throw me out if I gained five pounds. That he'd stick by me as we grew old together. That we'd have a chance.

I wasn't a good person. I wasn't sure if happiness was meant for someone like me, but I was going to try to grab a firm hold of it, was going to try to give it to this man too. Maybe that would be enough.

Happiness and love.

Maybe that would tie him to me when I grew old and gray—

I squealed as he applied some intense suction on my clit, and because I needed to bring this man to his knees as much as he did me, I took advantage of his ease with his body, with his masculinity. Grabbing my breasts, I slipped his dick between them before I trailed the tip of my tongue down to a place that was a 'no go' for a lot of men and women.

Nothing was TMI for me.

No place was verboten.

Not with this man.

Never again.

He grunted as I rimmed him, fluttering my tongue in concentric circles that had his ass rocking back into the bed. Cock leaking cum against my tits, coating them with his stickiness, I smiled as I noticed his Dyson lips took a break as he enjoyed what I freely gave him. No expectations, no price tag. Just... an act given with love for the man I loved.

His hand tightened on my thigh, and I rocked so that he could breathe and had enough air to rasp, "*Vita mia*, if you don't sink that pussy onto my dick, we're gonna have a problem."

His accent was thicker than frozen custard, and I moaned in response to how I'd fractured his control.

Feeling no need to tease, I immediately complied, lifting my head, cocking my leg around so that I was on his side, before I shifted to straddle his hips. But he was ahead of me. He twisted around so that he was sitting up against the pillow, his body higher up now, and he patted his lap.

"Come, *cara mia*. I want to see that *culu*," he rumbled, so deep and so low that I felt it in my soul.

Twisting around so that my back was to him, I grabbed his cock, slotted it to my slick, slick, *slick* pussy.

Clearly, now he was home, he changed his mind because he pulled me against his chest, rearranged me as he raised his legs, so that when he spread them apart, he dragged mine wide open.

His fingers toyed with my clit from the get-go, and I had zero traction, had no alternative other than to let him fuck me from below.

The pressure shifted, all of it focused on my clit and G-spot, so when I exploded, splintering into a thousand shards, I just flowed with it because he gave me no choice other than to absorb the ecstasy he weaponized and used to suffocate me with a pleasure that was more addictive than carbs.

As I screamed, he roared out his release too as we both came simultaneously. Bodies taut, minds shot, sexes bound, hearts joined in a way, I prayed, would be forever.

TWENTY-FIVE

LUC

THE FIERI ESTATE WAS A MONSTROSITY.

Horrendous.

Ugly.

From the little I'd seen of it on the night we'd, in a word, *conquered* it, I knew that already. The more I got to see of it, though, the more it made me want to hurl because it went against everything that represented good taste.

The obscene extravagance was something Stan found amusing, that was why he showed me the gold-plated facilities in the master bathroom, led me to a sauna that had a sex swing in it, and guided me to a library with a section filled with an erotic literature collection that might have belonged to the Marquis de Sade.

When he showed me the newly converted laboratory, I hummed, asked about the expense, praised him when he expected it, then asked, "How long until C-L-O is ready?"

He scowled at me. "You busting my balls already?"

"Just waiting for the wunderkind to reveal his wunderproduct," I mocked.

His scowl only deepened. "Give me a chance. I haven't worked in a lab regularly for years. It'll take time."

I didn't bitch at him because I was only giving him the shit he kept hurling at me when it came to Fi, and as he made excuses and justified the millions this lab had cost us, I merely nosed around, admittedly impressed with what he'd accomplished over the last couple of weeks…

Saying that, plenty of other things had happened in that time too.

Great-uncle Currau was now a free man. Well, as free as he could be while bedridden. He was refusing visitors, and the doctors were even saying that he should be moved to a shared room because being by himself wasn't good for his mental health.

Five days ago, as a result of Currau's freedom, Rory had taken the plunge. The DA's office was in her past, and her future was about to be sealed within the next hour.

If she deigned to show up.

"You nervous?"

I scoffed at Stan. "No. Are you?"

He shrugged. "First time speaking as the Don."

"You're the one who should be nervous, having all these cunts in here."

His lips twitched. "I sectioned off the meeting hall. They can only access the rooms that I allow."

"How very anal of you."

"I try, I try," he mocked. "I don't want them sneaking around the place."

"You sure that final sweep of the house caught every bug."

"I checked every goddamn crevice myself, and I tell you what, I'm not letting any fucker into my private quarters."

"Not even to clean?"

"Not without a Sicilian watching the housekeeper."

I snickered. "So, you're gonna have a Sicilian watching the house-keeper, and a Sicilian watching the Sicilian watch the housekeeper?"

"Don't forget cameras. I'm gonna have those too."

"Pervert."

He smirked. "Nothing wrong with watching home movies. All consenting adults, and hell, I ain't about to let that footage leak. I want my dick out there less than those girls want their pussies on PornLand."

"Don't voyeurism and exhibitionism go hand in hand?"

Though he flipped me the bird, he was grinning as he flicked a finger over one of the counters, checking it for dust.

"Good to be here?" I asked softly, not teasing him this time.

I knew how long he'd put this goal off.

Some dreams would never be fully realized, but with the money we had in the bank, certain hobbies could be toyed with, especially when they were more of a vocation than a pastime.

"Very."

"You sure? I know it must hurt after what happened with Accursio."

Stan's jaw tightened, but he didn't comment. "The council room is as good as new by the way. The repairs are finished and because Fieri didn't believe in minimalism, I've shoved some of the overflow of furniture in there."

Taking the hint, I nodded. "Good job." Another glance around the room had me asking, "Is it ready to work in?"

"Yeah." He shot me a sheepish glance. "I might have to take up some classes."

"I think we can afford for you to take some time off." Especially as getting him into school would put off the C-L-O project.

His education suddenly became a priority to me.

"I wish I'd finished my degree." He stared around the lab, and though he looked at home, I could tell that he didn't altogether feel like that.

"Some things aren't meant to be."

If he'd have graduated according to plan, Custanzu would have been one of the youngest ever graduates at the *Università degli Studi di Palermo*. It was his getting into college early that had caused the family so many problems.

"You don't have to work on drugs when you're in here, Stan," I told him quietly—I'd always thought his talk of C-L-O was weird considering his own addiction issues in the past.

"What else would I do?" he questioned gruffly.

Studying him, I said, "You can work on the cure for fucking cancer, Stan. You don't need to work on C-L-O. You know I'm only messing with you—"

Before I could finish, a guard cleared his throat from the doorway and muttered, "Don? The Carusos, Vitales, Puglisis, Messinas, Randaz-zos, and Brunos are here."

"Are the Favaros?"

He shook his head.

I pursed my lips at the slight, then said, "If they show up, tell them to turn back around and go home. They're no longer welcome."

Giovi nodded and slipped out of sight.

"That wise?" Stan queried. "They're the only Italians at the table."

"They're disrespecting me by showing up late." I gritted my teeth. "I'm not about to encourage that kind of behavior."

He shrugged, which told me he agreed with me, and together, we headed out of the lab and walked through the room that housed the indoor pool that had more bare-titted statues than the Louvre, and up through the house toward the meeting hall where the Fieris had held council.

The Fieris had always been seated at the top, much like kings of old, and they'd had families—the Rossis and the Genovicos—at their right and left that had supporting roles in underboss positions.

When they'd run the Sicilians out of New York City, some had returned to the motherland like my *nanna*, others had fled to the West Coast, some to the South.

In my grandfather's time, those who *had* run, who hadn't stayed to fight, would have been considered cowards. But now, with so few Sicilian families remaining in the life, I was trying to re-seed the rightful people within the mafia.

So, no, I wasn't nervous about being the head of these fuckers, nor was I nervous about the announcements I was about to make.

This wasn't a fucking democracy.

The old way, my *nannu's* way, was to have five families ruling together, instigating a system of checks and balances that kept a leader from turning power mad.

However, I reigned over the goddamn lot of them, and they were only here, only welcomed back within the city's limits because my power grab had unlocked the gates for them.

That was something they needed to remember.

They were only here now because they hadn't fought for my grandfather's cause, and they owed us. Things would never be how they once were, but I didn't want them to know that.

The thought fueled me, and as I stepped toward the meeting hall, Rory slipped into place beside Stan.

"Nice of you to show up," Stan muttered behind me, but I didn't make a comment.

Sarcasm aside, I'd known she'd come, but she knew what she was giving up and my sister didn't like being backed into a corner.

The men in the meeting hall would know who she was, *what* she was, but no one else would.

Considering how damn smart she was, that had to sting.

Lorenzo opened the doors for us, and unlike our greeting of before, we sailed through, finding a council room that had been returned to its previous grandeur. One that I could now see was as ornately overdecorated as the rest of the place.

Stuffed sofas had been slotted into every available space around a massive fireplace that belonged in a goddamn castle. There were even suits of armor, tapestries on the wall of grand battles, all surrounding a table that was ten feet wide and twenty feet long.

"*Cristo*," Rory grumbled beneath her breath because this was the first time she was seeing it. "They weren't allergic to chintz, were they?"

Yeah, that about summed it up.

There was little to no damage remaining from the night of our siege, not that that came as a surprise. Stan was incredibly efficient and always good for his word.

As the door boomed behind me as it closed, the men standing around the room, each taking up their own small patch of space in here, turned around to face us.

Each family was represented by their head, their second, a *consigliere*, and a *capo*.

With six families, that meant twenty-four potential enemies or allies were under the same roof as my siblings and me.

Letting my gaze drift over each *famigghia*, it was clear to see where they had situated themselves after their exile.

The Caruso head wore a fucking Stetson, the Vitale's looked like he'd walked off a film set—who the hell wore sunglasses inside and in the middle of a miserable day in February? The Randazzos showed up in plaid shirts, shearling coats, and jeans. Only the Puglisis, Brunos, and Messinas looked in anyway fucking normal. And by normal, I meant, each wore an expensive suit.

I moved over to the head of the table, seated myself while Stan and Rory remained standing at my back.

It was a power play, and when I swept my hand in front of them, I rasped, "Take a seat."

It was their choice how they sat down, and from a psychological standpoint, it'd let me know who was still integrated into the life.

Not unsurprisingly, each of the Randazzos and the Carusos' men took a seat around the table, whereas the Vitales, Puglisis, Brunos, and Messinas all remained standing apart from the head of the family.

I shifted my glance around the room and said, "You know why I called you to the city. I have to assume that you wouldn't have agreed to be here if you weren't interested in what I have to offer—" I bridged my fingers together and placed them on my stomach. "—a slice of the *Cosa Nostra* as we rebuild the city and reclaim what was taken from us."

Randazzo raised a hand and said, "We're not in the life anymore, *but* we heard about what went down with the Fieris and on behalf of my family, we'd like to congratulate you and celebrate you as the new Don.

"My grandfather, when he died, was bitter about being exiled from the city. He set up in Wyoming, and the line continued there, but we're ranchers now and not a part of this world.

"Respect for him and for your family brought me here, and I'd like to thank you for the opportunity even though I have to decline your offer."

Because I appreciated candor a lot more than ass-licking, I nodded. "Your thanks are appreciated, and your family is always welcome in New York City. You can leave with no dishonor or disrespect between us."

As one, the four men scraped their chairs back, getting to their feet, before they moved down the table toward me.

I held out my hand for Randazzo to take, we shook, and they left.

Simple as that.

Bruno murmured, "We're ready to take back the city."

Messina nodded. "Our family is too."

Vitale said, "My grandfather mapped out a piece of land for himself in LA, but the Camorra aren't making things easy for us—"

"We won't help you with a turf war over on the West Coast," I drawled. "That isn't our game. New York City is our patch, and it's more than enough for us to handle.

"You want to come home, then you're more than welcome. But you'll leave your old lives behind, and Manhattan will become your priority."

Vitale's chair scraped back as he stormed off, none of the politesse of the Randazzos, but as they headed out, the *capo* stayed behind and said, "I have to apologize for my father, Don. We lost my elder brother to a turf war with the Camorra last week. He isn't handling the loss well."

Though anger at the bastard's disrespect rippled through me, I nodded at his son. "I appreciate the apology. Please, accept my condolences and take them to your mother."

"I will. Thank you. Well done on taking back the city, sir. You honor our ancestors." He bowed his head, then took the same path as the rest of his family.

That left the Carusos and Puglisis.

Puglisi dipped his chin. "We're in."

Short and sweet.

Caruso said, "We're in, but my granddaddy was smart. He bought a lot of land and black gold was on that territory." He rubbed his chin. "I ain't about to sell all that and leave Texas behind just to come and play Godfather up here.

"However, I'm tired of not being welcome in the city, and my daughter wants to study here. If there's a compromise we can come to..."

"What kind of compromise?" I inquired.

Caruso grunted. "I'm too old for this shit, but my boy? He's interested." He motioned to a guy a little older than Stan, his eyes glittering as he nodded at me. "Would you be willing to have him represent my family?"

"More than interested." Young blood would suit my purposes better than old.

We'd gotten rid of the old, and I didn't want to cloud it up with traditional mindsets.

Not with Rory being here.

"I'm glad to hear it." Caruso's chair scraped back, and he got to his feet. "The Vitale boy said it a lot better than I can, but he was right—you honor our ancestors by taking back the city on their behalf." He strode down toward me and said, "I'll leave the city to you and wish you well with it."

I bowed my head. "Appreciated."

When he left, his family staying behind, clearly men who wanted to be involved in the business, I said, "Each line is Sicilian. I invited an Italian here, the Favaros, but they decided to fuck me around and be late.

"We still have a lot of Italians on our front line, and plenty aren't happy about having a Sicilian back in charge. I intended to ease their concerns by having Italians on the council, but if they're going to mess me around, then they can go fuck themselves."

"Agreed," Bruno muttered. "Wouldn't want Italian cunts on the fucking council anyway."

"It was smart," Messina countered. "The Don's right. I've looked into the situation in the city. Too many Italians still working as made men, on the front lines, doing the dirty work.

"With new leadership, it'd have been a good idea to have familiar faces on board. But the disrespect can't be tolerated."

"Why did you select them, Don?" Caruso queried.

"They were the family who were the least close to the Fieris with the largest population of living made men."

"Did they have hopes of taking your seat?" Puglisi asked.

"I would assume so. They've shoved themselves into obscurity with their disrespect, and I don't want to waste any time on them."

"For the best," Puglisi concurred, "but, Don, before we get down to business, do you think we should be having this conversation while your wife is in the room?"

I graced him with a look. "Aurora isn't my wife. She's my *consigliere.*"

For a second, there was silence, then the Puglisis all burst out laughing, a couple of the Messinas chuckled, but the Brunos and Carusos earned brownie points with their silence.

"Did I say something funny?" I snarled, leaning forward, temper making the vein at my temple tic with outrage on my twin's behalf.

"Don't I know you?" Caruso queried before any of the fuckers who thought my sister was a joke could answer me.

"I doubt it," Rory replied. "I've never been to Texas."

Caruso drummed his fingers against the table. "I'm sure I've seen you on TV."

"Maybe you have," I rumbled. "She was a DA for New York for the last four years."

Silence fell around the table, then Caruso smirked. "Smart, very fucking smart."

"That's why she's my *consigliere.*" I scowled at the Messinas and the Puglisis. "That's why, if you have a fucking problem with her, then you can walk straight out that goddamn door like the Vitales and Randazzos did."

Puglisi shook his head. "Now, Don, there's no need for that."

"There's every fucking need," I snapped. "Since the beginning, she's acted as my *consigliere.* However, I understand the precarious position this puts some of you in. We're a traditional people, and I'm not blind to that.

"Aurora has agreed to marry and, in public, her husband will act as my *consigliere.*"

Puglisi settled back, apparently appeased by that.

Caruso frowned. "This isn't the sixties. Women can be in positions of power too."

"I don't dispute that."

"My brother's reign has already been undermined by several clusters of Italians who seek to overthrow a Sicilian Don.

"I have no desire to cast aspersions on his abilities to lead. It isn't his fault the mafia is a sexist cesspool," Aurora bit off. "When I've proven myself, and the day will come, that's when I'll step forward but for now, I'm willing to play to the rules of the *Famiglia.* In public, at least."

"You *will* afford her the respect and the *fear,*" I emphasized, "befitting someone in her position, gentlemen. *Capisci?*"

Four sets of *capiscis* echoed around the meeting hall... I considered that a job well done for my first official day leading the *Famiglia's* council.

Now that was settled, we had real business to discuss.

TWENTY-SIX

JEN

AFTER AOIFE BLEW me off for the fourth time, I'd admit, I was starting to think up unusual ways of seeing her.

I nixed the idea of urban climbing, simply because their building was way too high up and I wasn't athletic by choice.

The prospect of waiting for her to go to the bakery she owned, only to leap out reminded me of *Punk'd*. Getting Finn to sneak me inside wasn't going to work seeing as Aoife was ignoring me for a reason, and he was duty bound to take her side.

I just wasn't sure what that reason was.

Logic dictated that I hadn't caused her miscarriage, but did logic matter when you were grieving?

I knew for a fact that it didn't.

Still, when I showed up at their apartment, I approached with the idea that I wasn't going to get in, and that I really needed to manage my disappointment levels because I was about to be crushed.

The doorman, however, when he saw me, waved and let me ride up to their floor, and when the doors pinged open, I blinked with surprise because I hadn't expected that.

Maybe I was the one who was about to get punk'd?

Peering out, I saw Finn at the end of the hall in the living room and watched as he strode toward me now the elevators had pinged their warning. When his eyes caught on mine, his brows rose.

"Jen?"

I frowned at him. "Yeah?" I wasn't sure why my name was a question. "I'm Jen. Is it that long since you've seen me that you don't remember what I look like?"

"No."

"Then?" I asked, when he carried on looking at me. "What's the problem?"

"No problem. You just look... happy." His gaze scanned me. Not because he was checking me out—for all his faults, I knew Aoife was literally the only woman he saw—more like he was trying to verify that I actually *was* Jennifer MacNeill.

"Did I look constipated before or something?"

"Maybe. You just look different."

"Is that Jen?" Aoife called out before she stepped into the hall, making my smile freeze when I saw how much weight she'd dropped.

Aoife was what I liked to think of as being pleasantly plump. I bet when she and Finn fucked, they bounced off each other. I'd always envied her her curves, but they'd disappeared some. Her face was drawn, a little gaunt at the cheeks, and I could tell that she hadn't been sleeping well.

I wanted to go and hug her, but I wasn't the hugger in our friendship, so I just hovered there awkwardly, until I blurted out, "You freezing me out, Eef, is a low blow."

Her eyes narrowed upon me. "I was just going through some stuff."

"Yeah, well, you don't cut out your BFF, bitch."

"Watch it, Jen," Finn growled out a warning.

"It's okay, Finn, she's right." Her chin tipped up. "I've been ignoring everyone."

"I'm not 'everyone.'"

"Agreed. Do you want some cake? I made some for a guest who's coming over this afternoon."

"Oh, shit. That's who the doorman thought was coming over, right? I figured he wouldn't let me up—"

"I didn't put a block on you coming up, Jen. Jeez. I just didn't feel like talking." Her smile was wan. "I still don't feel like it, but I have to get on with life, right?"

Finn frowned at that. "No. You take it as slow as you want."

"Flopping around the apartment crying isn't getting me anywhere." She wafted a hand at me. "Come on, let's eat. Padraig is coming to see Jake and Finn."

"That's not true. I'm sure he wants to get to know you too."

I almost froze up at the mention of Padraig because, in these parts, there were many Patricks, a helluva lot of Paddies, but Padraig? Nope.

And certainly not under this roof.

Gulping, I followed Aoife, well aware that Finn's concerned gaze clung to his wife, and as we made it into the kitchen, I plunked the gift bags I'd brought over onto the counter, tried not to stare at the floor where a puddle of blood had once been, and I flung myself at her.

I didn't care that she had her back to me, didn't give a damn that she tensed up or that she was bony. It just felt so damn good to be near her again. So much so that the non-hugger of our daring duo seriously needed a hug.

"I missed you," I groused, squeezing her waist.

"Missed you too, Jen," Aoife whispered.

"Then why cut me out?"

"Because I-I don't know..." She sighed, and I thought it might have been easier because her back was to me so I couldn't see her expression. "I just wanted to be alone."

"You're not made to be alone." She'd been raised with two women, and I'd almost always been hanging out too. Aoife was not a person who did well on her own. "I'd have come and hung out. You didn't have to isolate yourself."

"I did. I wasn't fit for company. I was crying all the time, either that or sleeping. I just..." She blew out a breath. "It was hard. I was really happy, and then, I just wasn't."

"I'm so sorry, Eef," I whispered, miserable for her. "I shouldn't have sprung my news on you. I just, well, I tell you everything."

"It wasn't your fault."

I didn't discern a trace of bitterness in her voice, so I knew she wasn't lying.

If anything, she sounded more resigned than anything.

"No?" I whispered.

"No." She patted my hand. "The OB/GYN said it was high risk. She even said..." Her gulp was audible. "She told me that I should terminate the pregnancy."

"Finn never said—"

"He didn't know. I went without him to that appointment." She bit her lip before she admitted, "I knew something wasn't right."

"Oh, my God, Eef." That was massive. Those two shared everything.

"I knew what he'd say. I didn't want to hear it. I knew what you'd say too," she muttered mulishly. "I didn't want to hear that either."

"Were you in danger?"

When she didn't answer, Finn did instead. "Yeah. She was. If she hadn't miscarried, and if the baby had gone to term, it could have killed her."

I heard his fury, heard his hurt, and I got it. Totally.

I also knew why Aoife had shut me out, had, perhaps, even shut Finn out.

She knew we wouldn't get it.

She knew what we'd say.

And, as she'd just told me, she didn't want to hear it.

"Our baby wasn't an 'it,' Finn," Aoife snapped, sounding angrier than I'd ever heard her before. Which made me realize that here was another reason why she'd cut me out—Aoife and Finn were at war over this.

Unused to seeing the loved-up couple at each other's throats, I commented, "I could really do with some cake."

Well aware that husband and wife were glaring at each other, my words crumbled into dust as Finn snapped, "What the fuck would Jake and I have done without you, Aoife? How the fuck would we have—" His voice broke off, and then he did the damnedest thing. His hands flopped up like he couldn't take anymore, and he walked away.

Finn.

Walked.

Away.

He didn't leave the apartment or anything, but he left the room, and as he did, it was like any spark that was left in Aoife fizzled into nothingness.

Those two were like living flames that kept the other burning bright. I'd never seen a more accurate representation of that than I did now.

Why did life have to throw curveballs like this? Why did it have to fuck things up for people when everything was going great?

Aoife sniffled before she shuffled away and pulled out a cake, and because everything was upside down right now, I actually ate the slice she served me when she placed the dish in front of me.

I hated lemon drizzle, she knew that, but I ate it anyway because, damn, I needed something—a pick me up—to help me find my equilibrium.

As she poured us both coffee, then sat down at the counter, we both heard the ping of the elevator once more.

She ignored it, but I didn't.

I perked up, just waiting to hear the voice of the man who was my father, and when it came, it was...

Well, it fell flat.

Maybe I thought my ears would tingle or the earth beneath my feet would tremble, but there was nothing like that. It was just a raspy voice.

A little old, a little gruff, like he'd smoked all his life or something.

Nothing special.

Nothing that made me think, 'That's my dad.'

"I heard about Padraig doing a resurrection." I forked up some cake and shoved it into my mouth to keep my tongue busy.

"The boys are the only ones who are happy about it," she replied softly, her focus on the coffee. "You should have seen their dad when Padraig showed up. Thought he was going to have a fit."

"He didn't?"

"No. Finn told me the brothers had a massive argument though."

"I'll bet. You don't pretend to be dead and think there won't be any repercussions when you return," I mumbled.

"He didn't want to. His son is that hockey player who got kidnapped." She cleared her throat. "He came to ask Sr. for some cash for the pay off."

"Is he home now?" I questioned.

"I think so. I haven't met him. He went back to Canada. It's the middle of the NHL season, and he didn't want to miss any games."

"Christ, he's just been kidnapped and he went straight back to work?"

"Guess he didn't want to mope around." She reached up and rubbed her eyes. "I know how he feels. I'm sick of this place."

"You haven't been going to the bakery?"

"No. Finn had Louise take over for a while." Louise was her assistant manager. "I should check in, start to get on with things. Life isn't over because my baby—" Her voice cut off and tears pricked my eyes.

"Let it out, Eef. You know this is a safe spot with me."

"Finn doesn't get it."

I shrugged. "I don't get it. But I don't have to, do I? It matters to you, and that's what counts."

When Aoife began weeping, I reached over and slid my arm around her shoulders. When she burrowed into me, I held her.

That was the only thing I could do.

Hold on, not let her go, and be there for her when she needed me the most.

I didn't say anything, but, I understood Finn's point of view.

Where would *I* be without her?

My stance didn't count, but Finn's did, and for the first time in their marriage, I knew I was going to play devil's advocate on his behalf.

Aoife didn't want to hear it, but Finn was right. She had no business taking such risks with herself when she had a toddler who needed her more than anyone else in this world.

I'd have to work on getting her to see that if she was going to be able to move on.

But for now, I just hugged her as she cried, as she let out her grief for the child that would never be, and for the future that would always be different than she'd planned.

TWENTY-SEVEN

LUC

"OH, GOD, LUC!" Fi screamed, her hands in my hair, her fingers tugging at the locks as I ate her out, savoring her like she was the finest Bordeaux, feasting on her—

My cell rang.

If I'd had my knife close by, I'd have stabbed the fucker straight through, but it was the ringtone I couldn't ignore.

Rachel.

As Fi sobbed through her orgasm, I stayed close, sucking on her clit until she was wriggling and writhing underneath me, her sensitive flesh unable to take any more attention.

With a soft kiss to her slick pussy, I started to pull back, and though I'd have liked to dive on top of her and press a kiss to her mouth, I didn't.

Instead, I dropped one on her inner thigh then shoved off the bed and grabbed my phone.

Wiping her juices off my jaw, I answered it, demanding, "Everything okay?"

"When I got your uncle out," she greeted, "I had to pull in a massive favor with the State's Attorney General."

Mind still fixed on my *riggina's* pussy, it took a second for me to process what she was saying.

Scrubbing my forehead, I asked, "He's called it in now? So early?"

She hummed.

"What does he want?" I asked, turning away from the temptation that was my woman on the bed, her legs splayed, her entire body replete with satisfaction.

"Do you still have that cabin in Nevada?"

If I sounded wary, then so be it. "*Se.*"

"He wants that."

"Fucking corrupt bastard."

Rachel's grunt was dismissive. "Like you didn't already know that. And let's be grateful that he is."

"You know what that cabin is?"

"A shelter made of wood? What's the problem? Go and build another one."

"It's a high-class resort for businessmen with certain proclivities."

Rachel scoffed, "It's a brothel?"

"*Se.* It is." I scrubbed my chin. "If he even knows about it, that means he has those kinks."

I wasn't sure if that made the prospect of losing a business that made over two million a year in profit—tax-free profit at that—more or *less* palatable.

"You're into sex trafficking?" Rachel growled.

"These women aren't trafficked," I jeered. "Jesus, they're there because they make half a million a year." I tried to imagine Madam Domina being beholden to anyone and failed. "Plus, it's Nevada. That's not illegal there. The only illegal shit going down in that place is tax evasion because I highly doubt those ladies are paying the IRS all their dues."

"Half a million?" Rachel questioned dubiously. "What are they doing to earn that?"

"Keeping secrets, mostly," was my dry retort. "People wouldn't like knowing that their Senator enjoys taking bright pink, ten-inch dildos up their ass while wearing a minidress and high heels."

"Christ. You know I have to work with the State's Attorney General, don't you? I'll never unsee that, and Foundry is already a goddamn sleaze ball."

"You shouldn't have asked then," I drawled, but I quickly conceded, "He might not be into that, but only a select number of men are even aware of that goddamn cabin. They don't let the news out to just anyone."

As far as I knew anyway.

That was Rory's side of things.

I didn't like the skin trade. Never had.

"I'll bet," she grumbled. "Anyway, are you going to hand it over to him?"

"He can have it."

"I'll let him know."

She cut the call, leaving me rubbing my chin as I contemplated telling Rory we'd just lost one of our prime sources of blackmailing material.

Shit.

Still, she'd needed that back in the DA's office. As *consigliere*, I wasn't going to say it wouldn't have been a useful tool in our arsenal, but she'd been fighting a damn sight longer than I had for Currau's release, so I knew she'd relinquish the right to the brothel without much argument.

"What is it?" Fi asked, and I twisted around, sighing at the sight of her decorating my bed.

"You're fucking gorgeous, do you know that?" I kissed my fingers. "*Bedda.*"

She blinked, but laughed. "Well, I'll take compliments like that any day."

"Good. You should." Tapping my cell phone against my chin, I answered her question, "There are complications from Currau's release."

"His health?" She sat up and leaned back against her elbows. "Is he still refusing to let anyone in to visit him?"

"He sure is," I agreed gruffly, appreciating her concern for a man she'd never even met. "But it's not that. The doctors said he's responding well to treatment." Amazing what they could do after Stan threatened to cut off their balls if they didn't fix our great-uncle. "Getting him out early came with a high price."

"You just learned how high?"

I shot her a smile. "You're astute this early in the morning."

She snickered and flopped back against the pillows. "Well, I'm not the one with the boner."

Because losing myself in her seemed a far more pleasurable pastime than dealing with Rory, I pressed one knee to the bed then growled when my phone rang again.

"I'm going to get showered," Fi muttered, rolling off the bed and striding to the bathroom.

I watched that ass go, but I didn't call her back because it was Hügel, and Hügel only contacted me when he had information for sale.

"I have good news, Mr. Valentini," he greeted me.

As suspected. "I wish I got more calls from you, Hügel. I like good news." I just didn't get it often.

Hügel grunted—he didn't appreciate small talk, and he considered jokes and social niceties to be small talk. Was it any wonder I liked this guy? "I believe I've found the Anjou ring."

"You believe or you know?" I didn't pay him to doubt.

"If I say, 'I believe,' you won't cut off my hand," Hügel drawled. "There is only one way to ascertain the truth and that is a lab test, as well you know."

"And the buyer won't agree to it?"

"The buyer doesn't want to sell," Hügel retorted. "She's quite content to keep the ring. It requires a man far more persuasive than myself to encourage her to sell."

I heaved a sigh—these goddamn rubies. "Where are they?"

"Monaco. Lady Francesca will be staying at the Hotel de Paris for the next ten days."

Mentally flipping through my upcoming schedule, I asked, "What information do you have on her?"

"The family isn't impoverished, but she lost her father and the death duties in Britain are crippling on an estate as large as the one her brother inherited."

Having owed them myself after Grandfather's death, I knew that *crippling* wasn't an understatement.

"She got the jewels?"

"Yes, unusual arrangement. The brother inherited the title, the estates, but Lady Francesca retained a smaller inheritance with some key, *expensive* pieces."

That she was being heavily taxed on.

"How much are we talking here on death duties?"

"If she sells the ruby ring, they'd be paid."

"But she doesn't want to?"

"No. It's understandable, Mr. Valentini. It's a beautiful ring."

"Being debt-free is better."

"Apparently she doesn't agree. She's been juggling these debts for the last two years."

My brows rose at that information, but I merely said, "I'll fly in today."

"I'll let her know you'd like a meeting."

Hügel fell silent, but I knew that if he was done, he'd have just hung up the phone. So I prodded, "What is it, Hügel?"

"She's a beautiful lady, Mr. Valentini. Key word there being *lady*. I hope you won't..."

"Cut off her hand?" I remarked, well aware of where he was taking this.

"Well, yes, to be frank."

"I make no promises."

I cut the call before he could say anything, then hearing a whooshing sound, turned around and found Fi watching me from the doorway to the bathroom as she brushed her hair.

"Into amputation now, are we?"

I smiled at her inclusion. "Will you hold the knife for me, *cara mia*?"

Her nose crinkled. "No. I've done enough slicing to last a lifetime."

Wincing, I said, "Sorry, Fi. I shouldn't have joked, not so soon after—"

"It's okay." Her smile was genuine. "I mean it, Luc. It really is."

She sounded like she thought she believed that, but Fi, for all that she had dubious morals in some regards, wasn't as *immoral* as she thought.

"I have no intention of cutting off anyone's hand. Not this week."

"Good to know," she said with a chuckle. "Where are you flying in?"

"Where are *we* flying in," I corrected with a tut, stepping over to her then hauling her against my chest so I could palm her ass. Fuck, I was sick of this cast getting in the goddamn way.

"We? I just got a new job, Luc," she mocked. "I can't leave on vacation now."

"Can't you though?" My eyes twinkled. "I need personal, hands-on assistance with my tax evading for the next couple days or so."

Laughing, she shook her head. "You're a nut. But I guess you're also the boss, so who am I to say no?" I'd have been a moron if I didn't see the gleam of anticipation in her eyes. "Where are we going?"

"Monaco."

Her eyes flared wide. "Monaco?" she breathed.

I smiled. "Yeah."

Her squeal of excitement would have woken the dead, but who was I kidding? She woke up the dead parts of my fucking soul every goddamn day and if the dead complained about a little noise, well, screw them.

She planted her mouth on mine, bestowing an excited kiss on my lips that ended with her laughing with glee as she danced away, talking about packing. I let her go, but only because I had to update Rory who, unsurprisingly, wasn't happy.

Not about losing the brothel, not about the ring, not about any goddamn thing.

"You're more of a grouch than usual," I chided.

"No, you're just annoyingly *filici*."

"Annoyingly happy? They're the words you're settling on? Aren't you happy that I'm happy?" I prodded, even though I wasn't offended.

I felt as if our family had been stuck in the stasis of mourning our father for so long that we didn't know how to get out of it.

That we were trapped within the vendetta we vowed to live by to avenge his death.

Grief had become our *carcere*—our prison.

Rory didn't answer, just sighed. "This is a setback, Luc. I mined that place for a lot of information, and you heading off to Europe when you're only just assimilating your forces here in the city isn't good timing."

"You and Stan will be here," I pointed out.

"You're the Don. Stan should be the one who goes."

I thought about the glee and the excitement in Fi's face and immediately nixed that idea. "No. I'll go. It'll be a three-day trip, Rory. No one will even know I've left."

"The second you file the flight plan, people will know," she argued.

"Then figure out how to make my trip incognito. What's the fear? Someone will blow me out of the sky? Don't think the Favaros have that level of power yet," I drawled.

"What if she doesn't want to sell?"

"I can be persuasive."

"Not *that* persuasive," she retorted with a huff. "I'll deal with it and send you some leverage."

"If it's too much trouble," I mocked, "I can pick up a phone myself."

"I said I'll deal with it."

"Like you're dealing with this mole situation with the Bratva?" I taunted.

She huffed. "I think I preferred it when you were a miserable bastard. I'm working on it. No one's showed their hand yet."

"Then fucking make them. If you don't want me getting involved and you want to handle this, strike back first." Before I ended the call, I told her, "I'm flying out today."

I had an appointment with Lady Francesca, and she had a ring that needed to be on my woman's finger.

Aieri—yesterday.

TWENTY-EIGHT

JEN

MONTE CARLO WAS EVERYTHING.

Literally, *everything*.

It was tiny, cramped, busy, but even though it was winter still, it was just extra.

Extra the adjective, not the adverb.

I was in love.

Absolutely in love.

It had nothing to do with this being my first time out of the States and in Europe. Nothing to do with how ultraluxe everything was. It was just... beautiful. And old. So old.

From our suite in the Hotel de Paris, named for Princess Grace, I stood on the glass-walled terrace and peered out onto the harbor, seeing the casino beside us with its twin turrets, the stormy navy blue of a still wintry ocean.

There were buildings everywhere—it was so tight and so clustered that it could have been claustrophobic, but from my place up here, it was just glorious. There were construction sites dotted here and there, modern condos that were the future homes of next year's tax evaders.

In the harbor, the real difference between billionaires and million-aires was on display in the form of superyachts that had basketball courts and private pools on them that neighbored baby yachts which were only capable of heading out into the water—talk about slumming it.

From the cramped roads, I could hear the booming engines of the hundreds of sports cars that were at a standstill thanks to a traffic jam of Lamborghinis and Ferraris.

Craggy cliffs were loaded with widespread mansions that looked over the principality, and at the center of the chaos, I stood in a small pool of sunlight, dressed in a pair of jeans, some boots, and a sweater because, while it was cold, it was definitely warmer than back home.

Leaning over the balcony rail, I absorbed my first real look at Europe and tried not to swoon—it was everything I wanted it to be, and so much more.

A soft exhalation escaped me, and I smiled when I felt Luc's heat at my back.

In full on ghost mode, he placed his hands on either side of my arms on the railing and settled his chin on my shoulder.

"You'll get cold."

"It's warm," I argued.

"It's cold," he grumbled.

"I'm warm. Can't you feel the sun on your head?" I sighed. "It's bliss."

"I figured that out when you didn't come inside the suite an hour ago."

A shocked laugh escaped me. "I've been out here an hour?"

"*Se.* I thought I'd lost you, but no, here you are. Staring out onto the ocean."

"Well, the ocean's boring. It's the town that's interesting. Look at it." I released a delighted sigh. "I love it."

"I'm glad, *vita mia.* Just wait until I take you to Catania." He pressed a kiss to the side of my throat. "You'll love the estate even more. We have views over the ocean and across the city, and there's so much more space than here."

"You don't like it?"

"It reminds me of New York. Cramped, crowded. Our estate is the opposite. Plus, it used to belong to the Anjou family. They sold it in the eighteen hundreds. It feels right being back where my people are from."

"That's because you're a history nerd."

"True," he agreed unapologetically.

"I'm guessing you don't have a Valentino store adjoining the house like this hotel though?"

He laughed. "I have a Valentini store."

"What does it sell?"

"Ohh, I don't know... anything your heart desires?"

That had me sighing even more than the spectacular view. "I probably don't deserve for you to be so kind."

"Says who?"

"Me? I'm not a nice person."

"You think I am?" His laughter was more of a cackle this time. "I'm not a good person either. If you were a good person too, then we couldn't be together. I wouldn't allow myself to tarnish you."

I snorted. "Is there supposed to be a compliment in there?"

"There is a compliment—I love you exactly how you are."

"Wow," I whispered, stunned by his words as I twisted my head to the side and rubbed my cheek against his temple. "That *is* a massive compliment."

He hummed, then teased, "Plus, we have a mailman. He comes by regularly so if you need anything you can just ship it in."

"I was only teasing about the Valentino thing. I'm sure I'll love your estate."

If he thought it was better than *here*, how couldn't I?

"We have an olive grove, then there are fields just filled with orange trees in the spring.

"For a few weeks a year, every tree is loaded with blossoms, and when you drive by, it perfumes the air. There are herb gardens and a patch of land where *Matri* used to grow vegetables..."

"Simple times?"

"*Se.* Before everything got so complicated."

"I'm sorry, love."

He stilled. "It's the first time you called me that."

"It is?" I kissed his cheek. "Well, I'll be sure to rectify that."

"*Bonu,*" he rumbled, sounding so frickin' Sicilian that I almost melted.

I still took it as a great sign when his voice grew accented.

"Are we going this time?"

"No. I have to get back to the city. It's still too early to be leaving it for long." He kissed my shoulder. "Next time."

"Promise?" I whispered.

"*Supra l'onori de mi matri.*"

"What does that mean? I understood the word *matri*. That's mom, right?"

"It means, 'on my mother's honor.'"

I whistled under my breath. "Damn, you're going hardcore with that promise, aren't you?"

"When I make *you* a promise, it's always *supra l'onori de mi matri*."

Well, there was no mistaking that.

"Luc?" I murmured. "I don't have much honor in my family, none really, but... when I make you a promise, I mean it too."

"I know, *cara mia*. Now, I don't have to meet with Lady Francesca for a few hours. Do you want to go out and shop?"

Smiling, I shook my head and said, "No. Can we just stay here?"

"Are you sure?"

"Positive. Tomorrow, there's some work I could do. Some connections that would be smart to make because I've spoken with them on the phone before, you know? But not today... today, I'd just like to be here."

"I will, but there's an 'if.'"

"Hit me with it."

"You'll eat lunch with me."

I tensed. "Okay."

He clucked his tongue. "I won't poison it."

"I know," I retorted. "I didn't think you would."

A hand pressed to my stomach. "One day, when this is big and round and full with our son, I'm going to bring you back here and fuck you over this railing."

My heart skipped a beat, an ache stirred to life in my core, and my soul just... God, I wanted to cry.

"You want that with me?"

"I think I already have that with you. You forget that first night together after Aspen?"

"No. But I don't know yet…"

"I do. I know. And if it didn't happen then, then we haven't been taking care to prevent it, have we?"

Unease filled me. "I haven't tried to trap you—"

His laughter was loaded with a warm amusement, no bitterness or anger.

"What's so funny?" I groused when he didn't stop with the chuckling.

"Nothing, *vita mia.*" He pressed a kiss to my cheek. "But this is why you have to eat."

Stung, I tensed up. "I eat."

"You need to eat more. It's all good. I'm Sicilian. I know how to eat. I'll teach you."

A snort escaped me. "I can eat."

"You just choose not to to stay thin." He grunted. "I know. But I'm Sicilian," he repeated. "Your curves won't offend me but turning away pasta will."

My body was my product.

Being slim was what men wanted…

I gritted my teeth, and the only concession I could make was, "I'll have a salad."

"*Bonu, bonu,*" he repeated, his tone hearty. "I'll go make an order with room service."

He left me there with a gentle squeeze around my waist, and as he left, I wondered if I felt different. If I really *was* pregnant or not. I'd had no signs. Not really. No morning sickness, none of the super sniffer shit that had plagued Aoife with Jacob.

But Luciu was so certain…

Which left me with the question of how a man so traditional, who believed a woman was pregnant with his child, who he said he loved… *hadn't* proposed.

For the first time in my life, I didn't want to hear the question for financial security. I *craved* it for emotional stability. Something I'd vowed to myself that I'd never leave in the hands of a man.

Men always break their promises, don't they?

My mother had lived her life learning that lesson one after another, and I'd been raised believing that I was worth less because I wanted more...

Would Luciu let me down like Padraig had let her down?

Was I destined to live the same life as her?

My mouth firmed at the thought, because *no*. Just, no.

Even if I was alone, I could be a great mom, and I had Aoife and Savannah. They'd help.

Under my breath, with the Mediterranean in front of me, the crystal blue skies overhead, I placed my hand on my stomach and whispered, "I'm not her, and I will *never,* ever be like her."

And I didn't make that promise for myself, but for the baby I almost *hoped* was stirring to life inside me.

TWENTY-NINE

LUC

HOURS LATER, my lips still twitched over our conversation on the terrace.

The notion that she'd tried to trap me was a hilarious one.

If anything, I was doing my level best to seal that particular deal. Not just every time I made love to her, but tonight.

I wanted that damn ring, and I wasn't about to take no for an answer.

Having left her at the casino with some pin money, I returned to the Hotel de Paris and made my way to the suite number Hügel had emailed me yesterday.

Reaching the room, I knocked on the door and waited until it opened to reveal a woman wearing a very beautiful red gown. Instinct had me checking her out for weapons, but when my gaze found her hand, that was where I faltered.

The ruby.

She was wearing it.

And I knew.

I fucking knew.

Much like I had with the tiara, I *knew.*

I needed no test to confirm it—this was the Anjou ring.

I'd seen it in pictures, but the resolution was too limited to get a strong idea of its true appearance.

A large cabochon ruby, not faceted but polished so that it was gleaming in the light from the hallway, over fifteen carats in size, dominated her finger.

It was heavy, the gold old and yellow, a faint brassiness to it as was indicative of its antiquity, but it was surrounded by small diamonds that seemed to enhance the blood red hue. There were no streaks of purple or orange to mar the sheer, unadulterated *red* of the stone, and it draped on the woman's hand as if the weight made it impractical to wear.

The second I saw it, I knew that it wasn't made for 'real life.'

Fi would never be able to roam around Manhattan wearing it. I didn't mind putting four or five extra guards on her, but it was the kind of ring that would fall down the drain after washing your hands. She could lose it and the *famigghia* needed it for our star to rise.

For all that it was an impressive piece, for all that I knew she'd only ever be able to wear her engagement ring on special occasions, I couldn't take my eyes off it.

Without even stepping into the room, I let my gaze return to Lady Francesca's, and I asked, "How much?"

Surprise had her lashes fluttering slightly, but she said, "It's not for sale, Mr. Valentini. My brother owed Hügel a favor. That was the only reason I decided to see you."

"What do you want for it?"

"My father gave this to my mother as a present when she gave birth to me. That kind of memory isn't something that can be bought."

"That ring was in my family for centuries. You can't talk about history without taking into account that that ring was stolen from my grandparents."

Her eyes narrowed. "You can't prove that."

"I don't need to. I'm just asking, politely, how much do you want for the ring?"

Mouth tight, she snapped, "It's not for sale."

"Everything's for sale, Lady Francesca." I smiled at her. "Now, we can do this the nice way where you claw yourself out of debt, or we can do this the nasty way and I tell you that I know where your brother lives, and I'm not afraid to use that information for my own gain."

"You're threatening me?" she squawked.

I nodded. "I sure am. However, I'm a fair man. I'm more than willing to pay your asking price, and considering both you and your brother are in debt up to your eyeballs and you clearly have expensive taste in clothes and hotel suites, I figure you need a payday. Consider me that."

"You can't afford—"

"I know your brother owes three million and you owe just under one million pounds to Her Majesty's Revenue & Customs," I mocked. "So, how about I give you five million for the ring that's worth a million max to ease the sting of having to sell it?"

"Why don't I just demand ten million to get you off my back?"

I reached for my cell phone, switched it on, then showed her my screen.

"What the hell—" Her voice waned as she squinted at the footage. "Is that my brother?" she squeaked.

"*Se*, it is. Seems to me that it would be very rude to disturb his..." I turned the phone back to me and watched him pick up a slice of pizza. "...meal."

"You bastard," she snapped. "This is extortion."

"I think you'll find me paying you five million for a ring that isn't worth that much is extortion, but I won't tell anyone if you don't."

My smile was cold, but it appeared to help her sense my bitter resolve because she gulped. "How do I know you won't hurt him?"

"Once I have the ring, you are of no consequence to me. Why would I waste my time on either of you?"

She took a step backward, moving deeper into the room, before she beckoned me inside. I complied, and five million lighter in the pocket, I retreated an hour later with the ring box in my hand.

My mother had always been wealthy, and the Fitzwilliam family estate in Cornwall was still there, ticking over, earning her money that was legitimate, that had no ties to the mafia.

Only for a snippet of time when my grandfather had cut her off for marrying my father had she ever had to live without wealth.

But the pride that filled me when I was capable of handing over that amount of money to retrieve an item stolen from my *famigghia* compounded the satisfaction I'd felt when I'd signed the papers that had my great-uncle Currau moved from a prisoner's ward to one of the best in Bellevue.

Everyone needed a *why*.

It was what got them up in the morning, what stoked the fire in their soul, and what pressed them to carry on when things seemed too difficult to resolve.

For so long, my *why* had been revenge. I'd slept it, dreamed it, awoken with that at the forefront of my mind. I'd worked it, beaten it, cut it. Every slash, every slice, every cheek scarred was a lasting memory of my rage against the people who'd devastated my family.

Reclaiming the title of Don should have been a momentous occasion, but it had paled in comparison to the years of hard work that had led to it.

Here, now, with the ring box in my hand, I knew my *why* was going to change.

It had to.

My father would never be avenged, and the blood I'd shed to counter his was grossly outbalanced. I'd taken back the city for the Valentinis by brokering peace with other factions, but was that supposed to be it?

I was just supposed to reign and nothing else?

As I stepped into our suite at the hotel to take a moment just to stare at the goddamn ring that was one of the pieces that had haunted my siblings and I for years, I recognized how Fi had come into my life at the perfect moment.

Where triumph was within my grasp, but the future was unwritten and could have led me down different paths, darker ones.

If a 'why' didn't change, then bitterness and malice could twist a person.

It was only now I had her in my life that I could see that I wanted more.

Not just for me, but for Rory and Stan too.

There was more to life than vendettas. Than a business that was founded on bloodshed and body counts.

Thinking of them, I instigated a group call.

It was only the afternoon in New York so the time zone was on my side—not that Stan would care, but Rory was a real bitch if she got woken up in the middle of the night.

When their faces shone back at me from across the ocean, I tipped up the ring box, which, in itself, was ancient. Made with a worn velvet, the little pod opened up onto a silk pillow that revealed the Anjou ring.

I let that be my greeting.

His eyes on the ring, Stan, his lab as his backdrop, flopped down onto one of the seats that ran along the counter of his workshop.

Rory, sitting behind my desk at *Russu*, stared blindly at the antique.

For a few endless moments, none of us said anything, we just stared at the ring that represented so much.

The tiara was one thing, but the ring was another—for us all.

We'd bought this.

We'd *earned* this.

It wasn't leveraged on favors, wasn't gifted to us at the risk of being snatched back.

We'd bought and sold and killed and cut and paid for this ourselves.

"Let our dynasty be reborn," Rory rasped, and from anyone else, the formal words might have been laughable.

But that was exactly what we were.

The start of a dynasty that was on the brink of rebirth.

THIRTY

JEN

GAMBLING WAS A FOOL'S GAME. I'd watched the *Ocean's Eleven* movie franchise far too many times not to learn that.

The house always won, and if you came out without remortgaging your apartment—if you were lucky enough to own one—then you'd been kissed by an angel.

As someone who had never been blessed with cash, I wasn't about to push my good fortune.

So, at first, when Luc left me at the casino with a couple of grunts trailing after me, I'd admit, I was more interested in the architecture.

The place was snazzy as fuck.

The main hall alone looked like it belonged in a museum, with marble columns that supported a mezzanine landing which was decorated with murals depicting the coastline.

The piéce de resistance was overhead, though. The domed roof set with glass that revealed the glow of lights from the city, while showing a few stars, took my breath away as I meandered into gambling halls that belonged in a Bond movie.

The roulette room had another massive domed ceiling, but this one spread out across the entire space, circular in shape, and it was mirrored by the royal blue carpeting.

Small tables with surprisingly poky wooden chairs were surrounded by dozens of people, and at one end of the hall, there was a bar.

Wandering over to it in my Morticia dress, all clinging black silk from wrist to ankle, with a fishtail skirt that made it impossible to walk without swinging my hips, I ordered a soda water.

Feeling the heavy weight of my guards' attention, I leaned my elbows against the bar's mahogany counter and stared at Monaco's elite.

"No locals are allowed in here," someone to my left told me in English. "Isn't that just crazy to you?"

It made perfect sense to me....

I cast the stranger a look and, by that alone, without him uttering a word, I'd have known he was American.

Most of the men here wore tuxedos with Oxford shoes, much as Luc did, but this one wore a suit with a shirt and an unfastened collar, and on his feet, he had leather sports shoes.

"Aren't they against the dress code?" was my reply.

He shot me a smile that was all white teeth—they'd probably glow in the dark like Ross's had in *Friends*. "You don't recognize me, do you?"

"No, I don't," I dismissed, uninterested in what he was selling.

Wunderdick might have appealed to me before, but in comparison to Luc, he paled.

I didn't give a damn if he was Hollywood's latest star or the big shit on Wall Street, he wasn't Luc.

"Ms. MacNeill, is everything okay?"

I took the out with both hands. "Pleasure talking to you," I lied, heading away from the bar with my drink as I wandered over to one of the roulette tables.

A guard pulled out a chair for me, one that was newly vacated and even though I was only watching, I slipped into it, figuring that would be the best way to keep me out of trouble.

I watched as, time after time, the ball spun around the wheel. Some gamblers cried out with glee, and others turned pale in the face with concern.

It was interesting from a mathematical perspective because I couldn't discern a means of turning the game to your favor. It wasn't like blackjack where you could count cards or poker where you could influence the game with a bluff.

There were probably hundreds of systems that could cheat the house, especially with modern technology, but I couldn't see any of them, not when this was a game of probabilities.

My heart sped up when a woman hollered as she collected fifty thousand euros, then proceeded to lose it over the next three spins.

The more I watched, the more the pull of the game hit me, and I found myself placing the five-thousand-dollar chip Luciu had left me with while he dealt with business on red.

I'd heard all kinds of terms as I sat there, 'straights,' 'baskets,' 'six lines,' 'squares,' *'rouges,' 'noirs.'* So I kept it simple for my first try.

I placed my chip on an outside bet—red.

Heart pounding as the croupier spun the wheel, I swore, my breathing was timed to the run of the ball as I watched it pass through the deflectors, spinning around and around until...

"Sept rouge."

I started hyperventilating at the sight of the ball sitting pretty in 'seven red.'

A tingle of glee shot up my spine when the croupier shoveled chips at me, and I was left with ten thousand.

As he called for more bets, I did another stupid thing and put ten on red again.

Excitement throbbed through my veins when the ball came to a halt at thirty red.

With twenty grand at risk, I decided to shake things up. Not by one iota did I think about backing away, which was probably how the rest of the losers who'd left this table for the past two hundred years had come away with nothing...

I cut my losses and decided not to tempt fate.

Shoving ten on black and ten on even, I watched, my heart racing with anticipation, as the clicking of the wheel started up—

"Dix-sept noir."

'Seventeen black.'

At the bottom of my back, I felt sweat beginning to bead, but I still had twenty left thanks to cutting my bet in half.

Biting my lip, I let the next wheel spin without me gambling a cent, but I watched the board and saw someone put a chip between two numbers.

He lost, but I mimicked the move, feeling crazy and brave and stupid all at the same time.

I placed my chips on the split between fourteen and seventeen.

With every chip on those two digits, the sweat was no longer just at the base of my back, it sprinkled the whole way up my spine...

The croupier spun the wheel, tossed the ball, and time seemed to freeze then speed up then settle...

"*Quatorze rouge.*"

Fourteen red.

Eyes wide, I clapped because I wanted to scream with excitement. This wasn't the kind of place where I figured screaming like I was at a Knicks' game would go down well, so I contained it.

And I contained it.

As chip.

After chip.

After chip.

After chip was pushed in front of me.

"That was a seventeen to one bet, *madame*," the croupier told me, his tone bored, when I asked how much I'd won.

I guessed he dealt with bigger amounts of money every day. Hell, so did I, but it was other people's money.

This was mine.

I did the math.

Twenty multiplied by seventeen?

Three hundred and forty thousand dollars.

I could...

Holy Christ, I could buy a house. Maybe not in New York City, but upstate. If I was pregnant and Luc pulled a Padraig, I could afford a small place, and I could pay off my debts.

Actually, I could do that anyway.

I still had the credit card with the fifty K on there, but as time passed, I felt weird about using it.

I'd been grateful to hand it over to my mom because that felt like it was being used for a worthwhile purpose—buying her out of my life had been one of my top priorities until Luc had dealt with her.

I sucked in a breath though. Because the only money I *really* needed was the fifty grand to cover my debts.

The rest... it was pin money.

Luc had given it to me to play with.

He thought nothing of it and wouldn't care if I lost the five grand he'd gifted me.

The money only mattered to me, and it mattered because security meant everything. Yet, I wanted it for a house. Because if Luc let me down, then I'd have somewhere to rest my head.

If one plus one led to two, that meant that I didn't trust Luc.

And if I didn't trust him, then what was the point of loving him?

Mom said men always broke their promises, but Luc's came with a side order of honor thrown into the mix.

"*Supra l'onori de mi matri,*" I repeated the words under my breath. Letting them sink in.

Resonate.

The wheel churned four more times as I sat there, having an existential crisis, arguing with myself over whether I should carry on playing when that was the dumb thing to do.

But it wasn't about losing the money.

It boiled down to trust.

Trusting in a man when I'd learned that they were the gender of the species I should never trust...

I eyed my chips, so colorful against the green baize, and that was when I came to a decision.

I retrieved five ten-thousand-euro chips and tucked them in my Judith Leiber clutch. That was my debt handled, and all without Luc feeling the pinch.

As for the rest, I decided to go big or go home because there was no harm done either way.

If settling a one-euro chip between two numbers earned me seventeen in return, I had to figure that one chip on one number doubled the bet to thirty-five to one.

Sucking in a breath, I picked two numbers and for the first time in my life, I went with nostalgia.

I placed half of my money on number twenty-three because that was Jake's birthdate.

The other half, I did something romantic.

I'd showed up at Luciu's nightclub on the first of the first, so I settled it on number one.

My mind was so focused on those numbers, on the wheel, on the ball, that I didn't notice the soft lull of the crowd around the table.

My heart pounded with every click of the deflectors running against the ball, and when it leaped and darted around the wheel, I swore I was going to be sick.

You just wasted two-hundred and ninety thousand dollars.

Stupid bitch, why the fuck would you do that?

When Luc tosses you to the curb, what the hell are you going to do?

No money, no job, maybe a kid because he's right, your stupid ass never insisted on a condom.

You're going to be just like Mom.

Maybe you'll be grateful some scum-sucking piece of shit like Vlad takes a shine to you as well.

The ball took its last few tumbles.

Drifting pass thirty-six, hopping onto eleven. It leaped onto thirty, then...

"I'm going to be sick," I whispered as I watched the ball hover on the eight.

Just beside twenty-three.

For the longest time, my heart was frozen, and gravity and everything else seemed to be as well. Then the ball skipped into the next slot.

Twenty-three.

For a second, I stared blankly at the wheel, trying to figure out what had just happened...

The croupier drew out a black cloth and placed it over the wheel.

Soft lips brushed against my ear, defrosting time *and* me, as I whipped around to shove whoever the hell was rubbing up beside me away.

That was when I scented his aftershave, and I melted.

"Luc?" I breathed.

I felt his soft chuckle in my core. "You just broke the bank, *cara mia.*"

Tears pricked my eyes. "How much did I win?"

"You're the accountant," he teased, his tone gentle like he knew how I was feeling. *Shook.*

"My brain won't work." I was going to be sick for real.

"Just over five million euros—"

Mouth trembling, nausea overtaking everything, I realized I was a...

Dear God.

I was a...

I was a millionaire.

So I did the only thing that made sense at that moment. I twisted around in my seat, came face to face with Luc, and asked, "Will you marry me?"

THIRTY-ONE

LUC

SHE BEAT ME TO IT, but I couldn't be mad. Not when she looked up at me with dazed eyes that were beginning to gleam with excitement.

Not when her expression was open and unguarded, and her question was earnest with her desire.

The gawdy Anjou ring was a heavy weight in my pocket, but it could stay there.

This mattered more.

The situation was unique; her security was solicited on her own merit.

She didn't need to look for a man to support her anymore—she could do that by herself.

There was no alternative but for me to murmur, "*Se.*"

Her expression twisted with relief, her eyes fluttering closed for a handful of seconds, before she breathed, "I almost thought you were going to say no."

"Every part of you belongs to me, *vita mia.* You're the crazy one if you think you needed a ring for that."

"You can't spoil my buzz by being a Neanderthal," she retorted, her arms sliding up and over my shoulders as she jumped to her feet.

"I never want to spoil your buzz," I countered, pressing a soft kiss to her lips when I really wanted to tongue fuck her in front of the smattering of Monaco's elite within the casino. "Let's collect your winnings."

"It can't be five million, can it?" she whispered to me. "It's a joke, right?"

"Well, it's seventy grand more than five million," I corrected. "I think I might get you to do my investments for me. I give you five thousand and you come away with millions?"

"I wasn't even going to play," she replied with a laugh. "Thank God I did." Then, she shivered. "I'm never playing ever again."

"Hush, don't say that too loud. The casino won't like that. They need repeat customers to stay open."

I winked at her as I whisked her away to arrange the collection of her winnings. When she was told that hers was the third highest payout in the casino's history, I thought she was going to faint, but instead, once everything was sorted out, we retrieved our coats before we began the short, meandering path back to the Hotel de Paris.

As we approached one of the fountains that glittered and gleamed in the lights from the casino, I tugged her to a halt then hauled her against my chest.

There were a few clusters of people walking around the gardens, the roar of sports cars rumbled along the sound waves, but I knew my guards would stop anyone who tried to come closer.

When I banded my cast-covered arm at her back, I slid my other hand along her waist then trickled it down to grab her fingers.

Beneath the gleaming moon, a chill in the air that made every breath feel crisp, with her triumph simmering in her veins, and the love between us flooding the air, I felt like doing something sappy.

Holding her against me, I moved us in a soft two-step, and as we danced beneath the moonlight, I decided to share something with her that I needed her to know. Someone with her background... I knew she craved security.

Stability.

My world was the exact opposite, but I'd figured out a way to give her everything she needed to feel better. To feel strong. To feel safe.

The five million she'd just won would definitely help.

"You beat me to it."

She smiled at me, her face tipped toward mine, joy making her beautiful face glorious as my Fi looked at me like she'd never seen another man before. Like I was the only one in the world.

For her, I wanted to be.

Just like she was the only woman I saw. The only woman I wanted.

"What did I beat you to? The roulette table?"

I shook my head. "I was going to ask you to marry me tonight."

She stilled but I moved her along, so we were swaying together. "You were?"

"I was. I got the ring—"

"You got the Anjou ring?! That's great news! I can't believe I forgot to ask."

"You had other priorities," I teased. "But I was waiting on the ring to propose... however, there's a problem."

"What with?" Fi queried, her brow furrowed.

"The ring... It's ugly as hell."

She laughed, her grin widening. "Oh, dear."

"*Se*, oh, dear. So, my grand gesture has gone to waste, and you're going to have to settle for Van Cleefs and Arpels."

"I'm sure I'll survive the shame," she joked, squeezing my hand so I knew she was only messing with me. "I'll wear the ugly ring. For you."

"Now *that's* true love. But no, it's too big. You can wear it on our wedding day, though, hmm?"

Fi swallowed. "Wow. Wedding day."

"Should I be offended that you forgot already?"

"No. I just, well, I actually want to marry you. It's kind of crazy."

I didn't chuckle or mock her, because I knew what she meant.

She'd always thought she'd marry for money, but instead, she was marrying the man she loved. Who loved her in return.

I pressed my lips to hers. "It's crazy in the best way, hmm?"

"In the *very* best way," she emphasized. "I have to tell Aoife and Savannah! I wonder how they'll duke it out to be my matron of honor."

But those plans were for another day. Another time. So I quieted her by kissing her and stemming the flow of words that sprang free with her excitement.

Beneath the moonlight and the glow from the casino, with the sticky spray from the fountains misting the air around us, I kissed the woman who was born to be mine.

The walk to the hotel took too long even though it was barely a few minutes away, and I shuffled her through the grand lobby into one of the elevators and into the privacy of our suite where we were alone at long last.

The second the door was closed, however, I pinned her against it. Using my hold on her hand, I raised first one arm against the door then the next, before I ordered, "Keep them there."

When she didn't argue, I shucked up her skirt until it was pulling taut around her hips, the fabric creaking and snagging as the seams creaked in response to my demands.

"Did I tell you how fucking delicious you look, *cara mia?*"

"No, my love," she told me breathily. "Should I be offended?"

To answer her, I slipped my fingers back between her legs, making her spine arch as she rocked into the door, butt bouncing against it as she parted her thighs to let me in.

My fingertips found her clit through her panties, and I stroked the nub, focusing all my attention on the most sensitive part of her as my mouth hovered above hers.

"You were always going to belong to me, *bedda mia.* Do you know that now?"

Her dazed eyes collided with mine. "I was..." She swallowed. "... scared."

"Of my life?"

"No. Of us being like my parents."

Irritation flashed through me, but she wasn't as blessed as I was with a mother and father who loved each other and who had loved their children.

That wasn't her fault.

It just meant it was my duty to show her the way forward, to show her how two people could be together when love bound them as a unit.

"We were never going to be like your parents."

Ceasing to tease her, I moved my hand from her panties then dropped to my knees, so quickly that the joints colliding against the marble made an audible click, and she squeaked.

From the floor, I stared up at her and pressed my face into her stomach. "We were always going to be like us. And that is perfectly imperfect. How it was always supposed to be."

I kissed her belly, loving when she disobeyed by dropping her hands and raking her fingers through my hair.

"I-I've always been easily discardable," she whispered. "I didn't want to—"

"Of course you were," I told her instantly, peering up at her with a scowl. "If you'd been with another man, then how would I have found you?"

Her smile grew at that, and she shook her head. "You're really crazy, aren't you, honey?"

I grinned at her. "Crazy, creepy... you know how to make a man feel good."

"I'll make you feel good for the next sixty years, how about that?"

"What if I can't get a boner when I'm ninety-six?"

She snorted. "Have you seen how fine I am? I'll be fine at eighty-six too. And if you're not, I'll get you some Viagra. That'll rattle your bones."

Laughing, I rocked my forehead against her stomach and murmured, "Your past is your past. I've never judged you for it, and I never will, just like I hope you'll never judge me for mine. But you mustn't let it taint the present or the future."

"I won't. I was just... if I'm pregnant..."

Pulling back to look up at her, I scoffed, "You're pregnant. I've worked hard to make sure that you are."

Her eyes narrowed upon me. "I could have told you to wear a condom."

"And you could have gotten the shot without me knowing." I shrugged. "Some things are written in the stars."

She swallowed then whispered, "You say things like that and I believe them."

"So you should." I pressed a kiss to her stomach, then surged onto my feet once more. "Turn around," I directed her, "arms over your head again."

Fi complied and burrowed her butt against me, flexing those sinful curves around my hardness.

"You're burning temptation, *cara mia*. How could I do anything other than tie you to me for the rest of our lives, hmm?"

A whimper escaped her, and she whispered, "Please, never stop tying me to you."

There was no fear of that.

I cupped her ass then scooped her skirt back up.

Leaning forward to kiss her shoulder, I whispered, "I will show you every day for as long as I live."

Gathering the fabric around my cast, I tugged at her panties, dragging them down to her knees before I hauled her forward a little so that I could bend her over better.

With her standing how I wanted, I pulled on my zipper and released my dick.

Like a magnet for her cunt, it bobbed between her folds. I let it hover there, twitching and flexing as I rumbled in her ear, "I should take your ass. It would be a fitting beginning and ending to our courtship, hmm? But this pussy..." I sighed. "This pussy is my fucking home."

I surged forward so the tip rolled through her folds and as she groaned, I pressed into her slit.

Each inch my cock claimed felt more victorious than the last time because someday soon, she'd be mine in all the ways under the sun.

Nothing would tear us apart.

No one. No law. Nothing.

As I sank all the way into her, I dug around in my pocket for the Anjou ruby, popping it out of the box by slipping it over the tip of my thumb.

Letting my hand slide over the curve of her waist, lower, and lower, I used the cool gem to run along her clit.

A squeal escaped her at the chill but as I moved the ring deeper between her folds, gathering her slick juices against it, I retreated to the nub and whispered, "You're more precious to me than this ring, *duci*."

The tremor that hit her was like a quake through her system. "No, I—"

"No, nothing. Purposes change, needs adapt... you're my reason for waking up in the morning, *vita mia*. When you get scared, remember that."

Before she could argue, I started to thrust into her, pounding harder while I stroked her clit.

Leaning over her so she could hear my breathing in her ear, I spoke to her in Sicilian, words she'd never understand, that she didn't need to.

She just needed to hear them.

And I needed to tell her in my mother tongue.

That I loved her.

That she belonged to me.

That I belonged to her.

That she was my sunrise and sunset.

Worth a thousand vendettas.

A treasure beyond anything my ancestors had coveted...

With each husky word uttered in her ear, her cunt clamped down on my cock.

I knew before she did when she was going to explode, and I sped up, thrusting harder, faster, going deeper so that we'd come at the same time.

When release both tore us apart and forced us together, our mutual cries filled the entryway of the hotel suite. The freedom that slipped through our veins was better than any high.

It belonged to us.

Uniquely ours.

Forever.

THIRTY-TWO

JEN

WHEN HE PASSED me the iPad the following morning, then bestowed the crown of my head with a kiss, murmuring, "Thank you," I squinted at the headline because I wasn't wearing my contacts or glasses.

"What is it?"

"Read it," he drawled, moving away to the table that could seat eight and which held a breakfast spread worthy of a buffet.

It could probably feed a full restaurant too.

Uninterested by the tablet, I watched him pick up a plate then wander down the array of platters.

He collected some fruit, put that in a corner, then came a croissant. He grabbed a bowl of yogurt, placed that on the dish, then sprinkled some nuts on top and drizzled honey over it.

Then, he placed that in front of me and kissed my head again.

"Eat, *amore mia*," he crooned softly, and as I looked up at him, a glance passing between us, I recognized that if I could trust him enough to risk nearly three hundred thousand on a bet, then I could trust him enough not to toss me out if I gained a couple pounds.

Licking my lips, I picked up a fork and ate some of the fruit.

When he took a seat with a plate a lot fuller than mine, I smiled as he sighed with enjoyment when he tucked into an omelet.

Behind him, the ocean was grim and gloomy but oh, so beautiful. The dark navy was totally unlike the gray of the Hudson, and even with barely any sun, the city was a wonderful sight to behold this early in the morning.

He ignored me to read the newspaper, and I switched my glance to the tablet, widening the screen so that the text was bigger.

Arching a brow when I saw Savannah had gone through with her article on Eva Kingston, I asked, "You can keep the tiara?"

"I assume. I think I'll hear from Martinez if he's unsatisfied," he drawled. "And it's your tiara. I want you to wear it to our wedding."

My lips twitched. "Well, that means we're having a fancy-assed ceremony, doesn't it?"

"Why does that come as a surprise? When a Don finds his Lady, the wedding has to take New York by storm."

His arched brow called me a fool for doubting him, and I snickered as I averted my attention to the article.

In this country, we revere the boys in blue as if they're gods who walk among us. We equip them as if they're an armed force all on their own, but what happens when the boys in blue turn on the girls in blue?

When a decorated cop, a legacy officer whose family has been in the NYPD for generations, her father the current commissioner, is cast out, her face lining the walls in posters alongside criminals she sought to take off her streets, we see a chink in the shield of the force we so revere.

This writer discovered the story of Eva Kingston quite by chance. Amid a folder of files regarding the New World Sparrows, her name slipped out and I remembered her.

The cop who decapitated a fellow cop.

At the time, I craved more information, never imagining the rabbit hole this story would take me down...

I peered over at Luc. "She's a little heavy handed, isn't she?"

"I don't care so long as it makes people ask the questions her husband wants them to ask."

"Did she do it?" I questioned. "Decapitate the cop, I mean?"

"You remember the case?"

"I looked her up before I approached Savvie. It made me remember how much it was all over the news. The NYPD were really hunting her down. I thought it was weird at the time because I remembered her story coming out when she escaped that serial killer."

"She has not had the best of lives," he concurred. "To escape the lair of a serial killer then to find her footing where she did..." He pursed his lips. "I'm under no doubt that she did it. Why is another matter."

Grimacing, I asked, "Isn't it difficult to cut off someone's head?"

He laughed. "*Cara mia*, you'll be relieved to know, I'm sure, that that is something I haven't tried out. Ask Lorenzo when we're back home. He'll tell you."

"Lorenzo?" I sputtered. "He's your driver!"

"So? Drivers can multitask." His eyes twinkled. "He'll be your permanent guard soon enough. You don't think I'd leave you underprotected again, do you?"

"No." Not that I was about to argue after the last couple of weeks. "Remember, you owe Savannah a favor for agreeing to write this."

"Trust me, I haven't forgotten," he grumbled. "I hate owing people favors. I'd prefer to pay."

"That's because money isn't a problem for you," I pointed out.

"It isn't a problem for you anymore either."

A shocked breath whispered from my lips. "Shit, you're right."

He laughed. "I wonder when you'll believe it."

"I don't think I will." My brow puckered. "Ever."

"It will settle soon," he assured me. "But remember, you don't have to touch it. You're mine... the money is yours."

"So, what's yours is mine and what's mine is mine?"

"Something like that."

"See?" I cackled. "Crazy."

"Traditional," he countered, making me roll my eyes.

"Well, I expect you to sign a prenup. I have assets now."

Laughter trickled from him. "I will sign one so long as it's on the explicit understanding that you're stuck with me even in heaven."

"You don't believe in heaven, do you? You're not the most religious of guys."

"I didn't believe," he corrected. "Then I met you, and I learned most things are possible."

I stared at him. Just stared. Before I croaked, "You need to write romance novels."

His lips curved as he rustled his newspaper. "For you, *cori mia*, why not?"

Well, hell.

Because he said it with such ease, I knew I'd have to get used to his romantic words. Maybe sixty years of them would lessen their appeal?

Somehow, I didn't think so.

"I need to learn Sicilian," I blurted out.

The paper crinkled as he peered over the corner he tipped down. "Why?"

"So I understand all the stuff you say. Plus, it'll be hotter in Sicilian."

He smirked. "First lesson: *vasu*."

"What does that mean?"

"A kiss."

"*Vasu*," I repeated with a grin, blowing him one and laughing when he pounded his chest to catch it. "Crazy."

"For you," he murmured absentmindedly as he carried on reading the paper, which made those two words even more powerful.

Continuing with my read of Savannah's article before I started bawling, I sent her a message when I was finished.

Me: *Thank you.*

Savannah: *My pleasure.*

Me: *I'm surprised you wrote it that fast.*

Savannah: *It's mostly made up. Lol. Like writing a story. Much easier when you don't have to fact check. Or, should I say, when the facts are ones you can make up and people can't dive into them.*

Me: *Egomaniac.*

Savannah: *Aren't you lucky that I am and that I don't mind leveraging favors for good causes?*

Lips twitching, I typed:

Me: *Very lucky. Do you know what you want? He's here. I can tell him.*

Savannah: *Nope, let him sweat. I might not want anything for forty years, but I like having something over a mafia boss.*

Savannah: *She did it. You know that, right?*

Me: *Luciu said the same.*

Savannah: *She's fucked up. Sad, really. That's another reason I didn't mind writing it.*

Savannah: *She survived that bastard who abducted her for thirty-three days, can you imagine?*

Me: *No. I can't. Just the thought makes me shudder. I read all the articles at the time.*

Savannah: *Honey, everyone did.*

Savannah: *He used to kill his other victims in front of her. During the court case, she said that she made him fall in love with her.*

Me: *That's so fucked up.*

Savannah: *Right? Talk about power though. Makes you wonder what else she's capable of.*

Me: *Nothing good, I'd imagine.*

Savannah: *I dunno. People can surprise us. The guy's dead, did you know that?*

Me: *The serial killer?*

Savannah: *Yep.*

Me: *In jail?*

Savannah: *No. The Whistler took him out.*

Me: *Jesus. I've heard about him. Don't they say he's like CIA or something?*

Savannah: *They say a lot about him, lmao. He's the bogeyman. Wonder if that had something to do with her husband...*

Me: *You sure you haven't been checking out conspiracytok?*

Savannah: *I'm positive.*

Me: *I have massive news to tell you.*

Savannah: *About Luc?*

Me: *About US.*

Savannah: *Oooh, what?*

Me: *You're not the only one who's gonna be queen of the mob.*

Savannah: *Fuck off. OMG. You're getting married?! Holy hell!*

Me: *I'm so excited!!*

Savannah: *I'm glad you are because I was about to check and make sure you actually wanted to marry him.*

Me: *Lol. I asked him.*

Savannah: *No way! Feminism FTW. Damn, I should have done that.*

Me: *Pfft. Beat you to it.*

Savannah: *Lmao. Wow. You know what that means?*

Me: *We're both insane?*

Savannah: *We knew that already.*

Me: *True.*

Savannah: *It means we're bagged and tagged.*

Me: *Speak for yourself, I'm not dead.*

Savannah: *NYC's dating scene is going to get a lot more boring.*

Me: *They should have snatched us up when they had the chance.*

Savannah: *Very true.*

As I started to type out,

Me: *You'll never believe what happened last night at the casino*

A message of hers came through, and it completely robbed me of my glee about my winnings.

Savannah: *Did you hear about Aoife and Finn?*

Concerned, I dropped my spoon against the bowl of yogurt and tapped out quickly,

Me: *What about them?*

Savannah: *She moved into a hotel suite with Jake.*

Me: *You're not being serious! What the hell? Talk about burying the lede, Savvie!*

Savannah: *Happened last night. Finn called Aidan. He was scared shitless when he got home and couldn't find her.*

Me: *I'll bet he was!*

Me: *I'm going to call her.*

Savannah: *If you learn anything, let me know? The family's going nuts. She won't let anyone into the hotel suite to see her.*

Me: *Will do. Speak later. xox*

Savannah: *Later xox*

"Cara mia, what is it?"

I barely glanced at Luc before I shook my head and said, "It's about Aoife and her husband. I think she might have left him."

I felt his eyes on me as I waited for Aoife to pick up.

Only, she didn't.

"Dammit, she's hiding again."

"Hiding?"

"She wouldn't answer her phone after the miscarriage. The last time I was there, I could tell they'd been arguing. It was weird because they're not the type to argue."

"Every couple argues."

"Not this one."

"It's three AM in New York, Fi, maybe that's why she doesn't answer, hmm?"

"I tried to call her last night when you were asleep. You know, to tell her the good news? She didn't answer." I bit my lip, wondering if she'd been checking into the hotel then. As I was getting a husband, she was leaving hers. What the fuck was going on? "I hope Eef is okay."

My stomach started churning with nerves, and I shoved the plate of breakfast food away, hoping that would help, but it didn't.

From out of nowhere, the need to puke hit me, and I scraped my chair against the floor in my hurry to get out of there.

Almost skidding in my haste to make it to the bathroom, I collapsed on the floor and puked up what little I'd managed to eat.

Was I surprised when I felt Luciu settle me on a towel so that my knees weren't on the marble?

When he gathered my hair and tucked it between my shoulders as I groaned like I was dying against the toilet seat, not even caring that my cheek was resting against it?

No.

As he maneuvered me, I let him, knowing that asking him to leave wouldn't work.

So when I started heaving again, I didn't even demand he get out. I didn't waste my energy. I just concentrated on trying to keep my stomach within the confines of my body.

When the wave of nausea faded, I heard the crinkling of a packet after he flushed the toilet.

With tired eyes, I turned to him and found him standing there, holding something out to me.

I palmed the test and whispered, "Prepared for every eventuality?"

"Always." He crouched down in front of me and helped me stand.

"I'll let you watch me puke, but I'm not going to pee in front of you."

His lips twitched. "I already know what it's going to say, but I thought you might need the confirmation." He pressed a kiss to my temple. "Remember, *ti ficci na promissa*, I promised to bring you back here when you're big and round, and I'm going to fuck you against the terrace..."

The prospect of being *bounced* had my stomach heaving again.

Softly, he murmured, "I'll wait for you outside, *cori mia*."

After I cleaned the toilet as best as I could, I plunked the seat down then collapsed against it, staring at the test... but I knew he was right.

It was the worst timing.

Horrible for Aoife.

But I pressed a hand to my stomach, knowing that there was never a right time for anything.

Life was one big dose of imperfect moments that you had to make work for you.

Somehow, out of one big wad of imperfect moments, Luc and I had come to be. Much like our child had.

And bad timing or not, that, I thought, couldn't be anything other than something to celebrate.

Even if I *was* nervous as hell.

AURORA

THE LAST WEDDING I'd been to had been my own.

When I looked back over the years, that felt as if it were the last time I was happy too.

My dad had been alive, my parents had been happy together, both sets of my grandparents had still been okay before illness and a broken heart had laid waste to them.

College had been going well; my life was on a set path... Work on freeing *prozio*. DA before I hit thirty. US Attorney before forty. Build my name. Break glass ceilings. Solid goals. Solid plans.

Then everything had gone to shit.

I plucked at my bottom lip as I watched my brother dancing with his new bride, then plucked it some more when I saw my mother, standing at the sidelines, watching them with stars in her eyes.

I knew what she was thinking—a love match. Like hers and *Patri's*. Before it had all gone wrong.

Things had a habit of doing that in our family.

Repressing the memories, I turned my focus on Jennifer. She'd surprised me; I'd admit it. Her work at our firm of accountants was superb, and she looked set to save us a fortune in taxes.

I didn't read people wrong often, and I disliked that I'd done so with her. Not because I needed her to like me—I didn't—but because it meant my brain had let me down.

I couldn't afford for that to happen.

The bump at her belly was noticeable, yet thanks to a cleverly placed waistline, it was meager, but I saw it.

My *frate* seemed happy, and I knew he wasn't the type of man who would be if she'd trapped him.

What Stan and I had done to protect him had been for nothing, it seemed. Luciu had brought her into the *famigghia* regardless of our approval. He'd even gifted her with the honor of the Anjou ring and tiara, uncaring that the crimson stones looked like blood spatter offset against her pale amber dress...

It was my own fault that I felt less a part of the family than she seemed to be.

I'd spent so many years on the outside looking in that I *was* an outsider.

The thought was not only goddamn disconcerting, it was depressing too.

All these years, I'd worked hard to get my great-uncle released, and now that I'd accomplished that... everything else had been shot to hell.

To have my family, I couldn't remain with the DA.

To be Luc's *consigliere*, I had to get married again.

To get married again, I had to forget about the past. Had to let a man into my life, had to let him do things to me... things I wasn't sure I could stand. Not after last time.

"You look like you just made out with a dog."

Stan's comment had me frowning at him. "Your imagination hasn't improved with age. I forgot how annoying you can be in real life. You keep a check on it over the phone."

"And you, darling *soru*, are as big of a pain in the ass as you ever were." He kissed the top of my head and made a loud smacking noise as he did so. "Although, to be fair, *you're* the one who looks constipated, not me.

"Why are you scowling? He's made his choice. Doesn't matter if we think he's fucking crazy, she makes him happy."

She did.

Stan was right on another matter too—I *did* think Luc was crazy, but then, weren't we all a little mad?

Our father's death had tipped us over the edge, I thought. Had made us deep dive into darker parts of our natures that would otherwise have remained unexplored.

The thought saddened me because my beloved *patri* was a cheerful man. Boisterous and loud, but loving and warm.

To think that, in his memory, battles had been committed, and death and chaos had happened under the guise of avenging him saddened me.

A lot about today saddened me.

"The end of an era," Stan remarked when I didn't reply, plunking his ass down at my side.

"It is," I agreed. "The start of a new one."

He hummed. "You decided who you're getting hitched to?"

"No." I scowled at the table. "I don't want to talk about it." Then, because it was near, I used my dinner knife to stab a rose that was trailing too close to my dessert plate.

The Victoria's banquet hall was loaded down with more flowers than a greenhouse, and it stank because of it. Maybe I could blame my desire to cry on my allergies?

The period room was set up around a dance floor where the newly married couple were currently in each other's arms for their first dance.

Flowers crept onto the floor as if they were growing all around them, and I felt sure the wedding planner was proud of the concept, but the creeping trails reminded me of zombie hands scrabbling over the side of a cliff to get to the poor human whose brains they'd scented.

"What did the poor flower ever do to you?" Stan chided, freeing the rose from my blade.

"It was either that or stab you."

"Now, now, Luc's the cutter, not you."

"Maybe I'm the stabber."

"You couldn't hurt anyone," he scoffed. "You fought for the goodies for too long."

My laugh was cold. "No one is truly good. Good is a relative concept."

"Don't get philosophical on me."

"Why not? I think you could do with a class on ethics."

A shift of movement from one of the guards over by the doorway caught my eye, and because we were on red alert, I took note of what was happening until Stan pressed a hand to my arm.

"It's okay. Latecomers."

"Latecomers?" I frowned because I'd gone over the guest list with a fine-tooth comb.

Alongside Jennifer and Luciu's close family and friends, there were the many factions that we couldn't afford to piss off.

Hence the red alert.

I wasn't sure New York City had ever seen such a showing of crime families outside of a Summit.

In one corner, there was a table of Bratva. The Pakhan hadn't moved from his seat apart from to use the bathroom.

Another corner housed the Irish. Aidan O'Donnelly Sr. wasn't here, but his son was, as were a few other couples that Jennifer was close with. Aoife O'Grady had been her matron of honor, while Savannah Daniels, the new bride of the O'Donnelly clan, had been a bridesmaid.

Not unsurprisingly, I hadn't been asked to take part in the ceremony.

Another corner of the ballroom housed the Triads, whom Luciu and Stan had helped a few months ago.

There were more foreign crime factions in here than our own families, and that was for a reason.

The Italians were slowly being purged. Disloyalty was being weeded out under my watch.

Some had died, others had left, a few had fled.

Luciu was ruling with an iron fist at my say so, and contrary to what Stan believed, I wasn't afraid to play nasty.

"Everyone's here who should be here," I argued, twisting around to look at him, a demand for answers in my tone.

"This is a name I added to the guest list. He didn't arrive in time for the church ceremony."

I blinked. "Who is he?"

Stan pursed his lips. "You're gonna get mad at me, but I can deal with that—"

"Why's that, I wonder? Because you pull dipshit moves and I have to clean them up?" I growled. "What the fuck have you done now?"

But the opening of the doors seemed to punctuate my question, and suddenly, his need to answer was no more.

"What have you done?" I rasped under my breath, staring at Hunter, a man I'd known since childhood.

A man I'd loved since childhood...

"You have to get married, Rory," Stan argued. "You're pushing it by waiting as long as you have. The council doesn't approve of you as it is, but you agreed to get married.

"Hunter's the only guy I've ever seen you with who can get through that thick layer of ice—"

"Is this a set up?" I snarled, twisting around to stare at him.

If we were alone, I swore to *Cristo* that I'd grab his hair and slam his head into the table.

"No, it's a blind date."

"A blind date?" I wheezed. "Does he know?"

Stan snorted. "What do you think?"

"I think you're fucking crazy."

But as I looked at Hunter, all those old feelings came back, and they seemed to highlight what I'd felt earlier. As if college was also the last time I'd been happy, and a part of that had been because of Hunter.

"How did you even get him here? He's Camorra."

"I told him you needed his help," Stan informed me unapologetically.

"And he came?"

"Immediately. Soon as I said you needed him, he was on the red eye."

My mouth twisted at that news, but as always, when I thought of him it was bittersweet.

Here was the man who'd introduced me to bison steak and green chili cheeseburgers.

Who I'd cheered on as he raced across the field, evading linebackers and cornerbacks.

But for all the good times, there was only one real memory that mattered.

And it flickered into being in my mind as if I'd just hit play on a video on YouTube.

Which, of course, was the moment he turned his head and found me in the crowd.

As our eyes clashed, I didn't see him *now*.

I saw him *then*.

His face spattered with blood.

My husband's blood.

LUC

SEPTEMBER

WHEN THE MIDWIFE placed her in my arms, I wasn't sure what to think.

That she was precious was a given—she was her mother's incarnation.

That she'd given her *matri* and I the run around with three different sets of false labor only to arrive after a five-hour stint in the birthing room when she'd decided to grace the world with her presence, made sense to me—she was Fi's daughter.

That she was noisy was natural—she was Sicilian.

But what stunned me the most was the great welter of love that seemed to flood me as I held her.

I knew what it was to go to war for someone I loved. I knew and still meant it when I told Fi that if anyone hurt her, Manhattan would turn to dust once I'd avenged her. But as I looked into my daughter's dazed eyes, I knew the entire US of A was in danger if anyone so much as—

"I can already see you planning wars," Fi muttered, her hands outstretched. "Let's not get into any fights before she's eighteen, hmm? We have plenty of time before then."

"She's your daughter."

"So?" She scowled at me. "Stop hogging her. I want to hold her too."

"So, she's your daughter," I repeated as I carefully placed her in Fi's arms. "That means she's trouble with a capital T."

A smile danced about her lips. "So long as you know nothing's changed on that front."

"I didn't doubt it, *cara mia*," I drawled. "That final trimester in the Sicilian heat slowed you some, but I know your return to raising havoc will be swift."

She snickered as she tipped her head down, but when her gaze glanced over our little girl, that was the moment I knew I was staring at my world.

My entire world, my everything, my goddamn universe was sitting on that bed. A bed that had seen dozens of Valentini births over the years, maybe even hundreds...

A bed that had forged a dynasty, and that my *vita mia* had continued by electing to give birth in Sicily...

This was my wedding present.

Our child would have a Sicilian passport first, then dual citizenship would come later.

Fi knew me too well and couldn't have gifted me with anything better.

Amid the old-world glamor of the ancient estate, tucked between newel posts of the four-poster bed that were as thick as some tree trunks, they fit in perfectly.

Mother and child.

Mine.

Mine.

"She will melt even Rory's heart," I cooed, looking forward to watching my icy cold *soru* meet her niece. "Stan will be a sap. It's in his genes. She'll twist him around her finger the second he sets eyes on her."

Fi's lips twitched. "You Valentini men are romantics."

"This is hardly a bad thing, *cori mia*."

"True." Fi's smile grew, but as it did, something shifted in her eyes. "Saverina."

I arched a brow. "Her name?"

She nodded. "It means 'new house.'"

Well aware of what she was saying, my throat choked up.

With the birth of our daughter, we both stepped forward into another phase.

She wasn't Irish.

I wasn't Sicilian.

We were something new, something tangled, a silent promise sworn to one another as our daughter grew in her belly…

Saverina was that oath personified.

"Perfect, *cara mia*."

She kissed Saverina's forehead. "*Mon cher*, did you doubt me?"

Ready for the next duet?
REVELATION
You can preorder the duet here: www.books2read.com/ValentiniThree
and here: www.books2read.com/ValentiniFour

AUTHOR NOTE

Hey there, lovelies!

How's you?

Ready for the next duet?

REVELATION

You can preorder them here: www.books2read.com/ValentiniThree and here: www.books2read.com/ValentiniFour

And for a **massive release week giveaway celebration**, be sure to join my Diva reader group: www.facebook.com/groups/Serena AkeroydsDivas or take part here: https://kingsumo.com/g/buxylr/the-don-release-day-giveaway

With that being said, yes, you did come across some names and faces in THE DON and THE LADY.

These are the books they belong to:

Aoife & Finn - Filthy (www.books2read.com/FilthySere
naAkeroyd) & Filthy Secret (releasing October
2021 www.books2read.com/FilthySecret)

Eoghan & Inessa - Filthy Rich (www.books2read.com/
   FilthyRich)

Declan & Aela - Filthy Dark (www.books2read.com/
   FilthyDark)

Brennan & Camille - Filthy Sex (www.books2read.com/
   FilthySex)

Savannah & Aidan Jr. - Filthy Hot (www.books2read.
   com/FilthyHot)

*Rachel Laker - Rex (www.books2read.com/RexSerena
   Akeroyd)*

Eva Kingston & Martinez - INFILTRATED (*Coming
   soon*)

However, for Infiltrated, you'll have to join my mailing list if you're interested in knowing when and how Eva Kingston became the 'cop decapitator.' www.serenaakeroyd.com/Newsletter

I hope you loved meeting the Valentinis and are stoked to meet up with them again in REVELATION.

Much love,

Serena

xoxo

Ps. If you're new to my books, read on to enjoy the first chapters of FILTHY, the first novel in my FIVE POINTS' MOB collection.

THE CROSSOVER READING ORDER
WITH THE FIVE POINTS

FILTHY
FILTHY SINNER
NYX
LINK
FILTHY RICH
SIN
STEEL
FILTHY DARK
CRUZ
MAVERICK
FILTHY SEX
HAWK
FILTHY HOT
STORM
THE DON
THE LADY
FILTHY SECRET
REX
RACHEL
FILTHY KING

REVELATION BOOK ONE
REVELATION BOOK TWO
FILTHY LIES
FILTHY TRUTH

RUSSIAN MAFIA
Adjacent to the universe, but can be read as a standalone
SILENCED

VALENTINI FAMILY

START THE FIVE POINTS' UNIVERSE FROM THE BEGINNING...

FILTHY

FINN

Obsessive habits weren't alien to me.

They were as much a part of me as my coal-dark hair and my diamond-blue eyes. Ingrained as they were, it didn't mean they weren't irritating as fuck.

As I rifled through the folder on the table in front of me, staring down at the life of one pesky tenant, I wanted to toss it in the trash. I truly did.

I wanted not to be interested in her.

Wanted my focus to return to the matter at hand—business.

But there was something about her.

Something. . .

Irish.

I was a sucker for my own people. When I was a kid, I'd only dated other Irish girls in my class, and though I'd become less discerning about nationality and had grown more interested in tits and ass, I'd thought that desire had died down.

But Aoife Keegan was undeniably, indefatigably Irish.

From her fucking name—I didn't know people still named their kids in Gaelic over here—to her red goddamn hair and milky-white skin.

To many, she wouldn't be sexy. Too pale, too curvy, too rounded and wholesome. But to me? It was like God had formed a creature that was born to be my downfall.

I could feel the beast inside me roaring to life as I stared at the photos of her. It wanted out. It wanted her.

Fuck.

"I told you not to get those briefs."

My eyes flared wide in surprise at my brother, Aidan O'Donnelly's remark. "What?" I snapped.

"I told you not to get those briefs," he repeated, unoffended. Which was a miracle. Had I been speaking to Aidan Sr., I'd probably have lost a finger, but Aidan Jr. was one of my best friends, as well as a confidant and fellow businessman.

When I said business, it wasn't the kind Valley girls dreamed their future husbands would be involved in. No Manhattan socialite, though we were wealthy as fuck, would want us on their arm if they truly knew what games we were involved in.

My business was forged, unashamedly, in blood, sweat, and tears.

Preferably not my own, although I had taken a few hits for the Family over the years.

"My briefs aren't irritating me," I carried on, blowing out a breath.

"No? You look like you've got something up your ass crack." Aidan cocked a brow at me, but his smirk told me he knew exactly what the fuck was wrong.

I flipped him the bird—the finger that I'd have lost by showing cheek to his father—and he just grinned at me as he leaned over my glass desk and scooped up one of the pictures.

That beast I mentioned earlier?

It roared to life again when his eyes drifted over Aoife's curvy form.

"She's like your kryptonite," he breathed, tilting his head to the side. "Fuck me, Finn."

"I'd rather not," I told him dryly. "Now her? Yeah. I'd fuck her anytime."

He wafted a dismissive hand at my teasing. "I knew from that look in your eye, there was a woman involved. I just didn't know it would be a looker like this."

I snatched the photo from him. "Mine."

My growl had him snickering. "The Old Country ain't where I get my women from, Finn. Simmer down."

Throat tightening, I grated out, "What the fuck am I going to do?"

"Screw her?" he suggested.

"I can't."

He snorted. "You can."

"How the fuck am I supposed to get her in my bed when I'm about to bribe her into selling off her commercial lot?"

Aidan shrugged. "Do the bribing after."

That had me blowing out a breath. "You're a bastard, you know that, right?"

Piously, he murmured, "My parents were well and truly married before I came along. I have the wedding and birth certificates to prove it." He grinned. "Anyway, you're only just figuring that out?"

I shot him a scowl. "You're remarkably cheerful today."

"Is that a question or a statement?"

"Both?" The word sounded far too Irish for my own taste. My mother had come from Ireland, Tipperary to be precise—yeah, like the song. I was American born and bred, my accent that of someone who'd been raised in Hell's Kitchen but, and I hated it, my mother's accent would make an appearance every now and then.

'Both' came out sounding almost like 'boat.'

Aidan, knowing me as well as he did, smirked again—the fucker. "I got laid."

Grunting, I told him, "That doesn't usually make you cheerful."

"It does. I just never see you first thing after I wake up. Da hasn't managed to piss me off today."

Aidan was the heir to the Five Points—an Irish gang who operated out of Hell's Kitchen. It wasn't like being the heir to a candy company or a title. It came with responsibilities that no one really appreciated.

We were tied into the life, though. Had been since the day we were born.

There was no use in whining over it, and Aidan wasn't. But if I had to deal with his father on a daily basis? I'd have been whining to the morgue and back.

Aidan Sr. was the shrewdest man I knew. What the man could do with our clout defied belief. Even if I thought he was a sociopath, he had my respect, and in truth, my love and loyalty.

Bastard or no, he'd taken me in when I was fourteen and had made me one of his family. I'd gone from being his kids' friend, the son of one of his runners, to suddenly being welcome in the main house.

All because Aidan Sr.—though I was sure he was certifiable—believed in family.

I shot Aidan Jr. a look. "Was it that blonde over on Canal Street?"

He rubbed his chin. "Yeah."

Snorting, I told him, "Hope you wore a rubber. I swear that woman has so many men going in and out of her door, it should be on double-action hinges."

He scowled at me. "Are you trying to piss me off?"

"Why? Didn't wear a jimmy?" I grinned at him, my mood soaring in the face of his irritation. "Better get to the clinic before it drops off."

Though he flipped me the bird as easily as I'd done to him—I was his brother, after all—he grumbled, "What are you going to do about little Aoife?"

I squinted at him. "She's not little."

That seemed to restore his humor. "I know. Just how you like them." He shook his head. "You and Conor, I swear. What do you do with them? Drown yourself in their tits?"

Heaving a sigh, I informed him, "My predilection for large tits is none of your business."

"And whether or not I wore a jimmy last night is none of yours."

"If it turns green and looks like a moldy corn on the cob, who you gonna call?"

"Ghostbusters?" he tried.

I shook my head, then pointed a finger at him and back at myself. "No. Me."

Grunting, he got to his feet and pressed his fists to the desk. "We need that building, Finn."

"The business development plan was mine, Aid. I know we need it. Don't worry, I won't do anything stupid."

He snorted. "Your kind of stupid could go one of two ways."

That had me narrowing my eyes at him, but he held up his hands in surrender.

"Fuck her out of your system quickly, and then get started on the deal," he advised. "Best way."

It probably was the best way, but—

He sighed. "That fucking honor of yours."

I had to laugh. Only in the O'Donnelly family would my thoughts be considered honorable.

"If I'm fucking someone over, I want them to know it," was all I said.

"That makes no sense."

"Makes for epic sex, though," I jibed, and he shot me a grin.

"Angry sex is always good." He rubbed his chin, then he reached over again and flipped through the photos. "Who's the old guy to her?"

"To her? Not sure. Sugar daddy?" The thought alone made the beast inside rage. I cleared my throat to get rid of the rasp there. "To us? He's our meal ticket."

Aidan's eyes widened. "He is?"

I nodded. "Just leave it to me."

"I was always going to, *dearthāir*." He tilted his chin at me, honoring me with the Gaelic word for brother. "Be careful out there."

"You, too, brother."

Aidan winked at me and, with a far too cheerful whistle for someone whose dick might soon be 'ribbed for her pleasure' without the need for a condom, walked out of my office leaving me to brood.

The instant his back was to me, I stared at the photos again. Flipping through them, I glowered at the innocent face staring back at me through the photo paper—if only she knew.

Hers was a building in Hell's Kitchen. Five Points Territory. One of many on my hit list.

Back in the 70s, Aidan Sr., following in his father's footsteps, had bought up a shit-ton of property, pre-gentrification, and it was my job to either sell off the portfolio, reconstruct, or 'improve' the current aesthetics of the buildings the Points owned.

This particular one was something I'd taken a personal interest in.

See, I was technically a legitimate businessman.

This office?

I had views of the Hudson. I could see the Empire State Building, and in the evening, I had an epic view of the sunset setting over Manhattan. This office building, also Points' property, was worth a cool hundred million, and I was, again technically, the CEO of it.

On paper?

I looked seamless.

The businessman who sported hundred thousand dollar watches and had a house in the Hamptons. No one save the Points and my CPA knew where the money came from. I liked that because, fuck, I had no intention of switching this pad for a lock-up in Riker's Island.

Still, this project cut close to home, and the reasoning was fucking pathetic.

I'd never admit it to any of the O'Donnellys. The bastards were like family to me, and if I admitted to this, they'd never let me hear the end of it.

Extortion?

I usually doled that out to someone else's to do list. Someone with a far lower paygrade than me, someone expendable. But the minute I'd heard of the troublesome tenant who was refusing to sell her lot to us? After not one, not two, not even three attempts with higher prices?

Five outright refusals?

The challenge to convince her otherwise had overtaken me.

See, I liked stubborn in women.

I liked fucking it out of them.

Throw in the fact the woman's name was Aoife? It had been enough to get me sending someone out to follow her.

If she'd been fifty with as many chins as she had grandchildren, she'd have been safe from me.

But she wasn't.

She was, as Aidan had correctly stated, my kryptonite. All milky flesh with gleaming auburn hair that I wanted to tie around my clenched fist. Her soft features with those delicate green eyes that sparkled when she smiled and were like wet grass when she was mad, acted like a punch to my gut.

Now?

My interest hadn't just been piqued.

It had fucking imploded.

Yeah, I was thinking with my cock, but what man, at the end of the day, didn't?

I'd just have to be careful. Just have to make sure I put pressure on the right places, make sure she'd bend and not break, and the old bastard in the pictures was my key to just that.

See, every third Tuesday of the month, Aoife Keegan had a habit of traipsing across Manhattan to the Upper East Side. There, at three PM on the dot, she'd enter a discreet little boutique hotel and wouldn't leave until nine PM that night.

Five minutes after she arrived and left, the same man would leave, too.

At first, when Jimmy O'Leary had told me that Senator Alan Davidson was at the hotel, I hadn't thought anything of it.

Why would I?

Senators trawled for donations in fancy hotels every fucking day of the week. It was the true luxury of politics. Sure, they made it look real good for the press. Posing in derelict neighborhoods and shaking hands with people who did the fucking work . . . all while they lived it up large with women half their age in two thousand dollar a night suites.

My mouth firmed at that.

Was Aoife selling herself to the Senator?

The thought pissed me off.

I couldn't see why she'd do such a thing. Not when I'd looked into her finances, had seen just how secure she was. But maybe that was why. Maybe the Senator was funneling money to her.

The only problem was that the lot Aoife owned—did I mention it was owned outright? Yeah, that was enough to chafe my suspicions, too, considering she was only twenty-fucking-five years old—was a teashop in a small building in a questionable area of HK.

I mean, come on. I loved Hell's Kitchen. It was home. But fuck.

Where she was? What kind of Senator would put his fancy piece in *that?*

My jaw clenched as I studied the Senator's and Aoife's smiling faces as they left the hotel. Separately, of course. But whatever they'd been doing together, it sure put a Cheshire Cat grin on their chops–that was for fucking sure. Jimmy being a dumbass, hadn't put the two together, had just remarked on the 'coincidence,' but I was no fool.

How did I know they were together in the hotel?

Jimmy had been trailing Aoife for four months—told you I was obsessive—and every third Tuesday, come rain or shine, this little routine had jumped out, and when Jimmy had picked up on the fact Davidson had been there each and every time, I'd gotten my hands dirty, bribed one of the hotel maids myself—and fuck, that had been hard. Turned out that place made even the maids sign NDA agreements, but everyone had a price—and I'd found out that my little obsession shared a suite with the old prick.

My fingers curled into fists as I stared at her. Butter wouldn't fucking melt. She was the epitome of innocence. Like a redheaded angel. Could she really be lifting her skirts for that old fucker? Just so she could own a teashop?

Something didn't make sense, and fuck, if that didn't intrigue me all the more.

Aoife Keegan had snared one of the biggest, nastiest sharks in Manhattan.

She just didn't know it yet.

✷✷✷

Aoife

"We need more scones for tomorrow. I keep telling you four dozen isn't enough."

Lifting a hand at my waitress and friend, Jenny, I mumbled, "I know, I know."

"If you know, then why the hell don't you listen?" Jenny complained, making me grin.

"Because I'm the one who has to make them? Making half that again is just . . ." I sighed.

I loved my job.

I did.

I adored baking—my butt and hips attested to that fact—and making a career out of my passion was something every twenty-something hoped for. Especially in one of the most expensive cities in the world. But sheesh. There was only so much one person could do, and this was still, essentially, a one-woman-band.

With the threat of Acuig Corp looming over me, I didn't feel safe hiring extra staff. I'd held them off for close to six months now. Six months of them trying to tempt me to leave, to sell up. They'd raised their prices to ten percent above market value, whereas with everyone else in the building, they'd just offered what the apartments were truly worth. Considering this place wasn't the nicest in the block, that wasn't much.

Most people hadn't held out because, hell, why wouldn't they want to live elsewhere?

Those who were landlords hadn't felt any issue in tossing their tenants out on the street. The tenants grumbled, but when did they ever have any rights, anyway?

For myself, this was where my mom and I had worked to—

I brought that thought to a shuddering halt.

Mom was dead now.

I had to remember that. This was on me, not her.

My throat thickened with tears as I turned to Jenny and murmured, "I'll try better tomorrow."

The words had her frowning at me. "Babe, you know I'm not the boss here, right?"

Lips curving, I whispered, "I know. But you're so scary."

She snickered then peered down at herself. "Yeah, I bet I'd make grown men cry."

Maybe for a taste of her. . . .

Jenny was everything I wasn't.

She was slender, didn't dip her hand into the cookie jar at will—the woman had more willpower than I did hips, and my hips seemed to go on forever—and her face looked like it belonged on the cover of a fashion magazine. Even her hair was enough to inspire envy. It was black and straight as a ruler.

Mine?

Bright red and curly like a bitch. I had to straighten it out every morning if I didn't want to look like little orphan Annie.

I'd once read that curly-haired women straightened their hair for special events, and that straight-haired women curled theirs in turn, but I called bullshit.

Curly-haired women lived with their straightening irons surgically attached to their hands.

At least, I did.

My rat's nest was like a ginger afro. Maybe Beyoncé could make that work, but I sure as hell didn't have the bone structure.

"I think grown men would cry," I told her dryly, "if you asked them to."

She pshawed, but there was a twinkle in her eye that I understood. . . . She agreed with me, knew it was true, but wasn't going to admit it. With anyone else, she might have. She had an ego—that was for damn sure. But with me? I think she figured I was zero competition, so she felt no need to rub salt in the wound, too.

I plunked my elbows on the counter and stared around my domain as she bustled off and started clearing the tables. It was her last duty of the day, and my feet were aching so damn bad that I didn't even have it in me to care.

This owning your own business shit?

It wasn't easy.

Not saying I didn't love it, but it was hard.

I slept like four hours a night, and when I wasn't in bed, I was here. All the time.

Baking, cooking, serving, and smiling. Always smiling. Even if I was so sleep-deprived I could sob.

Jenny's actually a life saver.

My mom used to be front of house before. . . .

I sucked down a breath.

I had to get used to thinking about it.

She wasn't here anymore, but just avoiding all thoughts of her period wasn't working for me. It was like I was purposely forgetting her, and, well, fuck that.

She'd always wanted to have a teashop. It had been her one true dream. Back in Ireland, when she was a little girl, her grandmother had owned one in Limerick. Mom had caught the bug and had wanted to have one here in the States. But not only was it too fucking expensive for a woman on her own, it was also impossible with my feckless father at her side.

I didn't want to think about him either, though.

Why?

Because the feckless father who'd pretty much ruined my mother's life, wasn't the only father in my life. My biological dad hadn't exactly cared about her happiness, but once he'd come to know about me, he'd tried. That was more than could be said for the man who'd lived with me throughout my early childhood.

"You look gloomy."

Jenny's statement had me blinking in surprise. She had a ton of dishes piled in her arms, and I'd have worried for the expensive china if I hadn't known she was an old pro at this shit. Just as I was.

We could probably earn a Guinness World Record on how many dishes we could take back and forth to the kitchen of *Ellie's Tea Rooms*. I swear, I had guns because of all that hefting. My biceps were probably the firmest part of my body.

More's the pity.

I'd have preferred an ass you could bounce dimes off of, but, when it boiled down to it, there was no way in this universe I could live without cake.

Just wasn't going to happen.

My big butt wasn't going *anywhere* until scientists could make zero calorie eclairs and pies.

"I'm not glum."

"No? Then why are your eyes sad?"

Were they? I pursed my lips as I let the 'sad eyes' drift around the tea room. I wish I could say it was all forged on my own hard work, but it wasn't. Not really.

"I was just thinking about Mom."

"Oh, honey," Jenny said sadly, and she carefully placed all the dishes on the counter, so she could round it and curve her arm around my waist. "It was only seven months ago. Of course, you were thinking of her."

"I just—" I blew out a breath. "I don't know if I'm doing what she'd want."

"You can't live for her choices, sweetness. You have to do what you think is right for you."

I gnawed at my bottom lip again. "I-I know, but she was always there for me. A guiding light. With Fiona gone and her, too? I don't really know what I'm doing with myself."

This business wasn't something that made me want to get up on a morning. It was my mom's dream, her goal. Every decision I made, I tried to remember how she'd longed for a place like this, but it wasn't my passion. It was hers, and I was trying to keep that dream alive while fretting over the fact my heart wasn't in it.

"I think you're doing a damn fine job. You have a very successful teashop. Your cakes are raved about. Have you visited our TripAdvisor page recently? Or our Yelp?" She squeaked. "I swear, you're making this place a tourist hotspot. I don't think Fiona or Michelle could be more proud of you if they tried."

The baking shit, yeah, that was all on me, but the other stuff? The finances?

I'd caved in.

I'd caved where my mom had always refused in the past.

With the accident had come a lot of medical bills that I just hadn't been able to afford. Without her help, I'd had to take on extra staff, and out of nowhere, my expenses had added up.

Mom had been so proud of this place, so ferociously gleeful that we'd done it by ourselves, and yet, here I was, financially free for the first time in my life, and I still felt like I was drowning because my freedom went entirely against her wishes.

"Is this to do with Acuig? I know they're still pestering you."

Jenny's statement had me wincing. Acuig were the bottom feeders who wanted to snap up this building, demolish it, and then replace it with a skyscraper. Don't get me wrong, the building was foul, but a lot of people lived here, and the minute it morphed into some exclusive condo, no one from around here would be able to afford to live in it.

It would become yuppy central.

I'd rejected all their offers to buy my tea room even though I didn't want the damn thing, not really. Mostly I wanted to keep mom's goals alive and kicking, but also, it pissed me off the way Acuig were changing Hell's Kitchen. Ratcheting up prices, making it unaffordable for the everyday man and woman—the people I'd grown up with—and bringing a shit-ton of banker-wankers and 1%ers to the area.

So, maybe I'd watched Erin Brockovich a time or two as a kid and had a social conscience . . . Wasn't the worst thing to possess, right?

"Aoife?" Jenny stated, making me look over at her. "Is Acuig pressuring you?"

I winced, realizing I hadn't answered—Jenny was my friend, but she also worked here and relied on the paycheck. It wasn't fair of me to keep her hanging like that. "They upped the sales price. I guess that isn't helping," I admitted, frowning down at my hands.

Unlike Jenny who had her nails manicured, mine were cut neatly and plain. I had no rings on my fingers, and wore no watch or bracelets because my wrists were usually deep in flour or sugar bags.

I spent most of my life right where I wanted it—behind the shopfront. That had slowly morphed where I was doing double the work to compensate for Mom's loss.

Was it any wonder I was feeling a little out of my league?

I was coping without Fiona, grieving Mom, working without her, too, and then practically living in the kitchens here. I didn't exactly have that much of a life. I had nothing cheerful on the horizon, either.

Well, nothing except for next Tuesday, and that wasn't enough to turn my frown upside down.

The money was a temptation. I didn't need to sell up and start working on my own goals, but that just loaded me down with more guilt and made me feel like a really shitty daughter.

Jenny squeezed me in a gentle hug. But as I turned to speak to her, the bell above the door rang as it opened. We both jerked in surprise—each of us apparently thinking the other had locked up when neither of us had—and turned to face the entrance.

On the brink of telling the client we were closed for the day, my mouth opened then shut.

Standing there, amid the frilly, lacy curtains, was the most masculine man I'd ever seen in my life.

And I meant that.

It was like a thousand aftershave models had morphed into one handsome creature that had just walked through my door.

At my side, I could feel Jenny's 'hot guy radar' flare to life, and for once, I couldn't damn well blame her.

This guy was . . . well, he was enough to make me choke on my words and splutter to a halt.

The tea room was all girly femininity. It was sophisticated enough to appeal to businesswomen with its mauve, taupe, and cream-toned hues, and the ethereal watercolors that decorated the walls. But the table-cloths were lacy, and the china dishes and cake stands we used were the height of Edwardian elegance.

Moms brought their little girls here for their birthday, and high-powered executives spilled dirt on their lovers with their girlfriends over scones and clotted cream—breaking their diets as they discussed the boyfriends who had broken their hearts.

The man, whoever the hell he was, was dressed to impress in a navy suit with the finest pinstripe. It was close to a silver fleck, and I could see, even from this distance, that it was hand tailored. I'd seen custom tailoring before, and only a trained eye could get a suit cut so perfectly to this man's form.

With wide shoulders that looked like they could take the weight of the world, a long, lean frame that was enhanced by strong muscles evident through the close fit of his pants and jacket, then the silkiness of his shirt which revealed delineated abs when his bright gold and scarlet tie flapped as he moved, the guy was hot.

With a capital H.

"How can we help, sir?" Jenny purred, and despite my own awe, I had to dip my chin to hide my smile.

Even if I wanted to throw my hat into this particular man's game, there was no way he'd choose me over Jenny. Fuck, I'd screw her, and I wasn't even a lesbian. Not even a teensy bit bi. I'd gone shopping with her enough to have seen her ass, and I promise you, it's biteable.

So, nope. I didn't have a snowball's chance in hell of this Adonis seeing *me* when Jenny was in the room.

Yet. . . .

When I'd controlled my smile, I looked over at the man, and his focus was on me.

My breath stuttered to a halt.

Why wasn't his gaze glued to Jenny?

Why weren't those ice-white blue eyes fixated on my best friend's tits, which Jenny helpfully plumped up as she preened at my side?

For a second, I was so close to breaking out into a coughing fit, it was humiliating. Then, more humiliation struck in a quieter manner, but it was nevertheless rotten—I turned pink.

Now, you might think you know what a blush is. You might think you've even experienced it yourself a time or two. But I was a redhead. My skin made fresh milk look yellow, and even my fucking freckles were pale. Everything about me was like I'd been dunked into white wax.

But as the heat crawled over me, taking over my skin as the man looked at me without pause, I knew things had rarely been this dire.

See, with Jenny as a best friend, I was used to the attention going her way. I could hide in the background, hide in her shadow. I liked it there. I was comfortable there. Sometimes, on double dates, she'd drag me along, and even the guy supposed to be dating me would be gaping at Jenny. As pathetic as it was, I was so used to it, it didn't bother me.

But now?

I just wasn't used to being in the spotlight.

Especially not a man like this one's spotlight.

When you're a teenager, practicing with your mom's blush for the first time, you always look like a tomato that's been left out in the sun, right?

I was redder than that.

I could feel it. I could fucking feel the heat turning me tomato red.

When Jenny cleared her throat, I thanked God when it broke the man's attention. He shot her a look, but it wasn't admiring. It wasn't even impressed.

If anything, it was irritated.

Okay, so now both Jenny and I were stunned.

Fuck that, we were floored.

Literally.

Our mouths were doing a pretty good fish impression as the man turned back to look at me.

Shit, was this some kind of joke?

Was it April 1st and I'd just gotten the dates mixed up again?

"Ms. Keegan?"

Oh fuck. His voice.

Oh. My. God.

That voice.

It was. . . .

I had to swallow.

Did men even talk like that?

It was low and husky and raspy and made me think of sex, not just mediocre sex, but the best sex. Toe-curling, nails-breaking-in-the-sheets sex. Sex so fucking good you couldn't walk the next day. Sex so hot that it made my current core temperature look polar in comparison. Sex that I'd never been lucky to have before, so I pined for it in the worst way.

Jenny nudged me in the side when I just carried on gaping at the man. "Y-Yes. That's me." I cleared my throat, feeling nervous and stupid and flustered as I wiped my hands on my apron.

Sweet Jesus.

Was this man really looking for me while I was wearing a goddamn pinafore?

Even as practical as they were, I wanted to beg the patron saint of pinnies to remove it from me. To do something, anything, to make sure that this man didn't see me in the red gingham check that I always wore to cover up stains.

And then I felt it.

Jenny's hand.

Tugging at the knot.

I wanted to kiss her. Seriously. I wanted to give her a fucking raise! As I moved away from the counter and her side, the apron dropped to the floor as I headed for the man whose hand was now held out, ready for me to shake in greeting.

There are those moments in your life when you know you'll never forget them. They can be happy or sad, annoying or exhilarating. This was one of them.

As I slipped my hand into his, I felt the electric shocks down to my core. Meeting his gaze wasn't hard because I was stunned, and I needed to know if he'd felt that, too.

From the way those eyelids were shielding his icy-blue eyes, I figured he was just as surprised.

It was like a satisfied puma was watching me. One that was happy there was plump prey prancing around in front of him.

Shit.

Did I just describe myself as 'plump prey?'

And like that, my house of cards came tumbling down because what the hell would this man want with me?

I was seeing things.

God, I was so stupid sometimes.

I cleared my throat for, like, the fourth damn time, and asked, "I'm Ms. Keegan. You are?"

His smile, when it appeared, was as charming as the rest of him. His teeth were white, but not creepy, reality-TV-star white. They were straight except for one of his canines, which tilted in slightly. In his perfect face, it was one flaw that I almost clung to. Because with that wide brow, the hair so dark it looked like black silk that was cut closely to his head with a faint peak at his forehead, the strong nose, and even stronger jaw, I needed something imperfect to focus on.

Then, I sucked down a breath and remembered what Fiona had told me once upon a time. When I'd been nervous about asking Jamie Winters to homecoming, she'd advised me in her soft Irish lilt, "Lass, that boy takes a dump just like you do. He uses the bathroom twice a day and undoubtedly leaves a puddle on the floor for his ma to clean up. I bet he's puked a time or two as well. Had diarrhea and the good Lord only knows what else. Just you think that the next time you see that boy and want to ask him out."

Yeah. It was gross, but fuck, it had worked. Her advice had worked so well I hadn't asked anyone out because I could only think of them using the damn toilet!

Still, looking at this Adonis, there was no imagining *that.*

Surely, gods didn't use the bathroom.

Did they?

"The name's Finn. Finn O'Grady."

My eyes flared at the name.

No.

It couldn't be.

Finn O'Grady?

No. It wasn't a rare name, but it was a strong one. One that suited him, one that had always suited him.

I frowned up at him wondering, yet again, if this was a joke of some sort, but as he looked at me, *really* looked at me, I saw no recognition. Saw nothing on his features that revealed any ounce of awareness that I'd known him for years.

Well, okay, not *known.* But I'd known his mother. Our mothers had been best friends. And as I looked, I saw the same almond-shaped eyes Fiona had, the stubborn jaw, and that unmistakable butt-indent on his chin.

At the reminder of just how forgettable I was, my heart sank, and hurt whistled through me.

Then, I realized I was *still* holding his hand, and as he squeezed, the flush returned and I almost died of mortification.

CHAPTER 2

FINN

GOD, she was perfect.

And when I said perfect, I meant it.

I'd fucked a lot of women. Redheads, blondes, brunettes, even the rare thing that is a natural head of black hair. None of them, not a single one, lit up like Aoife Keegan.

Her cheeks were cherry red and in the light camisole she wore, a cheerful yellow, I could see how the blush went all the way down to the upper curve of her breasts.

She'd go that color, I knew, when she came.

And fuck, I wanted to see that.

I wanted to see that perfectly pale flesh turn bright pink under my ministrations.

Even as I looked at her, all shy and flustered, I wondered if she was a screamer in bed.

Some of the shyest often were.

Maybe not at first, but after a handful of orgasms, it was a wonder what that could do to a woman's self-confidence, and Jesus, I wanted to *see* that, too. I wanted a seat at center stage.

My suit jacket was open, and I regretted it. Immensely. My cock was hard, had been since we'd shaken hands, and her fingers had clung to mine like a daughter would to her daddy's at her first visit to the county fair.

Fuck.

Squeezing her fingers wasn't intentional. If anything, I'd just liked the feel of her palm against mine, but when I put faint pressure on her, she jerked back like she'd been scalded.

Her cheeks bloomed with heat again, and she whispered, "Mr. O'Grady, what can I do for you?"

You can get on your fucking knees and sort out the hard-on you just caused.

That's what she could fucking do.

I almost growled at the thought because the image of her on her knees, my cock in her small fist, her dainty mouth opening to take the tip. . . .

Shit.

That had to happen.

Here, too.

In this fancy, frilly, feminine place, I wanted to defile her.

Fuck, I wanted that so goddamn much, it was enough to make me reconsider my demolition plans.

I wanted to screw her against all this goddamn lace, which suited her perfectly. She was made for lace. And silk. Hell, silk would look like heaven against her skin. I wouldn't know where she ended and it began.

When her brow puckered, she dipped her chin, and that gorgeous wave of auburn hair slipped over her shoulder.

If we'd been alone, if that brassy bitch—who was staring at me like I could fuck her over the counter with her friend watching if I was game—wasn't here, I'd have grabbed that rope of hair, twisted it around my fingers, and forced her gaze up.

Some guys liked their women demure. And I was one of them. I wasn't about to lie. I liked that in her, but I wanted her eyes on me. Always.

It was enough to prompt me to bite out, "Can we speak privately?"

She jerked at my words, then as she licked her bottom lip, turned to look at the waitress. "Jenny, it's okay. I can handle the rest by myself. You get home."

Jenny, her gaze drifting between me and her boss, nodded. She retreated to a door that swung as she moved through the opening, and within seconds, she had her coat and purse over her arm.

As she sashayed past—for my benefit, I was sure—she murmured, "See you tomorrow, Aoife."

Aoife nodded and shot her friend a smile, but I wasn't smiling. There were dishes on every table. Plates and saucers and tea pots. Those fancy stands that made any man wonder if he could touch it without snapping it.

Aoife was going to clear all that herself? Not on my fucking watch.

When the bell rang as the waitress opened the door, I didn't take my eyes off her until it rang once more upon closing.

Aoife swallowed, and I watched her throat work, watched it with a hunger that felt alien to me, because, God, I wanted to see my bites on her. Wanted to see my marks on that pale column of skin and her tits.

Barely withholding a groan, I asked, "Do you often let your staff go when you still have a lot of work to do, so you can speak to a stranger?"

Her cheeks flushed again, and she took a step back. "I-I, you're not —" Flustered once more, she fell silent.

"I'm not what?" Curiosity had me asking the question. Whatever I'd expected her to say, it hadn't been that.

She cleared her throat. "N-Nothing. You wished to speak with me, Mr. O'Grady?"

My other hand tightened around my briefcase, and though seeing her had made my reason for being here all that more necessary, I was almost disappointed. There was a gentle warmth to those bright-green eyes that would die out when I told her my purpose for being here. And her innocent attraction to me would change, morph into something else.

But I could only handle *something else*.

Some men were made for forever.

But those men weren't in my line of business.

I moved away from her, pressing my briefcase to one of the few empty tables. I wasn't happy about her having to do all the clearing up later on, and wondered if Paul, my PA, would know who to call to get her some help.

There was no way I was spending the rest of the night alone in my bed, my only companion my fist wrapped around my cock.

No way, no fucking how.

I paid Paul enough for him to come and clear the fucking place on his own if he couldn't find someone else.

I wanted Aoife on her knees, bent over my goddamn bed, and I was a man who always got what he wanted.

In this jungle, I was the lion, and Aoife? She was my prey.

I keyed in the code and opened my briefcase. The manila envelope was large and thick, well-padded with my documentation of Aoife's every move for the past few months.

It had started off as a legitimate move.

I'd wanted to know her weaknesses, so I could put pressure on her and make her cave to my demands.

Now, my demands had changed. I didn't just want her to sell the tea room we were standing in, I wanted her in my bed.

Fuck, I wanted that more than I wanted to make Aidan Sr. a fucking profit, and Aidan's profit and my balls still being attached to my body ran hand in hand.

Aidan was an evil cunt.

If I failed to deliver, he'd take it out on me. Whether I was his idea of an adopted son or not, he'd have done the same to his blood sons.

Well, he wouldn't have taken their balls. The man, for all his psychotic flaws, was obsessed with the idea of grandchildren, of passing it all on to the next generation. He'd cut his boys though. Without a doubt.

I knew Conor had marks on his back from a beating he refused to speak about. Then there was Brennan. He had a weak wrist because his father had a habit of breaking *that* wrist.

Without speaking, I grabbed the envelope and passed it to her.

She frowned down at it and asked, "For me?"

I smiled at her. "Open it."

"What is it?"

"Leverage."

That had her eyes flaring wide as she pulled out some of the photos.

A gasp fell from her lips as she grabbed the photos when she spotted herself in them, jerking so hard the envelope tore. Some of the pictures spilled to the ground, but I didn't care about that.

Leaning back against one of the dainty tables once I was satisfied it would take my weight, I watched her cheeks blanch, all that delicious color dissipating as she took in everything the photos revealed.

"Y-You've been stalking me. Why?"

The question was high-pitched, loaded down with panic. I'd heard it often enough to recognize it easily.

I didn't get involved in wet work anymore. That wasn't my style, but along the way, to reach this point, I'd had no choice but to get my hands dirty. Panic was part of the job when you were collecting debts for the Irish Mob. And the Five Points were notorious for Aidan Sr.'s temper.

He wasn't the first patriarch. If anything, his grandfather was the founder. But Aidan Sr. was the type of guy that if you didn't pay him back, he didn't give a fuck about the money, he cared about the lack of respect.

See, you owed the mob and didn't pay? They'd send heavies around, beat the shit out of you, and threaten to do the same to your family, and usually, that did the trick. You didn't kill the cash cow.

Aidan Sr.?

He didn't give a fuck about the cash cow.

Only the truly desperate thought about borrowing money from Aidan, because if you didn't pay it back, he'd take your teeth, and your fingers and toes as a first warning. Then, if you still didn't pay—and most did—it was death.

Respect meant a lot to Aidan.

And fuck, if it wasn't starting to mean a lot to me. The panic in her voice made my cock throb.

I wanted this woman weak and willing.

I wanted it more than I wanted my next breath.

Ignoring her, I reached for my phone and tapped out a message to Paul.

Need housekeeping crew to clean this place.

I attached my live location, saw the blue ticks as Paul read the message—he knew better than to ignore my texts, whatever time of day they came—and he replied: *Sure thing.*

That was the kind of reply I was used to getting. Not just from Paul, but from everyone.

There were very few people who weren't below me in the strata of Five Points, and I'd worked my ass off to make that so.

The only people who ranked above me included Aidan Jr. and his brothers, Aidan Sr. of course, and then maybe a handful of his advisors that he respected for what they'd done for him and the Points over the years.

But the money I made Aidan Sr.?

That blew most of their 'advice' out of the window.

The reason Aidan had a Dassault Falcon executive private plane?

Because I was, as the City itself called me, a whiz kid.

I'd made my first million—backed by the Points, of course—at twenty-two.

Fifteen years later?

I'd made him hundreds of millions.

My own personal fortune was nothing to sniff at, either.

"W-Why have you done this?" Aoife asked, her voice breathy enough to make me wonder if she sounded like that in the sack.

"Because you've been a very stubborn little girl."

Her eyes flared wide. "Excuse me?"

I reached into the inside pocket of my suit coat and pulled out a business card. "For you," I prompted, offering it to her.

When she turned it over, saw the logo of five points shaped into a star, then read Acuig—in the Gaelic way, ah-coo-ig, not a butchered American way, ah-coo-ch—aloud, I watched her throat work as she swallowed.

"I-I should have realized with the Irish name," she whispered, the muscles in her brow twitching as she took in the chaos of the scattered photos on the floor.

Watching her as she dropped the contents on the ground, so she was surrounded by them, I tilted my head to the side, taking her in as her panic started to crest.

"I-I won't sell." Her first words surprised me.

I should have figured, though. Everything about this woman was surprisingly delicious.

"You have no choice," I purred. "As far as I'm aware, the Senator has a wife. He also has a reputation to protect. I'm not sure he'd be happy if any of those made it onto the *National Enquirer's* front page. Not when he's just trying to shore up his image to take a run for the White House next election."

She reached up and clutched her throat. The self-protective gesture was enough to make me smile at her—I knew what the absence of hope looked like.

There'd been a time when that had been my life, too.

"But, on the bright side," I carried on, "this can all be wiped away if you sell." As her gaze flicked to mine, I added, "As well as if you do something for me."

For a second, she was speechless. I could see she knew what that *something* was. Had my body language given it away? Had there been a certain raspiness to my tone?

I wasn't sure, and frankly, didn't give a fuck.

There was a little hiccoughing sound that escaped her lips, and she frowned at me, then down at herself.

"Is this a joke?"

"Do I look like I'm the kind of guy who jokes, Aoife?" Fuck, I loved saying her name.

The Gaelic notes just drove me insane.

Ee-Fah.

Nothing like the spelling, and all the more complicated and delicious for it.

"N-No," she confirmed, "but . . ."

"But what?" I prompted.

"I mean . . . you just can't be serious."

"Oh, but I am." I grinned. "Deadly. You've wasted a lot of my time, Aoife Keegan. A lot. Do you think I'm normally involved in negotiations of this level?"

Her eyes whispered over me, and I felt the loving caress of her gaze as she took in each and every inch of me. When she licked her lips, I knew she liked what she saw. I didn't really care, but it was helpful for her to be eager in some small way—especially when coercion was involved.

Aidan had called it bribery. I preferred 'coercion'. It sounded far kinder.

"No. That suit alone probably cost the mortgage payment on this place."

I nodded—she wasn't wrong. I knew what she'd been paying as rent, then as a mortgage, before some kind *benefactor* had paid it all off. Free and clear.

"I had to get my hands dirty, and while I might like some things dirty . . .," I trailed off, smirking when she flushed. "So, as I see it, we have a problem. I want this building. You don't want anyone to know you're having an affair with a Senator. Or, should I say, the Senator doesn't want anyone to know he's having an affair with someone young enough to be his daughter . . ."

If my voice turned into a growl at that point, then it was because the notion of her spreading her legs for that old bastard just turned my stomach.

Fuck, this woman, the thoughts she made me think.

Because I was startled at the possessive note to my growl, I ran a hand over my head. I kept my hair short for a reason—ease. I wasn't the kind of man who wasted time primping. It was an expensive cut, so I didn't have to do anything to it. Even mussing it up had it falling back into the same sleek lines as before—a man in my position had to look pristine under pressure. And very few people could even begin to understand the kind of strain I was under.

The formation of igneous rock had less volcanic pressure than Aidan Sr.

She licked her lips as she stared down at the photos, then back up at me. "And you want me to sell the place to you, even though this is my livelihood and the livelihood of all my staff, and then sleep with you?"

Her squeaky voice, putting suspicion into words, had me crossing my legs at the ankle. "We wouldn't be doing much sleeping."

Another shaky breath soughed from her lips, then, those beautiful pillowy morsels that would look good around my cock, quivered.

"This is crazy," she whispered shakily.

"As far as I'm concerned, all of this could be avoided if you'd just sold to me a few months back. Now you have to pay for my time wasted on this project."

"By spreading my legs?"

Another squeak. I tsked at her question, but in truth, I was annoyed at her using those same words I had to describe her with that old hypocrite of a Senator.

I didn't move, though. Didn't even flex my arms in irritation, just murmured, "Small price to pay. And, even though it's ten percent above market price, I'll stick to the last offer Acuig gave you. Can't say anything's fairer than that."

She shook her head, and there was a desperation to the gesture as she cried, "I need this business. You don't understand—"

"I understand that some very powerful and very dangerous businessmen want this building demolished. I understand that those same powerful and dangerous men want a skyscraper taking up this plot of land. I understand that a four hundred million dollar project isn't going to be put on hiatus because one small Irish woman doesn't want to go out of business . . ." I cocked a brow at her. "You think I'm coming in hot and heavy? These kinds of men, Aoife, they're not the sort you fuck around with.

"Take my check, and my other offer, before you or the people you care about are threatened." I got to my feet and straightened my jacket out. "This suit? These shoes? That briefcase and this watch? I own them because I'm damn good at what I do. I'm a financial advisor, Aoife. Take my word for it. You're getting the best deal out of this."

She staggered back, the counter stopping her from crumpling to the floor. "You'd hurt me?"

"Not me," I repudiated. Not in the way she thought, anyway. "But the men I work for?"

Her gaze dropped to the one thing she'd retained in her hand—my card. "Acuig," she whispered. "Five in Gaelic."

My brows twitched in surprise. She knew Gaelic?

"The Five Points." Her eyes flared wide with terror. "They're behind this deal."

I hadn't expected her to put one and one together, but now that she had? It worked to my advantage.

Nodding, I told her, "Any minute now, there'll be a team of house-keepers coming in here to clear up for the night." When she gaped at me, I retrieved the contract from my briefcase, slapped it on the table, and handed her a pen as I carried on, "I suggest you let tonight be your last night of business."

What I didn't tell her, was that my suggestions weren't wasted words. They were like the law.

You didn't break them, and, like any lawmaker, I expected imme-diate obeisance.

***

Aoife

SO, the beautiful man just happened to be an absolute cocksucker of a bastard.

Still, this couldn't be real, could it?

The dick could have anyone he wanted. Jesus, Jenny was panting after him like a dog in heat. She would have gone out with him if he'd so much as clicked his fingers at her.

But he'd had eyes for me.

Like he wanted me.

He thought he'd bought me. Or, at least, bought my silence, and yeah, to some extent he had. But . . . why buy me, why not just drop the price on the building if he wanted me to pay for the time he'd wasted on me?

The arrogance imbued in those words was enough to make me pull my hair out, but that was inwardly. I was a redhead. I had a temper. But that temper was mostly overshadowed by fear.

Senator Alan Davidson wasn't my boyfriend, my lover, as this dick seemed to believe. He was my father, and as Finn O'Grady had correctly surmised, he was aiming for the White House.

How could I put that in jeopardy?

My dad was a good man. He'd made a mistake one summer when he'd come home from college, one that only some careful digging by his campaign manager had uncovered. Dad himself hadn't known of my existence, not until his CM had gone hunting for any nasty secrets that could come out and bite him in the ass.

This had been five years ago when he'd run for Senator. Now, Dad's goal was the presidential seat, and I wasn't going to be the one who put a wrench in the works.

When Garry Smythe had approached me back then, I'd thought he was joking. I was out on the street, heading home from work. At the side of me, a black car had driven in from the lane of traffic, just to park, or so I'd thought. As he'd held out his hand with a card, one of the car doors had opened up, and I'd been 'invited' inside.

Had I been scared?

At first.

But when Garry had told me my country needed me, I hadn't been sure whether to laugh or tell him to fuck off. He hadn't shuffled me into the car, though, hadn't tried to coerce me. He'd just asked if I'd voted for Senator Alan Davidson in the elections, and because he was one of the only politicians out there who wasn't a complete douche, and that was the name printed on the card in my hand, I'd shuffled into the back of the car.

Where the Senator himself had been sitting.

Now, when I thought about that day, I realized how fucking naive I'd been to get into the back of a limo for such a vague reason. But I'd been fortunate. Alan *had* been waiting for me. Waiting to tell me a story that still shook me to my core.

I'd made a promise to my dad that I wouldn't tell anyone. He'd offered me money, and I hadn't accepted it. I guess I should have, but back then, I'd been haughty and proud, and because the good guy I'd thought him to be hadn't been so good when he tried to buy my silence, I'd told him to fuck off. I'd been disappointed in him, frightened by the lifelong lie I'd been living, and equally hurt that the man who'd sired me was just concerned that I was a threat to his campaign.

I'd walked out of that car never expecting to see my dear old Dad ever again.

Then, the day after he'd been elected, he'd been sitting in the booth of the cafe where I worked part-time to get me through culinary school.

Seeing him, I'd almost handed that table off to one of the other waitresses, but I hadn't. Not when every time I'd passed the table, he'd caught my eye, a patient smile on his lips, one that said he'd wait for me all day if he had to.

Ever since that second meeting, I'd been catching up with him every three weeks.

And this bastard thought he could use our limited time together against my father? The one politician who could make a difference in the White House? One who didn't have Big Oil up his ass, a pharmaceutical company sucking his dick, or any other kind of corporation so far up his rectum that he was a walking, talking lie?

No.

That wasn't going to happen.

Which meant I was going to have to sleep with this stranger.

Before this conversation, hell, that hadn't been too disturbing a prospect. Because, dayum, what woman wouldn't want to sleep with this guy?

Even with an ego as big as his, he was delicious. Better than any cake I could bake, that was for fucking sure.

More than that, I knew him.

And I now knew that the life Fiona would never have wanted for her son was one he'd been drawn into.

The Mob.

The Five Points were notorious in these parts. Everyone was scared of them. I paid protection money to them, for God's sake. I knew to be scared of them, and having been raised in their territory, it was the height of stupidity to think paying them wasn't just a part of business.

Still, Fiona had never wanted that for Finn, and her Finn was the same as the one standing before me here today. In my tea room, which looked far too small to contain the might of this man.

She'd be so disappointed. So heart-sore to know that he was up to his neck in dirty dealings with the Five Points, and as he'd pointed out, the cost of his shoes, his clothes, and his jewelry, was enough to speak for itself.

If he wasn't high up the ladder in the gang, then I wasn't one of the best bakers of scones in the district.

Like Jenny had said, I had five star ratings across most social media platforms for a reason. I was good. But apparently, this man wasn't.

Before I could utter a word, before I could even cringe at how utterly sorrowful Fiona would be about this turn of events—not just about the Five Points but what her son was making me do—the door clattered open.

Like he'd predicted, a team of people swarmed in.

Finn motioned to the floor. "Want anyone to see those?"

With a gasp, I dropped to my knees and collected the shots, stuffing them back into the envelope with a haste that wasn't exactly practical.

Two shiny shoes appeared before me, followed by two expensively clad legs, and I peered up at him, wondering what he was about. He held out his hand, but I clasped the photos to my chest.

"You're making more of a mess than anything else, Aoife." His voice was raspy, his eyes weighted down by heavy lids.

For a second, I wondered why, then I saw *why*.

He had an erection.

An erection?

I peered around at the staff, but they were all men. Not a single woman in sight, well, save for the seventy-year-old with a clipboard who was barking out orders to the guys in what sounded like Russian.

So that meant, what?

The erection was for me?

The blush, the dreaded, hated blush, made another goddamn appearance, and to cover it, I ducked my head, then pushed the photos and the envelope at him.

For whatever reason, I stayed where I was, staring up at him as he calmly, coolly, and so fucking collectedly pushed the photos back into the torn envelope—it was some coverage. Better than none at all, I figured.

Being down here was. . . .

Hell, I don't know what it was.

To be looked at like that?

For his body to respond to me like that?

It was unprecedented.

I'd had one sexual experience with a boy back in college, and that had not gone according to plan. So much so I was still technically a fucking virgin because, and this was no lie, the guy had *zero* understanding of a woman's body.

Craig had spent more time fingering my perineum than my clit, and every time he'd tried to shove his dick into me, he'd somehow managed to drag it down toward my ass.

I'd gotten so sick of him frigging the wrong bits of me, that I'd pushed him off and given him a blowjob. It had been the quickest way to get out of that annoying situation.

Yeah, annoying.

Jenny, when I'd told her, had pissed herself laughing, and ever since, had tried to get me to hook up with randoms, so I could slough off my virginity like it was dead skin and I was a snake. But life had just always gotten in the way, and I'd had no time for men.

Shortly after *that* had happened, we'd lost Fiona. Then, I'd graduated, and after, Mom and I had set up this place thanks to some insurance money she'd come into after her husband had died. It had been crazy building the tea room into an established cafe, and then mom had passed on, too.

So, here I was. Still a virgin. On my knees in front of the sexiest man on Earth, a man I knew, a man whose mother had half raised me, one who wanted me in his bed as some kind of blackmail payment.

Was this a dream?

Seriously?

I mean, I'd been depressed before Finn O'Grady had walked through my doors. Now I wasn't sure whether to be apoplectic or worried as fuck because he wasn't wrong: you didn't mess with the Five Points.

God, if I'd known they'd been behind the development on this building, I'd have probably signed over months ago.

The Points were. . . .

I shuddered.

Vindictive.

Aidan O'Donnelly was half-evil genius and half-twisted sociopath. St. Patrick's Church, two streets away, had the best roof in the neighborhood and the strongest attendance because Aidan, for all he'd cut you into more pieces than a butcher, was a devout Catholic. His men knew better than to avoid Sunday service, and I reckoned that Father Doyle was the busiest priest in the city because of Five Points' attendance.

"I like you down there," he murmured absentmindedly.

The words weren't exactly dirty, but the meaning? They had my temperature soaring.

Shit.

What the hell was I doing?

Enjoying the way this man was victimizing me?

It was so wrong, and yet, what was standing right in front of me? I knew he'd know what to do with that thing tucked behind his pants.

He wouldn't try to penetrate my urethra—yes, you read that right. Craig had tried to fuck my pee-hole! Like, *why?*

Finn?

He oozed sex appeal.

It seemed to seep from every pore, perfuming the air around me with his pheromones.

I hadn't even believed in pheromones until I scented Finn O'Grady's delicious essence.

It reminded me of the one out of town vacation we'd ever had. We'd gone to Cooperstown, and I'd scented a body of water that didn't have corpses floating in it—Otsego Lake. He reminded me of that. So green and earthy. It was an attack on my overwhelmed senses, an attack I didn't need.

With the envelope in his hand, he held out his other for me. When I placed my fingers in his, the size difference between us was noticeable once more.

I was just over five feet, and he was over six. I was round and curvy, and he was hard and lean.

It reminded me of the nursery tale Mom had sung to me as a child—Jack Sprat could eat no fat, and his wife could eat no lean.

Did it say a lot for my confidence that I couldn't seem to take it in that he wanted *me*? Or was it simply that I wasn't understanding how anyone could prefer me over Jenny?

Even my mom had called Jenny beautiful, whereas she'd kissed me on the nose and called me her 'bonny lass.'

Biting my lip, I accepted his help off the floor. My black jeans weren't the smartest thing for the tea room, but I didn't actually serve that many dishes, just bustled around behind the counter, working up the courage to do what Mom had done every day—greet people.

I wasn't a sociable person. I preferred my kitchen to the front of house, hence the jeans, but I regretted not wearing something else today. Something that covered just how big my ass was, how slender my waist *wasn't*.

Ugh.

This man is blackmailing you into his bed, Aoife. For Christ's sake, you're not supposed to be worrying if he likes the goods, too!

Still, no matter how much I tried, years of inadequacy weighed me down as I wiped off my knees.

"Do you have a coat?" he asked, and his voice was raspy again. "A jacket? Or a purse?"

I nodded at him but kept my gaze trained on the floor. "Yes."

"Go get them."

His order had me shuffling my feet toward the kitchen, but as I approached the door, I heard his strong voice speaking with the old woman with the clipboard: "I want this all cleaned up and boxed. Take it to my storage lot in Queens."

With my back to him, I stiffened at his brisk orders. *Was I just going to let him do this? Get away with it?*

My shoulders immediately sagged.

Did I have a choice?

If it was just him, just Acuig, then I'd fight this, as I'd been fighting it since the building had come to the attention of the developer. But this wasn't a regular business deal.

This was mob business, and it seemed like somehow, I'd become a part of that.

FML.

Seriously, FML.

TO READ MORE, Filthy is free on KU: www.books2read.com/FilthySerenaAkeroyd

FREE BOOK!

Don't forget to grab your free e-Book!
Secrets & Lies is now free!

Meg's love life was missing a spark until she discovered her need to be dominated. When her fiancé shared the same kink, she thought all her birthdays had come at once, and then she came to learn their relationship was one big fat lie.

Gabe has loved Meg for years, watching her from afar, and always wishing he'd been the one to date her first and not his brother. When he has the chance to have Meg in his bed—even better, tied to it—it's an opportunity he can't refuse.

With disastrous consequences.

Can Gabe make Meg realize she's the one woman he's always wanted? But once secrets and lies have wormed their way into a relationship, is it impossible to establish the firm base of trust needed between lovers, and more importantly, between sub and Sir...?

This story features orgasm control in a BDSM setting.
Secrets & Lies is now free!

CONNECT WITH SERENA

For the latest updates, be sure to check out my website!
But if you'd like to hang out with me and get to know me better, then I'd love to see you in my Diva reader's group where you can find out all the gossip on new releases as and when they happen. You can join here: www.facebook.com/groups/SerenaAkeroydsDivas. Or you can always PM or email me. I love to hear from you guys: serenaakeroyd@ gmail.com.

ABOUT THE AUTHOR

I'm a romance novelaholic and I won't touch a book unless I know there's a happy ending. This addiction is what made me craft stories that suit my voracious need for raunchy romance. I love twists and unexpected turns, and my novels all contain sexy guys, dark humor, and hot AF love scenes.

I write MF, menage, and reverse harem (also known as why choose romance,) in both contemporary and paranormal. Some of my stories are darker than others, but I can promise you one thing, you will always get the happy ending your heart needs!